Forbidden Love

Haunted by the mysterious deaths of his two brothers, Grant Roberson, 10th Earl of Straithern, fears for his life. Determined to produce an heir before it's too late, Grant has promised to wed a woman he has never met. But instead of being enticed by his bride-to-be, Grant can't fight his attraction to the understated beauty and wit of her paid companion.

Gillian Cameron long ago learned the danger of falling in love. Now, as the companion to a spoiled bluestocking, she has learned to keep a firm hold on her emotions. But, from the moment she meets him, she is powerless to resist the alluring and handsome earl.

Fighting their attraction, Gillian and Grant must band together to stop an unknown enemy from striking. Will the threat of danger be enough to make them realize their true feelings?

By Karen Ranney

THE SCOTTISH COMPANION • AUTUMN IN SCOTLAND
AN UNLIKELY GOVERNESS • TILL NEXT WE MEET
SO IN LOVE • TO LOVE A SCOTTISH LORD
THE IRRESISTIBLE MACRAE
WHEN THE LAIRD RETURNS • ONE MAN'S LOVE
AFTER THE KISS • MY TRUE LOVE
MY BELOVED • UPON A WICKED TIME
MY WICKED FANTASY

If You've Enjoyed This Book,
Be Sure to Read These Other
AVON ROMANTIC TREASURES

BEWITCHING THE HIGHLANDER *by Lois Greiman*
THE DUKE'S INDISCRETION *by Adele Ashworth*
HOW TO ENGAGE AN EARL *by Kathryn Caskie*
JUST WICKED ENOUGH *by Lorraine Heath*
THE VISCOUNT IN HER BEDROOM *by Gayle Callen*

Coming Soon

IN MY WILDEST FANTASIES *by Julianne MacLean*

KAREN RANNEY

The Scottish Companion

An Avon Romantic Treasure

AVON

An Imprint of HarperCollinsPublishers

This is a work of fiction. Names, characters, places, and incidents are products of the author's imagination or are used fictitiously and are not to be construed as real. Any resemblance to actual events, locales, organizations, or persons, living or dead, is entirely coincidental.

AVON BOOKS
An Imprint of HarperCollins*Publishers*
10 East 53rd Street
New York, New York 10022-5299

Copyright © 2007 by Karen Ranney
ISBN: 978-0-06-125237-2
ISBN-10: 0-06-125237-9
www.avonromance.com

First Avon Books paperback printing: October 2007

Avon Trademark Reg. U.S. Pat. Off. and in Other Countries,
Marca Registrada, Hecho en U.S.A.
HarperCollins® is a registered trademark of HarperCollins Publishers.

Printed in the U.S.A.

10 9 8 7 6 5 4 3 2 1

The Scottish Companion

Chapter 1

Rosemoor
Scotland, 1850

A funeral was the culmination of a contest—sickness, accident, age, it mattered not—in which Death was the victor. The deceased was the vanquished, and Death's prize was a black-draped catafalque.

In this case, the coffin of James Roberson.

Grant Roberson, the 10th Earl of Straithern, stood beside a marble-encased pillar, unwilling to join his mother in the family pew. He would be trapped there while the rest of the congregation stared at the back of his head, no doubt hoping for a reaction. They would be doomed to disappointment. He had no intention of expressing his grief for his brother in public.

The chapel was a sea of black: hats, veils, mourning suits, and dresses. The hundreds of candles could do nothing to illuminate the shadows since even the day was leaning toward darkness. The fog outside seemed to permeate the very brick, pool at the feet of the congregation, and hover below the casket as if impatient for the moment of his interment.

"My condolences, Your Lordship."

Grant turned his head slightly, glanced at the man who'd been the Roberson family physician for two decades, and nodded.

Dr. Fenton's appearance was such that people tended to overlook him. He was short and bewhiskered, with a bulbous nose and a rounded chin. His brown eyes were often filled with kindness, but their expression was hidden behind thick spectacles. When he was distressed or anxious, or most insistent upon a point, he removed them and polished them with his handkerchief or his cuff, or whatever piece of clothing presented itself.

Now he was diligently rubbing at the frames with the hem of his waistcoat.

"I did all that I could to save him, Your Lordship."

It hadn't been enough. But now was not the time to condemn the man's methods or the fact that he'd also been unable to save Grant's other brother six months earlier. The physician would be the first to explain that medicine was an imperfect science.

Perhaps Grant should have enlisted the aid of the nearest wise woman instead.

"We need to examine you at your earliest convenience, Your Lordship," Dr. Fenton said in a low voice.

Grant took advantage of the choir's interruption. A dozen angelic boyish voices spiraled toward the vaulted ceiling, marking the beginning of the service.

Dr. Fenton, however, was not daunted. "The sooner, Your Lordship, the better."

Grant folded his arms and stared down at the stone

floor. "I hardly think this is the proper time to discuss my health, Dr. Fenton."

"I can think of no better place, Your Lordship."

Was the man joking? A swift glance assured Grant that he was not. There was nothing remotely amused about Dr. Fenton's sober expression. Instead, the man's gaze met his directly, forcing Grant to think about something he didn't particularly care to consider at the moment.

In a month, a week, a few days, he might well be the one resting on the catafalque before the altar. Who would mourn him? His overburdened mother? By rights, no woman should have had to endure the death of a husband and two of her sons. Would his death be the final blow? Or would she simply endure as she was now, stiff and silent, unbending in her grief?

"Tomorrow," Grant said. "That's time enough. Surely I'll survive until tomorrow. You can examine me then."

The physician nodded, and had the tact to move away, leaving Grant to his contemplation of mortality.

A blood disease. In the midst of attending James, Dr. Fenton had hinted as much. A hereditary anomaly. Grant was, like his two brothers before him, doomed.

James had died five days ago, just as Andrew had six months earlier. Their symptoms had been eerily similar: lethargy, followed by an unearthly paleness as if the body were being readied for the state of being an angel. During the last week, James had been unable to keep anything on his stomach. When he'd died, he'd looked like a skeleton.

He could not be dead. James was annoying and boisterous, forever ridiculing those things Grant held so dear. His laughter and wit were sometimes too cutting, his appreciation of women and drink too encompassing. There was too great a silence in the world now and there was a yawning hole in Grant's life.

He could almost imagine his brother's comments at this moment, as if James stood beside him watching his own funeral.

Older brother, must you look so dour? I know we Scots are supposed to be a somber race, but you can crack a smile for me at least. If for no other reason than in memory. Surely there are some good times you can recall.

Grant felt tears pepper his eyes and stared resolutely ahead, refusing to give in to a public demonstration of grief. Whatever he felt was private, not to be shared. The 10th Earl of Straithern must, at all times, remember his position in life.

Not one whisper must carry about his behavior. Not one rumor be repeated, or one story told.

Chilled air wafted along the floor, crept up his trouser legs. If he didn't know better, he'd think that James's spirit was trying to get his attention.

Come, Grant, how difficult is it to get a smile out of you? I swear, you've got the fiercest look on your face.

He couldn't smile. He'd somehow lost the ability in the past few weeks, ever since he'd sat at James's bedside and watched him slip away.

He'd been his brothers' protector ever since he'd returned to Rosemoor on holiday from school at sixteen. The second night home he'd been awakened with the news that the 9th Earl of Straithern had taken his own life. A few days later, he'd stood at the grave site with his brothers, still children, and counseled them in a low voice.

"It looks dark now," he'd said. "But we're together. We'll overcome this, and soon there will be brighter days ahead."

How many times was he to bid a member of his family farewell?

His fingernails dug into the palms of his hands. Let him concentrate on physical discomfort rather than grief. Let him think of the future, of the design for the electric magnet he was perfecting, anything. Perhaps, then, he could endure the pain of this moment.

James's spirit was finally mercifully silent.

"As you can see, Dr. Fenton, I'm in the peak of health." Grant fastened his shirt, taking some time with his cuffs.

"Your brothers no doubt felt the same, Your Lordship," said Dr. Fenton. He moved to the other side of the room, standing in front of the fire.

After a moment, Grant finished dressing and joined him.

"Well, is there anything wrong with me?"

"Not that I can see, Your Lordship. But I would have given the same answer after examining James and Andrew." He studied the fire as if the solution for this particular dilemma were there in the orange and blue-tipped flames. "One moment they were well, and the next they were sickening."

"So, you think this blood disease, or whatever it is, will afflict me in the same manner? Why visit Andrew first? And then James? I'm oldest, why didn't it begin with me?"

"Your Lordship, I have no idea. I hesitate to be so honest with you, but I doubt any other medical practitioner in the whole of Scotland could give you a more truthful answer. We do not know so much about the human body. Perhaps one day we will be able to predict, at a child's birth, exactly what maladies will plague him. But at this moment, we do not know."

"Either a disease is killing us, or it isn't. Either I have it, or do not. Either I will die, or survive."

Grant turned away, moved to his desk.

"Your Lordship, so it is with all of us. None of us is more knowledgeable about our ultimate fate."

"Have you any idea how this mythical blood disease will affect my heirs, should I decide to have any?"

"That I cannot say, Your Lordship." Dr. Fenton shook his head as he spoke.

"So what do I do?"

The doctor turned to face him. "Your Lordship, I don't know the answer to that, either. But I would suggest that you go about your life. But do not leave important decisions to the future."

"In other words, act as if I'm dying?" Grant said.

"Aren't we all, Your Lordship?"

"Then I should prepare to be wed, Fenton."

The doctor smiled. "Marriage is not the fate some men think it is, Your Lordship. I was married to my dear Catherine for twenty-five years."

"You have a daughter, do you not?"

"I believe I've spoken of her to Your Lordship on numerous occasions," Fenton said. "I'm very proud of

her. If she were a boy, she'd be a fine physician. As it
is, however, she has a talent that can never be utilized,
regrettably."

"If she were the Countess of Straithern, she could,"
Grant said.

He was accustomed to rendering people speechless.
Simply being the Earl of Straithern had that effect on
quite a few people. Altogether, it wasn't a bad experience, and he'd grown accustomed to some deference.
Now, however, Dr. Fenton's fish-eyed stare and stark
silence were tiresome.

"I'm sorry, Your Lordship," the man finally said. "I
do not understand."

"I would think it would be eminently understandable, Doctor. I must marry. You have a daughter of
marriageable age."

"You want to marry my daughter?"

Grant settled in behind his desk. He pointed to the
chair opposite, and Dr. Fenton sat without comment.
He took off his spectacles and polished them on the
edge of his coat before carefully replacing them.

For a long moment he regarded Grant before finally
speaking. "I don't believe you've ever met my daughter, Your Lordship."

"She's healthy, is she not?"

"Very healthy, Your Lordship. And a beautiful girl,
if I may say so. But you, sir, could have your pick
of any woman in Scotland as well as England. Why
would you choose my daughter?"

"Am I that diseased that you would refuse the
match?"

"You misunderstand me, Your Lordship. You do
not seem to be suffering from the affliction that took

your brothers. But I cannot be certain. That is not why I'm surprised, however."

"Your reaction is a great deal more than surprised, sir."

"You are the Earl of Straithern, Your Lordship. You hold a long and venerated title. My daughter is not of the peerage."

"I frankly don't care, Dr. Fenton. I've neither the inclination nor the time, evidently, to search out a bride on my own."

"I doubt the countess will feel the same, Your Lordship."

The man had the sense to look away just then. If he'd not, Grant would have skewered him with a glance. His wife was no one's concern but his own. His mother's wishes did not enter into his decision. He doubted his mother would care if he married for property or wealth—the Roberson fortune was legendary in Scotland. Perhaps she'd have him marry for love as she was so fond of saying about her own union.

Look what happened when emotion was allowed to triumph over reason.

"I've been in Italy for the past five years, Doctor. Prior to that, I was not inclined to socialize. Nor has my mother left Rosemoor since my father died. We do not have social contacts and I've neither the time nor the willingness to court a bride. I simply want to wed. As a physician, you should understand the bluntness of my request. I need heirs. For that, I require a wife. Are you telling me that you do not wish your daughter to marry me?"

Dr. Fenton continued to stare at him, his wide brown eyes reminding Grant of one of the Rubenesque murals in the chapel. The physician was evidently at a loss for words, a rarity in the time since Grant had known him. Dr. Fenton was never without a comment or opinion.

"The match would be a good one for your daughter."

Dr. Fenton put the tips of his fingers together and studied them.

"Not to mention your charities," Grant added.

"Are you thinking to buy my cooperation, Your Lordship? I would not trade it for my daughter's happiness."

"Did you have your mind set for a love match for her, then? Tell me, is there anyone she would prefer to marry?"

"She doesn't have her mind on things that women commonly think of, Your Lordship. She'd much rather be involved in medicine. Ever since she was a little girl, she has studied my books and my journals."

"As the Countess of Straithern she would have the entire staff of my five homes to practice on. In fact, their health would be her concern. Her duty. Nor would it be amiss to have a wife with medical training as far as my own health is concerned, Doctor."

"I don't understand." Fenton waved his hand in the air. "I would be a fool to decline, Your Lordship."

"But you still think I'm a fool for proposing it," Grant said.

The doctor didn't answer.

"Let me be frank with you, if I may, Dr. Fenton. I want my countess to be of similar disposition as myself. That is to say, someone who is not ruled by emotion. I am a man of science. If my wife is of a similar nature, all the better. I want a wife who will have her own life, separate from mine, who will have her own interests, apart from me. Being the Countess of Straithern will give her sufficient income to do whatever she wishes to do. My requirements for her are very simple. She will not shame me or my family. She will not bring a hint of scandal to Rosemoor, and she will bear me a suitable number of children so that I can be assured my heritage will continue. That is all I ask of her.

"From what you've said about your daughter over the years, she will suit as well as anyone."

"She will not know what is expected of her, Your Lordship. We do not travel in exalted circles."

"Neither do I, Dr. Fenton. But if you're concerned about her role as my wife, bring her to Rosemoor. We will become acquainted in the month before our marriage."

"A month, Your Lordship?"

"Is there a reason for delay?"

Dr. Fenton shook his head. "I cannot think of one."

"Good," Grant said, standing. "The sooner it's done, the sooner I can concentrate on other matters."

"Other matters, Your Lordship?"

Grant studied him for a moment. "I have done as you suggested, Dr. Fenton, and not delayed my future. But perhaps it's time for even more honesty between us. I don't believe I'm dying. I don't believe there's a malady that has afflicted my family. I think James and Andrew were murdered, and I intend to find out who poisoned them, and why."

Chapter 2

The study was so quiet that Gillian Cameron could hear the squirrels chittering to one another outside the window. The day was a brilliantly beautiful one. A chilled breeze brought the hint of spring; the sky was blue and cloudless. Everything about the day had been pleasant, until this particular moment when shock rendered Gillian speechless.

"I expect you to assist her, Gillian. My daughter needs your help."

She stared at Dr. Fenton, aghast. "Sir, I counsel you not to insist upon this marriage. Arabella is not prepared."

Dr. Fenton frowned at her. "This is a very advantageous union, Gillian. It's not often such elevation is possible." He swiveled his chair to face her. "If she's not ready for marriage, then I expect you, as her companion, to teach her what she needs to know, tutor her in those social niceties she requires. Make her presentable. You have a month to do so."

She was so startled that for a moment she couldn't even frame a question. A month? Finally, she found her voice. "Sir, Arabella cares nothing at all for feminine pursuits. All she wants to do is study her books."

How often had she thought she was the only person in this household who did not seem to be fascinated with dying and death?

"His Lordship is not averse to allowing Arabella to pursue her studies, Gillian. In fact, he was quite willing to allow her to treat his staff. Tell her that if she balks. It's the only way she'll ever be a physician."

He turned away.

"You would use that, Dr. Fenton?" she asked, more calmly than she felt. "You would use Arabella's . . ." What did she call it? Obsession? Desperation? Nothing existed for Arabella but medicine. From the moment she woke in the morning until she fell asleep, exhausted, with a book in her hand, she was consumed with the idea of learning everything she could learn about the human body, about the treatment of disease. A broken bone delighted her, an inflammation fascinated her, and pus rendered her ecstatic.

"I've agreed, and as her father I've only Arabella's best interests at heart. You, of all people, Gillian, should know the foolishness of a woman turning against her upbringing."

She clasped her hands together so tightly that her knuckles were white.

"I beg you, Dr. Fenton, please do not insist upon this. Whether or not it's an advantageous union is of no difference. Arabella will not agree. And if she does, by some miracle, accede to your wishes, she'll be miserable."

"Then you must plant the idea in her head that it is for her greatest good, Gillian. I expect you to be able to influence her to accept her future. Her very bright future."

Since Arabella barely spoke to her, and since she had not once exerted any influence over the young woman since the day she entered Dr. Fenton's employ nearly two years ago, Gillian could only stare helplessly at him.

Finally she left the doctor's study and took the stairs to Arabella's room. Even though it was already midmorning, the girl would not have left her chamber. Instead she would be at her desk, a lamp lit despite the brightness of the day, poring over yet another text featuring gruesome illustrations and even more hideous descriptions.

Life was much more pleasant when she controlled her feelings. As Gillian made her way to Arabella's room, however, she found herself growing more and more disturbed. Perhaps it was anger. At Dr. Fenton, when he'd alluded to her past? Or at his wish to be aligned to an earl? Or was she annoyed at herself for feeling a surge of unexpected grief when he'd mentioned family?

Nearly three years ago, she'd left her stepmother clutching her lace-trimmed handkerchief, and her father frowning into the bowl of his pipe. They'd said not one word to her as she'd left the manor house that had been her home all her life.

One last time, she'd turned back, optimist to the end, and said, "Do you hate me so much, then?"

Time was arthritic, ticking by on bent and crooked hands.

"Not hate, Gillian," her father had finally said. "Not hate. But you've lost the right to be in the company of decent people."

Decent people? A stepmother who could watch her walk away and not say one word? A father who cared more for his new family than his daughter? Was that decent?

They wouldn't listen to her words, however. They hadn't from the beginning. Nothing would sway them, nothing would soften their iron hearts. So she remained mute and almost sullen, feeling a terror so deep and cold that she was stiff with it.

Perhaps that's what she felt now. Perhaps it was fear, and not anger. If Arabella married, what would happen to her? Arabella, as the Countess of Straithern, wouldn't need a companion. In all honesty, she didn't need her now. Arabella certainly didn't want Gillian in her room, in her life. Whenever Gillian spoke, it was to silence, and the two women rarely shared a conversation. To converse required the participation of both people.

The only time Arabella talked to her was if Gillian mentioned some discomfort. She'd stuck herself with her needle when embroidering. Her woman's time was difficult this month. Then Arabella's eyes would light up and Gillian could not stem the flow of questions.

The problem was, Gillian was exceedingly healthy. Nor was she about to imagine ailments in order to converse with Arabella. Therefore, most of their time together was silent, Arabella studying, and Gillian engaged in her embroidery.

A very proper, if boring, existence, and one that was about to drastically change.

How odd that she missed it already.

She knocked on the door to Arabella's sitting room, waited a moment, and opened the door. It would be a waste of time waiting for Arabella's response. She neither welcomed nor forbade Gillian to enter. She simply ignored her.

Gillian entered the room and closed the door behind her. Without a word, she went to the chair beside the window, sat, and picked up her embroidery. Arabella didn't turn from her position at the desk.

Long moments passed while Gillian stared out the window, wishing she could be anywhere but here. Perhaps on the moor, standing among the heather. A hardy plant, it scarcely seemed to need anything. Instead, it just planted its roots into the ground, impervious to wind or rain or sun. Would that she could be like the heather.

She turned her head and regarded Arabella. Her head was bent, intent on the notes she was writing. The sun was bright today, and seemed to add gilt to the girl's blond hair.

"Your father wished to speak to me," Gillian said.

Arabella didn't stop writing.

"About your coming marriage."

Arabella's head came up, but she didn't turn. She only stared at the drawers of her secretary in front of her.

"I told him you would object."

"Did you?" Arabella asked.

"He said it was quite an honor to marry an earl." Those weren't his exact words. Dr. Fenton was a bit more avaricious than that, but the gist was the same.

"You really do not have a choice, I'm afraid," Gillian said. "Your father is set on the match. I have to agree that it seems very advantageous."

Arabella glanced at her, her mouth curved in a smile. "What would an earl want with me?"

Did the girl not ever look in the mirror? She was perhaps the most beautiful creature Gillian had ever seen. She looked like an angel from a medieval painting with her heart-shaped face and striking green eyes. There was nothing about Arabella out of place, not one imperfection. Of course an earl would want her for his wife.

"He says you can continue your studies. Did your father tell you that?"

Arabella nodded. "I don't believe him, of course." She returned to her notes. "Most people say things they don't really mean to make you do what they want."

"How horribly cynical," Gillian said. "Surely you don't actually feel that way?"

"I do. My own father is not averse to the technique." She glanced at Gillian again, looking supremely bored by the subject as if they were not discussing her future.

"What if he were telling the truth?" Gillian asked. "Would you consent to the union?"

Arabella smiled again.

"Regardless of what I feel, Gillian, I haven't a choice. I may rail and protest and shout to the rooftops, but in the end my father and the earl will make it come about. We women have no say in our lives, not truly. When a man asks you what you want, it is only a waste of time. If you tell him, he'll quickly dismiss everything you've just said out of hand."

She turned her attention to her notes, but she didn't begin writing. "I don't want to be married, Gillian, but I shall be. I have no choice in the matter. I'm like a trapped animal, and no amount of prettying it up will change that fact."

"You might find love, Arabella. It might be possible to find love in such a union. If not, a measure of contentment. No, we do not have a choice, I agree, but in some matters you do. You could choose to be happy, in some way. The earl has said you might practice medicine. Surely you could find some contentment in that?"

"How silly you can be, Gillian. You're such a child in so many ways."

Stung, Gillian could only stare at her.

"Sometimes, the price for contentment is too high. He will touch me. He will bed me. I think I shall die if that happens."

"One doesn't die," Gillian said, compelled to speak by the utter hopelessness in the girl's voice. "In some situations, with some men, it's pleasurable." More than pleasurable. The act of love could exalt the senses, transport a place, a room, a mood into something almost hallowed.

"There is nothing you could say to make the situation more bearable, Gillian. I do not have your childish view of the world. I see it as it is, not as I wish it to be."

This conversation was the longest she'd ever had with Arabella. In fact, it was the most she'd ever heard Arabella speak.

Gillian glanced at the girl, knowing there was nothing further she could say. Arabella had it right. In the end, she'd be married, regardless of what she wanted.

But what Arabella didn't know was that marriage was so much more preferable to other alternatives. Being alone, for one. Being left adrift without anyone to love, or to love her.

But she had loved well, and that memory must sustain her for the rest of her life. Yet, at times like this, when others were rejecting love's potential and promise, she felt increasingly lonely. She would have been satisfied to be in Arabella's place, to be given so much without any effort, to be promised respect, and protection. All Arabella had to do was marry.

For the first time, Gillian truly envied the girl, and wasn't that a foolish emotion?

Chapter 3

Gillian sat back against the cushions of the carriage, wishing suddenly that Dr. Fenton had not requested that she accompany them to Rosemoor. Requested? Hardly the correct word. It wasn't a request—more a command, rather. What other choice had she? If she wasn't Arabella's companion, she'd have no occupation at all.

She should have taken advantage of the occasional trips to Inverness and visited a few of the milliners there. She could have seen the newest styles, perhaps practiced decorating a few of her own bonnets. Then she could have taken the results and solicited a position. She was talented in embroidery, evident from the fact that her work could be found in abundance throughout Dr. Fenton's house. Surely she could have shown her work to a few dressmakers, and obtained a position with one of them.

Or perhaps she was only being foolish, and there was nothing she could do, no talent she possessed significant enough to support herself. Therefore, she packed her trunk and watched as it was lashed to the wagon holding all of Arabella's belongings.

Gillian couldn't help but wonder what the earl would think of Arabella's trousseau: two trunks of books; one of her personal belongings, such as the silver-backed mirror and brush she'd inherited from her mother, and a porcelain tooth cup from France. One trunk held her clothing, and the last—or the most important, according to Arabella—was a trunk containing a male skeleton.

Not that it was possible to tell, from even a studied glance, what gender Roderick had once been. Gillian had not spent an appreciable time contemplating him. She could still remember when she'd opened the bureau in Arabella's sitting room the first time and found herself facing a grinning skull. She'd taken one look at Roderick and clamped her hand over her mouth to contain a scream.

"Oh, do not be childish, Gillian," Arabella had said. "It's only a skeleton. We shall all look like Roderick one day."

"There are certain things I don't wish to know," Gillian had retorted. "The exact hour and day of my death, for one, and my appearance after that moment."

She'd ignored—or tried—the skeleton after that day.

Now Arabella sat at Gillian's side, opposite her father. Her head was bent, her attention directed at the open book on her lap. Gillian knew she wasn't reading, however. Arabella grew ill when reading in a carriage—one of the few personal details she knew about the girl. Arabella disliked greens, and favored lamb with mint jelly. She liked warm milk in the evening, and preferred wearing a particular nightgown with blue flowers embroidered on the yoke. She had no patience for card games, or conversation of any sort, and if she did speak it was to that hideous skeleton in her sitting room. That, and her growing dislike of the idea of marriage, was the extent of her knowledge of Arabella.

There was a flash of white beyond the trees. Leaning forward, Gillian caught a glimpse of something pointed. The top of a tower? The tops of two towers, to be precise. Narrow and round, they were built atop a brick wall now covered in lichen or ivy. Beyond the towers were two other pediments, these square and cumbersome, as if they'd been added as an afterthought to the wall.

"Is that it?" she asked, stunned at both the size and the majesty of Arabella's new home. "Is that Rosemoor?"

Dr. Fenton sat up and glanced out the window. "Indeed it is. Rosemoor, the seat of the Earls of Straithern. A most impressive edifice, don't you think, Gillian?"

The house was a jumble of buildings, all connected together, some high, some low, some topped with towers, some flat. The whole of Rosemoor was faded red sandstone, with large arched windows where there were windows, and tiny slits where there were none. She started to count them, and stopped when she reached twenty.

"It's very large."

"Indeed it is. Seventy-two rooms, to be precise. I myself have seen only a quarter of them. But I expect you, my dear," he said, shooting a fond look toward his daughter, "will grow to know them well."

Arabella said nothing. Nor did she look up from her book.

* * *

"Your bride will be here any moment, Grant."

Grant stared at the paper in front of him, wondering if he should engage in conversation with his mother, or ignore her. She was, after all, the Countess of Straithern, and free to speak her mind. But that didn't mean he had to listen, or even agree. Although he'd occasionally solicited her opinion, he wasn't interested in what she had to say now.

He glanced up from his ledger. "I have given word that I'm to be notified when she arrives."

"Are you no more interested than that? A wife is not a horse, Grant, however much you've bargained for the filly."

He stood, unwilling to sit behind his desk while she advanced on him. He really should have left for his laboratory early this morning, but he'd been kept behind by his correspondence.

"The subject isn't open to discussion, Mother. I've done what I feel is necessary."

"Have you?" She took a step back as if to equalize their height, but he was at least six inches taller. Nor was he cowed by the ferocity of her look as he had been when he was twelve and guilty of some misdeed.

Living in Italy had been a pleasure in more ways than one.

"The subject is not open to discussion," he repeated. "Is there anything else I can do for you?"

She clamped her lips shut and narrowed her eyes. "You've become insufferably arrogant, Grant. I dislike that quality in you."

"Perhaps if you listed all my faults, we could meet

soon to discuss them. I'm not averse to improvement, Mother."

"Then at least tell me why you've chosen Dr. Fenton's daughter. Are you set on this course, Grant?"

He studied her for a moment. "Are you prepared to go to Edinburgh, Mother? Renew your acquaintances, enter society once again?"

She didn't respond.

"Arabella Fenton will suit well enough. Is there anything else I can do for you, Mother?" He brushed his fingertips against the letter he was writing, wondering when, exactly, he could finish with this chore and escape. He liked routine, the act of finishing one task before beginning another. If he wasn't so methodical, he would have bolted from the room before she'd advanced on him.

She stood her ground, frowning at him. "Have you fallen in love?"

He was almost amused by that question, enough that he felt the corners of his lips curve up in a smile. "No, Mother, I'm not in love. I've yet to meet the girl."

"Then why?"

"Because it would be wiser if I married as soon as possible," he said.

They exchanged a long look, and he wondered what was in his eyes. Some knowledge, something that she saw and recognized, some emotion that made her nod and look down.

Perhaps his marriage to Dr. Fenton's daughter would leave his family open to gossip, but no more so than his sudden appearance on the Edinburgh marriage mart. He could imagine that speculation.

"She will be arriving soon. If you cannot welcome her, Mother, then I can accept that. But do not make her miserable. I would think that you would train her, instead. Mold her into what you think she should be."

Her dark eyes were filled with an emotion he didn't want to decipher. Without another word, she turned and left the room.

He stared after her, wondering if he should have shared his suspicions.

Someone had wanted his brothers dead. But who? And did their murderous intent extend to him? Who was next in line to inherit the title? An obscure second cousin who'd immigrated to America. He hadn't heard of the family for years, wasn't even certain the man was alive. But his solicitors would somehow manage to find him if anything happened to Grant.

If anything happened to him. What a warming thought.

His mother would be protected by the enormous Roberson wealth. But she would be forced to leave Rosemoor if an obscure relation inherited the title. The estate was entailed, so wrapped up in codicils and provisos that the most skillful of Edinburgh lawyers couldn't disentangle it.

His attention was caught by a movement outside. A carriage pulled slowly into the drive. He stood and walked to the window, watching as the vehicle stopped in front of the stone steps. One of the footmen opened the door. Dr. Fenton emerged, extending a hand inside the vehicle.

A woman descended the steps. As he watched, the hood of her cloak fell, revealing her features. Her face was pale, a delicate rose tinting her cheeks. Her hair was brown and arranged in a tight coronet at the back of her head.

She stared off into the distance, and he wondered what had captured her attention. He stepped to the side and looked to where her attention was directed. A tree. She was looking at a tree, a small smile playing around her lips.

What kind of woman was amused by a tree?

As he watched, she was joined by another female. This one carried a book, and seemed uninterested in her surroundings. But she was even more beautiful than the first woman. An angel, with golden hair to match and a face that had him staring. She was perhaps the most beautiful woman he'd ever seen. She looked up from her book, and he wished for a set of binoculars so that he could determine the color of her eyes.

Should he join them? Welcome them at the broad stone steps? Or should he remain in his study, the arrogant taskmaster with a reputation of disliking interruptions?

One of these women was going to be his wife. Which one? They were both beautiful, a fact that annoyed him. He hadn't expected Dr. Fenton's daughter to be beautiful. Why hadn't Fenton mentioned her appearance? Or perhaps the man had, and Grant had simply taken his posturing for the words of a proud father.

A beautiful woman would be a detriment to the life he'd planned for himself. A woman of beauty expected a certain amount of attention, a certain obeisance. She wouldn't be content with his routine, his involvement with his work.

The blond woman glanced toward Rosemoor, her attention momentarily distracted from her book. Her face was solemn, her mouth unsmiling. He wondered what would amuse her, what would banish the look of caution from her features.

Suddenly, the prospect of marrying a beautiful woman didn't seem so abhorrent.

A curving brick staircase in the shape of a horseshoe rose to the double doors, above which stood a crest no doubt belonging to the Earls of Straithern. Topping the entrance was a square tower, the clock in the center of it bearing Roman numerals against an ivory face.

When Arabella made no move to leave the carriage, Gillian stepped out. The shrubberies surrounding the house were trimmed; the trees were arching tidily over the road. Even the gravel path was orderly, as if it had been swept clean of extraneous leaves. One lone tree sat in a circular island, its branches left to grow naturally, its leaves still curling in the cool spring air. As if it were a sentinel, a warning to all what might happen if nature were left to itself. It was, perhaps, the most welcoming part of Rosemoor.

The air of Rosemoor smelled different, somehow, as if the Earl of Straithern had commanded only the best scents to be present for their arrival: grass, newly born flowers, the sweetest breeze from the south.

Gillian turned and faced the edifice, thinking that she'd been wrong. This was no house, but a castle. All the towers and crenellated patterns along the roof spoke of defense, barely needed now in this peaceful age.

Arabella finally left the carriage. Dr. Fenton extended his arm to her, and she placed her hand on his sleeve. The two of them preceded Gillian up the curving steps while two footmen followed. What must it be like to have servants around every hour of every day? Gillian wanted to stop and tell them that she was no more important than they. She, too, was a servant, for all the title of companion. Her role would not change despite Arabella's elevation in rank.

"You will like this, Gillian." Dr. Fenton stopped and glanced back at her. "There are bits of needlework at Rosemoor that were worked by Mary, Queen of Scots."

"Truly?"

He nodded. "I am not certain which ones they are, but I shall find out for you. Also, one of the bedrooms is said to have been occupied by Bonnie Prince Charlie during his retreat from the English." He looked up at the broad double doors. "A home steeped in history, Arabella. And you will be the chatelaine of it."

Arabella said nothing, and although Gillian couldn't see her face, she would wager that it was expressionless. Arabella had a way of hiding her feelings so deep that no one really knew what she was thinking. How very odd that Gillian had adopted the trait over the last year. It was easier to pretend, wasn't it?

The doors suddenly opened, and they were greeted by a portly man with white hair, attired in a gray suit that fit his corpulent form perfectly. For a horrified moment, Gillian thought he might be the earl. If so, this marriage was even more understandable. He was old, and Arabella was young and beautiful.

But he bowed to Dr. Fenton and stepped aside. Of

course, he was the majordomo. How foolish of her. An earl would not greet them at the door.

"Good day, Blevins," Dr. Fenton said. "His Lordship is expecting us."

"Indeed, sir. The earl will welcome you in the Flower Room."

Dr. Fenton smiled brightly. "My favorite room."

The majordomo led the way, with Dr. Fenton keeping up a running commentary about all the treasures to be found at Rosemoor.

He stopped beside one table, oblivious to the fact that Blevins eyed him with some disfavor.

"This writing table was made by Gole, the cabinetmaker to Louis XIV of France. It was a gift from the king to the Earl of Straithern who was an ambassador to Paris at the time."

The majordomo pulled out his pocket watch and glanced at it with great ceremony, a none too gentle reminder that one did not keep an earl waiting.

Gillian glanced at the table as she passed. The inlaid pewter, brass, and mother-of-pearl made for a gaudy display. Everything old was not necessarily beautiful.

Of her two companions, Dr. Fenton was more enamored of Rosemoor than his daughter. Arabella had been silent during most of the journey. Now her demeanor was stiff, her shoulders straight, her posture leaving no doubt that she was a reluctant guest, and an even more reluctant bride.

Blevins hesitated before a set of double doors, and nodded to a footman who stood beside one. With military precision, the young man turned, opened the door, and then bowed to all four of them before stepping aside.

The Flower Room was a drawing room featuring numerous sketches of flowers mounted in frames along the walls. The walls were adorned in a deep crimson patterned silk. Mahogany cabinets and tables sat next to the pale yellow silk upholstered chairs and sofas. But it was the carpet that no doubt gave the room its name. In the center was the Straithern coat of arms, but the border design was entirely made up of flowers, all so perfectly woven they looked ready to pick.

Gillian stood admiring the carpet for a moment before becoming aware that Dr. Fenton was addressing her. She glanced up to see him gesturing toward the fireplace.

A man stood there, attired in immaculate black, his stiff white collar fastened at the throat with a black onyx pin. The silver buttons on his coat were so polished that they glinted in the sunlight from an adjoining window. His hair was as black as his suit, and she half expected his eyes to be dark as well. But as her glance traveled upward, past a square chin and an aristocratic nose, she was startled to discover that his eyes were gray.

Or silver. Silver like his buttons, and the buckles of his shoes. Silver, like clouds after a storm, like a river in the sunlight.

Grant Roberson, the 10th Earl of Straithern.

He looked like an earl, a man set apart from others. Of course his home was a showplace, a relic of the past. His ancestors had been part of Scotland's history.

Why on earth would he want to marry Arabella Fenton?

"Miss Cameron." He glanced at her momentarily, and then at Arabella.

Had they been introduced while her mind was wandering? Evidently so, because he paid her no further attention.

"Your Lordship," she said, wondering if she should curtsy. Why hadn't she studied how to greet an earl?

He nodded at Blevins, and the man disappeared. Dr. Fenton led Arabella to a sofa, and Gillian followed, uncertain of the protocol. Did she sit beside her? In another chair? Did she excuse herself from the room entirely?

She chose to sit on an adjoining sofa, and realized that she'd made the wrong decision when the earl sat next to her.

His hands were large and square, the fingers long, his nails cut straight across. She tended to notice hands on a man, as well as the back of his neck. Odd things, really, since physical characteristics gave no indication of a man's character or temperament.

She smiled at herself, and then realized the earl was looking at her.

"Are you amused, Miss Cameron?"

"In a way, Your Lordship. At my own peccadilloes, perhaps."

He looked startled by her answer.

"I'm pleased that you find Rosemoor amusing, Miss Cameron. That isn't the reaction it normally inspires."

"No doubt people are awestruck, Your Lordship," she suggested. "Or perhaps simply rendered dumb."

He looked at her intently, as if to gauge whether she was joking. How odd that she had the strangest desire to laugh. He was not a particularly amusing sight. In fact, the Earl of Straithern was rather imposing, if not arresting.

"How many gardeners do you employ?" she asked.

Once again, he looked startled.

"Twenty. Why do you ask?"

"I was simply curious. Everything looks very tame, Your Lordship."

"Is that why you were staring at a tree?"

It was her turn to be surprised. He had been watching her and she'd not known.

There was something decidedly wintry about his gray eyes. Perhaps Arabella might inspire their warmth, but Gillian doubted it. Arabella was as cold in her way.

The two of them would make a pair, wouldn't they?

She looked away, attempting to free him from any more politeness, real or feigned, on his part.

It was all too clear that he was a match to Arabella in attractiveness. They would have exquisite children—if Arabella allowed him into her bed.

"Was your journey pleasant?" he asked Arabella.

"Very much so, very much so," Dr. Fenton answered. "Thank you for sending your carriage for us."

"What do you think of Rosemoor, Miss Fenton?"

There, a more frontal attack. The earl's quick glance at Dr. Fenton was almost a warning for the man not to answer for his daughter.

Gillian stifled a smile. The doctor had met his match in the earl. Or perhaps been bested.

"Lovely," Arabella said, the one-word answer faint, as if she breathed more than spoke the word.

At that moment, Gillian decided to set aside a few examples of her embroidery in the next week or so, and arrange travel to Inverness. Surely there she might obtain an offer of employment.

Anything but watch this disaster of a marriage transpire.

As if he'd heard her thoughts, the earl turned to her. "And you, Miss Cameron, was the journey acceptable for you as well?"

She glanced at him, surprised. What did he care for her comfort? Perhaps he was more egalitarian than the doctor, to whom she was nothing more than a paid servant.

"It was acceptable, Your Lordship," she said.

Gillian stood, moved to the window, wishing she could transport herself magically anywhere but here. The silence in the room was awkward, embarrassing, almost a personage in its own right.

Blevins appeared with a maid in tow, carrying a silver tray heaped with refreshments. While the others were being served, Gillian remained where she was at the window, her back to all of them, deliberately isolating herself. Was she being rude? She didn't know, and at the moment, truly didn't care.

She was the companion: the extra woman, the chaperone, the one who made arrangements, offered excuses, and protected, but was otherwise useless. She was as valuable as a fireplace andiron on a summer day.

How very strange to be feeling out of sorts right now.

She was wearing her darkest, most serviceable dress, a dark blue with a white detachable collar and lace cuffs. A perfect choice in which to travel. When she'd dressed this morning, she'd given no thought whatsoever about appearing at her best. She'd simply wanted to get Arabella to Rosemoor before she'd rebelled.

Gillian glanced in the earl's direction to find him studying her. His face was stern and unsmiling, his gray eyes intent.

Why on earth was he looking at her? Had she done something unpardonable? What was the required etiquette when dealing with an earl? He couldn't be all that different from other men. Look at his reaction to Arabella. Surely she wasn't jealous. She was as far from an earl's eye as a ladybug was from an eagle.

They exchanged a long look before she finally turned away. She clasped her hands together, staring out the window, wondering why she was trembling.

Fatigue, of course. That's all it could be. Even though the journey here had been a scant hour's duration, she hadn't slept well the night before.

She could still feel him staring. Surreptitiously she glanced down at herself. Was a button unbuttoned? Her fingers brushed against one cheek and then the other. Had she some dirt on her face? Was there something wrong with her?

What did she say to an earl to get him to stop staring?

Your Lordship, if you would, please, look at Arabella. Study her with the intensity you are now studying me. Or look at this magnificent table beside the window. Mosaic, is it not? From where did you acquire it? Was it another gift from a king? If nothing else, perhaps you might investigate the view outside your own window. It's indeed worthy of awe, Your

Lordship. Anything would be preferable, Your Lordship, than to stare at me.

"Blevins?"

Blevins halted in the act of serving Dr. Fenton, and glanced at his employer. "Your Lordship?"

"See that Miss Cameron is served as well."

The earl's voice sounded like chocolate, rich and dark and warm.

Blevins bowed. "Assuredly, Your Lordship."

"I'm not hungry, Your Lordship," Gillian said, wondering if her face was as flushed as it felt. "But thank you."

Dr. Fenton frowned at her. Evidently she'd irritated him somehow. Would this entire visit be as wearying as the last five minutes? Would she have to be concerned about pleasing everyone?

The Earl of Straithern loaded two biscuits and a small piece of cake on a plate and stood, delivering it to her himself.

"Are you very certain?" he asked. "Our cook is renowned for her pastries."

His gray eyes were alight with an emotion she couldn't decipher. Humor? Did she amuse him? Or was he daring her to be rude in the face of Dr. Fenton's obvious displeasure?

She took the plate from him, their fingers brushing. She glanced up to find him looking at her again.

"Please do not," she said in a low enough tone that Dr. Fenton would not hear.

"Do not what?"

"Stare at me so." She looked away, still holding the plate in front of her.

"I wasn't aware that I was staring," he said.

"What rubbish, Your Lordship. You know perfectly well you were staring."

He looked startled again, but he didn't counter her observation. Instead, he smiled.

"Please let any of my staff know if Miss Fenton requires anything."

"Of course, Your Lordship."

"Her well-being is of great importance to me."

"Of course, Your Lordship." Since Arabella had avoided looking in his direction, she evidently didn't feel the same degree of caring for the earl as he did for her. But Gillian carefully restrained herself from saying anything of the sort. She was, after all, only the companion, and a reluctant one at that.

"You look as if you'd like to escape to the veranda, Miss Cameron."

Was he *daring* her?

"Not at all, Your Lordship," she said calmly.

"You may, of course, if you wish." With a gesture, he indicated the door that led to the outside.

Dr. Fenton would not understand. Arabella might, if she ventured an opinion as to her companion's actions, which she rarely did. Arabella was so completely within herself that it was difficult to tell if she even noticed anyone else.

"Thank you, no," Gillian said.

"A very proper response."

She glanced at him. "Have I given you any reason to think I'm not entirely proper, Your Lordship?" She pushed down the fear that seemed to clench her throat like an unseen hand.

"Not at all, Miss Cameron."

"Then please do not say such—"

"Have I offended you?" He looked amused, which irritated her.

"You have," she said, loud enough that Dr. Fenton turned and looked at her, the expression on his face one of concern.

"Then I apologize for that as well, Miss Cameron."

"As well as what, Your Lordship?" Would he just simply go away?

"For implying you were not proper. Propriety is very important to me."

"Is it, Your Lordship?" She turned and faced him directly, annoyed that she had to look up at him. "Then I would think you'd be careful to direct your attentions to Arabella and not to me."

He smiled slightly, almost a self-deprecating expression, before leaving her without a word.

After he left her side, Gillian took a deep breath, wishing that he wasn't quite so handsome. Or so very much a presence. He filled the air around him, and made people notice him. Or perhaps she was the only one to feel this way.

The sooner Arabella was married and settled, the better for everyone.

Chapter 4

Dinner that night was a tray in Arabella's sitting room, a concession to Arabella's stated exhaustion. Gillian wasn't tired from the journey but she was exceedingly tired of being in Arabella's presence. An Arabella who was pointedly ignoring her.

"You should not hold your cup in such a manner," Gillian said gently. "Hold it by the handle, like this." She demonstrated, hoping that Arabella would cease planting both elbows on the table and glaring at her.

Had the girl always been so sullen? Or was her attitude somehow emphasized by the strangeness of their surroundings? Either way, Gillian was growing increasingly impatient with Arabella.

"Do not lecture me, Gillian. I do not care one whit about the manners of the gentry at the moment."

"They are not simply the manners of the gentry, Arabella," Gillian said. "Holding your cup with both hands is not polite. Which you would know if you ever bothered to look around you."

"I don't care."

"You should," Gillian said, annoyance slipping into her voice. Let Dr. Fenton lecture her on patience if he must. "You're to be the Countess of Straithern in less than a month."

"Not because I wish it." Arabella stood and walked to the window.

"Yes, yes, I know," Gillian said. "You wish to save yourself for your studies. Medicine calls to you. Life beckons to you as a healer. You are meant for better things. God save us if you have to be a wife or mother when there's a boil to be lanced or a bedsore to be treated."

She stood and circled the table, intent for her own room.

For a moment, Arabella didn't speak. Finally, she said, "Why are you so irritated, Gillian?"

"Because you are irritating," Gillian answered. "You may not wish to be married, but such is the way of the world. You should thank God you're to be married to an earl, a man who can give you anything you desire."

"Money does not influence me."

"Because you've never been without it. Or protection," Gillian said bitingly. "You've never known what it was to have to choose between dignity and survival, Arabella."

Arabella turned and stared out at the night. "Dignity and survival. You're talking about what happened to you in Edinburgh, aren't you?"

"I don't discuss my past with anyone, Arabella, even you."

The other woman smiled, an oddly sad expression. "Nor I. But sometimes it intrudes, even so." She placed both hands flat on the window, and leaned closer until her nose almost touched the pane. "You do not know how much I hate this place, Gillian. I hate Rosemoor with a deep and abiding loathing. I never wished to live here."

Startled, Gillian watched her. "How do you know you hate it? You've been here a matter of hours only."

Arabella turned and looked at her. "Do you realize, Gillian, that I'm only here to act as a broodmare for the Earl of Straithern?"

A broodmare? She could look at the man and think that?

"Would you be alone all of your life, Arabella?"

"I would be the arbiter of my own fate."

Gillian sighed, pity winning out over annoyance. Arabella had not yet been tested by life. She wanted something that could never happen, even in a perfect world.

"No one is the arbiter of his own fate. You are subject to the dictates of society just as we all are. You must do what is expected of you, Arabella. But you can find pleasure in that, if you will. The earl seems like a good man, an interesting man." A fascinating man, but that comment she didn't make.

"You are determined that I should marry and be happy, aren't you? Even though I am certain that I will be miserable?" Arabella turned to look at her.

"You will be what you wish, Arabella. If you are set on being miserable, you will be miserable."

Arabella turned away from her, staring out at the night.

Gillian bit back any further comments at the entrance of a maid who began unpacking Arabella's trunks. She filled the armoire and the dresser with the trousseau Dr. Fenton had ordered from three over-worked seamstresses.

"Do not unpack that one," Arabella ordered, gesturing to the trunk nearest the door. The maid stepped back, curtsied, and left the room, making Gillian grateful that she didn't have to explain about Arabella's prized skeleton. She could just imagine the talk below stairs about that.

When Arabella retreated into a book, Gillian left for her own room, an adjoining chamber easily as beautiful as Arabella's.

A beige flower-patterned wallpaper softened the room, and seemed to add warmth to the chill. Spring might have come to the Highlands, but winter had not yet vanished completely. A taste of it was there in the wind, and the clear, crisp night.

Her room held an armoire as large as the one in Arabella's chamber, along with a bureau, and a curtained bed on a raised dais. The biggest surprise, however, was a door leading to a private washing area.

Rosemoor was a startling combination of history and new advances.

Gillian finished unpacking her trunk in only minutes. She glanced at the clock on the mantel. Beyond time to retire, considering that she'd begun her day at dawn. But she was in a very strange, almost demented, mood. What she wanted to do was wander through this magnificent place, study the portraits in the hall and the landscapes in the stairwell. There was a bronze urn in an alcove in the hallway that she'd wanted to examine, but Arabella had been too impatient to reach her room for her to do so.

However, she was not exactly a guest here. She

was only at Rosemoor because of Arabella, her only duty to ensure Arabella's . . . Her thoughts ground to a halt. She was not here to make certain Arabella was happy. She doubted if Arabella could really *be* happy. Instead, she was here to guarantee that Arabella fit into the new world that circumstance and tragedy had acquired for her.

Envy was a foolish emotion.

"Your Lordship," Dr. Fenton said. "Ever since the time of the Medicis, and possibly even before, man has created poison to kill his enemies. However, a man with murder on his mind can dispose of a rival quick enough. He needn't have poison to do it."

"Are you being deliberately obtuse, Dr. Fenton?" Grant asked. "Or is it simply because you don't know the answer to my question? Is it possible to give a man poison and have him evince the same symptoms as either James or Andrew? A simple answer will suffice. Yes or no?"

Dr. Fenton took too long to answer for Grant's peace of mind. Just as he was on the brink of ordering the older man from his study, the doctor finally spoke again.

"I suppose it is. But I am not versed in poisons, Your Lordship. Although I have a few books on the subject, I have not taken the time to study them."

"Do you know of anyone with such an expertise?"

"I suppose it would be possible to inquire among my former students. Perhaps someone has a keen interest in poisons. Although I do not see merit in such studies. We are trained, as physicians, to heal, Your Lordship, not kill."

"Pursue your inquiries, Doctor, but only on the condition that you do not mention Rosemoor. I want no hint of rumor or innuendo."

Dr. Fenton bowed slightly. "Of course, Your Lordship. I shall send letters to only those who can hold their tongue. But I had thought you resigned yourself to the illness of your brothers. Has something changed in that regard?"

"Are you speaking of your daughter, Dr. Fenton?"

The older man nodded.

"I didn't choose to wed because of a blood disease. I decided to marry because I was concerned someone might achieve their aim to kill me. Hopefully, before they do so, I've created an heir for Rosemoor."

Dr. Fenton looked shocked. "If such a person should succeed in killing you, Your Lordship, what would stop them from killing your heir as well?"

"Absolutely nothing," Grant said. "Which is why I need to discover the identity of the person doing this."

Dr. Fenton nodded. "Then I shall correspond with some of my colleagues in Edinburgh, Your Lordship. I will ask them, as well, if they have any knowledge of any new treatments of blood diseases."

"New treatments?"

"Purges, Your Lordship. Perhaps you should drink more wine."

"By all means, seek out any new treatments. In the meantime," Grant said, "I've taken a few precautions of my own." He only smiled, having absolutely no intention of telling the physician what he'd done.

He didn't care if Fenton was a healer or not. Grant couldn't trust anyone.

After the doctor's departure, Grant stared at the list of relatives he'd made a month ago. His solicitor had recently sent word of another death in the family, this one from old age and not a blood disease. He scratched off Derrick Roberson's name, and made a notation of the man's age of eighty-four. Of the remaining names, three lived in Scotland, one in England, and two had immigrated either to Australia or to America.

His father's will had been surprisingly generous. Ranald Roberson had awarded a distant cousin a stipend for his lifetime. In addition, there were various other bequests, each one of which Grant had his solicitor investigate. He wanted to know the whereabouts of every relative. Common sense, however, told him to look elsewhere. He couldn't see how the males remaining on the list could be perceived as a threat. One was an octogenarian; a third cousin was seven, and the remaining relative had been stricken by apoplexy. Nevertheless, he wanted to know their current circumstances. Had penury made them desperate?

"You've made a mistake, Grant."

He glanced up to find his mother standing in the doorway to his study.

"In what regard?"

"You should have chosen the plainer one. If you must marry so far beneath you, choose the companion."

"You used the peephole, didn't you?" he asked. Should he be amused, or irritated? It was often difficult to decide with his mother. "You should have joined us, Mother."

"Tomorrow is soon enough, Grant."

She turned to leave the room.

"Why do you think I should have chosen Miss Cameron?" he asked.

"Because she would have run you a pretty race, and that's exactly what you need. A little passion is what makes life worth living." She hesitated. "The right kind of passion, Grant. The kind between a man and woman. You need that, and I think Miss Cameron would have given it to you."

Since this comment was so unexpected, he could only stare at her.

"I do not like Miss Fenton," she said, further surprising him. "I cannot rid myself of the notion that I should know her."

"Is that entirely fair?"

"Perhaps not," she answered, and shrugged. She didn't say another word as she left him, leaving him staring after her and wondering if she was right.

Had he made a mistake? The worst kind of mistake?

Miss Cameron's smile had captured his attention, it was true, and he'd been fascinated by the way she had of looking at him as if she were mocking him.

She'd studied his hands.

She wasn't as beautiful as Miss Fenton. Her eyes were a soft blue, commonplace certainly. She had brown hair, not blond. Simply brown. An unremarkable shade, really. She had a peculiar smile, one that did not quite meet her eyes.

She'd deliberately separated herself from the rest of the group, almost as if she were physically acknowledging the gap between them. But Miss Cameron's apartness had an aura of sadness to it. Or mystery.

Perhaps that's why he had gravitated toward her—she'd simply sparked his curiosity.

No, his mother was wrong. His own instincts were momentarily skewed. He was going to marry Miss Fenton. But it wouldn't hurt if he avoided the temptation of Gillian Cameron in the meantime.

Chapter 5

Gillian awoke the next morning feeling pampered and blessed. For a short matter of minutes, she allowed herself to believe that she would always wake in such a chamber, with the sight of a young maid bustling about with a smile on her face, and the smell of morning tea being brought to her bedside.

"I've brought you hot water for washing, miss," the maid said, bobbing a curtsy, "and tea and toast. If there's anything else you'd like, you've only to ring."

"This is wonderful," Gillian said, rising up on one elbow to survey the bedside tray.

"I'm to give you a message," the maid said, bobbing another curtsy. "You and Miss Fenton are to meet with the countess in the Italian Room, miss. This morning." She turned away, and then turned back, bobbing yet another curtsy. "Nine o'clock, miss. The countess holds great store for everyone being on time."

The feeling of being steeped in luxury abruptly disappeared, leaving only dread. A feeling that was, unfortunately, more precognitive than she wished.

Arabella was late, but then Arabella was often late. She'd forget the hour, being immersed in one of her books. Even after being reminded of the time, she often didn't appear either to care about being late or to be conscious that her behavior altered other people's schedules.

Today, of all days, she was more slow-moving than usual, to the extent that Gillian almost shouted at her to hurry. But losing her temper with Arabella would have been an exercise in futility—it wouldn't have made the girl faster in her dressing and could well have made her more mulishly slow.

The consequence was that they were fifteen minutes late for the audience in the Italian Room. Gillian pulled Arabella through the door, startled to find that they were not the only ones in attendance, but evidently the last to arrive. As the entered the room, the earl stood along with Dr. Fenton, both men looking displeased.

This drawing room was a blur of gilded and upholstered furniture that filled the space and yet appeared almost too delicate to use. The deep blue curtains on the tall windows looked to be silk, matching the color of the sofas, while the walls were covered in a dark wood. Landscapes occupied the middle of every panel, each vista one of sun-splashed hills and deeply green groves.

The greatest feature of the room, however, was the countess herself.

The Countess of Straithern stood beside the fireplace, her right hand resting on the mantel, a pose no doubt designed to be imposing.

Despite her short stature, she was a formidable-looking woman. Her face was round, and she looked to have at least two chins. Perhaps the rest of her was as plump, although it was difficult to tell in the voluminous dress she was wearing. Of black silk, with long puffy sleeves and an overskirt divided in the front to show a panel of lace, it also bore something that looked like a train. Attached at the shoulders, the swath of material fell behind the countess and puddled on the floor.

Her eyes, an arresting blue, were fixed on Arabella with narrowed intensity. Her mouth was unsmiling, the corners hidden beneath doughy cheeks.

When Dr. Fenton brought his daughter forward, the countess simply inclined her head very slightly, just as if she were a queen being introduced to one of her subjects.

Arabella appeared oblivious to the stare from her soon-to-be mother-in-law. Gillian knew the younger girl would much rather be in a small, secluded chamber, perusing one of her books. Give her an elderly manservant to treat, a set of rheumy eyes to examine, or a pus-filled sore, and she would soon be smiling.

The countess, however stern her appearance or advanced her age, did not look as if she were suffering from ill health. However, Arabella was taking the occasion to examine her visually. Her gaze encompassed the other woman from the top of the countess's hair to the tips of the shoes that peeped beneath her skirts.

Nor was that the only spot to which her attention was directed. Arabella appeared fixed on the older woman's chest, as if she were counting the rising and falling of that not inconsiderable bosom. She even stared at the countess's ears, and Gillian knew she was not intrigued with the glittering diamond earrings.

Arabella was no doubt wondering if there was a way to test the older woman's hearing.

In the meantime, the expression on the older woman's face had not softened. She continued to stare fixedly at Arabella, who seemed blissfully unaware of the tense atmosphere in the room or the fact that the countess was growing more and more irritated.

Dr. Fenton looked at Gillian, who knew that she would soon be at the receiving end of a rather long and involved lecture about Arabella's shocking lack of manners.

After all, her only duty was to render Arabella presentable.

Her defense was already prepared, although it sounded weak even to her ears. *She wasn't actually doing anything wrong. She was simply looking at the countess.*

She could only imagine Dr. Fenton's reply.

For five minutes?

Arabella did look as if she would like to take out her journal and begin writing about the countess's color. Or, heaven forbid, ask the countess to open her mouth so that she might examine her teeth.

She swerved her gaze from Arabella to Dr. Fenton and back again, and somehow she accidentally looked at *him*. The earl wasn't finding the situation humorous in the least. In fact, he looked as if he never smiled, or as if the idea of amusement had never once occurred to him in his entire life.

She found it rather disconcerting to return a man's stare while attempting to hide any hint of her thoughts. But she managed to do so nonetheless, even tilting her head just a little so as to appear as haughty as he.

How odd that while Arabella was being rude, staring at the countess without a word, the earl was doing the very same thing to her. Who would call him to task for his behavior?

Dr. Fenton cleared his throat.

Gillian took a step, positioning herself directly behind Arabella and poking her gently in the back with one finger. Normally such a physical manifestation of her impatience was enough to capture Arabella's attention. Not today, evidently.

She glanced at Dr. Fenton, whose complexion was becoming more and more florid as the seconds passed.

Did Arabella not have the sense God gave a goat?

Twice the countess tapped her cane on the patterned carpet, the sound an odd punctuation to the otherwise stilted silence.

Gillian leaned close to Arabella and whispered, in a tone she hoped only the younger girl could hear, "Arabella, you are causing a scene. Say something polite."

Arabella turned her head only slightly. Her gaze met Gillian's, and a look of irritation crossed her face.

"Why should I not use every situation to improve my powers of observation, Gillian? This woman might be a victim of apoplexy. She has the color for it. I suspect her diet is too sufficient in cheeses and meat. I think she would benefit from a few glasses of ale in the evening. Or wine, perhaps, as a morning tonic. A week's regimen of purgatives would not be amiss."

Purgatives? Dear God.

"Young woman, can you pour?" the countess said.

Arabella blinked. "What?"

The countess raised her cane and pointed it at Arabella. "Can you only talk of private matters in public, young woman, or can you behave as befitting a woman of some manners?"

For once Arabella remained silent.

"Well?"

"Arabella is schooled in good manners, Your Ladyship," Gillian said, stepping to Arabella's side. "She sometimes forgets, however, in her quest to be a healer."

"A physician," Arabella corrected, sending her an annoyed look.

The countess pointed her cane at the adjoining sofa. "Sit."

Gillian didn't think twice, but Arabella was somewhat slower. Gillian sighed, bit back a comment, and tugged on Arabella's sleeve.

The countess sat opposite the sofa, while Dr. Fenton and the earl sat on adjoining chairs.

Just then, the door opened as if the countess had performed some secret signal. A footman came in, struggling under the weight of a massive silver service.

Arabella sent her a look, not of desperation, but of annoyance.

"Use your common sense," Gillian whispered to her. "If you can stitch a wound, you can certainly pour a cup of tea."

If only her words had been remotely prophetic. But Arabella proved to be abysmal when it came to making other people around her comfortable. She did not indulge in casual conversation. Other than asking the countess, the earl, and her father exactly how they wished their tea, she didn't speak at all.

Gillian did not even receive the courtesy of being asked. Without a word, Arabella simply handed her a saucer and a full cup, tea sloshing over the rim.

Gillian thanked her and sat back in the corner of the sofa, feeling grateful, for the first time, that she was not in Arabella's position, and was therefore spared from being on the receiving end of the countess's stare.

It was all too obvious that Arabella was failing in her first test. The entire gathering was awkward, and so filled with painful silence that Gillian would have done anything to escape it.

"You shall learn everything that you need to know," the earl said unexpectedly. "All you need is a little practice."

"I have no desire whatsoever to practice," Arabella said. "I would much prefer to spend my time serving mankind."

"Well," Gillian said, "think of it as serving mankind. Only a smaller number of them."

She hadn't meant the remark to be amusing. She knew how to appeal to Arabella's skewed sense of logic. The earl's sudden smile was startling, as was the countess's precipitous departure. The woman stood, looked down at Arabella as if she would like to say something particularly scathing, and then simply made her way to the door without a further word to anyone—not to her son, not to the doctor, and certainly not to Arabella, who looked faintly relieved at the other woman's absence.

Arabella turned to her. "May I return to my room now?"

The earl stood. "Would you prefer a tour of Rose-moor instead, Arabella? I believe you would find the library particularly interesting."

Gillian sent him a look of gratitude.

Arabella did not look in his direction. "I would prefer to return to my chamber, Your Lordship," she said.

"May I escort you, then?"

"I can't think why," Arabella answered. "I'm not about to become lost."

To his credit, the earl simply bowed slightly in response. If he was annoyed at her answer, he didn't reveal it.

Gillian stood and made her way to the door to accompany her, but Arabella didn't wait, simply left the room with the hauteur of the countess.

Was she supposed to follow her? Did she remain behind?

The earl reached out his hand, staying her with a gesture. She was sure he didn't mean to touch her, because he pulled back his hand the moment his fingers brushed beneath the lace at her elbow. She was certain the gesture wasn't meant to be one of reassurance or even intimacy but rather one of arrogance.

He had not meant the moment to mean anything at all, but it did. She stopped, frozen into place by his touch. Nor did he speak, and she couldn't discern anything from his expression except for an almost imperceptible flinch of surprise.

She wanted him to touch her again, to press his fingers along the top of her arm where she seemed especially sensitive. Or perhaps he might encircle her wrist with his fingers, and create a prisoner out of her. As if she would walk away.

How much ruin could she endure?

"If I may have a moment of your time, Gillian."

She turned toward Dr. Fenton. "Of course, sir."

She left the earl at the door, managing to cross the room without looking at him once. But he was there, nevertheless. She felt him staring at her, could feel his glance between her shoulder blades and on her bare neck, right at the nape where her hair had been gathered up and was now restrained with a tortoiseshell comb.

As Gillian sat on the sofa facing Dr. Fenton, she prayed for composure, and a little propriety. If nothing else, then let memory flood her mind. Let her recall those two days of fear when she'd been abandoned, terrified, and with child in Edinburgh.

The earl hesitated, and for a moment she wondered if he was going to remain in the room and listen to Dr. Fenton's words. But then he simply closed the door behind him, leaving her feeling relieved.

The minute they were alone, Gillian turned her attention to her employer.

She pressed her hands together and willed herself not to betray any emotion. No annoyance, irritation, or anger would show on her features.

"Arabella does not seem inclined to take on the role of countess."

Since she had told him that very thing for the last two weeks, Gillian remained silent now.

"She needs to be made aware of what a superlative opportunity this is for her, one that most women would not get."

Gillian was growing irritated, and annoyance was an infinitely preferable emotion to fear. "Whenever I speak to her about her manners, Dr. Fenton, Arabella merely ignores me. What am I to do?"

"I'm not asking that you treat her as you would a sister, Gillian. I know that is impossible. But I would not wish her to be shamed by her own behavior."

Gillian didn't think that was possible. Arabella was so completely unconscious of the entire world that she doubted the other girl noted when it rain or snowed or was otherwise a fair day. If it was not within Arabella's small frame of reference, she simply paid no attention to it.

"I fear the countess was not impressed by Arabella," Dr. Fenton added. "It is imperative that all of Arabella's deficiencies are eliminated, Gillian, as quickly as possible."

What could she say to that? It was all too evident that Arabella was not prepared for the role she was to assume and didn't seem to notice or care.

"Very well," she said. "I will try a little harder."

"See that you do, Gillian." He studied her for a moment. "The Earl of Straithern is very conscious of his position in society."

She remained silent.

"Should he be informed of your past, I do not doubt that he would ask me to dispense with your services."

Aghast, she stared at him. "Why would you do such a thing, sir?"

"I trust that it will not be necessary."

There was a look in his eyes she'd never before seen, a glance that almost conveyed dislike. "I have told you that I will try with Arabella," she said, hoping that her voice was even and conciliatory. She had learned one valuable lesson in the past, and that was to protect herself. Until she had a new position, she could not afford to alienate the doctor.

"You are Arabella's dutiful companion, someone with Arabella's interests at heart. That is what you are and that is what I want everyone at Rosemoor to think."

She clenched her hands together again.

"Not a woman with wildness in her heart, Gillian. Not a girl who would forget that she was a gentlewoman."

"No. Sir."

"You have a habit of looking at him too well, Gillian. Anyone could see he interests you."

Ah, the true reason for this tête-à-tête.

"See that your history does not repeat itself, Gillian, that no hint of scandal comes to Rosemoor because of your actions. If you cannot remember, then I will be forced to confide in the earl. You will find yourself on the streets of Edinburgh again."

A curt nod was all she could muster before leaving him.

Grant opened the letter with some trepidation, hoping it wasn't bad news. Instead, it was the very best news of all. He began to smile as he scanned his friend's scrawled handwriting, easily discerning from the labyrinth of loops and swirls exactly what Lorenzo was trying to say. His friend had been delayed in London, but would arrive at Rosemoor as soon as he was able.

In the meantime, he had some advice to impart to Grant. A list of remedies followed, some of which Grant thought he might as well attempt in the interim. He found himself nodding in agreement toward the end of the letter.

It is very rare that such a malady makes no appearance until just before death. Had your brothers been sick often as children? And you, my friend, were you sickly as well before coming to my country? If it is not so, then I would be doubtful of an illness such as you described.

Unfortunately, he hadn't been in Scotland when Andrew had fallen ill and died. Nor had he noticed James becoming sick before the illness that had claimed his life. But then, he'd been involved in his own interests, spending countless hours traveling back and forth to Perth to ensure that his machinery had arrived safely from Italy.

James might well have been ill long before he knew it. Unfortunately, his brother had been one of those individuals who never complain until complaints would do no good.

He folded the letter and put it away, thinking that it had been too long since he'd seen Lorenzo. There were a few people he could trust, and although he trusted Count Paterno more than any other man, even Lorenzo did not know all his secrets.

Oddly enough, contentment permeated Rosemoor. The servants seemed pleased to be employed at the great house, and there were many smiles among the staff. She'd also heard laughter along the corridors, and it was such an odd sound for this place that she stopped and listened for it.

Was she the only one who could see beneath the smiles to the true evil?

The gray eyes of the Roberson males were the color of smoke, of slate. The devil's colors, as if he lived inside each of them.

True, they were all charming, the Roberson men. Each one of them, from the patriarch on down, had the grace of Gabriel, and the slyness, too. They smiled with ease, and it took great practice to see beyond their pleasantries to the sin residing in their hearts.

It wasn't that voices told her how evil they were. True, there were voices she heard in her mind, voices that she knew other people didn't hear. Sometimes she thought that the voices were the various entities of God Himself: the Holy Spirit, the Son, and God the Father. But then they would change and seem almost like children, and she'd know exactly who they were. Mostly she knew that what she heard was her conscience, goading her to duty.

Practice had made her fingers nimble at their task. She uncorked the cobalt bottle, inserted the long-handled spoon, and removed a small quantity of powder. Every day she ingested a little, placing it on the tip of her tongue. If she survived to the following day, she knew she should be about her mission.

When it was time, she would add a larger quantity to the earl's food or beverage and watch him die with a true and deep sorrow. People would come to join her in mourning such a man, and they would marvel at her composure, at her dignity.

There was no rancor in this act. It was simply something that needed to be done. A task that needed to be carried out for the good of all. Such evil could not be allowed to exist in the world. Such horror must have a consequence.

The bloodline must be eliminated.

Chapter 6

Arabella was claiming a headache, and said she'd taken one of her powders. Short of dragging her from her chamber, there was nothing for Gillian to do but wish her well.

It was a blessing that the girl had chosen to barricade herself in her chamber. For a few hours, Gillian would be free of her, free of any duties, free of pretense. Free, most of all, of being the guardian of Arabella's future.

What would Dr. Fenton say if she was truly honest about Arabella? Did he really wish to know all of Arabella's deficiencies?

Arabella must learn to be kind. She should pay attention to others, in order to notice their sadness or irritation. If she could not dredge a drop of sympathy for another living soul, then she should pretend to care. Pretense was sometimes necessary, especially if another's feelings were to be spared. There is no virtue to brutal honesty. Arabella must guard her tongue. The world truly did not care for her opinion, especially if it was unduly harsh. A little tact went a very long way, and silence even farther.

Arabella must look beyond the boundaries of her books. There was a world outside the printed page, or the bones of her skeleton. There was music in the wind, in the sounds of the birds, in the silence of the countryside. There was beauty all around them, especially at Rosemoor, and she was foolish to ignore it so unremittingly.

Arabella must learn to exhibit some enjoyment in the world, in a manner that did not include disease, suffering, or death.

There, that was enough to start with, and she'd not yet begun on Arabella's social graces. The girl needed to be slowed when it came to eating. She gobbled up her food as if it were going to disappear, or as if eating were a chore that, although necessary, was not enjoyable. She needed to learn to talk to other people. A simple inquiry as to the weather would suffice. She must not ask a stranger about his intestines, and please, for pity's sake, let her learn that a diagnosis of impending death was not socially acceptable.

Playing the pianoforte was perhaps more than Gillian could hope for, as was any skill in watercolors, but Arabella was certainly capable of learning how to do many of the Scottish country dances.

But for now, she was tired of Arabella. She had a few hours of freedom, and instead of retiring to her room, she wanted to explore.

Gillian wasn't entirely certain that what she was doing was proper or even acceptable. She was constrained by manners in the fact that she was the Earl of Straithern's guest, but that thought did not stop her now. Curiosity drew her out the front door of Rosemoor and down the sloping lawn to the lake she'd seen on her arrival.

The lake was a perfect oval and quite obviously created by man at the lowest point of the lawn, and designed to reflect the building it fronted. The water-fowl didn't seem to mind that the lake was created for artistic purposes. Instead, the geese and ducks were absolutely content to paddle around on the glassy surface.

Cattails surrounded the lake at the narrowest point and were obviously trimmed from time to time. So they would not mar the purity of the scene?

The building opposite the lake was large and square and constructed of white stone that gleamed in the morning sun. On either side of the tall arched doorway was a vaulted recess, each filled with a life-size alabaster statue of a woman dressed in a diaphanous garment. On the second floor was an entablature consisting of four statues: two men dressed only in a loincloth and holding spears, flanked by two women as scantily dressed.

Above the door, directly beneath the steeply pitched tile roof, was another statue, this one of a pair of lovers. The woman was bent back in the embrace of a powerful-looking male who was plundering her with a kiss. The inscription, carved into a ribbon of stone at the base of the figures, read "Virtue and Vice."

It was all too easy to recognize that Vice was winning that particular battle.

Upon first seeing the building, she'd thought it to be some sort of crypt, but it was much too large. The structure was larger than Dr. Fenton's house, but was dwarfed by Rosemoor.

The spring morning was chilly but not uncomfortably so. The call of the birds was the only sound, the soft swaying of the cattails the only movement. She might have stepped into a painting, something appropriately titled to reflect the earl's wealth and prominence.

Slowly she encircled the lake, taking the path worn in the grass to the front door of the structure. At the bottom of the steps, she hesitated for a moment before grabbing her skirts in her fists and lifting them slightly. She took the first step, ignoring the voice of her conscience that warned her against being where she didn't belong.

No one protested her arrival. No human voice called out in anger. No ghostly denizens decried her actions. She was alone with the statues, with the tall, arched, black-painted door and its brass knocker.

She pushed in the door, surprised to find that it was unlocked. Surely, if such a place was not open to visitors, it would be locked tightly? One last whisper of caution sounded in her ear. How could she possibly guide Arabella if she was as lacking in social graces?

She had every intention of closing the door, walking down the three wide steps, and returning to Rosemoor. But just at that moment, a shaft of sunlight illuminated the room through a rounded window in the roof.

Breathless with wonder, she pushed aside the door, her attention captivated by the light and what it revealed: a large area sunken into the floor below the glass dome, surrounded by a series of columns, and ringed by concentric circles of steps.

Slowly she crossed the floor, carefully descending the steps, until she stood bathed in the light. This would be a sunny refuge in winter, or even in this chilly spring.

"You're trespassing, you know."

She whirled, and looked up to find the earl standing on the edge of the steps looking down at her.

"Did no one tell you this was my laboratory?" he asked.

She felt a sudden surge of caution as she stared up at him. He was dressed in a white shirt and black trousers, his black boots gleaming in the sunlight. He was as dark as the devil, with his black hair and gray eyes. He had a smile tinged with self-mockery even in the midst of genuine amusement. His face was perfectly formed, all the features neither remarkable nor forgettable, but somewhere in between. A normal, average face that managed not to be either normal or average at all. Somehow, he managed to appear all at once extraordinarily handsome and particularly dangerous.

Words were simply beyond her. Finally, blessedly, she found her voice. "I apologize, Your Lordship. I thought the building empty."

"It is not," he said curtly.

"I apologize," she repeated, ascending the steps.

"How long have you been here, Miss Cameron?"

She looked at him. "You know when we arrived, Your Lordship."

"A day. A scant day, is it not?"

She nodded.

"Yet in that short time, you've managed to find the palace and invade my privacy."

"The palace?" she asked, confused.

"It's a name that was given to the place a very long time ago. The Pleasure Palace, to be precise."

"I did not intend to invade your privacy, Your Lordship. But I did see the palace when we arrived and was curious about it. If you consider curiosity to be a bad trait, then I am doomed to be in your disfavor. Surely as the Earl of Straithern you're accustomed to people being in awe of Rosemoor?"

He studied her for a moment. "Are you always so direct, Miss Cameron? Such honesty is dangerous, you know. I could forgive you anything for it."

It was her turn to remain silent, but only until curiosity surfaced yet again.

"Even my curiosity?"

"Has it not been satisfied?"

She smiled. "If anything, Your Lordship, it has only been whetted. What, exactly, is the palace used for?"

"I am a scientist, Miss Cameron."

At her silence, he continued. "Had you no idea?"

She shook her head.

"For the last several years, I've been living in Italy. Did you know that?"

She shook her head again.

"What do you know of me?"

"You are an earl and you wish to marry Arabella."

He looked startled. "That is the extent of it?"

"Perhaps your financial condition might be mentioned as well," she said, as tactfully as possible. "You are quite wealthy, I understand."

"Nothing as to my nature, my character?"

"You have suffered a loss, Your Lordship. Other than that, I've no knowledge of you."

"Nor I you, Miss Cameron," he said, his voice sounding as harsh as a millstone.

He strode away from the rotunda, leaving her staring after him.

"Well?" His voice echoed through the cavernous space. "Are you coming? If you've no wish to see my laboratory, leave now."

"The three of you make me feel woefully inadequate," she said, racing to catch up with him.

"The three of us?" he asked over his shoulder.

"You, Dr. Fenton, and Arabella. All of you are scientists to some degree."

"I would differ with you. Fenton is a doctor. Arabella wishes to be one. I study electrics."

She stopped and stared at his back.

"Electrics? What are electrics?"

He turned to face her. "Do you truly wish to know? Or is that simply an idle response? I do not mind addressing a scholarly interest, Miss Cameron, but I haven't time for chatter. Nor do I have an interest in it."

"I truly wish to know," she said.

"Then come with me."

Without glancing to see if she was following, he turned and walked away.

See that your history does not repeat itself, Gillian, that no hint of scandal comes to Rosemoor because of your actions. Dr. Fenton's words echoed in her mind, but it wasn't his warning that slowed her footsteps. Her own memories stopped her there in the shadowed hallway, staring after the Earl of Straithern.

"Well, Miss Cameron?" He slowed, glancing impatiently back at her. "Are you coming?"

He was not tempting her to sin, only to curiosity.

She nodded, and followed him.

Chapter 7

He was damned if he knew what he was doing. There was no reason to welcome Gillian Cameron into his laboratory, the haven he'd created out of necessity.

True, there was something about her that appealed to him, some look in her blue eyes that made him wonder at its source. He found himself studying her mouth, as if certain a plea would soon be uttered between those full lips. What would she say to him? *Stay? Talk to me? Converse with me upon a myriad of subjects, only do not leave me to the solitude of my own thoughts.*

Or was he only mimicking his own thoughts? Perhaps he'd been alone too long, and that's why he slowly opened the door to his laboratory before turning to her.

"I would appreciate it, Miss Cameron, if you would give me your word before entering."

Gillian stopped and wrapped her arms around her waist, staring up at him as if she were gathering her thoughts. Or was she simply arming herself with her dignity?

She was so controlled that he wanted to bend down and jolt her out of her composure by doing something idiotic like grinning at her, or making a sudden strange noise. In a word, he wanted to act suddenly unlike himself, unrestrained and defiant, coaxing some sort of reaction from Miss Cameron.

"What is that, Your Lordship?" she asked in a very composed voice. A very mannerly, quite austere tone of voice.

"I would ask that you keep what you learn within these walls to yourself and not discuss this room with anyone."

"Is what you do so special, Your Lordship? What exactly do you do here that you would ask such a promise of me?"

"I haven't the slightest idea why, Miss Cameron," he said as he stepped back to allow her to precede him into the room, "but I'm about to show you."

"Perhaps I will not understand, Your Lordship, and any concerns you have are simply misplaced."

"Perhaps," he said, amused at her sudden look of indignation. Did she think she could goad him so easily?

His laboratory was a large rectangular room with two tall windows in the long wall, and a red brick fireplace at the shorter end. At the opposite end of the room was a door, now closed.

A scarred wooden table, easily ten feet long, sat in the middle of the room, and on it rested a dozen or so strange machines, one prepossessing structure nearly four feet high, crafted of wire, wheels, and metal parts.

"What is that?" she asked, pointing to one of the machines.

He stopped, reached out, and turned a crank. Sparks emerged from it so fiercely that she stepped back in precaution.

Another apparatus had glowing wires emerging from it. Without a word, he walked across the room and extinguished the gas lamps on the wall and then pulled the curtains closed over each of the windows. The room was filled with shadows, the better to illuminate the wires and the trail of light on the table.

He was amused by her wide-eyed glances. Or perhaps he was gratified, instead, and pleased that she seemed so amazed. To the uninitiated, his experiments were grandiose and a little frightening. To those of a similar experience, they were familiar in some respects and startling in others.

Why, though, did Gillian Cameron's impression seem to matter more than the opinions of the men with whom he corresponded?

If he had any sense at all he'd simply banish her from the palace completely. He wouldn't keep himself still so that when she passed by he could play a game with his senses. He wondered how many petticoats she wore beneath her full skirts. By the swish of them, he guessed two. What did she wash her hair with, that it boasted gold highlights? And what scent did she wear? She smelled of something feminine, a sweet, virginal scent that he would forever be able to recall and label Gillian.

He hadn't lied to her about his confusion, although he had muted it somewhat. Now it returned in full measure, forcing him to admit that she was a distraction.

A dangerous, unsettling distraction—a curious and beautiful woman.

She turned and smiled at him, and he dared himself to banish her. What a fool he was as the moments passed and he did no such thing.

"You're doing it again," she said.

"Staring at you," he answered. He nodded and walked to the other side of the room. "Perhaps you are worthy of my regard, Miss Cameron. Perhaps I simply have something else on my mind."

How on earth was she to take that? She decided to ignore him and concentrate on his experiments instead.

"Why does it light up like that?" Gillian asked, walking closer to the table. She focused on the strange glow coming from the wires.

"It's a way of creating energy," he said.

"How does it work?"

"Are you truly interested?" he asked.

The obvious surprise in his voice annoyed her.

"I am not devoid of intelligence, Your Lordship. For all that I am Arabella's companion. I do have a mind, you see."

"I also suspect you become very annoyed when you are patronized, Miss Cameron."

"I do not like people to think I am without intellect."

"I should never be so foolish," he said. "Come around here and let me show you."

As she walked around the table, he opened the curtains, and then returned to one of the machines. "This particular device is a zinc-acid cell. An energy cell," he added. "Each cell contains two electrodes immersed in a solution. When the cell is at rest, it doesn't produce current, and at that point there is a difference in the energy between the two electrodes."

She nodded, not entirely certain she understood.

"Let me show you this one instead," he said, evidently correctly deciphering her confusion. "This is called Volta's pile."

Volta's pile was a series of wire frames containing stacks of metal disks. Each frame was connected to the next with a metal strip.

"There are two types of discs here, one silver and the other zinc, separated from each other by pieces of cloth soaked in salt water. One pile can only generate a small amount of energy, but connected together, they can be quite powerful."

He reached out and opened a bottle, pouring a little of the mixture into the tray at the bottom of the machine. A small plume of smoke hid the damage from view for a moment, but when the acrid odor disappeared and the air cleared, she leaned forward, surprised.

"There's a hole where you poured," she said.

"A warning, Miss Cameron. Sulfuric acid can also blind or burn the skin. Normally I choose to use copper sulfate, but I am attempting to generate even more current with the acid."

"And the danger is why you prefer to work in the palace?" she asked, drawing back.

He smiled again. "Actually," he said, "I choose to work here because I'm left alone. I prefer to perform my experiments without the company of people, Miss Cameron. Does that make me sound cold and unfeeling?"

"No, Your Lordship," she said, wondering how

much of her honesty he could tolerate. "It makes you sound lonely."

He looked at her again. Moments ticked by in silence. Was he going to dismiss her from his laboratory? Or from Rosemoor entirely?

"Would you like to help me in my experiments?"

Surprised, she could only nod. "Tell me what to do." She looked dubiously at the bottle of sulfuric acid. "Will it require working with that?"

"I have another task." He reached below the table and withdrew a heavy burlap bag that he placed on the scarred wooden surface. "I am building a larger apparatus, and I need to have each of the silver disks polished. They conduct current better if the surface is clean."

She took possession of the disks, a soft rag, and a bowl filled with a blue-tinged liquid. She eyed the solution with caution.

He pulled up a stool and sat beside her.

"It's safe, Miss Cameron. Do you trust me?"

She nodded, the answer surprisingly instantaneous. For a few moments they worked in silence, she polishing the disks, and the earl occupied with arranging them in their wire cages.

"What will you do with it when it's finished?"

"Prove that it's possible to generate massive amounts of electricity, and store it as well."

"But why?"

"Can you not imagine, Miss Cameron? Think of a world in which you needn't be near a river or a stream to mill your flour. Or a machine that provides light and all you must do is simply turn a handle."

"No oil? No candles?"

"None. Simply electrics."

His face was animated, the sparkle in his eyes almost mischievous.

"Can something like that really happen?"

"It not only will, it must. There are countless discoveries we will make in our lifetimes, Miss Cameron. All things we've never thought would ever come to pass."

"If you have your way," she said.

"If I have my way. I'm a scientist."

She didn't comment. What could she say?

"How can you bear to spend your time on anything else?" she said, bending forward again to study the apparatus.

"I have been accused of being too involved in my work," he said. "Some who don't understand consider it an avocation or nothing more than a pastime, something to while away the hours between my duties as earl."

"It seems to me that it would be vastly more interesting to be a scientist than an earl."

"Were you an only child, Miss Cameron?" he asked abruptly.

She turned to look at him. How very odd that he was even more arresting in the bright sunlight. He probably should have been more handsome in shadows.

"Why would you ask that, Your Lordship?'

"To rectify our ignorance of each other."

Was that entirely wise? Probably not, but she answered him regardless.

"Actually, I'm not," she said. "I was an only child," she admitted, "for a number of years, until my father remarried." And then their home was suddenly full of children. Six brothers and sisters, all of whom she was responsible for at various stages in their lives.

"A very close family, I'd wager."

She nodded. "My father and I were very close until he married."

"And then you had a stepmother."

"All girls need a mother to guide them."

"Were you guided, Miss Cameron?"

"In a way, Your Lordship. My stepmother believed I should make an advantageous marriage."

"But you chose a life as Miss Fenton's companion instead?" He looked dubious, but she was not about to illuminate him as to her past. "What do your parents think of your choice, Miss Cameron?"

She didn't answer him.

"Do you not see them, Miss Cameron?"

Not since she'd been banished from their home, another comment she would not make.

"Not often, Your Lordship," she said, lying.

"Do you miss them?"

How did he manage to ask the most difficult questions? "Yes and no," she answered, hoping he wouldn't demand more of an answer.

"I miss my brothers," he said, offering a hint of vulnerability so that they were equally matched. How brave of him, and how surprising.

"How terrible to lose both of them in one year," she said.

"I was in Florence when Andrew died. I didn't know about his death for two months."

"How very terrible for you."

"I often wondered what I was doing when he died.

Was I working on my experiments, or having dinner with friends? What was so important that I somehow didn't know he was dead?"

"You couldn't have been expected to know," she said, wishing that she could ease his grief somehow.

He didn't reply, and she wondered if he regretted his comments.

She turned her head and looked at him. "I'm so very sorry for your loss," she said. Neither a fortune nor a title protected him from the pain of living. Everyone loves, everyone loses, and even being an earl could not insulate him from that.

For a moment he remained silent, and then he spoke, his voice sounding rougher than usual. "Thank you, Miss Cameron. I appreciate your kindness."

"It wasn't kindness, Your Lordship," she said. "I, too, know what it's like to lose someone you love."

"Whom do you mourn, Miss Cameron?"

That she would not tell him, and he didn't press the issue after she shook her head.

For an hour she sat beside him, watching out of the corner of her eye as he adjusted the wires on his machine. From time to time he would explain what he was doing, but for the most part they sat in companionable silence.

When she was done with the bag of coins, she folded the burlap into a square, wiped her hands on the rag, and stood.

"I should be going. Arabella's headache must have eased by now."

"Is she often subject to headaches?"

Only when she wished to be alone, but it would not be proper to say such a thing, would it?

"Are you certain you wish to marry, Your Lordship?" An even more improper question.

He studied the wires he was wrapping around a copper spool. "Why would you ask that, Miss Cameron?"

"Arabella prefers her own company, Your Lordship. She is involved with her books, her medicine. She would, I think, infinitely prefer to remain single all her life."

"You have described a woman who would be my exact match in all ways."

"Do you dislike being touched, Your Lordship?"

He looked startled at the question.

"Arabella does. She cringes if anyone accidentally brushes by her, if a maid touches her hand, or even if her father pats her on the shoulder."

"Will you come tomorrow?"

The change of topic was so jarring that she understood immediately. She was not to bring up the subject of his marriage or Arabella.

She forced herself to look directly at him. Although it was harder this way, it was more courageous. "I don't think so," she said. "It would be wiser if I didn't."

"Do you always do the wisest thing?" he asked.

"No. Perhaps it's for that reason that I won't come tomorrow. Experience has taught me to be wary."

"Very well," he said dismissively. "Enjoy life in fear, if you must, Miss Cameron."

Surprised, she could only stare at him. "I beg your pardon? Are you ridiculing me because of my decision?"

"Yes," he said, "I suppose I am."

"That's hardly fair, is it?"

"You're afraid of something imaginary. I would never allow my electrics to harm you, Miss Cameron, or any of the experiments I perform. If they're dangerous, then I will simply wait until you are not here to perform them."

"You think I'm afraid of your experiments?"

"I think you should have a measure of caution about them, that is true. But not fear."

"I can assure you, Your Lordship, that I am not afraid of your experiments. Or of your electrics."

"Then what are you afraid of?"

He looked up, focusing directly on her, all his attention given to her as if she were one of his machines. She found it disconcerting to be subjected to his intensity, but not enough to guard her words.

"You," she said simply.

Strangely enough, he didn't look surprised by her answer. He remained silent for a moment and then spoke. "Have I given you any reason to fear me?"

What would he say if she gave him the complete truth? She enjoyed his smiles too much, and she could sit and study the color of his eyes for hours. Beyond his attractiveness, she was fascinated with his mind, and that seemed even more dangerous. Why had he become interested in electrics? What did he want to accomplish in his life? When did he know that he wanted to be more than simply a titled and wealthy man? All questions that veered into the realm of too personal and too intrusive.

So, yes, he had given her ample reason to fear him, simply by being who he was. She knew only too well that she was lonely and vulnerable. He was the very last person she should be around.

"I promise not to harm you, Miss Cameron."

"I'm not altogether certain that you can promise that, Your Lordship."

He came around the table and approached her, and she made herself stand exactly where she was beside the door.

"Anyone would tell you," he began and then stopped, frowning at her. "I'm exceptionally impatient in my laboratory, Miss Cameron. But I have found it quite pleasant to have you assist me. If I give my word as the Earl of Straithern, would you return?"

"And what sort of word would that be, Your Lordship?"

"What word do you require?"

"Could you cease being so charming?" she asked, and then wanted to call the words back the moment they were spoken.

He looked amused by her comment, and she wanted to tell him he was right to smile—it was only a jest. Instead, she turned and left the laboratory.

"Miss Cameron?" She halted in the corridor without turning around, waiting for him to speak.

"Will you come back tomorrow?"

She really shouldn't. She glanced over her shoulder at him. "If I can, Your Lordship. If Arabella does not need me," she said, and wondered if she sealed her doom by those few words.

Gillian opened the massive door to the palace and pulled it shut behind her, standing there for a moment with her hand flat against the carvings.

She'd always been an avid student, finding refuge in books when her father was suddenly too engrossed with his new wife to pay her much attention. If she was overlooked by her stepmother it was because the woman soon enough had a child of her own. The dame's school she attended was more intent upon passing down the skills of housewifery than Aristotle's lessons. Therefore, Gillian's education had been allowed to continue, for the most part, at her own pace.

Her father's library was a treasure of unexplored lands and treatises from long-dead philosophers. In the soft quiet of an afternoon, the sunshine muted by the dark printed drapes of the library windows, she first explored the words of others and then the thoughts and wonderings of her own mind.

It was the complexity of her curiosity that amazed her, and then amused her as she would follow one thought to the next as if they were tumbled skeins of yarn.

How very odd that for the last two years she'd missed intellectual curiosity and only just now realized it.

As she walked swiftly away from the palace, Gillian had the absurd thought that she'd been wrong. The earl might have summoned her into his laboratory to appease her curiosity, but he'd trapped her with his charm. She could easily be fascinated with the Earl of Straithern, and not simply because of his scientific ambitions or pursuits. The man interested her, the man with the enigmatic smile and the silver eyes occasionally betraying a hint of pain.

Wasn't that the best reason to leave Rosemoor, as quickly as she was able?

Chapter 8

His mother frowned at him. The countess was quite the termagant when she wished to be, but Grant wasn't compelled to change his mind. He'd endured the fiery temper of more than one tempestuous mistress in the past five years; he could certainly tolerate his mother's well-mannered tantrum.

"We must introduce Arabella to the neighborhood, Grant. If you're determined to go through with this marriage, she must, at least, be welcomed."

"I would think that the neighborhood would be talking more about our entertaining so soon after James died than about my new bride."

"There are exceptions to every rule, Grant, even this. I have lost my child, and yet I think introducing Arabella is the correct thing to do. A small soiree, nothing tastelessly extravagant."

"No."

She frowned at him again. "Are you ashamed of her, Grant? Do you want this wedding to be a hole and corner affair? Are you wishing yourself quit of her already?"

"Arabella is a beautiful girl," he said easily. "Any

man would be pleased to have her for a bride. I simply want no hint of scandal to touch Rosemoor. Our wedding must, by necessity, be a private affair. There's time to introduce her to the neighborhood later."

She eyed him with a watchful look that was beginning to be annoying. He glanced down at the paperwork on his desk and wondered at the years he'd delegated such tasks to Andrew. His brother had a head for figures and was happiest tallying the sum of a column of numbers. Grant would much rather be involved in his electrics.

"You cannot erase the sins of the past by your behavior today, Grant."

He didn't look up for a moment. When he did, he was startled to see tears in his mother's eyes.

"You are not your father, and no one thinks you are."

What the hell did he say to that?

For a long stretch of moments they regarded each other. When he'd first returned from Italy, he'd been surprised to find that she looked exactly the same as when he'd left Scotland. Now, however, she was noticeably older, as if she'd aged each day since James's death. On the temples and crown, her black hair had whitened, and the corners of her lids drooped as if to reach the pouches beneath her eyes. But it was the expression in her eyes that disturbed him the most—as if she held all the grief and pain of the world within their blue depths.

An expression, oddly enough, that reminded him of Gillian Cameron.

He stood and forced a smile to his face.

"Have your ball, Mother. Entertain who you will."

"Will you attend, Grant?"

He made his way to the door, suddenly feeling as if the library were too warm and too small. "Yes," he said, "I'll attend, and be the dutiful bridegroom."

Even if being solicitous was an act and being near Arabella was a chore.

"I cannot treat you, Blevins, if you insist upon attempting to escape me."

Arabella followed the majordomo from room to room, Gillian trailing behind.

"I can assure you, miss, that I am fine. It is nothing but a little lumbago. An aching in the joints that comes to us all."

"On the contrary, Blevins, I will be the one to make that diagnosis. It is to your best interest to allow me to examine your knee."

"I would appreciate it, miss, if you just let me get about my duties. The silver needs polishing, and the housemaids have to be set to the dusting."

"You might as well surrender, Blevins," Gillian said. "Arabella is determined to treat your injury."

The majordomo turned and looked at her, mildly outraged. "I have no injury, Miss Cameron. If anything, old age has visited me."

"Nonsense," Arabella said briskly. "You're still a relatively young man. I know several topical ointments that might assist your knees."

Blevins looked affronted. The fact that he did not give Arabella a dressing-down was due more to Arabella's role than to his inclination. One did not, after all, lecture the future Countess of Straithern.

"Please, Arabella," Gillian said, feeling sorry for

the man. "If Blevins needs any assistance, I'm certain he will come to you." She looked to him for assent, and he reluctantly nodded. "There, you see? Blevins will not only seek you out if he needs you, Arabella, but he will be certain to send any of the staff to you if they have an injury. Won't you, Blevins?"

Again the man nodded reluctantly. It was a devil's bargain she made between them, but she wanted Blevins to understand that Arabella was not to be ignored. When she wanted a patient, she would obtain one.

Arabella did not look as pleased with the arrangements. She folded her arms and looked at Gillian, her lips pursed into a tiny line. Gillian wanted to warn her that such a look was not attractive at all. If she continued doing it for many years, she would gain two little pouches on either side of her chin. One day, as age advanced, she would look like a squirrel with a mouthful of nuts.

As Blevins moved away, Gillian turned to the younger girl.

"Arabella," she began.

"It does no good to frown at me in that fashion, Gillian," Arabella interrupted. "The man was limping. I know exactly what to do to treat him. Why he persists in remaining in pain, I do not know."

"Just because you know how to treat a person, doesn't mean you have the right to do so, Arabella. It is, after all, his knee, and it's his decision whether it should be treated."

"That's ridiculous. Illness should be stopped wherever it is found. Disease cannot be allowed to roam rampant through the countryside."

"I doubt if Blevins's knee is going to multiply," Gillian said, careful not to smile. "In the meantime, you and I have our lessons."

"You are not my governess, Gillian. You are my companion. A *companion*," she repeated, emphasizing the word. "Not my conscience, and certainly not my teacher."

Gillian took a deep breath. There were moments, as now, when she would just as soon walk away from the girl than attempt to reason with her. She had, however, promised Dr. Fenton.

"You must be fitted for your trousseau."

Arabella looked mutinous but remained silent.

"Especially your ball gown. The earl has arranged for a ball to be held in your honor."

"The family is in mourning," Arabella said. "There will be no ball."

Gillian took another deep breath. "Not from what I have been told," she said. "The countess has agreed that there should be a small ceremony to introduce you to the countryside. It will not be a lavish entertainment, true, but it will be a ball. You will be expected to be in attendance and pleasant and courteous and attired as the future countess."

"What a waste of time, energy, and money, Gillian. Surely they know my measurements. Take one of my old dresses and make a gown from that."

Arabella was staring at one of the footmen. Had the man grimaced? Held a hand to his jaw, blinked rapidly? She looked as excited as if she'd been given a present.

"It's the earl's money to waste, Arabella. Discuss it with him. As for me, I've promised your father that you will be at the fitting, and you will be there."

Her gaze locked with Arabella's. She could be just as stubborn as the other girl. In addition, she was feeling a little out of sorts this morning, and would not mind winning a confrontation with Arabella.

She'd awakened from a fitful sleep, certain that her dreams of Robert had been for one purpose—to remind her that flouting the rules of society had ended in ruin. Passion was all well and good, but it would not protect her, feed her, or keep her safe and warm. Passion was an addiction, a weakness, and she was well quit of it.

Being around the Earl of Straithern was as risky as opium.

"My father indicated that this was a marriage of convenience, Gillian. Convenience mainly for the earl, I think. I was to be allowed to practice medicine, while he was to be allowed to practice being a husband." She waved her hand in the air. "As to a ball gown, I have no interest."

"Then you must pretend, Arabella," Gillian said, fast losing her patience.

"Have you no other ladylike occupations to teach me? I would be interested in learning how to sew. My stitches are not as neat as they could be."

"I doubt sewing will be among those talents required for a countess," Gillian said.

"I do not like him," Arabella said abruptly.

"I doubt you would have liked anyone your father selected for a husband."

"He is rather unfriendly, don't you think, Gillian?"

"He is an earl, Arabella. I believe they are supposed to look a little off-putting. It's one of the requirements of the position. Do you not look as stern when you're treating one of your patients?"

"I have neither inherited that role nor simply accepted it. I have studied very hard for what I know. I have done as much or more than any man."

"I know that, Arabella, but now is not the time to engage in conversation on the rights of women. It's time to be fitted for your dresses."

"I do not like him," Arabella repeated.

Was the girl a complete idiot?

"You just have to get to know him, Arabella. Stop avoiding the earl at every turn. Spend a little time talking to him. He's a fascinating man."

Oh dear, had she already said too much? Did her words betray her own fascination with Grant, Earl of Straithern? Or her envy?

She was suddenly so annoyed with herself that she wanted to be away from Arabella, away from Rosemoor completely. The future yawned before her, terrifying and empty, but it must be faced.

How very foolish she was. How very foolish they both were. Arabella, for refusing to see the blessing she'd been given. And she, for wishing she was Arabella.

"You are spoiled, Arabella," she said. "Spoiled and foolish. You think the world will stop and obey you simply because you think it should. The world can be a cold and heartless place, Arabella, and I hope you do not ever discover that on your own."

Arabella whirled and faced her. The girl's complexion was suddenly pale except for twin spots of color on her cheeks. "What makes you think I haven't already discovered just how cold and heartless the world can be, Gillian?"

Gillian didn't have a response. Nor did she have an

answer for the sudden and surprising fear she felt at that moment, looking into Arabella's green eyes.

Dorothea, Countess of Straithern, stood at the top of the stairs looking down at her son's soon-to-be-wife. There was something about the girl that disturbed her, something that niggled at her during the day, and especially during her prayers. As if God were chastising her for feeling such antipathy for a girl so intent on doing good. Blevins had been an old stubborn fool, but it looked as if he'd won that battle. She should retreat to her parlor where she would decide upon the guest list for the upcoming ball, but for some reason she remained where she was, studying the girl.

What, exactly, was it about Arabella Fenton that disturbed her so much?

Her hand gripped the railing tighter as she watched the two of them, Arabella and Gillian. Some might say that it was the fact that the girl would relegate her to dowager status, but she was more than ready to give up being the Countess of Straithern for Grant's sake. There was something else about the girl, something beyond her fascination with medicine and her shocking insistence upon becoming a physician.

Dorothea shrugged. Perhaps it was nothing more than resentment. That, and a little envy of the girl's youth. Or perhaps not. She watched Arabella leave. There was a look on the companion's face as she stared after Arabella, a look that disturbed Dorothea even more than her own thoughts.

She knew fear when she saw it.

* * *

Miss Cameron wasn't coming, which only proved that she was wiser than he.

Grant moved around his laboratory restlessly, feeling an unwarranted dissatisfaction in his current experiments. Normally he could lose himself in his electrics in a way that transcended anything else surrounding him.

If he was lonely, he worked. If he was annoyed with some facet of his life, he worked. If he was numb with grief, it even helped to go through the motions of work.

Work had always given him solace, until recently.

Life was a series of uncomfortable moments punctuated by joy. Lately, however, he'd experienced more uncomfortable moments than interludes of happiness. Why was that? Because he was back in England?

For years he'd made Italy his home. Occasionally he'd ached for Scotland, for his family, for the history that was his, for Rosemoor. But Italy had given him what Scotland could not: the absolute freedom to be simply Grant Roberson.

In Scotland, he was always the Earl of Straithern, with the responsibility of being earl and the compromises attendant to the title.

He should not be here now, in his laboratory, beginning what should be a series of fascinating experiments. Instead, he should be meeting with his steward, and making any number of decisions. The outbuildings needed painting and he had to choose the color. The irrigation ditches were choked with weeds and he needed to choose in which order they were to be cleaned. Next year's planting schedule had to be ordained, as well as the date the cattle were sent to market. Not to mention that the roof required repairs—who did he select for that task?

He was needed as Earl of Straithern, but today he wanted to be a scientist.

Perhaps that's why his conscience was so silent when dealing with Gillian Cameron—it was too occupied with finding excuses for his procrastination. Perhaps that's why he didn't concern himself with the reason he wanted her in his laboratory, as much as the fact that it was quite evident she was not going to return.

Why wasn't she?

And why did he care?

Instead of worrying about Gillian Cameron, he should instead concentrate on Arabella. She was going to be his wife, a decision he'd made of his own free will.

Arabella was as fierce and determined as he. Her drive and ambition were similar as well. But what might serve a friendship well, or even a business partner, did not seem appropriate for marriage.

When he'd first proposed the union to Dr. Fenton, he had simply wanted convenience. Now he wanted so much more.

He needed someone in his life who could laugh, who could enter a room and enliven it with her presence. He wanted a woman who knew how to smile, whose tongue could be occasionally barbed, but someone who could remind him that he, too, was human and fallible.

He had a low tolerance for a great many things: willful stupidity, for one. Cruelty, giggling, insipid comments, boredom, all made him yearn for the silence and blissful serenity of his laboratory. Gillian Cameron had not irritated him. Not once, and that singular feat made her stand out as unusual among women.

How odd that he'd been able to consider his death with a great deal of equanimity a month ago. Now the idea of his own mortality enraged him. Perhaps he shouldn't entirely discount Dr. Fenton's diagnosis after all. Perhaps he did have a blood disease and his days were ticking away. Had he lived longer than he had left to live? Another thought that didn't please him, along with the fact that he'd made the choice to share however many more days were left to him with Arabella Fenton.

What the hell had he done?

Gillian thought him charming. No one thought him charming. Oh, perhaps a few women in Italy, but no one in Scotland. He was the Earl of Straithern, unapproachable, arrogant.

She thought him charming.

Where was she?

Chapter 9

The sitting room attached to Arabella's bedchamber had been turned into a fashionable modiste's salon. Fabric swatches and dolls attired in the latest fashions littered the room. No fewer than three seamstresses were engaged in pinning Arabella into a pale yellow silk dress, adorned with puffy sleeves, pearl buttons, and Beeston lace.

Gillian sat on the sofa near the window, present among the chaos only because she was very much afraid that Arabella would banish everyone and return to her books if she left the room.

"I have no desire whatsoever, Gillian, to engage in what I consider a very silly pastime for very much longer," Arabella announced now, speaking over the head of one industrious young woman. Gillian wanted to warn the seamstress that Arabella would not stay still for much longer, so the pinning on the front of the dress had better be completed soon.

"Being correctly attired is not a silly pastime, Arabella," Gillian said. "You must wear something to the ball. Everyone will be looking at you."

Arabella looked as if she would like to protest further, but Gillian held up her hand. "Please, Arabella, just let these women do what they've come here to do. I've promised Dr. Fenton that I will do my utmost to see that you are ready for the role of countess."

"I'm not willing to spend any more than the absolute minimum amount of time required to get this farce of a marriage over and done. I do not want to give the earl the impression that I go into this alliance with any eagerness whatsoever."

"I truly don't think he's under the impression that you're an eager bride, Arabella," Gillian said dryly. "All that I ask is that you do not frighten the poor man off before he even has a chance to approach the altar."

One of the young women pinning Arabella's hem turned to look at her, an unspoken warning that she was being too frank in the company of others. Gillian felt a flush of embarrassment and sat back, determined to be silent.

"Why do you show such sympathy for him? Do you have a *tendre* for him yourself?"

She turned to look at Arabella. "Don't be ridiculous," Gillian said, feeling compelled to respond.

"I wouldn't mind, truly, although I can't imagine that you would want that sort of relationship. Being a wife is one thing, but a mistress is something else entirely. You have no protection. You have the censure of society. But then, you already know that, don't you?"

Was that comment meant to be as cruel as it sounded? Or had Arabella just stated the truth as she knew it? Or even worse, had Arabella meant to shame her? Regardless of the motivation, she'd only stated the truth.

"Yes," Gillian said, ignoring the curious glances from the other women. "I do know what that's like."

Since becoming Arabella's companion she'd had numerous occasions to moderate her words. There were times, however, as now, when she would just as soon stand, leave the room, and never again set foot in a chamber occupied by Arabella Fenton.

Unfortunately, without prospects or employment, such a decision would be suicide. Many more afternoons like this one, however, and she would seriously consider it.

"Are they nearly finished?" Arabella asked.

Since a woman was pinning the left sleeve into place, and the right one had not yet been started, Gillian guessed not.

"It won't do, Gillian." Arabella brought her foot down smartly on the box on which she was standing. Because she was attired in soft leather dancing slippers, the gesture made absolutely no sound, which seemed to infuriate Arabella even further.

She began to extract the pins from the side of the gown, half tossing them to the poor woman kneeling at her feet. The hapless seamstress pinning on a sleeve put up her hands to block Arabella's destruction, and all she got for her troubles was to be stabbed in the palm.

The resultant blood and cry of pain halted Arabella's tantrum immediately.

"I am sorry," she said. "I didn't mean to inflict an injury. Here, let me see it."

The seamstress was having none of it, drawing back when Arabella would have examined her hand.

"I am a doctor," Arabella said sternly.

"Begging your pardon, miss," the seamstress said,

"are you really a physician? I have never heard of a woman doing such."

"I said I was, didn't I?" Arabella said. "Now give me your hand."

The patient stretched out her hand timidly. Arabella examined the palm with great precision, seemingly uncaring that several drops of blood dripped to the floor, threatening the beautiful yellow silk she was wearing. The dressmaker, however, saved the garment by hurriedly draping a length of muslin between the two women.

"It's not as severe a cut as I thought," Arabella declared. "Time will heal it well enough. I've a salve I'll get for you," she added. She frowned at the dressmaker. "If I'm allowed to move."

"I'll get it," Gillian said, anxious to escape.

She entered Arabella's chamber and retrieved the basket of her medicines, returning to the sitting room within a period of minutes. For the first time since the women had arrived, Arabella looked pleased.

The poor woman would be treated, Arabella would be content, and Gillian would garner a few minutes to herself.

A terrace ran the length of the second floor of this wing, and she escaped to it, drawing the first deep breath she'd taken all day.

Rosemoor stretched out in front of her, the lawn falling away to the woods to the left, and to the right, to the road that led to the Pleasure Palace. How apt a name for the façade of the building, but not for its interior.

"You didn't come to my laboratory, Miss Cameron. Are you not a woman of your word?"

She didn't turn, didn't greet him, merely kept her attention on the vista in front of her.

All in all, she would much rather have concentrated on him. His face was infinitely more interesting than the rolling valley in front of her. But staring at Grant Roberson was not considered proper, and she was trying to be proper, God help her.

"Arabella needed me, Your Lordship. She is being fitted for her ballgown."

"Did it not matter that I might have needed you?"

Her heart really should not race as it was, and she truly should have been able to breathe correctly in his presence.

"Being Arabella's companion is my position, Your Lordship. I could not shirk it."

"Yet I am your employer."

She glanced at him and then away.

"The moment you arrived at Rosemoor, I assumed all of Arabella's obligations, including paying your rather parsimonious salary, Miss Cameron."

She had absolutely no comment for that.

"Would Arabella truly miss you?" he asked.

"The only one who might comment on my absence is Dr. Fenton," she told him honestly. "I doubt Arabella would even notice I was gone."

She stared ahead. To the right was the walled garden filled with fruit trees, the countess's favorite roses, and herbaceous borders. To the left was the original tower house, a structure she'd been told had been erected in the late fourteenth century.

"It must be a wondrous thing to be steward over such magnificence, Your Lordship."

He didn't answer.

A footman emerged from a doorway, and Grant waved him off. The man stopped, clicked his heels, and disappeared again as quickly.

"Such obeisance," she said. "What must it be like to have everyone in the world wishing to serve you?"

"Hardly everyone in the world," he said. "But it is a great deal of responsibility."

She glanced at him and then away.

He watched her for a moment.

"That young footman may remain here or go somewhere else, but what he does in his future life may well be determined by these months in my employ."

"What's his name?" she asked, guessing that he truly didn't know.

"James. James Arthur Ferguson. His uncle was my stable master for years before an accident put him in a chair."

"And you feel a duty toward the nephew?" she asked, turning and surveying him.

"I feel an obligation to ensure that he—or any young man in my employ—comes to no harm," he said, a small smile turning up the corners of his lips. "I insist that my staff attend church services every Sunday. I also insist they save a portion of their salaries and send it to a bank in Edinburgh."

"Yet, for all your stewardship, you remained in Italy."

"I did not abdicate my duties wholly, Miss Cameron," he said, frowning. "My brother and I maintained ample correspondence. He informed me of important decisions. I was not completely without influence."

"Forgive me, Your Lordship. I did not mean to annoy you."

"I am not annoyed," he said curtly.

"I have the habit of being at odds with you, have you noticed?"

"If you are, you have never conveyed it to me."

"Perhaps I have only imagined your irritation, then."

"Let us just say that I'm not used to someone with your candid nature."

She turned and faced forward again, placing her palms on the balustrade.

"I'm capable of some restraint in speech, Your Lordship. Not an excessive amount, I will admit, but some. Not every thought leaves my mind to travel to my lips. Some things are kept in abeyance."

"Then I would be very curious to hear what you do not say to me, Miss Cameron. They are, no doubt, very entertaining comments."

"Perhaps it's best if I remain silent, Your Lordship."

"What a pity," he said. "A beautiful woman's repartee is worth hearing, even if it results in irritation."

"Are you attempting a courtly compliment, Your Lordship? If so, I can assure you that the effort is appreciated but not necessary."

"By which you mean, I take it, that either I didn't succeed in being courtly, or you don't believe in your own attractiveness."

"I hardly think this topic of conversation is suitable, Your Lordship."

"Which means, of course, that I have failed abysmally at being complimentary."

"You shouldn't try. Or is that being too honest?"

He didn't speak for a moment. She glanced at him

out of the corner of her eye to find that he, too, had turned and was now surveying the view.

She didn't mind that he questioned her, but what was odd about this conversation was an absence of the proper kind of questions. He didn't ask Gillian about Arabella. There was no curiosity, as if his future wife were no more important to him than one of the andirons, or the frescoes on the ceiling.

Nor did Gillian immediately furnish him with information that she should have, perhaps. If she were truly a loyal employee, she would have hastened to explain to him that Arabella often had more weighty thoughts on her mind than the whereabouts of her companion. Or she might have gone on to enumerate the reasons that Arabella would make an acceptable wife. Her love of reading, for one—although she preferred only medical texts. Or the fact that she abjured fashion—which might save him a pretty penny with dressmakers. But Gillian did none of those things, only remained as silent as he.

"Do you not like fashion, Miss Cameron?" he asked suddenly.

"I do," she said.

He glanced at the windows of Arabella's chamber. "But you deliberately leave a room filled with seamstresses. Why?"

"Perhaps I dislike groups more than I like clothing."

"I, too, find myself avoiding people," he said.

Surprised, she glanced at him. "How very unsociable of you."

He smiled. "Do you think so? People, on the whole, disappoint me greatly. Science rarely does. I can measure what goes into an experiment. What goes into it is what comes out of it. People are rarely so pure."

"An experiment cannot hug you, cannot smile at you, and congratulate you for a successful day. A scientific equation cannot give you love."

"But a scientific equation does not bore me, Miss Cameron."

"You really should leave me," she said, feeling absurdly lighthearted. "Before I bore you."

"Now it is I who has annoyed you. Will you tell me? Or will you be restrained in your speech?"

He placed his hands on the balustrade next to hers, so close that she could feel the warmth of his fingers.

What would it feel like to reach out and place her hand atop his?

She stepped away.

"I think it best if I leave, Your Lordship."

"Why?"

His gaze was direct and penetrating. She held her mouth still against a tremulous quiver.

He knew quite well why.

"You are to be married, Your Lordship."

"Indeed I am, Miss Cameron, and how wise you are to remind me. Are you always so proper?"

"Always, Your Lordship."

For a moment they simply looked at each other. He turned and without another word strode from the terrace, leaving her standing there alone, untouched, and unsullied, at least on this occasion. His wisdom had saved her when her inclination would have quite possibly urged seduction.

Three years ago, she'd gone willingly to her downfall, enjoying every second of it. Not for her a shocked exclamation upon learning of the act of love. She was fascinated, not repulsed. She adored every stroke, every touch, every quiver, and every gasp. She was, as her lover maintained, adept at lust, and instead of finding shame in such a pronouncement, she'd felt only pleasure.

Did she somehow betray her knowledge? Did she have a certain look? Could any man, upon looking at her, know that she was neither virginal nor innocent? Would he suspect that she was ripe for misadventure? Was she more wanton in her walk than another woman? Or did the way she comported herself somehow convey to a man that she wished to be bedded?

Or did any man simply view a woman as a challenge? A wall that he must scale, an impenetrable fortress he must conquer?

If so, then she should be more like Arabella. Perhaps she should study how Arabella acted, moved, and dismissed all male companionship so effortlessly.

Or perhaps she should simply avoid the Earl of Straithern at all costs.

At the door he looked back at her. Gillian stood facing the front lawn. How much he hated that damn view. She'd thought it a pleasure to be steward of Rosemoor. If she only knew the full brunt of the responsibility he bore. But she was not privy to that part of his life, and with any luck she wouldn't know more than he chose to tell her.

He'd spent years of his life keeping Rosemoor safe from rumor or speculation.

Was that why he'd escaped to Italy? Not because he craved freedom as much as he wanted a release from the almost palpable aura of evil that clung to his childhood home. The deaths of his brothers had only added to Rosemoor's miasma.

Every moment he spent in Arabella's company only added to the certainty that she was exactly the wrong choice for him and for Rosemoor. He was growing to dislike Arabella Fenton with an intensity that shocked him. Normally he never felt such raw emotion about any woman, other than the curiosity he now felt about Gillian Cameron.

No, not simply curiosity. Delight. He felt lighter in her company, as if she banished the ghosts of his past, and the worries of his future.

Leave her alone.

How very odd that the command might well prove impossible.

Arabella watched the two of them from the window, making careful note of Gillian's flushed face and the look she gave the earl when he turned away. She was no better than a strumpet, a woman of loose morals, encouraging him so. Didn't she know that all she needed to do was to smile at a man in a certain way, and he would immediately deem a woman infatuated?

Gillian must be taught that her actions were like tinder to flame. She must comport herself with propriety at all times, with the dignity that womanhood demanded. Men could be rutting beasts, but women must be their masters. Women must civilize the world, must demonstrate by word and act that human beings could be creatures of intellect.

But would Gillian listen? She doubted it. Gillian

was changing, becoming more annoyed, more irritated with her role. Or was it something else?

Grant Roberson was proving to be as earthy as any of his subordinates, down to the stable boy and the gardener's helper. Such a discovery was both a disappointment and a secret relief. Had he been a paragon of virtue, an example for all other men to follow, she would have had no choice but to attempt to welcome this marriage. As it was, however, he was as far from virtuous as Gillian was proving to be.

This union was going to be worse than a sham; it was going to be a horror.

Chapter 10

Each day of the next two weeks was marked by a strange sense of waiting. Each morning Gillian awoke wondering if today would end the disconcerting feeling of anticipation. Would today be the day she finally lost her temper with Arabella and told her what a spoiled and ungrateful wretch she was? Or would she tell Dr. Fenton that she did not need another lecture on comportment or manners—she knew only too well who she was. Would today, perhaps, be the day when she allowed herself to begin to feel again? When she admitted, if only to herself, that Grant Roberson was the most fascinating man she'd ever met?

Gillian allowed herself a few moments of dreaming, before banishing any errant happy—impossible—thoughts. Perhaps if she did this day after day, there would come a time when she'd awake from the mists of a dream knowing that her lot in life would be exactly what it was now, at this moment, in this time, forever.

As if Arabella had discerned Gillian's short temper, she began to settle into her role. She no longer chased Blevins from room to room, although the man did eye her with caution when she came into view. She attended the last of her fittings and wore a few of her new dresses without a tirade on the restrictions of stays and the absurdity of the new fashions. On this point, Gillian would have agreed with her—collars were too large and sleeves were too puffy at the shoulder, and too snug between the elbow and wrist. Nor did Arabella constantly appear in company with a book, although there were still too many occasions when she did so. The most striking consequence of their daily lessons, however, was that Gillian overheard her comment to the earl about the beauty of the spring climate.

Arabella had never before remarked upon the weather.

While Arabella was beginning to act like a pleased soon-to-be bride, Gillian likewise behaved with perfect decorum, never once indicating that she would like to step out of the carefully proscribed role she'd assumed. She and the earl met at dinner, of course, and those other social occasions when she was required to accompany Arabella. She avoided any circumstance when they might be alone together, however. Nor did she return to his laboratory.

She was determined to avoid temptation.

Tonight a deep purple twilight fell over Rosemoor. The air was thick with scent from the adjoining gardens and the pines from the nearby forests. Night beckoned on a slender finger, coaxing her to dream of better days and happier times. Dreams, however, would never make up for the fact that Robert was gone, her parents had shunned her, and her friends had been shocked at her abandon.

The price she'd paid for being too free with her affections had been high, indeed.

She stood at the window staring out at the vista of Rosemoor being slowly encased in darkness. The great house was too quiet. She needed tumult and confusion. She needed the noise of Edinburgh, the cacophony that was London. Give her the sound of a house filled to the rafters with people and she would be happy enough.

At Rosemoor there was no need to line the streets with hay. The house was so vast that the inhabitants would never hear a carriage on the gravel drive.

Night deepened, a soft drape of nature to ensure the earl slept well. A princely rest for a man with noble blood in his veins, a man of such immense power that the world no doubt hesitated at the mention of his name.

As she did.

Whenever Arabella spoke of him, Gillian walked away or found another occupation. It would not do to think of him too often, to encourage feelings that were causing her to remain awake, as now.

More than once she'd told herself she was a fool. But the urgings of her conscience vied with a more disturbing voice, this one not quite so pure or driven by higher thoughts. This errant whisper urged her to lose her caution, be adventurous, even daring.

The rest of her life would be spent, in one form or fashion, in service to others. She had, by the feckless actions of her youth, determined her fate. She would no longer be a proper young matron of Edinburgh. She would no longer maintain her house, her husband, and her stature in society. If she married, somewhere in the far distant future, it would not be for position but simply for security. Nor would it be for love. She wasn't entirely certain that she trusted love anymore.

Or perhaps it was that she didn't trust herself. That was part of it, wasn't it? If her judgment had been so wrong in regard to Robert, then how could she be trusted to fall in love again?

How could she trust herself to know the difference between love and affection, or between physical desire and a deeper yearning?

She opened the window, wishing it were winter. The air would be bitterly cold; the snow would be piled high on the ground. She would be immediately reminded of sorrow. Winter was the season of death. Yet she needed no reminders.

Sleep would come late tonight, if at all.

Tonight, sadness was too close, and her mood too bleak. Loneliness felt like a ghost standing behind her, whispering in her ear, reminding her of the past.

Was it such a sin to want to be loved?

She turned away from the window. The maid had readied the bed, folding down the sheet and comforter on both sides, fluffing up the pillows. The room was a lovely one, a testament to Rosemoor's wealth and taste. She could fault neither her accommodations nor the warmth with which she had been welcomed to the earl's estate.

Perhaps her role in life would have been easier to bear had she been relegated to the servants' quarters and treated with disdain. This way, she actually had moments in which she dreamed Arabella's role might be hers.

At dinner tonight, the earl had watched her for too

long until she wanted to warn him that other people were noticing his interest. He'd questioned her opinion during the conversation, and when she'd retreated to silence, he'd sought her comments so pointedly that she had no choice but to answer him. Through it all, he'd never quite lost that small smile of his, as if he ridiculed her for her caution, or chastised her for her lack of courage.

She was no coward. But she couldn't quite forget one very important fact. Had it not been for Dr. Fenton's intervention, she would now be a woman of the streets. A poor creature whose night's lodgings or sustenance was paid for by the rent of her body.

She paced, restless, dreading the coming hours. A moment later, she grabbed her wrapper and left the room.

Rosemoor was a labyrinth of hallways and rooms. In the last two weeks she'd learned her way around by using the formal gardens as a landmark. They were located to the east of the structure. Therefore, she could readily find her way to the west and north wings, where the most commonly used rooms were located.

The gallery was long, one hundred fifty-two feet long, as measured by her footsteps. The plaster ceiling was deeply carved with trailing vines. The oak floor was set with alternating blond and dark wood strips, the shading illuminated by moonlight streaming in through the dozen or so floor-to-ceiling arched windows.

Delicate tables no larger than a foot square sat between each of the curtained windows. Some held deeply hued Chinese vases. A few bore intricately carved ivory statues, now a study in cream and gray shadow. One table sat empty, and as she walked to it, she realized the top itself might be considered a work of art since it was crafted of rare Blue John stone. Her father had ordered a vase made of the purple, yellow, and gray material and had to wait several years before delivery.

She moved to the middle of the corridor, studying the shadowed portraits mounted on the wall to her left. The Earls of Straithern had evidently prized their horses and their dogs, because both were prominently featured. Not so their wives.

A sound at the end of the room made her turn her head. Was there a footman in attendance? She cleared her throat and spoke, "Is anyone there?"

"Are you given to wandering around at night, Miss Cameron?" an imperious voice asked. "And if so, perhaps I should station a footman outside your door. It would not do for one of the guests at Rosemoor to be shot as an intruder."

"Does that happen often, Your Ladyship?" Gillian asked, searching the shadows.

A moment later, the woman stepped forward into the pale moonlight.

"Why are you awake, Miss Cameron?"

"I could not sleep," Gillian said.

"You should ask Miss Fenton for one of her sleeping powders. She has advised it for my maid, and now she snores throughout the night, keeping me awake."

"I can't help but think that if I am awake, there's a reason for it."

"Do you feel that God is punishing you for some errant thought or deed, Miss Cameron? I doubt God has the time to mete out such punishment in that manner. Time enough when we die and are called upon to answer to St. Peter for all our sins."

"Perhaps I would much rather settle my debts as I go, Your Ladyship. There might be too great a score after my death."

"Are you that sinful?" the countess asked.

"Some would say I am."

"You are an impertinent young woman, are you not? I thought so upon first viewing you."

What on earth did she say to that?

The countess turned, and for a moment Gillian didn't know what to do.

"Are you coming, Miss Cameron? If we are both to be awake, we might as well keep each other company."

Gillian descended the grand staircase behind the countess, holding on to the polished banister tightly. Only one small gas lamp illuminated the descent, and the marble steps could be dangerous.

The older woman began walking toward the back of the house. "I find that chocolate works when all other things fail, Miss Cameron. Will you join me?"

"However do you find your way in the darkness?" Gillian asked after an encounter with a small table. She rubbed at her thigh and followed the woman.

"Twenty years of making the same journey." From the sound of her voice, it was evident the countess was far ahead. Gillian increased her pace, only to stumble into another table. She was going to be bruised in the morning.

"Are you coming, Miss Cameron?" the countess asked with a touch of humor to her voice. "Or should I send a footman to escort you to the kitchens?"

"I believe I can navigate there, Your Ladyship," Gillian said.

"See that you do," came the disembodied voice. "Or else the chocolate will be cold by the time you arrive."

Gillian made her way through the clutter of the hallway and down a series of steps. She turned left, and then some distance before turning left yet again. Unlike the other rooms, this space was brightly lit by gas lamps.

"You'll find the journey a little easier," the countess said, appearing at the end of the corridor. "My son has insisted upon lighting the entire kitchen." She looked up at one of the sconces on the wall. "They smell abominably, but it is pleasant not to have to worry about candles. Grant tells me that such a thing will be commonplace in most homes in a matter of years. We live in a very progressive world, Miss Cameron. I suppose it's necessary to accept that fact, however difficult it might be."

"You must be very proud of the earl."

A shadow flitted over the countess's face, but she smiled a second later. "I am, Miss Cameron. He is a son any woman would admire. I missed him a great deal when he lived in Italy. I implored him to come home. I did not know that he would do so . . ." Her voice trailed off, and she shook her head as if annoyed at herself.

She turned and made her way into the kitchen. Gillian followed her, looking around the room, amazed. She'd never before seen such a large room. A huge table, not unlike the one in the earl's laboratory, sat in the middle of the space. On one wall was a massive fireplace, large enough that a dozen men could stand upright inside it. On the other walls were wooden shelves on which pots, pans, and other cooking utensils were kept.

"We can feed everyone at Rosemoor from this kitchen," the countess said, correctly interpreting Gillian's awe. "A not inconsiderable feat, Miss Cameron, since we have over a hundred people on staff at Rosemoor. You'll discover that they eat appreciably better than most. Whatever is served at the main table finds its way to the servants' dining room. Regrettably, there is little food left over to feed the poor. But I can proudly say that we have never turned away anyone in need of sustenance. Did you know that we have one entire building given over to the storage of foodstuffs?"

"I didn't," Gillian said.

"Miss Fenton did not know that fact, either. She has expressed not one iota of curiosity about the running of Rosemoor. I am very much afraid that she feels it is simply beneath her. But as countess, she will have to supervise every single aspect of the running of this estate. Fairies do not appear at twilight to scrape the pots, Miss Cameron. Nor do cobblers' elves ensure that all the servants are fed or clothed."

In other words, Arabella must evince some interest, even if false, in the duties of countess. She must also, if Gillian could convince her, express some curiosity about Rosemoor, at least to the Countess of Straithern.

The countess went to the shelf, procured a long-handled pot, and returned to the stove.

"You are looking at me very strangely, Miss Cameron. Did you expect me to call my maid?"

"Actually, I had expected one of the cooks to be awake, Your Ladyship."

"Then you'd better settle yourself in for the sight of a countess making her own chocolate. I am a duke's daughter, but my father was a firm believer in not rearing helpless children. After all, he'd seen what happened during the Revolution in France. All of those aristocrats, some of them unable to button their own shoes." She shook her head. "Self-sufficiency is a wonderful thing, Miss Cameron. I daresay you have it in abundance. I've watched you, you know."

"Have you?"

The countess nodded. "I have asked a great many questions about you as well, Miss Cameron. Dr. Fenton, however, seems uncharacteristically restrained when speaking of you. I sense a mystery there."

Gillian moved to the table, sat at one end of the bench. She placed her hands on the table, palms together, her fingers pointing in the countess's direction. "There is no mystery, Your Ladyship."

"How did you become companion to a very whiny and spoiled woman?"

"Arabella has a great many flaws, true, Your Ladyship, but they are of youth, I think, rather than inclination or character."

"And now you correct me. Perhaps you have carried your self-sufficiency a bit far."

Gillian didn't respond.

The countess opened a jar, poured something into the pot. A few moments later, the room was filled with a sultry chocolate smell.

"Why were you roaming the halls of Rosemoor, Miss Cameron?"

"I couldn't sleep, Your Ladyship."

The countess looked over her shoulder, her expression irritated. "I believe we have already established that fact, Miss Cameron," she said briskly. "I'm asking you why you couldn't sleep. Do you have a troubled conscience?"

"I will allow as how my conscience is not unblemished, Your Ladyship. But it has not yet kept me awake at night."

"You are either a very fortunate young woman, Miss Cameron, or you're an accomplished liar. Are there no actions you regret? Not one thing you've done that you wished undone? Are you one of the few unblemished souls, Miss Cameron? An example for all other young women to follow?"

"Hardly, Your Ladyship. But nighttime does not bring me any greater degree of regret than I feel during the day."

"A very careful answer, Miss Cameron." The countess kept stirring. "I'm awake because I find it sinful to be sleeping while my children are dead. I will, no doubt, awake in the morning, greet God's dawn once again, be refreshed, and without care for a matter of seconds. While I am gradually coming awake, I will hear the birds singing in the tree outside my chamber and I will glory in the sound of morning."

"And then it will strike you as a hideous thing that you've done," Gillian said, "to awake when what you love, what you care about, is dead. For a moment you close your eyes, and wonder if you can will yourself to death."

The countess's eyes were too sharp, but she said nothing. For some time she continued stirring, and then she poured the chocolate into two cups, one of which she pushed across the table to Gillian. She sat on the opposite bench. The two remained silent, each woman sipping at her chocolate.

"You know loss, Miss Cameron," the countess finally said.

Gillian didn't reply. It wasn't a question, after all.

She studied the pool of chocolate in her cup, careful to smooth her face of any expression. How strange that it became easier to hide what she felt from people she knew, and more and more difficult to shield herself from strangers.

How very different it would be to live somewhere where people weren't afraid to reveal themselves, where emotion was prized instead of hidden. She'd heard the Italians were that way. She should ask the earl if such a thing was true.

"Grant doesn't like to talk about his brothers," the countess said after several moments had passed. "He thinks that to do so would be to encourage my grief. But simply because my sons have died does not mean they ceased to live. I need to speak of them. To tell tales of them. To boast of their adventures, perhaps. I need to mark their presence in the world, in my heart, and never mentioning them does not make them invisible to me.

"I found it strange to be the mother of three boys. But I think I was blessed. No," she amended, "I know I was. There could have been no better sons in all the world."

She sat back, closed her eyes, and sighed deeply. Gillian couldn't help but wonder if she fought back tears.

"Tell me about them," Gillian said, leaning forward.

The older woman opened her eyes. "You needn't be kind, Miss Cameron. I appreciate it, but I do not require it.'

Gillian smiled. "Did they all have the earl's eyes?"

"The Roberson gray eyes?" The countess smiled. "All of them. And yet, sometimes I think that was all they had in common. They were so different from each other. James was the joker, the one who enjoyed life by celebrating it. Too much, I often thought. Andrew did not play enough. He was the studious one, who reveled in numbers. James and Andrew were so much younger than Grant, but they were all devoted to one another." She hesitated again, wiping at her cheeks, and this time Gillian had no doubt that she was weeping.

"Would you like to see a miniature of my sons, Miss Cameron?"

Gillian nodded.

"Then I shall show you. Tomorrow, after we've had a good night's sleep."

What an odd place Rosemoor was. Outwardly it was an estate fit for a prince, lavishly decorated, beautifully appointed, and surrounded by magnificent grounds. Inside, however, emotions swirled and seemed to color the air: grief and loss, and perhaps fear, coupled with an almost fierce determination to put a brave face to the world.

She herself knew only too well that sometimes intentions were not enough.

Chapter 11

Rosemoor was lit up like a fairy castle for the ball to introduce Arabella. The gas lamps at the eaves and porticoes were lit; wind-proof sconces were mounted at the windows. A trail of lanterns stretched all the way down the serpentine gravel drive to the massive brick gates of Rosemoor. Footmen were stationed at the entrance to give directions to the carriage drivers, and then again at the steps, one of them holding a silver tray on which goblets of warm wine had been placed, a traditional welcome to the Earl of Straithern's home.

The third floor had been opened up, aired out, and polished from the oak floors to the four great sparkling chandeliers with their sixteen candle arms and glittering crystal pendants.

The musicians had arrived three days ago from Edinburgh and had taken direction from the countess on what to play and when. Occasionally Gillian had seen members of the orchestra on the veranda outside the ballroom, but she'd never ventured closer.

The night of the ball, Gillian had supervised Arabella's dressing, surprised when the girl had made no more than a token protest. When the maid was finished with her hair, Gillian was in awe.

Arabella had always been pretty, but tonight she was beautiful, a perfect princess.

The soft yellow gown emphasized her curves and the alabaster of her skin, while the décolletage revealed what Arabella's plain blue and brown dresses did not. She was amply endowed, and her cleavage was marked by a delicate brown mole to one side.

Her blond hair was arranged in a coiffure that swept away from her face, with ringlets pulled free to soften the look, and flowers woven through her curls. Her complexion was a perfect porcelain, warmed with a delicate rose blush. Her green eyes sparkled as she regarded herself solemnly in the mirror, and Gillian couldn't help but wonder if she was pleased with the result.

Would the Earl of Straithern be smitten with his bride?

Gillian's soft pink gown was lovely as well, but she had no illusions that her appearance could compare to Arabella's. Her features were unremarkable, her figure slender but not noticeable. She was simply average, neither beautiful nor ugly.

She and Arabella walked to the ballroom together, but when it was time to enter, Gillian stepped back to allow Dr. Fenton to escort his daughter inside. When a footman offered his arm, she shook her head. Instead she walked to the end of the corridor and stared, unseeing, through the window.

How utterly foolish I am, God, to be envious of someone else. We cannot live the lives of other people. We must live the lives we have made for ourselves.

But was it so sinful to wish, for a matter of hours only, to be carefree and thoughtless again? Was it so horrible to wish to be the girl who'd balked at so many Edinburgh entertainments, who questioned why she must dance with that man or this? A heedless child who was feted and charmed as the daughter of one of Edinburgh's most successful and wealthiest merchants, and through it all never saw that attention as unusual or special in any way—but accepted it as her due.

When she scolded Arabella, she was really scolding the girl she'd been. But she'd paid the price for being spoiled and silly. Every moment of stolen joy was matched with an hour of silent grief. Every unmindful act was countered by endless regret.

Until she came to Rosemoor, Gillian thought her lessons well learned. Yet tonight she found herself envying Arabella.

Dear God, she must leave Rosemoor quickly.

Reluctantly she returned to the ballroom, grateful when Dr. Fenton separated from the crowd and escorted her to the side of the room. A footman arrived in front of her, offering her a cup of punch from a silver tray. She took it from him, more for something to do with her hands than because she was thirsty.

The dance floor was crowded with people in various stages of proficiency dancing the Strathspey and Half Tulloch. How many times had she negotiated the complicated patterns of the dances, feeling a quick impatience when one of the other three dancers was not as nimble?

What a silly girl she'd been.

Gillian had no difficulty in singling Grant out. Nor did it seem that he was alone. Others gathered around him, two men and three women, vying for his time and attention.

Gillian pressed her hands around the cup of punch and wished her skirts were less voluminous and easier to manage. Instead she was constrained by fabric and lace into being a model of womanly comportment, however much she wished otherwise.

If someone, a sage of the world, perhaps the oldest living man, or the wisest one, would come and ask her one question: what would she like to be now, right this moment, she would be forced to answer with the truth. Free, she'd say, an economy of speech, but a largesse of thought.

Perhaps she'd dress in a style reminiscent of twenty years ago, a long column of fabric gathered beneath her bosom and trailing to the floor. She'd adorn her hair with a simple ribbon to keep it from blowing in her face, and she'd dispense with a sun shade or parasol or bonnet. Her shoes would be supple leather, something that conformed well to her feet. Beneath her dress she would wear only a soft chemise. No corset, no stays, no itchy garments. She would have nothing to do but what she wished. She'd sketch the plants God created, or marvel at the passing of a day, from the brilliance of dawn to the subtle nuances of nightfall. With her new freedom she would go forth into the world and scandalize everyone who knew her. She would sing at the top of her lungs if the spirit moved her to do so. She'd eat what she liked, and drink sherry in the mornings and tea at midnight. She'd ridicule others if she felt cruel and petty. Or she'd be generous with her praise and her money.

Most of all, she'd love with abandon and dance to the sound of the wind.

She would be that most glorious of creatures, a human being with failings and flaws, and accepting of them. Instead she was forced to pretend, by the very requirements of survival, to be someone other than she was.

She didn't want to be here, but her attendance had been mandatory. A ball gown had been prepared for her almost without her participation. In fact, she'd not known about it until the very end of Arabella's fittings. The dress was a rose pink, not the color she'd choose, but she was still appropriately grateful to Dr. Fenton for his kindness.

Or should she be grateful to the earl, instead?

She slid her glance to him, and then away again before he noticed. Jealousy was an absolutely insane emotion, especially since she had no reason to be jealous. The world would not look upon her feelings as prudent or wise. What sort of woman lusted after a man she could not have? Not just any man, but an earl?

Dear God, please help me. Please help me understand that there are some things I cannot have. Let me understand, with my whole heart, that wishing for circumstances to be different is as nonsensical as wishing for the moon.

Perhaps one day she would find love. Perhaps one day she would have children. If that day ever came, she would make some grand and glorious gesture, some way to tell the world that dreams did come true and prayers were answered.

But until then, she was doomed to stand here and watch Grant pay attention to all the women guests at Rosemoor. He danced as he did everything, carefully, controlled, with almost mathematical precision, as if he counted the movements in his mind.

He was wearing gloves, as she was. If they danced, they would not feel the touch of each other's palm. They could be circumspect and proper. What about looking at his face? She would look away, directing her attention to the walls of mirrors or the windows that led to the veranda overlooking the terrace where once they'd stood and chatted as almost friends.

If they danced with each other, their feet would fly over the highly polished wooden floors together, in tandem, a proper, restrained, and acceptable union of their bodies.

Her heart beat so tightly that it felt as if someone were wrapping a cord around her chest. She felt as if she were weeping inside where the casual observer could not see. She was angry and she wasn't certain who she was angrier at: him for being so fascinating or herself, for being lured too easily.

Grant hadn't said another word about the ball to introduce Arabella to the neighborhood. Nor had he objected to taking a few hours from his schedule, filled though it was. He hadn't even caviled at being reintroduced to countless people he'd known all his life but hadn't seen since his return from Italy. Except for James's funeral, he'd not socialized, and he could understand their curiosity about him. This evening's entertainment, modest though it was due to their mourning, was considered a monumental social event, according to his mother. Therefore he forced himself to smile, to welcome people to Rosemoor, and to hide his increasing irritation.

He was being ignored by Gillian Cameron. Pointedly ignored, in fact, as if she were going out of her way to be annoying. Whenever he looked in her direction, she glanced away. When he moved toward her, she scurried to the other side of the room.

Someone addressed him, and he turned to the man, annoyed.

"I beg your pardon, Your Lordship," the man said, awkwardly bowing. Any other time, Grant would have told him that he wasn't the damn king; stop being so servile. Now he only nodded before glancing at Gillian.

Irritating woman.

He turned his attention to Arabella instead. He went to her side, inclined his head, and the crowd of people surrounding her obligingly parted.

"Would you care to dance, Arabella?" he asked.

She looked as if she would refuse, but gave him her hand instead.

With an uncharacteristic feeling of doom, Grant led her out to the middle of the room.

Dr. Ezra Fenton watched his daughter dance with a feeling like amazement. The earl was actually touching her hand, and she was allowing it. Arabella looked like an angel, and she actually had a smile on her face. Earlier, he'd heard her laugh.

Not for the first time since the earl had made his surprising proclamation, he thought of his dear wife. Catherine should have been there to witness the changes of the last few years. The little girl who barely spoke, who was terrified of night, had blossomed into a beautiful young woman, one who was to marry an earl.

Arabella appeared truly happy this evening. Of course, she was the princess of this ball, charming more than one young man. Even the earl appeared pleased, which was, all in all, a difficult thing to ascertain since he rarely smiled.

Nor did Gillian. How odd that the two of them were spending the entire night on opposite sides of the ballroom, but their expressions were almost identical.

He would have to talk to Gillian. She must remember exactly who she was, simply Arabella's companion. Perhaps at one time she would have been on a higher social level, but no longer. She was his daughter's companion, little more than a servant. She must maintain a distance between herself and the earl. While it was very possible she would be living at Rosemoor for the rest of her life, it would not do for there to be discord among the three of them.

Perhaps he should make some overture toward his future son-in-law. The idea had merit, but at the last moment, he decided against it. One did not approach Grant Roberson without an invitation. Even now, at his own ball, people appeared and then seemed to fade away.

The earl and Arabella had a great deal in common, if they could only communicate well enough to understand each other. Arabella was as driven as Grant, in her way. She was as intense, as dedicated to learning. Perhaps this union would prove successful after all.

He beamed, thinking himself the luckiest man in

the world. He caught sight of the countess. Although still in mourning, she'd put aside her grief to plan this ball for Arabella. He caught her gaze and smiled and nodded, and was elated when she returned his look with a small smile of her own.

Her face was too pale, but then she'd always had too little color. Otherwise she was a very healthy woman of a somewhat older age than she admitted to being. But she was still a very fine figure of a woman.

He had loved her for years, and for years he'd told himself that it was foolish to feel such emotion for a woman so high above him in rank. If he could only convince her to dance. Perhaps one day, but not tonight. One wish fulfilled was good enough for now.

Dorothea had smiled at him.

"You and I have not spent very much time in conversation this evening," Grant said when the break in the music accommodated speech.

Their dance was finished, but he didn't move away. Why was it so difficult to talk to Arabella, and so incredibly easy to talk with Gillian?

His innate caution surfaced when he was around Arabella. She was not, for all her devotion to healing, a nurturing type of woman. He could not, for all his efforts, envision her cradling a child to her bosom.

"Is it necessary that we speak, Your Lordship?" Arabella asked. "It's my understanding that you do not wish for me to be personable as much as fertile."

He stared at Arabella, wondering how he was to respond to that. She wasn't attempting to shock him. In fact, the expression on her face was one of extreme boredom.

He suspected that the only way to incite her curiosity or even her animation was to bring her someone ill.

"You dance quite well," he said.

She didn't respond to the compliment. "And you are very beautiful tonight."

"A result of artifice, I fear," she said. "A bit of paint. My eyebrows have been tweezed, and I have been constrained in this gown to the extent that my curves are not natural. I do not doubt it will alter my digestion and cause my stomach fluids to sour."

"As bad as all that?"

She frowned at him.

"I like your hair, especially with the flowers entwined through it," he said in the silence.

"Your mother's maid did that to me. She said I would be like Aphrodite. I have no earthly desire to be modeled after one of the Greek goddesses," she added. "If she must pattern me after someone, why not Hippocrates?"

"I believe Hippocrates was a man, and she wished you to appear as a female tonight."

She didn't comment.

"Would you consider another dance, Arabella?"

"I would prefer not, Your Lordship. I have managed to avoid your mother's censure by achieving a balance between my duty and my tolerance."

He could not help but smile at her answer. She really did hate socializing. "My brother Andrew was the same," he said. "He hated any manner of gathering and would hide out in the library."

"Indeed, Your Lordship?"

He had lost her again. Her interest level evidently

flagged when talking of anyone other than herself. Or perhaps he was simply being unkind, and she was merely uncomfortable speaking with him.

"Have you found any patients at Rosemoor who require your skills?" There, a subject she would like.

"The gardener's son has a very bad cut on his hand. I believe it is suppurating," she said. "I do not know if he will be able to regain the use of his fingers, or if I shall have to amputate two of them."

"Good God," he said, shocked. "I hope that will not be necessary."

"A physician does what one must, Your Lordship. The details of his wound are difficult for a layman to understand, or indeed to bear without a strong stomach."

"I have a great deal of forbearance, Arabella, but also some measure of compassion. Mark needs to be able to earn a living. How will he do so without the use of one hand?"

"Better than he will if he dies of infection, Your Lordship."

She turned away, facing toward the ballroom, as if dancing were more preferable than his company.

The question he asked her was unwise, but he asked it nevertheless. "Do you think we shall suit, Arabella?"

She glanced at him. "Are you seeking my opinion? It is the first time anyone has done so in this entire adventure."

"That's what you think it is, an adventure?"

"For lack of a better term. What would you call it, Your Lordship?"

A disaster. But he didn't say the word aloud.

As they stood at the edge of the room, she kept pulling at her gloves and pushing her hair off her cheek. Her puffed sleeves evidently bothered her, because she kept moving them upward on her arm. When she was studying her books, or treating a patient, Arabella appeared composed, controlled, and in her element. Now, however, he was struck by how uncomfortable she seemed.

He reached out and touched her on the shoulder, his fingers trailing along the curve in a reassuring touch.

She froze. "Remove your hand, Your Lordship. We are not yet wed. I do not belong to you yet."

When he did not instantly comply, she stepped away.

"I have never done you any harm, Arabella. Nor would I. You needn't be afraid of me."

She stepped back, away from him, a repudiation of his words and of him.

"You are to be my countess. That point alone should bring you a measure of reassurance."

He wanted to reassure her, banish that haunted look on her face. There was suddenly something about her that was innocent and almost childlike, an aura that made him abruptly realize he would probably never feel passion for her. But he might well be able to feel some degree of protectiveness. That would have to be enough for a marriage, and it was probably more than his parents had.

"I just want you to leave me alone."

"Hardly encouraging words for future husband, Arabella."

At her silence, he spoke again, "Do you wish me to release you from our upcoming marriage, Arabella?"

"I could not ask for you to do so without disappointing my father," she said, reluctance evident in every word. "Therefore, I think we must suit, Your Lordship."

"Perhaps a delay, then?"

She looked absurdly hopeful.

"That would be acceptable, Your Lordship. Thank you."

"A condemned prisoner might have more enthusiasm, Arabella."

"I do not wish to be married at all," she said. "To anyone."

"At least I suppose I should consider myself fortunate to be in such good company."

At her quizzical look, he smiled. "With the rest of the male gender."

"You do not understand, Your Lordship. How can you?"

"Then, pray, enlighten me."

"No," she said simply, and abruptly left him, skirting the dancers and pushing through the guests.

Grant was left to survey the ballroom and tamp down the feeling of relief Arabella's absence instantly produced. He looked for Gillian, and found her easily on the other side of the room.

Gillian was being personable, perhaps even amiable. She was obviously attempting to be charming and succeeding too well. Grant ignored the people congregating around him and frowned at her. If he approached her directly, she'd have nowhere to hide. What would she say if he asked her to join him in a dance? Perhaps he would coax her outside, into the moonlight. The shrubs, the trees, and the flowers would be witness to their meeting, but only nature, because humans caused too much grief with their speculation and gossip.

He was not given to poetic moments, despite the years of living in Italy. But she made him want to be a man of sonnets, a talent he'd never before desired until this moment. He wished he played the mandolin, or some other instrument that would allow him to serenade her. With music he could mute the confusion of his mind, communicate to her in a way that transcended words. Unfortunately, he had no such talent, never having given music any time at all.

He could lecture on a variety of subjects. Would she like to know his theory of magnetism? Or read his recent paper, "On the Motion of Heat and Its Validity to the Mathematical Theory of Electricity"? He could orchestrate a spark for her, perform another experiment to demonstrate his various hypotheses, but what woman wanted such an exhibition instead of a little romanticism?

Perhaps Gillian. Perhaps she would understand, of all the women he'd ever met. With her self-deprecating humor, and her aura of sorrow, with her layers of personality, one stacked upon the other like a fine Italian pastry. She was a conundrum; she was a puzzle, and he was as dedicated to solving her as he was his electrics.

That was not a very romantic declaration, perhaps, but he didn't have any right to make declarations of any type.

He was the Earl of Straithern, the last of the line of lecherous men who made no secret of their proclivities. The last in a long line of men who'd used their title and position to obtain anything they wanted. A line of men who'd been granted nobility by their birth, but hadn't done anything particularly successful with their lives.

He'd wanted to be different. He'd always wanted to be better than his father. He would be wise to remember that, but he wasn't altogether certain that with Gillian he was wise.

What was it about her that so fascinated him? Her brown hair was styled very simply, the thick curls arranged in a demure fashion. Her soft blue eyes? She was pretty in an average, nondescript sort of way. But she had a way of looking at him that made him wonder if she had the ability to peer into his very soul.

What utter rot.

She was no more and no less than any other woman he'd ever met. He was simply lonely, that was all, and marriage to Arabella Fenton suddenly did not suit at all. He was behaving no better than any of his ancestors, with the sole exception of his father, whose sins so far outweighed anything that Grant could attempt.

Yet when Gillian smiled, he wanted to respond in kind, or to laugh, relieved that she found humor in life instead of pain.

She was taking the time to amicably chat with the young men who made their way to her side. Why was she doing so? His mother was there to ensure that the gathering proceeded smoothly. Gillian had no need to be pleasant to all those toothy young males.

Why wasn't she dancing? And why did he feel so enormously pleased about the fact?

This night was interminable.

Now one of his neighbors was talking to Gillian, and the man was standing entirely too close. Why, exactly, was Barton spending so much time on an impecunious companion? Everyone knew the man needed a rich wife. He really should warn Gillian that she was making a spectacle of herself, being so pleasant to the man.

He had other things to occupy his mind rather than standing here being seen, being civil, being annoyed. Before his emotions could overwhelm him completely, he left the room.

Chapter 12

Grant walked down to the lake, stood on the other side, and stared at the palace. In the moonlight, the statues arrayed along the colonnade appeared almost like people, dressed in Roman togas, secretly congregating when there were no other witnesses to their meeting. They seemed to guard the structure jealously, as if they reveled inside and wanted no human eyes to witness their nocturnal celebration.

When he was a child, he'd been afraid of this building, possibly because of his father's dictate that he was never to come near it. Later he'd felt an aversion based on knowledge of what had gone on inside these walls. But twenty years of emptiness had made it simply a building again, and although it carried memories, mostly it was just a structure an ancestor had built and he used because it was convenient.

In the moonlight, and the silence, with the distant sound of the music coming from Rosemoor, the palace seemed almost an enchanted place.

Good God, but he was being fey tonight.

For the first time in a very long time, he was dissatisfied with his life, his choices, and his decisions.

He missed Andrew and James. His brothers had the ability to tease him from his dark moods.

Grant found himself walking toward Rosemoor's chapel.

Twenty-five years ago, his father had conceived of a structure that rivaled Versailles, and it had taken nearly all of that time for the architect and team of builders to achieve his dream. The chapel was an example of supreme excess, gilt, marble and Rubenesque murals depicting selected scenes from the Bible painted on the ceiling. The walls were adorned with floor-to-ceiling stained glass panels while the altar gleamed with gold, a huge gold burnished cross resting in the middle of the pristine white lace cloth. Hundreds of workmen had toiled day and night for a decade to carve the gargoyles perched near the roof, and the ornate carvings stretching from the ground to the turrets. Larger than life-size lions perched near the door, as if to remind each entering worshipper that he was in the presence of greatness—a family descended from English nobility who'd made their home in Scotland.

For a few moments, he stood at the end of the aisle, remembering only too well the occasion of his last visit: James's funeral. He hadn't been back since then, and as he stood there he knew only too well the reason why.

Sadness clung to the air like the final notes of a hymn. He could smell the lingering scent of too many flowers, the peppery incense, and the beeswax of the candles.

Slowly, he walked toward the altar. Once there, he mounted the five steps, and then turned, facing the empty pews. He began to light the candles on the altar before descending the steps, lighting candles at the wrought-iron stands throughout the chapel.

He moved to the end of one pew and sat, his concentration fixed on the altar.

Why did man assume that God was present only in sanctified structures? Could He not be felt in other places as well: a forest, the deserted cottage in the glen, the top of the nearest hill? Had the Robersons tried to imprison God in this place, the better to be spared judgment as to their acts throughout Rosemoor?

The God of Scotland was too fierce to be contained.

Too philosophical, brother.

He could almost hear James's teasing voice. Damn, but he missed him, and Andrew, too.

Grant wished, suddenly, that they were ghosts, that his brothers had become spirits. If so, perhaps he could coax them to speak to him, give him advice, tell him what to do to avenge their deaths and solve the mystery of their murders.

Only silence answered him.

Tears were for women, for children. His anguish needed no physical counterpart to be felt. It was there in his memory, in the imaginary voice echoing through the silent chapel.

This place was too damn large to belong to a family home, even one as sprawling as Rosemoor. Perhaps the chapel was Ranald Roberson's entrance fee into heaven. Could God be bribed? And would He wash clean that particular filthy soul?

Grant doubted it. His father's sins were too hideous to be easily forgiven.

He raised his gaze to the ceiling, and the pennants

flying there. Even in his act of contrition, his father could not help but brag a little. No one could doubt that the Earls of Straithern occupied this space.

"James." His voice carried too well throughout the chapel and was carried back to him by the stone walls and the marble pillars. James wasn't here, and that knowledge bit at him. Andrew. This time, he didn't bother speaking his brother's name. It was actually too painful to do so.

Why the hell was he here? What did he hope to gain? A little peace, perhaps? Absolution? Neither was to be found in an empty chapel.

Leave her alone.

The thought was so strong that it was almost a spoken command. He remained still, knowing that the voice he heard was not God's, but his, emerging from his conscience. Would Gillian be happy to know that he was condemning himself for his interest in her? Or would she, instead, be horrified to know that he thought of her at all?

Such a fixation was unwise, bordering on foolish, perhaps more. His path was laid out before him, firm and fixed, hardened by resolve. He was the Earl of Straithern, a fact that he'd never forgotten in all those years in Italy. A title that seemed to weigh heavily on his shoulders now.

Dr. Fenton was suddenly at Gillian's side, nodding affably to a few of the guests. His expression, however, was not quite so friendly when he turned to her.

"I think, perhaps, my dear, that it's time for you to be leaving. You would not wish to overstay your welcome."

You are, after all, only the companion. Words that needn't be said.

She grabbed her shawl. "Shall I say good night to our hosts, sir?" she asked, hoping that her voice sounded submissive enough for Dr. Fenton. "Or shall you say it for me?"

"There is no need for you to do so, Gillian." He frowned at her. "You should not presume upon acquaintance with the earl. Anything you need to say to him can be directed to Arabella or myself."

Gillian wrapped the shawl around her shoulders, taking more time at the task than it required. "I will just say farewell to Arabella," she said.

"Arabella will not miss you, I think." He smiled in fond acknowledgment of his daughter's popularity.

"Very well, sir. I'll bid you good night."

Gillian turned, nearly desperate to leave the ball. Arabella probably wouldn't notice her departure; she doubted anyone would. The only person in the corridor was the footman stationed at the top of the steps, and he avoided making eye contact as she nodded to him, and then descended the staircase. Did he think himself witness to an assignation? She was not meeting anyone—only trying to escape from herself.

She stepped through the front door, into the night, seeking an unknown refuge. Turning left, she began to walk, taking the gravel drive to the end of the main building. Once she stepped onto the path, she realized where she was heading—the chapel. Communing with God might be what she needed. Doing so would certainly take her mind from sin.

The arched chapel door, flanked by gas lamps, groaned slightly as she opened it.

Someone had lit the candles on the altar. The pool of light illuminated the gold of the altar plate, and snowy linen etched in lace.

The now darkened stained glass windows occupied most of the wall on the eastern side of the chapel. During the day, the room was probably bathed in multicolored light. She'd chosen to avoid the service the past two Sundays, but had been regaled with tales of the magnificence of the structure. Arabella had seemed impressed for the very first time since coming to Rosemoor.

She didn't see him until she was midway to the altar. Seated at he was behind a massive pillar encased in marble, he gave the impression of someone who had deliberately sought privacy. One hand fluttered at her side while the other gripped her shawl. She didn't know whether to go, or to stay, to speak, or to remain silent. In the end, it didn't matter anyway. He spoke in a voice barely above a whisper.

"Is it you again, Miss Cameron?"

She hesitated for a moment, Dr. Fenton's words prominent in her mind. If she truly had a servant's heart, she would turn and leave the chapel. She would return to Rosemoor, barricade herself in her room, and pray for divine intervention to remove this fascination.

Instead she turned toward his voice.

"It is, Your Lordship. Forgive my intrusion."

"Is there no place at Rosemoor that is forbidden you? Would you care to examine the wine cellar? Or the old dungeon? It's reputed to be haunted, and I do not doubt that you would be fascinated with it."

Stung, she retorted in kind, "If there are places

where I should not be, Your Lordship, pray tell me where they are. I did not know that I was invading your laboratory. Is the chapel now forbidden me?" She looked around at the cavernous space. "Is this the preserve only of earls? Is God not for all of us to worship? Or do the Robersons claim a special relationship to the Almighty?"

"If anything," came his dry reply, "we have no affinity for God. Nor has God any affinity for us, evidently."

There was such sadness in his tone that it occurred to her that he might be here for the very same reason as she, to seek comfort of a sort.

She turned, and without another word, began to walk toward the door.

"Whom do you mourn?"

The question stopped her cold.

"I asked you before, do you recall?"

Without turning, she replied, "How do you know I'm mourning anyone, Your Lordship?"

"By the paucity of that reply, for one," he said. "And because there is sadness in your eyes, Miss Cameron."

"I have thought the same about you," she said.

"Then we are a pair, are we not? Avoiding levity to mourn those who have gone."

She turned and walked forward until she could see him again. "I didn't know you'd left the ball."

"I found myself oddly lonely in the midst of others. Do you ever feel that way, Miss Cameron?"

"Yes," she said simply.

"I find myself missing my brothers more today than I did the day they died. Is that very odd?"

"No," she said. "The more you come to the realization that no matter how you wish it, the person you love will never be alive again, the more pain you feel. Death is permanent, and it seems that's the most difficult part to understand about it."

"You are my betrothed's companion, Miss Cameron. When did you become so very wise?"

"If I were wise, Your Lordship, I would not be here with you."

He surprised her by laughing. A dry, husky sort of laugh that made her wonder how long it had been since he'd felt amusement.

"So, you consider consorting with me a bit of foolishness?" he asked.

What a very dangerous question. Of course she shouldn't be here with him, and from his glance, he knew it as well. A small smile played around his lips, and he looked as enticing as sin.

"You ignored me at the ball, Miss Cameron. Why?"

"I thought it prudent."

"Do you always take the most prudent course?" he asked.

She had not been a model of restraint for all her life, but for the last two years she'd practiced it diligently. Yet he seemed to beckon her to forbidden places with his questions and tempt her to be foolish enough to say what she truly thought.

She was no wiser at this moment. "I attempt to do so, Your Lordship."

He motioned his hand toward a pew. When she hesitated, he smiled. "We are in a chapel, Miss Cameron. In the sight of God. Surely you can relax your guard sufficiently for a moment."

She sat down, drawing her skirts around her ankles, placing her hands on her knees, and exhibiting the posture of which she'd always been so proud.

He came, sat in the pew in front of her, and turned to face her, his arm on the carved back. "Shall we pretend that we have never met each other?" he asked.

"To what purpose, Your Lordship?"

He didn't answer her question.

"I shall be an acquaintance of your father's. And you shall be someone he has long wished for me to meet."

"Will you still be an earl, Your Lordship?"

"I think I shall be a plain mister," he said. "But we knew each other before, as children. You shall call me Grant, and I will call you Gillian."

"Your Lordship," she began, but he held up a hand to forestall her. "I am Grant," he said, "and you are Gillian. Where did we meet for the first time? At a gathering for your grandmother, I recall."

"No," she corrected, entering into his game, "a very ancient friend of hers, I believe. A woman who was very taken with your father, as I remember. Being, as he was, a bookseller in Inverness."

His smile broadened. "A bookseller in Inverness?"

"You aren't an aristocrat," she said. "But I often remember thinking that, as a boy, you were insufferably proud."

"Did you truly think so?"

"Oh yes," she said. "But I believe it was an affectation only, and not a true reflection of your character. After all, you went to school with boys who were destined to serve in the House of Lords."

"I wonder, did I make their life miserable in school?"

"Was yours?"

"No worse than for anyone else in a similar position," he said easily. "I learned to defend myself and to not mind being away from Rosemoor."

He was telling the truth, she was sure of it, and she wanted to give him something of herself in return.

"I was very studious when I was young," she said. "Perhaps you remember that I used to hide in the corner of my father's library."

"A well-read man, I'd often thought."

She shook her head. "I suspect that my father wished other people to think so. Unfortunately, I think he bought the books by the yard to impress others, rather than to read any of them. But they suited me, and I vowed to make my way through each and every volume."

"Did you?"

"I confess to having no interest whatsoever in horticulture or farming methods, and there were several philosophers who bored me beyond belief. But I adored the novels. I could have read novels endlessly. In fact, I was often accused of wishing to read my life away."

"Because the one you lived was too difficult?"

The questions were becoming too personal, but she answered him anyway. "My father remarried when I was ten. My mother had died at my birth, you see. My stepmother was a very nice woman, and very civil, in her way. But she had a child quite soon after they were wed, and their attention was rightfully directed to the baby."

He didn't say anything, merely stood up, went into the aisle, and then surprised her by sitting in the same pew she occupied. He didn't look at her, merely stared ahead at the altar.

"Were you a fanciful child?" he asked

She thought about the question for a moment. "I don't think so," she said. "I was a lonely child, though, so perhaps I was."

"So, not fanciful as much as forgotten."

"Perhaps," she said.

"You seem reluctant to speak of your youth. Why?"

"Perhaps I don't wish to revisit it," she said, looking at him.

"Was the question rude?'

"Not excessively so," she answered. "But I prefer to live in the present, Your Lordship. Not a fabricated past."

He stretched out a hand, and captured one of hers.

"I would have liked you as a child," he said. "I might've teased you out of your quiet. I might've told you my deepest, darkest secrets."

"Did you have so very many back then?"

"I had a few," he said. "But like you, I had no confidantes. I was the heir, you see, and treated differently from my brothers. More was expected of me than James and Andrew, so our paths in life were not the same."

"I'm glad that I didn't know you as a child," she said. He glanced at her but didn't speak.

She gently pulled her hand away. "As an earl's heir, you would have intimidated me. I would have said to myself: There is a boy, a quite handsome boy, who seems to be as alone as me. If he wasn't to be an earl, I would talk to him. But, of course, you were, and I would never have escaped my shyness."

For a few long moments they sat in companionable silence. Just when she thought he must be impatient to leave, he spoke again.

"I see you in my mind, Gillian. A very bookish, silent child who no doubt looked at the world with very wide eyes, marveling at everything and commenting on nothing."

"I was indeed that child," she said, smiling.

"And now?"

"Perhaps I am less wide-eyed, but I still marvel at a great many things. This chapel for one," she said, tilting back her head and examining the shadows of the buttressed ceiling. "What an absolutely glorious place this is."

"I think I hate it," he said, staring straight ahead.

Surprised, she lowered her head and looked at him, remaining silent and wondering if he would comment further.

"The funeral for my brother was the last ceremony to be held here," he finally said. "There was a soloist, a young boy, and his voice traveled through the entire space as if he were an angel exhorting us to be silent and think upon our mortal souls. I can still hear his voice. Or maybe it's only the faint screams of angels."

Startled, she stared at him. "Why would you say that, Your Lordship?"

"Perhaps it is my conscience speaking. An overused organ, that. Perhaps I'm simply tired and talking nonsense."

He dropped her hand and stood.

She wanted to approach him and then place her lips so very sweetly, so very gently against his.

"I was wrong to tell you to relax your guard, Miss Cameron. It was not wise of me," he added, his voice clipped and stern. In a matter of seconds he'd gone from being an affable companion to reverting to his role as an aristocrat.

"Am I being chastised for being here? You didn't seem to scorn my company a moment ago, Your Lordship."

Perhaps it was better if he didn't regard her as any more than a servant. Let him see her as an urn, a set of fireplace tools. Even a log in the grate. Let him be very surprised when she deigned to speak from time to time, that an inanimate object might be given voice.

"I apologize for disturbing you," she said, her voice sounding remarkably calm, almost disinterested. "I won't visit the chapel again." She stood, drawing her shawl around her shoulders, clutching it tight.

"Miss Cameron," he said. "You misunderstand."

Oh, she understood quite well. She was Arabella's companion. What more was there to say?

"Miss Cameron, you are unattached, with no male relatives to protect you. I am not yet married, although my intentions have already been announced toward Miss Fenton. The world would not understand our being alone together."

She really did understand. But she had been so captivated by the man that she'd forgotten her vow to be decorous.

"Besides all that," he said, his voice holding a note of what sounded amazingly like tenderness, "you are a very attractive young woman, Miss Cameron. And you have a mouth that looks made for kissing."

Shocked, her gaze flew to his. The grip on her shawl

lessened, and it almost felt the floor before she caught it with one trembling hand.

"I found myself wanting very much to kiss you, Miss Cameron, and that would, regrettably, dishonor both of us."

"You want to kiss me?"

Another woman, a wiser one, perhaps would not have asked that question.

His face changed. Whereas a moment ago there had been sternness, now there was a softening of his features, a curve to his mouth.

"Yes," he said simply.

She really should leave this place. She really should run away, as far and as fast as her feet could carry her. But wouldn't it be wonderful if she could simply forget for a moment, and indulge in a little wickedness? Oh, but a little wickedness had nearly ruined her. She could not endure any more scandal.

"I think it would be a very good idea if you left now, Miss Cameron. And please, do not look at me with such somber gaze, as if you're actually giving credence to the thought of our kissing."

"Would you prefer I looked shocked, Your Lordship?"

"I think it would be wiser."

He took one step toward her, and she took a precautionary step back. A curious dance to be held in the aisle of the massive chapel.

Did God witness their thrust and retreat, and was He amused? The distant thunder indicated that perhaps He was not.

Her heart felt as if it were racing, attempting to match the pace of her indrawn breath. Where the blood beat close to the surface of her skin she felt heated, but her extremities were as cold as if they'd been encased in ice.

How could a simple man cause such damage to her equilibrium?

Because he wasn't a simple man. He was an earl, the owner of everything she could see. Yet he was mortal, and not imbued with the qualities of angels. Nor was he a monster, however fierce his frown. He was neither misshapen nor ill formed. His physique was truly magnificent, if she allowed her thoughts to travel in such a direction.

Ah, but then, she was supposed to be ruined, was she not? A man's physique was not an entirely forbidden subject.

His eyes were, by degrees, either very warm or they were cold, as cold as snow. His mouth was as capable of revealing his emotions, tight with irritation, or as now, smiling slightly.

She'd begun to look for his smile.

The wind blew the door ajar, and for a moment she was startled into looking beyond the earl to the entrance. Were spirits adrift in this place, or had she simply not fastened the door well enough?

She turned back to him, to find that the distance had closed between them. He breathed quietly if a little rapidly, as did she. She wondered if his heart beat as quickly as hers.

She wanted so desperately to be kissed.

No, she wanted *him* to kiss her.

"Miss Cameron. Gillian," he whispered.

Now would come the condemnation. Now he would lecture her about her comportment. Now he would issue her a warning, or even worse, he would dismiss her from Arabella's employ. All those horrible things traveled through her mind in a flash of a second.

"I want to put my mouth on you," he said instead.

And then he did, so softly that his lips felt like a breath. She inhaled a sigh, and leaned toward him, placing both palms against his chest. He extended his arms around her, pulling her closer, and she, fool that she was, walked eagerly into his embrace.

A kiss should not be magic. A kiss should not feel like the spark from Volta's engine. But this one did. This kiss was a gate, swinging open slowly, beckoning her to part her lips, and angle her head just so. His face seemed to be a magnet for her two hands, her fingers gently touching his jaw as if to keep him from ending the kiss.

Slowly, softly, endearingly, he lured her to passion. His mouth promised delight as he deepened the kiss; his hands slid to her waist as if testing her receptiveness. Through it all, as her body warmed, her mind remained carefully numb, her thoughts blanked by the taste of desire.

He was the one to end it.

She could hear his breathing, as rapid as hers.

Now was the time for recriminations, but she felt none. She missed passion, regretted the absence of it in her life, and understood the eagerness she now felt. In a strange and remarkable way, the shadows seem to approve. The air was warmer, and perhaps even God, if He had entered and lingered here, was more inclined to forgive them their human frailties. But the world looked askance at sybarites, and she was not the type of woman who endured society's censure with ease.

She bent and retrieved her shawl from where it had fallen, leaving him before she could beg him to continue, before she could say the words to lure him to her bed.

He remained silent as she walked down the aisle, perhaps knowing that a word would have held her there.

She closed the door to the chapel and ran all the way back to Rosemoor, needing the exertion, needing something to overcome the panicky feeling deep inside her chest. She was out of breath before she reached her room, her stays digging into her side.

Twice she stopped in the hallway to regain her composure, and more than once she waved away a solicitous footman. When she reached her room, she closed the door and sagged against it.

Tonight, at least, regret would fuel her dreams instead of grief.

Chapter 13

The countess was escorting Arabella from room to room, explaining the history of Rosemoor and the duties she would need to assume. Dr. Fenton was occupied writing letters. Everyone seemed to have a purpose, duties to perform and tasks to do.

Gillian had only her thoughts for company.

She was tired of seeking refuge in her room. Five days had gone by since the night of the ball and she'd barely seen the earl, except for catching sight of him in the corridor occasionally. She'd always slip into an adjoining room to avoid him. She refused to attend dinner, claiming that she wasn't hungry. Thanks to the complicity of a maid who brought her a nightly tray, she didn't miss a meal. What had she gained for all her efforts? A healthy dose of misery, and the approval of Dr. Fenton.

"I commend you on your taking our little talk to heart, Gillian," he'd said, just this morning. "I trust that you will continue to remember your place."

"Of course, sir." Fallen woman. Foolish woman. She'd forced a smile on her face and left the room as quickly as she could.

Today, however, even nature seemed to chide her for hiding. The sky was a cloudless deep blue, the air was cool, and the morning promised a lovely day. She escaped to the rose garden, slowly walking the graveled paths, admiring the various species of roses the countess had collected over the years.

"*Buon giorno.*"

Startled, Gillian turned around to find her herself the object of a stranger's regard. She stared at him for a moment, as her mind tried to make sense of what, exactly, she was seeing.

A man was standing in the middle of the path grinning at her. His waistcoat was scarlet, embroidered in gold thread. His jacket was black and a longer style than what was popular, but expertly fitted over trousers that looked to be the same fine wool. His shoes were nearly eclipsed by bright silver buckles. But that was not the only place he sparkled. The man was a walking jewel case. A gold fob on his waistcoat was sprinkled with diamonds, and he wore a very large ruby ring on the third finger of his right hand. To top off the picture, his left hand rested on the jewel-encrusted top of a mahogany walking stick.

"You are a vision of loveliness, a rose in a common English garden." He placed one hand over his heart and bowed.

"I beg your pardon, sir?"

Her tone was, perhaps, too sharp, but he'd surprised her, and she didn't like being surprised, especially when she was indulging in a bit of silliness like feeling sorry for herself.

"He is one of my friends, Miss Cameron, and a man with whom you should be appropriately cautious."

Grant came into view, almost as if he were waiting for her in the rose garden. A foolish thought and one she immediately pushed away.

The stranger laughed, sending a smile toward the earl. "It is true, my dear," he said, turning his attention once more to Gillian. "I am not given to English sensibilities. I have too much passion. Count Paterno, at your service," he said, bowing once more.

"Scottish, Lorenzo. If you must insult my nationality, at least get it right."

The other man laughed. "I meant no insult, my dear friend. But I am simply not as rigid as you. Especially when it comes to the women.

"Tell me," he said, turning back to Gillian once more, "are you to be Grant's bride?" He cocked his head, regarded her, and smiled.

When she didn't answer, he laughed again. "Grant, she is a very pretty girl. With some spirit, if I do not mistake that look of ire in her eyes. I am delightfully surprised. Shocked, perhaps, by your wisdom. I approve of your choice, my friend."

"Lorenzo," Grant began.

"I know, my friend, I know. I wander where I do not belong. You'll have to forgive me, my dear, for my frankness. But you see, I think my friend is a fool. He has many responsibilities, and he works very hard. Too hard, perhaps. But he has no fun while doing it. But now, perhaps, he can have some fun, true?"

"Miss Cameron is not my bride, Lorenzo." Grant's tone was sharp. "She is, however, under my protection."

"Not your bride? Is this true?" Lorenzo asked, turning to her.

Gillian nodded.

"What a pity. I hope your bride is as lovely, my friend."

Lorenzo smiled at her. "I notice he is very protective of you, is he not?" he said in a low voice. Grant, however, could still hear him, evidenced by his frown. "I wonder if he's as careful of the maids in his employ?"

Gillian didn't know whether to laugh or to be shocked, so she opted for the most proper course. She left the rose garden.

"What was that demonstration all about?" Grant frowned at his friend. "Are you and Elise no longer together?"

Lorenzo smiled. "We will be together until the day one of us dies, and then, no doubt, the other will cock up his toes as you English—Scottish—say. But I cannot push aside my curiosity, my friend. I have a great deal of curiosity. What is it with you and the little Scottish kitten?"

"There is nothing between me and Gillian," Grant said. "Although I would appreciate it if you would leave her alone. Your devotion to Elise notwithstanding, I don't like that you are flirting with the women in my household, Lorenzo."

"That is another thing, my friend. Why is she among your household? And why is it that I have met her, and not your soon-to-be bride? Where is the woman who has so ably trapped my friend?"

"Miss Fenton did not trap me, Lorenzo. It is a marriage of convenience, nothing more."

"Sometimes those unions turn to love. Although

the tone in which you said your beloved's name was not quite so loverlike."

"And sometimes they don't," Grant said. "Witness my own father's aversion to my mother."

"Which surprises me all the more," Lorenzo said. "You have told me infinite times, my friend, that you are a practical man. I have never believed it as much as I do this moment. Your future is at stake, yet you seem to have no part of it. I do not understand this Scottish compulsion to marry for lands and riches."

Grant smiled.

"Miss Fenton has neither. What she does have is an excess of practicality, a certain way of looking at the world. She has no requirements of me, and I have none of her. It is simply enough that we marry and produce sons. Nothing more. When I say that it is a marriage of convenience, Lorenzo, you must understand that's exactly what I mean. I have no time to seek out a wife, and Miss Fenton has no inclination for a husband. The situation fits us both perfectly."

Lorenzo's shrewd gaze seemed to peer beneath Grant's words, but he forced himself to return the other man's look.

"I am honored to be your friend, Grant," the other man said surprisingly. "Because I do not think you have many."

What the hell did he say to that?

"Would you like to examine me today? Or tomorrow?"

"You wish, do you not, to change the subject? It is painful for you?"

"Have you been able to do any research into poisons?"

Lorenzo smiled. "Very well, my friend. We will talk death and not women."

Grant nodded, feeling a sense of relief out of proportion to the circumstances. His future was not something he wished to discuss, even with a friend. He was well aware of the leanness of it. Either someone was going to succeed in wiping out the last of the Roberson males, or he was going to be tied to Arabella Fenton for the rest of his life.

Neither prospect seemed palatable.

"Gillian!"

She heard Grant's voice behind her and didn't turn. However, she did glance around to see if Dr. Fenton was in earshot.

"Were you ignoring me again?" he asked when he reached her side.

"Yes, Your Lordship, I was. Are you trying to get me dismissed?"

There were times when she didn't mind his aristocratic tone. In fact, it was so much a part of him that she rarely noticed. Today, however, it was grating on her nerves.

"Who would do that?"

"Dr. Fenton."

"He has no power at Rosemoor, and certainly not if I decree it."

She glanced at him out of the corner of her eye. "That would be unwise, Your Lordship." Foolish woman. Foolish man.

"I am your employer, Miss Cameron. I thought we had established that."

Until you know my past. Until you are as shocked

*as the rest of the world, and then you will dismiss me
without a second thought.*

"What has he said to you?"

"He thinks me too familiar."

"Too familiar?" he asked.

"We converse more than you and Arabella do, Your
Lordship. He has, no doubt, seen us talking."

*And if he knew we'd kissed, I would have been dis-
missed for certain.*

"Your Lordship," she said as she kept walking,
"please go away."

"It won't do you any good to barricade yourself in
your room. I have a key to all the chambers at Rosemoor."

Finally she turned back and glanced at him. "Has
no one ever told you that you can be insufferable
sometimes?"

"I believe you have, on more than one occasion. If
you have not exactly said the words, they were certainly there in your expression."

She was silenced by that comment. Unfortunately,
he wasn't. "If you wish to converse further with
Lorenzo, then by all means do so. But he is very happily married, despite his charm."

He turned and began to walk in the direction of his
laboratory.

"Are you daft?" she called out, ignoring the interested gazes of the gardeners.

He glanced over his shoulder at her, stopped, and
turned.

"I have no interest in your friend. I was merely admiring your mother's roses."

He slowly walked back to her.

"Why have you been hiding?"

She ignored that question, asking one of her own. "Who is he?"

"A friend from Florence." He regarded her impassively. "A scientist."

"He doesn't seem like a scientist."

"One would think that he hadn't a brain in his head that didn't somehow involve women, but he's very intelligent. And very much devoted to his wife."

"I haven't a scintilla of interest in your friend or his wife."

He continued looking at her in that way of his, his eyes betraying nothing. What was he thinking? Sometimes she wanted to goad him into speech, simply to learn what he had to say.

"He's a very charming man."

"So are you, Your Lordship. When you wish to be. Did you leave many women pining in Italy? Or were you known for your haughty disposition?"

He didn't smile, the stern expression on his face didn't lighten, but she had the impression, however odd, that her question had pleased him in some manner.

"Would it matter to you if I had?" he asked.

"No. You're to be married soon. Two weeks, is it not?"

He didn't answer her, only asked a question of his own. "Why is Arabella afraid of me? I have not, to the best of my knowledge, attained a reputation for being a brutal man. While it's true that I've been out of Scotland for a number of years, there are people in Italy who can attest to my affable nature."

She glanced over at him.

"Very well, not affable," he corrected, "but not cruel, either."

"Arabella has never liked the touch of others, Your Lordship. It does not matter if you are male or female. Arabella does not like touch in any form. A hug, a kiss, an accidental contact, it's all the same. She stiffens and trembles."

Was there no one in Italy he might have chosen? He was an earl; he might have his choice of hundreds—thousands—of women the length and breadth of Scotland and England. Arabella would make his life miserable.

He took a few steps toward her. "It would not matter if I left a score of women in Italy?"

"Your Lordship," she said, "please go away."

"Not at all?"

Wisely or not, she gave him the truth. "Not one whit. I've found that the past is better left there. It has little bearing on our actions of today."

"I lied," he said. "I would not want you involved with Lorenzo."

"Because you don't want my heart broken."

He kept approaching her, slowly, like a large, predatory animal stalking a much more defenseless one. She was not, however, without resources. If she screamed, anyone might come running. Rosemoor was filled with people.

"Because you care for those in your safekeeping. I am a female in your household, and you're responsible for me."

"To my great shame, I cannot even claim that. While it's true I do care about your happiness, it is not because you are in my employ. Or even a guest at Rosemoor."

He stopped only inches away from her.

"There is a footman at the end of the walk," she cautioned him. "And a maid brushing the urns at the gate."

"What do you think I'm going to do, Gillian?" he asked softly.

She answered in a whisper, "Kiss me."

"As I did before?"

"A very unwise move, as I recall."

"Very unwise. It would be foolish for me to do such a thing again," he said.

"Yes, it would."

"I can't help but think of it, however."

She looked away, down the long path. The rose garden was built upon a slope of land near the house. Beyond was the view of the Pleasure Palace, and even farther, the road to Edinburgh.

"Please."

He stepped back.

"I would not shame you, Gillian. Such is not my intent."

"Then what do you wish of me, Your Lordship? To play some sort of game, again? To pretend we know each other better than we do? That we are of the same rank? You are the Earl of Straithern, and I am your betrothed's companion. What do you want of me?"

He didn't answer her, and she didn't remain behind to hear an explanation for his silence.

Dr. Fenton looked perfectly at home in his father's library, a fact that Grant did not share with the physician. They were not dissimilar in appearance, although his father had chosen to dress befitting his rank and wealth, and Dr. Fenton often looked as if he had for-gotten what clothes he donned in the morning. His appearance was not, evidently, of primary importance to him, but Grant did not hold that against the man.

"Do you have a moment, Doctor?" Grant asked.

"I did not mean to be presumptuous, Your Lord-ship," the older man said, standing, "but the countess said that I might take advantage of the space."

"I use this room only when I must, Doctor," Grant said, closing the door behind him. "If you're able to do so, then I'm glad of it." Grant waved him back into position. "Please sit."

Dr. Fenton did so, folding his hands on the desk in front of him, his bearing erect, shoulders squared, for all the world like he was a student in school, and Grant his headmaster.

Grant took a chair in front of the desk, remem-bering when he'd been summoned to this room as a youth. His father preferred London to Rosemoor. When the 9th Earl of Straithern did come home, it was with an entourage, a dozen or so men who elected to remain in the palace during the month-long visit. Grant was never punished by his father, and the few times he'd been called to his library had been to sim-ply show himself. Once his father was assured that his heir was alive and well, he proceeded to ignore Grant once again.

If there was a disciplinarian in Grant's life, it was the headmaster of the school to which he was sent as a young boy.

"Do you supervise Arabella's treatment?" he asked now, pushing his memories away to address the mat-ter at hand.

Dr. Fenton looked startled by the question, but he answered quickly enough. "I do, when there is a need for it. Are you talking generally, Your Lordship, or is there some particular case that you have in mind?"

"A particular case," Grant said, leaning back in the chair and stretching out his legs. He surveyed his boots, and made a mental note to have his valet send his measurements to Edinburgh. He needed a new pair, and it was easier just to buy a half dozen of the damn things rather than be concerned about something as mundane as shopping. "The gardener's boy. I understood from Arabella that he has a wound on his hand. I've been to see him myself, and I'm not satisfied that he's healing as he should."

"I have not seen the injury," Dr. Fenton said. "There wouldn't be a reason for me to see it, Your Lordship, unless Arabella has questions. I have the greatest faith in my daughter. She knows nearly as much about medicine as I do."

"She didn't seem very positive about the outcome. I would like you to supervise, at least until I am assured of the boy's welfare. I don't want his fingers cut off just because Arabella wants to practice her skills."

Dr. Fenton looked shocked. "I can assure you, Your Lordship, that she would do no such thing. Why, I've often put her in charge of my surgery when I'm forced to stay with a patient overnight."

"All I am saying, Doctor, is that I would like you to see the boy. Assure yourself that everything is being done for him that should be done. That you would do no differently."

"Your Lordship, she is a good girl."

"I'm not questioning her character, Dr. Fenton. I am questioning her ability."

"Very well, Your Lordship, I will see to him."

Grant hesitated. "There is one more item we need to discuss, Dr. Fenton."

The other man looked vaguely uncomfortable, as if he had some inkling of Grant's words. There was nothing to be done but to say it.

"Arabella does not appear to be acquiescent with this arrangement."

"Nonsense," the doctor said. "She is simply shy. She will make you a good wife."

"She doesn't seem all that eager to be a bride."

Dr. Fenton began to speak, but Grant interrupted him. "I don't know your daughter. Part of that is my fault. Part of it is regrettably hers. A month seemed like long enough when I proposed the marriage, but perhaps I was hasty. Do you think another month will give her enough time to become accustomed to the idea of being a wife?"

"Would you be willing to delay, your lordship?"

A delay of a decade did not seem long enough, but Grant nodded.

Dr. Fenton's smile was one Grant could only call relieved. He stood and studied the doctor for a moment. "One more thing, Doctor, if you will."

The other man looked up, the expression on his face one of earnest acceptance.

"Leave Miss Cameron alone. Do not threaten her with dismissal again."

Fenton stood. "Your Lordship, there is much you need to know about Miss Cameron."

"Then I shall allow her to tell me, Doctor."

He left the room before Dr. Fenton could comment further or before Grant could launch into an impassioned defense of Arabella's companion. That wouldn't be prudent, would it? Nor would voicing the thought that an additional month was not likely to change Arabella Fenton into a warm and caring woman.

Chapter 14

Attending dinner that night was mandatory. Not only were Grant, Arabella, Dr. Fenton, and the countess present, but Lorenzo was in attendance as well.

Gillian had tried to claim illness and request a tray in her room, but the countess was having none of it. That august personage actually came to Gillian's chamber to ensure that she would be there.

"I truly do not think that I would be missed, Your Ladyship. I am only the companion."

The countess did not answer, but the look she sent Gillian was sharp, and almost condemnatory.

"You will come to dinner, young woman," the countess said. "I will have no argument about it."

And that, it seemed, was that.

Should she simply be honest with the countess? Her thought lasted the length of time it took for Gillian to close the door behind the older woman. What would the countess say if she told her the complete truth? She'd learned some very difficult lessons in the past two years, but one lesson evidently had not been strong enough.

Her emotions would be the ruin of her.

Perhaps now she would be able to speak to Lorenzo, and to learn something of Grant's life in Italy. That would be infinitely better than trying not to betray her envy of Arabella or her interest in the earl.

She changed into her second-best dress, a gown that had once belonged to Arabella, but that suited Gillian better. Of blue silk, it was etched with ivory lace at the wrist and at the square neck. A maid assigned to her helped with her hair.

"Would you like to entwine some flowers through the curls, miss? Several of the spring roses would look lovely."

"No," Gillian said. In all honestly, she wished she had diamonds or pearls or rubies, something to sparkle and attract the attention. Instead, she should be circumspect, companionlike, the nondescript woman whose sole purpose in life was to accompany Arabella, the future countess.

Why Arabella and not her?

Gillian stared at herself in the mirror, seeing the blankness, the hopelessness of her own expression. Arabella's life was not hers. Nor did Arabella have her experiences. They were two separate people, with two different pasts, and two entirely different futures.

Whenever she was tempted to feel the least bit sorry for herself, she should lecture herself sternly. There was no one to blame but herself for the situation she was in. She had dared convention; she'd been a rebel, she had defied those who loved her and cared for her. She had demanded her own way, and she'd received exactly what she wanted.

She'd gotten Robert only to realize that she really

didn't have him. Did anyone ever possess another human being? Robert had done nothing but take advantage of the situation. She was the one who had given up the whole of her life for love, only to understand that love was not an infinite emotion. Instead it grew or shrunk according to the attention it received. If love was returned, then it flourished and prospered. If it was never reciprocated, it was like a plant left arid or a rose bush that never saw the sun.

Yet she had paid with more than regret, hadn't she?

Whom do you mourn?

"You look lovely, miss," the maid said, interrupting her reverie. "As pretty as any guest to Rosemoor."

"Thank you, Agnes," she said. Perhaps it would have been wiser to wish she were ugly, but she found it very difficult to wish for such thing, especially tonight.

How utterly foolish she was.

A handsome man smiled at her, and her heart beat faster. He whispered into her ear, and her thoughts immediately conjured up passion. He touched her wrist with his fingers, and desire curled up in her stomach, a tiny little flame that seemed annoyingly eternal.

Perhaps she should seek out a nunnery, or devote herself to good works for the rest of her life. If nothing else, she should find a household where there were no men at all. But it wasn't simply any man, was it? No, it was only a rather striking earl with fascinating eyes and a deep voice that gave her shivers to hear it.

"Miss?"

She looked up to find Agnes staring at her in the

mirror, an expression of concern on her face. "I was asking, miss, if you would like a shawl? These spring evenings can be chilly at Rosemoor."

"Yes, please," Gillian said, standing. She didn't give herself a last look. If something was askew or out of place, then good, all the better. Perhaps he would think her slovenly, or uncaring. Perhaps he would remark to himself that she had no sense of decorum, that she had no inclination on how to dress or comport herself in public. Perhaps he wouldn't speak to her at all tonight, and she needn't be bothered having to school her features or arrange her smile so that it was no warmer toward him than to a footman.

Agnes handed her the shawl, and she took it from her with a smile. She left the room, walking down the corridor to the wide marble steps. There was no one in sight except for a footman who stood with his back to the staircase. Beside him, a gas lamp glowed brightly, illuminating the foyer and the bottom of the steps.

Gillian hesitated halfway down the stairs and looked around her. Rosemoor was a home designed for entertaining, for long weekend parties and guests who stayed for months. She could easily hear the voices of people raised in laughter and conversation.

What was she doing here? She didn't belong at Rosemoor any more than Arabella. Arabella had challenged her fate from the beginning; Gillian was only now feeling the cold hand of doom. She couldn't remain here after their wedding. She couldn't see him every day and know that he returned to Arabella's bed at night. She couldn't, God help her, watch as Arabella bore his child.

Although she was normally punctual, she saw no

advantage to being on time for this gathering. She would spend the entire dinner, as she did most nights, wishing that it were over. She wouldn't taste what she was served, and she would be too conscious of the undercurrents at the table. Arabella would be sitting as narrowly as possible, her elbows tucked against her sides in case she accidentally touched someone. She would keep her head bowed, her focus on her food, in case Grant should smile at her. Dr. Fenton would be jocular; the countess would be ever watchful, and Grant . . . Grant would be too intense, too focused. He would seize upon a topic of conversation, and he and the doctor would discuss it for the duration of the dinner. Occasionally the countess would contribute her comments, but Arabella would never speak, and no one would ask Gillian's opinion.

Perhaps Lorenzo would change the tenor of the conversation.

She went into the dining room, and to her surprise, none of them was seated. Instead they milled around the fireplace at the end of the room.

The countess was holding a very small glass of something that looked purplish brown. A type of sherry, no doubt, something to settle her stomach. Gillian didn't doubt that it also aided in settling her nerves, and wished someone would offer her a glass. Unmarried women, however experienced they might be, were not offered sherry.

"We are waiting for Lorenzo," Grant said from behind her. She turned to find him standing there easily commanding the room. He was taller than the others and dressed plainly in a black suit and snowy white shirt. His shoes were brightly polished, and there was a gold chain hanging from his waistcoat pocket. She knew, from seeing him consult it before, that it led to a diamond-encrusted watch.

She turned away from him deliberately, putting a few feet between them. She didn't want him to be charming or personable. It would make this evening even more difficult to endure.

She walked to the window, watching him in the reflection. He was staring after her, and his expression was as carefully neutral as hers. Could emotions travel through the air? Could longing itself be felt without a word being spoken? Would anyone looking at her know what she was thinking?

Grant turned suddenly, greeting Lorenzo. Lorenzo, who was even more resplendently dressed than he'd been this afternoon.

The man wore a dark suit like Grant's, but there the resemblance ended. A bright red sash ran diagonally across his chest, fastened by a scarlet and gold brooch. She'd never seen jewels quite so large or sparkling, and couldn't help but wonder if they were real. But then, her knowledge of rubies was somewhat lacking.

"Ah, the little signorina," he said, coming to her side. He bowed over her hand, making too much fuss over her. "Little one, have you had a good day, a pleasant day here at Rosemoor?" Since she towered over Arabella, it was hardly the proper soubriquet, but she nodded.

"I have, sir."

"Ah, but you must call me Lorenzo."

"Must she?" Grant said easily from beside him. He nodded to Gillian and she nodded back, for all the world as if they were strangers on an Edinburgh street.

They found their seats at the dining table, and exactly as she had hoped, Lorenzo was seated next to her. Instead of being forced to listen to Grant and Dr. Fenton, she was able to ignore everyone but Lorenzo. It was an enchanting experience, being subjected to the Italian's charm. Just as Grant had said, however, it was obvious he was in love with his wife.

"Seven boys?" she asked, after the fish course.

"And another baby to be born soon."

"Why would you think of coming all the way to Scotland at such a time, sir?"

"Grant needed me," he said simply. "He is my friend. I owe him a debt such as I could never repay."

She was hoping her silence would encourage him to speak, but he didn't say anything further.

"So you say you have never been to Italy, Miss Cameron?"

"I have not," she said. "I would like to go to Rome," she said.

"You must see Florence, Miss Cameron. It is the splendor of Italy. And the Palazzo Vecchio is not a sight to miss. The Hall of Lilies, the courtyards, the statues by Michelangelo." He sighed theatrically. "The Uffizi Square, by Vasari, all such treasures to see before you die."

He glanced in Grant's direction. "You should ask Grant to tell you. He has a villa in Florence, and has spent many years there."

"Do you help Grant with his experiments?" she asked.

"I am a scientist as well," he said. "But in a different field." He said nothing further, leading her to wonder if there was a great deal of mystery surrounding Lorenzo, or was it an impression he cultivated on purpose.

He smiled down at her. "My friend does not allow just anyone into his laboratory. He tends to isolate himself there, and is completely happy to do so."

She glanced up to find Grant looking directly at her, and only then did she realize that the conversation at the table had halted. Had everyone been listening to the two of them?

"That was only occasionally, Lorenzo," Grant said. "Otherwise, I consider myself a very civilized sort."

"He lies," Lorenzo said in an aside to Gillian. "His valet had to distract him with scientific questions in order to get him to change his clothes. Anyone who is going to share Grant's life should be versed in science," Lorenzo said, stealing a quick look across the table to Arabella.

At his comment, she looked directly at him. "I am of a scientific mind, sir. Indeed, my father and I both engage in scientific pursuits."

"Then I do not doubt that you and my friend will suit quite admirably, Miss Fenton. Perhaps on your honeymoon, you and Grant can discuss Volta's memoirs. I obtained a set for your wedding present, Grant," he said. "But you must pretend to be surprised, for the sake of my Elise."

Grant only smiled in response.

"And you, Miss Cameron, are you of a scientific mind?"

"I regret to say, sir, that I'm not."

"Gillian does not have an analytical predilection, sir. She prefers novels to texts that would improve her intellect. I have seen her spend hours arranging her hair and staring at herself in the mirror."

"Hardly hours, Arabella," Gillian said, embarrassed. Surely this was not the topic of conversation that should be allowed at the table? But neither the earl nor the countess seemed interested in stopping Arabella, and Dr. Fenton thought anything his daughter said was worth hearing.

"I confess to my share of vanity, Arabella, but I doubt if even I would be interested in spending hours in front of the mirror."

Lorenzo smiled. "A woman is not to be criticized because she pays attention to her appearance," he said, a gentle rebuke toward Arabella.

"Neither is a woman to be criticized because she wishes to learn," Grant said.

His comment stung, but Gillian did not indicate her feelings either by her expression or by commenting.

Lorenzo, however, had no such reticence. "Are you not being too harsh toward Miss Cameron? Simply because she doesn't wish to study medicine doesn't mean she lacks a curious mind."

"I was not singling out Miss Cameron. On the contrary. She has proven to be quite an able assistant."

"You allowed her to work on your electrics?"

"I have. And I hope to convince her to assist me in the future."

"You are to be commended, Miss Cameron," Lorenzo said, turning to her. "Grant does not issue such an invitation lightly."

"Nor has he issued one to me," Arabella said quietly.

"Then you should both come," Grant said.

"To the laboratory?"

"To the marsh," he said.

"The marsh?" Gillian glanced at him.

"I visit the marsh periodically. I need to go tomorrow morning."

"There is no necessity for Gillian to accompany you, Your Lordship," Dr. Fenton said.

"Indeed not, Grant." Arabella smiled. "I would be more than happy to do so."

Dr. Fenton looked pleased at Arabella's comment. Grant and Lorenzo looked rather noncommittal. The countess, however, surprised Gillian by just staring at Arabella, her expression that of someone who'd just received unpleasant news.

"I'm afraid you will not have any time to spare, my dear girl," she said, her voice more tremulous than Gillian had ever heard it. Grant glanced at his mother, and she wondered if he, too, remarked on the oddity of the older woman's sudden paleness. But the countess ignored both of them, her attention focused on Arabella. "You must be trained in the running of Rosemoor. There are duties you must assume upon your marriage to Grant that are more important than even your medicine."

Arabella looked as if she would like to say something in response, but after a quick glance toward her father, she stifled her comment. She only nodded, and concentrated once again on the food on her plate.

"I would be more than happy to be of assistance, Your Lordship," Gillian said. There, a very pleasant, if innocuous comment, betraying nothing of what she truly felt.

Dr. Fenton glanced at Gillian, his expression one of

disapproval. A lecture was coming, she was certain. A diatribe as to her past, and her future, and no doubt a section on her manners as well. Fallen woman. She'd heard that before. Foolish woman. She'd called herself that often enough after arriving at Rosemoor.

She should speak up right this moment and decline any invitation issued by the Earl of Straithern. But she was silent, a fact that evidently continued to irritate Dr. Fenton, if the looks he gave her were any indication.

Dinner was a blur after that, the conversation shifting between the weather, Italy, Lorenzo's children, and a dozen other topics, each one of which was more interesting than the personal dissection of her intelligence.

The gentlemen did not stay behind, but joined them in the parlor immediately following dinner. Occasionally the countess graced them with a performance on a pianoforte. Tonight, however, she waved away the request framed by Dr. Fenton and sat, instead, in one of the wing chairs by the fireplace. Uncharacteristically, she summoned the footman to her side, and gave him instructions to light the fire.

"Are you ill, Your Ladyship?" Gillian asked, coming to her side. She had felt kindly disposed toward the countess ever since the night they'd shared hot chocolate, but had never presumed upon the acquaintance until now.

For a moment, she thought that the countess would dismiss her, and harshly, but then Gillian realized the woman was still in the grips of some discomfort.

"Is there anything I could bring you?" She moved a footstool a little closer so that the countess could use it.

"Mother," Grant said beside her, "if you are feeling ill, we shall make your excuses." He bent toward her solicitously.

"I am not feeling ill, Grant," she said, her voice still weak. "Let us just say that the past has visited me without warning."

He looked as if he would like to say more, but a quick glance toward Gillian warned her that he would not do as long as she was standing close. She moved away, a gesture that summoned a frown from him. Could she not please him at all?

She moved to the other side of the room, taking a chair along the wall. A clear notice to any who would engage her in conversation that she wasn't disposed to be pleasant. What she really and truly wished to do was retire to her room, but as the paid companion to Arabella Fenton, she couldn't very well leave before Arabella did.

Grant was coming toward her.

Gillian looked out the window, wishing he would stay away. She glanced back to find that he'd stopped to say something to Dr. Fenton, and then to Lorenzo. But the next moment, he was still coming closer.

She pasted a smile on her face with some difficulty, and held it there with great deliberation.

"Forgive me," he said, stopping in front of her. "I did not mean to be boorish."

"At dinner? Or just a few moments ago at your mother's chair?"

"Both, perhaps."

"Do you think to disarm me by using the truth, Your Lordship?"

"Is that what I was doing?"

She didn't bother to respond.

"You will have to forgive me; I was annoyed at Lorenzo, and I took it out on you."

She continued to look out the window, a difficult feat since it acted more like a night-darkened mirror.

But he had incited her curiosity, which annoyed her further. She wanted to ask why he was so annoyed at his friend, but she remained silent.

"He was flirting with you, and I disliked it."

She stopped studying the window, and glanced at him. "He wasn't, and you know it."

"I told myself that he wasn't, but it didn't seem to make a difference to my irritation. It kept growing the longer he kept smiling."

Something in her chest opened, like a giant cave that had never been seen in the light of day. And the warmth of her heart, perhaps, was the sun. Or maybe it was simply his words. Or even worse—or better— the look in his eyes.

Arabella was barely a dozen feet away.

"You are the one who is flirting, Your Lordship. And I don't think it's well done of you. You should not have invited me to be your assistant. Nor should you be talking to me now."

"I am the Earl of Straithern, Miss Cameron, and this is Rosemoor. I can damn well do anything I like."

He looked angry, and very intimidating. An earl, with all his power, wealth, and might.

She was a foot shorter than he was, poor, and certainly not his equal in experience. But she had courage, and at this moment, anger. "I am not to be cowed, Your Lordship. You cannot treat me as you would a maid or a footman."

"I never intended to, Gillian. But I dislike being told what I can and cannot do."

"Then we are the match in that," she said. "Do not presume to dictate to me what I will or will not do, Your Lordship. I may be, as you say, under your employ, but I will not be treated with disdain."

"So we are a match in arrogance. I can't help but wonder how else we are well matched."

"You should be saying that to Arabella, Your Lordship, not me."

"Will you join me in the marsh?"

The change of subject made her blink at him. How could he go from being so annoyed to suddenly so affable? He was smiling at her now, as if he approved of her show of temper.

The man was insufferable, irritating, and too fascinating for her peace of mind.

"The marsh?"

"I haven't been there for months."

No. That's what she should say. A simple no, an uncomplicated no. A polite no, a respectful decline. *I have letters to write*, she would say, although there was no one to whom she could address her correspondence. Her parents would not read her letters, nor would the cousin with whom she'd stayed for a few weeks. Robert, of course, was married by this time, and her friends would be scandalized if she dared to address any of them. Better she should claim some mending. Would he respond with the comment that there were dozens of servants at Rosemoor who could perform exactly the same chore? *I have personal things to attend to*, she might respond, and he could not hope to counter with any comment. He would be forced to silence, and she would return to her room feeling virtuous and proper.

"I warn you, however, that it's messy work. In the spirit of being completely honest."

"Your Lordship, there is something to be said for a little restraint. In this case, of honesty. Perhaps it is not wise to tell someone everything."

"I must beg to differ, Miss Cameron," he said reverting back to propriety in addressing her. "I think it's the best policy to always speak with as much honesty as possible. Otherwise, there is some doubt about motive, or intent."

If she were totally candid with him, it would no doubt make both of them very uncomfortable. She would tell him that he should not look at her in such a fashion, and counsel him that he should remember, more often, that he was to be wed to Arabella. But of course, one did not lecture an earl, especially an earl who took such umbrage at being corrected. Yet he balanced that arrogance with a disarming charm, which made him even more devastating to be around.

"Tomorrow," he said, turning to leave her. He glanced over his shoulder at her. "Before dawn."

"Your Lordship," she began, but was interrupted by his smile.

He stopped and turned. "We will have two footmen with us, Miss Cameron. And bring your maid, if you wish further protection."

"Shall I bring Arabella?"

"Shall I be completely honest, Miss Cameron? Or shall I exercise a little restraint?"

"I think perhaps restraint would be better, Your Lordship," she said.

"Then by all means," he said, "bring Arabella." He smiled and left her.

The Countess of Straithern dismissed her maid with a wave of her hand. She was attired for night, although not necessarily sleep. Her wrapper was fulsomely edged in lace, imported, she'd been told, from a convent in the South of France.

Nothing was good enough for the Countess of Straithern. Wasn't that what her husband had always said? He'd repeated it so often that she could almost hear his voice even after all these years. She had thought, with the naïveté of the very young and very innocent, that such a sentiment meant that Ranald loved her, and wanted only the best for her. Regrettably, such was not the case, but she didn't understand that until a decade after their wedding.

She knew now, with a hard-won wisdom, that Ranald had simply been accustomed to the best clothing, the finest furniture, and the most desired wife.

When he proposed, she'd deluded herself into believing that he'd fallen in love with her after her first season. And she, naturally, had been infatuated with him. Who would not have been? Ranald Roberson, the 9th Earl of Straithern, was an exceptionally fine specimen of man. He was blessed with gray eyes that seemed to search a woman's soul, and black hair, both attributes he'd passed on to Grant. Grant did not have his easy manner, however, or his ready smile. Or the laugh that still seemed to echo through the halls of Rosemoor. But Grant had something his father had not, a quality that had taken her years to discover lacking in her husband. Grant had decency, and a well-developed sense of morality, honed, no doubt, by his father's horrible deeds.

As she did every night, she moved to her secretary, and began to write in her journal. The small desk was a repository for her paperwork of a personal nature, those letters that she did not want anyone else to see. She'd often turned down Grant's offer to employ someone to assist her with her correspondence. She didn't like the idea of relying on a stranger to transpose her words to paper. Her old friends would simply have to endure her increasingly shaky writing.

She opened her journal and began to write. As usual, her diary entries were of a prosaic nature. The plant she was cultivating in her garden, including details on the fertilizer used, and pruning methods employed. She wrote of the menu Cook had devised for the week, and either her approval or disapproval. She wrote of Miss Fenton and Miss Cameron and her disappointments about both women. Nowhere, however, did she divulge any hint of her inner torment. What she felt was not for posterity to read, and she was of an age where Death was looming around the corner, peering at her from time to time to see if she was ready. She was not, and would not be, she had already decided, for many long years. But her decision did not stop Death from intrusively peeping at her.

Her journal entry done, she snuffed out the candle and moved to the prie-dieu in the corner of the room. Here was her sanctuary, so much more intimate than the lofty family chapel Ranald had built. She knew, now, why he met with the architect for months and spent a fortune on the construction of such a lavish edifice in the Scottish Highlands. She knelt, folding her hands and bowing her head.

She did not seek forgiveness for herself. She prayed for her children, the infants she'd borne in pain and optimism and joy. The two young men who had been such a source of happiness in her life, and yet they were no more. She prayed that God would not seek vengeance on them but would forgive them their parentage.

James and Andrew. In her mind's eye they were boys still, their smiles bright and their laughs infectious. Beneath her closed lids she saw them as she did every night when she allowed herself to remember. Only in this short hour, when darkness fell over Rosemoor, and the house quieted around her, did she allow herself to fully grieve.

Were her sons angels now, waiting for her arrival in heaven? They might have to wait for eternity. God would have His say about where her soul was transported, and she doubted, very much, that it would be to heaven.

She ignored the pain in her knees, sacrificing comfort for this hour. Perhaps the pain was a type of atonement. God would forgive her or not for the sin of being too foolish to see what was happening under her very nose. Or for seeking out her husband's bed—surely that was a sin for which she should be punished. If God ever did forgive her, it would be with the understanding that she had truly been a fool.

Wisdom must come to everyone, and hers had come in searing pain and shock. Gradually, the disbelief had worn off, but the agony and shame still lingered, so deeply that she felt its echoes even now.

Night surrounded her, but it was never truly quiet at Rosemoor. She'd learned to accept the noises as part of the ritual preceding sleep, just as she knew that she wouldn't rest for the full night. After a few hours, she'd awaken, either crying or suffering from the effects of a particularly troubling dream. Then, just when she thought she'd fall asleep again, the voices and tears of children would come to her.

God forgive her, she knew why.

Chapter 15

Gillian was awakened two hours before dawn by a sleepy Agnes. "Miss," she said, shaking Gillian's shoulder gently. "The earl is waiting for you. Outside."

The earl?

For a moment, nothing made sense, until she surfaced from her dream. A dream, strangely enough, that had featured the earl.

"He's waiting for me?" she asked, before remembering the conversation of the night before. Of course, he'd asked her to accompany him to the marsh.

Agnes placed the small lamp she was holding on the bureau.

"Does the earl have a great many servants with him?"

"He has Michael, miss, and one other footman."

So she would be chaperoned well enough. "If you will fetch my gray dress for me, please," Gillian said, swinging her legs over the side of the bed. "It is the oldest thing I own, and the most threadbare, and I have the distinct impression that my appearance is not going to matter."

"What are you about, miss? And why did the earl send Michael to my room to wake you?"

"I'm about to go on an adventure, Agnes," Gillian said, wondering at the sense of excitement she felt.

It seemed foolish to fuss with her hair, so she braided it and wrapped the braids in a coronet at the top of her head before pinning it into place. Agnes had laced her into her dress and helped her with her shoes, all the while looking worried at Gillian's choice of adventure. Gillian wanted to reassure the young woman that she wasn't doing anything untoward, but she wasn't absolutely certain that was true.

At the door she turned. "Would you like to accompany me, Agnes?"

Agnes shook her head. "If it's all the same, miss, I'd like to go back to bed."

Gillian smiled and left her, walking quickly through the corridors and nearly racing down the steps.

Excitement flowed through her as she nodded to one of the footmen. Regardless of the time of day, there was always a staff of servants waiting to assist at Rosemoor, and at this moment she was grateful for it. The tall oak doors were almost unmanageable by herself. She slipped out before the door was fully opened and stood at the top of the steps to find Grant looking up at her.

"Is Arabella going to join us?" he asked.

She hadn't given a single, fleeting thought to Arabella.

She shook her head, but he didn't comment on her absence. Instead he asked, "Are you ready for the marsh, Miss Cameron?"

"With a few reservations," she said. She took the

granite steps with more decorum than she'd used descending the interior staircase.

"How many petticoats are you wearing, Miss Cameron?"

The question so took her aback that she could only stare at him in the light of the lanterns. When he repeated it, she shook her head. "I have no intention of telling you, Your Lordship."

"I merely thought that you might dispense with one or two. They will only drag you down."

"Am I going wading?"

"Not unless you're clumsy," he said, his smile mischievous in the lantern light. "But there is a distinct possibility that you will get wet, yes."

"I have a manageable number of petticoats, Your Lordship, and I promise not to be clumsy."

He turned and began to walk away, leaving her no choice but to follow him.

"Why are we going to the marsh? And why in the middle of the night?"

"It's not exactly in the middle of the night," he corrected. "Merely an hour or two before dawn. I've found it's the best time to capture the marsh gases."

She remained silent, hoping that he wanted to explain that comment. But he didn't, merely turned and nodded to Michael. He led the way down the path almost to the palace, but before they could reach the lake, he turned left, following Michael's bobbing lantern. Behind them came the second footman, a long pole resting on his shoulders, his wrists dangling over the ends. Hanging from the pole by a thick rope were six bell-shaped glass jars, cushioned from clanking against one another by thick cotton wadding.

What a very strange procession they made: two servants, an earl, and a companion.

Finally, unable to bear the curiosity any longer, she turned to Grant. "What are marsh gases and why do you want to capture them?"

He glanced at her.

"All living things give off a gas when they die. From animals to birds to plants. It's possible, in the marsh, to actually trap these gases because they hover near the water. They are heavier than air but lighter than the surface of the water, so they can be contained in a glass vessel."

"But why would you?"

"It was one of Volta's experiments that I occasionally repeat, simply to see if I can do it better. I run an electrical charge through the gas and cause it to explode."

"Isn't that dangerous?"

"Of course it is," he said with a smile.

"You say that as if it doesn't concern you at all."

"Miss Cameron, it is my belief that someone is trying to kill me. Why should I worry about a little explosion?"

She stopped in the middle of the path and stared at him. She stood there for so long that the footman behind her was forced to stop as well. Ahead of them, Michael was blithely unaware that he was going on alone.

"I beg your pardon? Someone is attempting to kill you?"

He folded his arms and regarded her, and for several moments they simply looked at each other. She was as stubborn as he, and perhaps he became aware of that fact the longer they stood there in silence. She wasn't going to back down, and he didn't seem to be forthcoming in his explanation. But finally he smiled, his expression visible by the faint light from the footman's lantern.

"I believe my brothers were murdered, Miss Cameron. I believe that someone wished them dead. And it follows that if someone killed them, then I should be next."

"They died of a blood disease." She had heard Dr. Fenton explain it to Arabella in somewhat nauseating detail.

"That's Dr. Fenton's explanation. It is not mine."

"Do you think them truly murdered? And not simply ill?"

"I think them truly murdered. Despite the fact that Dr. Fenton believes that I may have the same malady, and that each of my days is numbered."

She could barely breathe, and her heart was beating much too quickly. "You cannot die," she said, unable to hold back her thoughts any longer. "You are in the prime of life, Your Lordship. You are handsome and strong, and anyone who looks as vigorous as you cannot die. You are the most vibrant man I've ever seen. You cannot simply die."

His smile had disappeared, and in its place was an oddly somber expression. He reached out and touched her face, his fingers trailing along the curve of her cheek. He cupped his hand beneath her chin and smiled into her eyes.

All forbidden gestures, and all thoroughly shocking.

"I had no idea, Miss Cameron, that you'd been watching me with such assiduousness."

"Forgive me," she said breathlessly.

Abruptly, he dropped his hand, and turned.

Michael waited for them at the slope of the next hill holding the lantern aloft. Without speaking further, the earl headed toward him.

"Come, we are almost there."

She'd not been paying much attention to the scenery, but she looked around her now, realizing that this part of Rosemoor was strange to her. The woods began to her right, with the land sloping downward on all four sides like an inverted bowl. At the deepest part was the marsh. Tall grasses rimmed the perimeter, and moss and bits of algae floated on top of the water, creating the illusion that the area was nothing more than a bit of soggy ground.

Matthew belied that impression by holding the lantern aloft and wading knee-deep into the middle of the marsh.

While the second footman carefully lowered the jars to the ground, the earl was evidently preparing to follow Michael, looking as enthused as a boy about a new adventure.

His decision to marry Arabella was suddenly more understandable.

"Wouldn't it be better to pair yourself with someone you love?" she abruptly asked. "Especially if you believe you're about to die. Wouldn't passion in your last days be infinitely preferable to aversion?"

"Are you speaking of Arabella, Miss Cameron?" He turned to face her, his smile no longer in view.

They were delving into dangerous territory. Every time they exchanged words they seemed to do so. She concentrated, instead, on the sodden ground beneath her feet.

"Have you a candidate, Miss Cameron? Someone with whom I could share passion?"

There they were again, entwined in a net of words.

Did he actually think she was about to answer him? She was not that foolish. What would he say if she abandoned all decorum, faced him boldly, and answered, *Me.*

"What do we do now?" she asked, changing the subject.

"We perform a small experiment," he said, "to ensure there is gas is present. You might want to step back, Gillian, and hold up your skirts just a little, in case you need to run."

What on earth that she gotten herself into? She took a precautionary step back and grabbed her skirts with both hands, picking them up until they almost exposed her ankles.

He retrieved the lantern from Michael, along with a paper cone he then lit. Bending down near a tall clump of grass, he touched the lit end to an area above the water. A burst of orange light flared for a second before being extinguished. So quickly did it appear and then disappear that Gillian thought she must have imagined it. But he bent again, and another plume of orange flame appeared against the dawn sky.

"You have to come to the marsh at night," she said, suddenly understanding. "Otherwise, you would never see the flame."

"Absolutely correct. If you were my student, I would reward you for your observational abilities."

"But how will you get the gas into the jar?"

"In a very convoluted siphon," he said. Over the next hour, she realized exactly how complicated it was, and how potentially dangerous. More than once, she wanted to shout out cautions to both Grant and the footman, knowing how flammable the gas was. And more than once, she restrained herself, realizing that the Earl of Straithern was going to do exactly what he wanted to do in the way he wanted to do it.

As the morning lengthened and dawn made its appearance, Gillian began to realize that what she'd thought was the Earl of Straithern's autocracy or arrogance was simply a certainty of self. He knew exactly what interested him, what challenged him, and what he wanted to accomplish in his lifetime. Ignorance was an anathema to him, and in that regard, he and Arabella had a great deal in common. If Arabella had stood here, she wouldn't have been concerned as to his safety, as much as encouraging him to learn more, do more, solve more riddles.

It was quite possible that Arabella would be a perfect match for him.

"You look excessively thoughtful, Miss Cameron. What intrigues you so on such a beautiful morning?'

She glanced over to see him standing on solid ground, the dawn sky behind him. For a moment, she was taken by the sight of him, mussed and disheveled, and yet so perfectly handsome that he took her breath away. He would have been as handsome as the head of a mercantile company, a ship's captain, or a soldier.

"Do I?" she asked. "I must confess that I cannot even remember what I was thinking."

"I'm sure it was a weighty matter," he said, smiling.

"I'm not so sure," she said, answering his smile with one of her own. "I am given to flighty thoughts just like any person. Surely, Your Lordship, you cannot say that every thought that comes through your mind is worth sharing with someone else."

He seemed to be considering the question for a moment. "I honestly do not know how to answer that," he said. "If I confess to silly thoughts, then that makes me seem like a dilettante. But if I confess that I never have less than vast, important thoughts on my mind, that makes me sound stodgy, doesn't it? Excessively tiresome, if not boring."

"Then I shall have to simply retract my question. I confess that I was thinking of the stars and the moon, and wondering if Galileo was correct."

He laughed, and she liked the sound of it, feeling absurdly pleased, as if she'd accomplished something grand by amusing him.

"You truly did read your father's library, didn't you?"

"I'm curious and dislike the fact that other people know something I do not," she confessed.

"Then I'm surprised you haven't taken up the study of medicine like Arabella."

"You are determined to learn all of my secrets, aren't you?" She smiled. "I have the oddest trait. I cry when others do. I cannot seem to help it. What kind of physician would I be if I dissolved into tears all the time?"

"Some would say you have an excess of empathy."

"Can empathy ever be excessive?" she asked.

"Oddly enough, Miss Cameron, I have the greatest curiosity as to your thoughts, even if you deem them flighty."

She turned away from him then, unable to bear his smile or the warmth in his gray eyes.

"Forgive me," she said, focusing on the sopping hem of her skirt. "I should not have said what I did about Arabella either today or yesterday. I ask your forgiveness. And hers, in absentia."

"It's entirely possible that Arabella would have thanked you for your efforts on her behalf," he said, surprisingly. "It's no surprise to me that Arabella is not overjoyed by this marriage."

Overjoyed was not a word she would have used in conjunction with Arabella in any situation, but she didn't say so. Arabella was rarely moved to happiness or even sadness, for that matter. Arabella's aspect was forever constant and unchanging. If she felt deeply about anything, it was medicine. Beyond that, she didn't reveal much of herself to anyone.

It was light enough to see him quite well by now, and once again she was struck by how handsome he was. Even rumpled, with bits of grass clinging to him here and there. She reached out and pulled a long strand of grass from his sleeve, and then brushed the fabric with her fingertips.

He looked bemused by her actions, and she realized just how intimate a gesture she'd just performed. A wife would do such a thing for a husband. She had often treated Robert in the same way, tending to him, caring for him, being concerned.

She deliberately took a step backward, away, so she could not touch him.

* * *

He was not given to self-flagellation. He didn't believe in punishing himself for his actions, even if they were ill-formed and wrong. Grant always made a point of learning from each misadventure. If his errors in judgment affected other people, he made amends where he could, and vowed not to duplicate his mistakes. He found that such techniques assisted him in his work and his personal life.

So what the hell was he doing now?

Someone should give her a good talking to. Someone should tell her that she really should not smile at a man with such warmth. And whatever she used to rinse her hair should certainly be forbidden, at least until she was married. Let her captivate her husband. Certainly she would marry one day, just as his nuptials were already planned. Why should he get such a sour feeling at the thought?

She should have worn a shawl over that dress. The bodice was entirely too snug. He could see the outline of her nipples. At least he thought he could, and God knew he'd looked often enough in the last few minutes.

He was like a boy who had never seen the female form before, and ached to stroke her with eager palms. He wanted to know if all the softest spots were really soft. Were her curves as enticing as he thought, and those long legs of hers, were they as shapely as he guessed?

Good God, he was over thirty. Surely enough time had passed since he was an adolescent? God knew he'd bedded his share of women. Why couldn't he remember one at the moment?

He shouldn't be alone with Gillian, and he shouldn't be talking to her: plumbing her mind in lieu of her body.

He should be concerned about his own health instead of traipsing through the marsh. Yet he'd never felt better, more energetic. Nor had he ever been as reluctant to face his future.

An earl did not renege on an arrangement. The 10th Earl of Straithern especially did not dishonor his bargain. His father had already blighted the family name; Grant had spent his lifetime attempting to not add to the shame.

He would marry Arabella Fenton and find something to champion about the union. But he would forever wonder about Gillian Cameron.

He gave the order for the men to convey the glass vials, now cloudy with gas, back to his laboratory. Only then did he turn to Gillian.

"Whom do you mourn?" he asked. A question she'd never answered and one that had niggled at him for days.

She looked startled. He waited until the footmen were sufficiently far away to ask the question again.

"Why do you wish to know?" she asked.

"I find I'm excessively curious about you, Miss Cameron. Perhaps I should not be, but there it is."

She hesitated for a moment, before turning and preceding him up the path.

There was something about Miss Gillian Cameron that led him to believe that his being an earl held absolutely no allure for her. She was extraordinarily self-possessed, given to seeking her own counsel rather than the company of others. He not only admired that trait, since he was also possessed of it, but he wanted to understand how a woman like Gillian could have acquired such aplomb. There were flashes of animation in her gaze sometime, expressed as humor or irritation. What incited his curiosity the most, however, was the sadness she occasionally evinced with a glance or a faraway stare.

She was an enigma, and he was fascinated with puzzles.

He was not averse to silence, and he would wait as long as it took. Several minutes later she halted, turning in his direction.

"My life," she said softly. "I mourn my existence, Your Lordship. The life I knew in Edinburgh. I mourn my innocence and my youth."

He stood in front of her, silent and waiting.

"We all do that, Miss Cameron, in various degrees."

She nodded. "I fell in love with a man who did not love me in return. Or not enough."

"A regrettable tale," he said, finding himself oddly irritated by her confession. "Do you love him still?"

She shook her head.

Just when he thought she would say nothing further, she took a deep breath and quite obviously forced herself to face him. Her gaze was intent, her face white.

"Did I not warn you, Gillian?"

She turned to find Dr. Fenton standing on the path facing her, his expression leaving no doubt as to his displeasure.

"I suggest you return to Rosemoor, Gillian," he continued, "and see if there is some task that you can perform for Arabella, something that does not involve cavorting through the meadows with your skirts above your ankles."

"Why do you presume to speak to Miss Cameron in such a fashion, Fenton?" Grant asked. He slowly stepped between them, standing in front of Gillian as if to protect her from a volley of arrows. Didn't he realize that words could hurt as much as any spear?

"Your demeanor should be such that you do not shame me, or by reflection, Arabella," Dr. Fenton said. He turned to Grant. "I apologize for her, Your Lordship," he said, his tone modulated somewhat in speaking to the earl. "She is a forward girl."

"It is not her demeanor that surprises me, Fenton, but yours. I have not judged Miss Cameron to be forward. If anything, I find her too retiring."

"And well she should be, Your Lordship. But the very fact she is here with you this morning is evidence of a rebellious nature. Arabella should be with you, not her companion. She does not warrant your defense, Your Lordship. I have tried to be a compassionate man, but her actions of late have proven that I was wrong to be swayed by pity."

Grant turned to look at her. "She does not seem to be such a base sort, Fenton. Has she stolen from you? Or perhaps imbibed some of your rum?" He smiled at Gillian, and any other time she might have returned the expression, but not now. "Have you drowned a sack of kittens, Gillian? What heinous deed have you performed that has Fenton in such a lather?"

The mottled color of Dr. Fenton's face revealed his temper.

"She has not told you of her past, has she, Your

Lordship? She has not divulged the totality of her wickedness?"

Gillian had never before been given the ability to read the future, but she knew what the next few moments would bring as if she'd written the scene herself. She took a deep breath and clasped her hands together.

"You are a doctor, Fenton, not a clergyman. Why should you be so concerned about divulging Miss Cameron's past? Or her wickedness, as you say?"

"Because I do not wish you to judge Arabella by Gillian's actions, Your Lordship. My daughter is a good girl, who would not indulge in wantonness with you like Gillian." Dr. Fenton frowned at her.

"Should I not be the judge of whether or not Miss Cameron has indulged in wantonness? And it seems that if you tar her with that brush, you cannot help but paint me as well. Are you accusing us both, Fenton?" Grant folded his arms and stared at the doctor impassively.

"I am not accusing you, sir," Dr. Fenton said. "Gillian was a woman of the street. A female of low inclination. She turned away from her family and her friends and all the tenets of her upbringing to pursue earthly pleasures, and it is my belief that she intends to the same again with you. When I found her, she was living in Edinburgh, willing to sell her body for a coin."

What a pity that she couldn't close her eyes and simply wish herself away from this particular place. But she still felt the soft morning breeze on her cheeks, and the smell of the marsh grasses clinging to the hem of her skirt. The air was laced with the acrid scent of sulfur.

She opened her eyes to find herself the object of intense scrutiny from both men.

Grant didn't speak, and those eyes, those remarkable, wonderful gray eyes of his, held no expression at all and were suddenly as hard and cold as pewter.

"Enough," Grant said suddenly, turning back to the doctor. "Enough, man, your tale is told. You should be satisfied with the result of your morning's effort."

"I shall not be satisfied, Your Lordship, until Gillian knows her place. You should be sharing your hours with Arabella, and not this creature. I rue the day I allowed charity and pity to bring her into my home if she draws your attention and affection away from my daughter."

"Since you are so adept at honesty, shall we have a bit more between us, Doctor? There is no affection between your daughter and me. Nor do I ever expect there to be any. Arabella does not seem to be of a nature to share affection."

When Dr. Fenton would have spoken, no doubt in protection of his only child, Grant held up his hand as if to forestall him. "I have no intention of discussing the matter further, sir. Instead, I shall escort Miss Cameron back to Rosemoor."

Dr. Fenton hesitated.

"We require neither your permission nor your presence, Fenton," Grant said.

With obvious reluctance, Dr. Fenton left them.

Gillian turned away, facing down the path toward the marsh. When she spoke, it was calmly and without emotion, as if the words were read from a well-known book in her mind.

"I was not quite a woman of the streets," she said. "Although I was certainly a figure of scandal. An example of impropriety." She bowed her head and clasped her hands together.

He still did not speak. In actuality, he was uncertain what he should say.

She nodded. "I wouldn't be at all surprised if mothers warned their daughters not to become like me."

"Why did you become like you?"

"I fell in love," she said. She looked away again, and he was tempted to reach out and grip her chin, turn her face in his direction, and look into her eyes. What would he see there? A glimpse of remorse, perhaps longing? He realized he didn't want to know.

"You needn't tell me, Gillian," he said.

She nodded. "I know. It doesn't matter. I fell in love," she repeated. "But I think that I loved Robert because he loved me." She raised her head and looked at him, and he wasn't surprised by the sadness in her eyes.

"I don't require any admissions from you," he said.

She nodded once again, and once again continued speaking. "It had been a very long time since I'd felt loved. Perhaps all the scandal I brought about was based on nothing more than gratitude."

Life was imperfect, imprecise, too fleeting, and by the time an individual got it correct, fate or mischance had stripped life away. His was a life made special by circumstance, and he was continually aware of that fact. From the moment he opened his eyes in the morning, until he slept at night, he was the Earl of Straithern. He was as conscious of his heritage as he was of his responsibilities. But along with the monumental burdens placed on him were also the great advantages. He never failed to remember those, either.

One of the greatest assets of being the Earl of Straithern was the power of his inclination. Whatever he wanted, he received. A word, a softly voiced request, an imperiously crooked finger, that's all it took for his wishes to be conveyed and fulfilled.

Now he wanted the power to banish the grief in her eyes, bid her smile to return, but he could do nothing but reach out and touch her arm in gentle, and proper, support.

"Was it enough of an adventure?" he asked.

She blinked at him.

"Today," he said. "The marsh. Was it adventurous enough for you?"

Silence stretched between them.

Finally, she spoke again. "You have it in your power, Your Lordship, to send me away from Rosemoor."

"Yes, I do," he said, nodding.

"On the basis that I am unfit company for Arabella. That I might corrupt your children."

"Which is a consideration, perhaps," he said amiably. "Are you quite finished with your confession?"

She nodded.

"Stop looking so stricken, Miss Cameron. I have no intention of banishing you from Rosemoor. I've never heard such drivel in my life."

She looked bemused.

"Did you learn anything today?"

"I learned a great deal today," she said slowly.

"Then the adventure was a success," he said. "Every day you should endeavor to learn something."

She frowned at him.

"Would you like to know what I learned?" he asked.

She nodded cautiously.

"I learned that Dr. Fenton is a despot, and that you are living too much in the past."

She didn't respond. He might have told her more, had he been more honest or had the moment been suitable for it. He might have told her that he thought her lovely at that moment, with the morning sun filtering through the trees and falling on her hair. It wasn't plain brown at all, but a curious shading of gold and red and brown, like the colors of a leaf. Or he might have told her that the sorrow in her eyes reminded him of his own. Even in the midst of life, he would remember his brothers, but perhaps the memories would become easier to bear with time. Or perhaps he'd even welcome them, knowing that as long as they lived in his mind and his heart, they would never truly die.

But because she was viewing him with caution, he only smiled and held out his arm.

"Would you like to view the second part of the experiment?"

"Where you create explosions?" she asked.

"I confess to liking explosions. But," he hastened to say, "there will be no danger. I promise."

That statement evidently decided her. She stretched out her hand and placed it on his arm, and he led her down the path as if they were very proper companions and not two people with secrets.

For long moments they didn't talk. He didn't think he'd ever shared silence so companionably with anyone.

They topped the rise, and the palace was finally in view.

"Will you kiss me?" she finally said, studying the statues mounted near the roof.

"Not unless you wish it," he said.

"Promise me that you'll not."

"Even if you wish it?" he asked, smiling.

"Even so."

"Then I promise. Not even if you beg me."

"I'm not a fallen woman," she said a moment later.

"Did you think I would test your morals? I have my own sins, it's true, but I have never taken advantage of the weak or the defenseless."

"I am not weak. Nor defenseless."

He only smiled, unwilling to enter into a debate with her.

"Then I'll come," she said resolutely.

"And no more nonsense about my banishing you from Rosemoor."

"You're a very strange man, Your Lordship."

"Am I?"

She nodded. "Just when I think I understand you, you do something to confound me utterly."

"I enjoy having that effect on people," he said. "But you are the same, you know."

"I am?"

He nodded, pleased when he saw a wisp of a smile on her face.

"In the interest of honesty, Miss Cameron, there's something I must tell you."

She glanced at him.

"There is nothing to prevent *you* from kissing me," he said, and smiled.

Chapter 16

Of course she was foolish to accompany him. Yet her feet seemed to fly over the path, and her hand never moved from his arm. Together they headed for the palace, and she determinedly silenced the voice in her mind that urged prudence and virtue and caution.

What could happen to her that had not already occurred? What could life do to her that had not already been done? She might fall in love, and that was a danger.

She was an idiot. Had she no sense? If she could not heed the experiences of her past, if she'd not learned from them, could she not at least listen to the warnings she'd given herself?

Did she think herself immune to him?

Love was a horrid emotion if it blinded her to reason so adeptly.

She couldn't even banish the absurd desire to smile. Even though Gillian knew she should be cautious, fear was only a word. There was no substance behind it. This feeling—whatever it was called: love, confusion, lust, anticipation, delight, misery—had dulled her wits and edged out any fear she should feel. It had stripped from her any vestige of sanity and rendered her imbecilic. Not to mention that it cushioned her in an armor of foolishness, and yet this invisible protection felt as strong as iron.

She also suspected that whatever she was feeling was a fierce and carnivorous emotion and that it would demand a price.

Gillian followed Grant into the building, and was once again struck by the palace's beauty and serenity.

Sunlight poured in through the stained glass ceiling of the cupola, bathing the space in cobalt and gold light. She walked slowly toward the recessed floor, and stood looking down at the marble circle.

Grant, however, was intent upon reaching his laboratory. She glanced at him over her shoulder and wondered at this small yet telling tableau. He was immune to this beauty, probably having seen it all his life. Yet she was enthralled.

At that moment, he looked over and returned her gaze. He halted in the doorway.

She wanted to say something profound to him, something that would ensnare him, and cause him to abandon his scientific inquiry and come to her side. But she doubted if any words could sway him once he was intent on a goal.

Who was she, Gillian Cameron of Edinburgh, to intrigue the 10th Earl of Straithern?

He hadn't thought her shameful. Nor had he thought her wanton. Or perhaps he had, and that's why he invited her here. Why should she care for her reputation, when it was so very clear that she'd none left? Perhaps her youthful improprieties would lead to a greater freedom. If Grant did banish her from his property, then perhaps she would open a salon in London, become a famous courtesan.

Otherwise she'd have to remain at Rosemoor, and watch him marry Arabella.

Slowly he began to walk toward her.

"You look like something ethereal standing there, with the light behind you."

"It's a beautiful place," she said, smiling. "It's a shame more people can't experience it."

"I actively discourage visitors."

"Except for me," she said.

"This was an invitation. You cannot be simply a visitor if you're invited."

"What shall I be?" she asked.

He'd reached her now, and stood so close that she could touch him if she wished. Oh, she did wish, but she kept her hands at her sides.

"My apprentice?"

"Your friend?"

"Have I need of one?"

She tilted her head up to view the cupola roof. "I think you would need a friend occasionally, Your Lordship. Despite your rather prickly exterior, you are just like everyone else."

"Prickly? Like a hedgehog?"

"An aristocratic hedgehog," she corrected. "A very haughty-looking one, who's quite aware he's an earl, with a long nose, perhaps, and a supercilious air."

"Do you think my nose too long?"

"No, I don't. But I can imagine a hedgehog with a very long nose." She glanced at him. "I wouldn't change one of your features. They're all perfect. But of course you know that. How could you help but notice the attention you get from women. At the ball, for example. All of your female guests were staring at you."

"Women don't stare at me," he said, clearly uncomfortable with her comment.

"Nonsense," she said, "of course they do. They sigh when you enter a room. They start adjusting their skirts immediately, and angle to glimpse themselves in the mirror. They flirt with you outrageously, and you can't help but notice."

"They do not. Or if they do, it's because I'm an earl."

"Do not stand on modesty with me, Your Lordship. I don't care one way or another. I don't think it has anything to do with your rank. I think they would feel the same if you were a footman."

"But you don't," he said.

"On the contrary," she said, giving him the truth. "I think you're devastatingly handsome."

He looked flummoxed, as if no one had ever complimented him before this moment. Instead of arguing with her, he stepped down into the circle of light. His arms were at his sides and his head was tilted back, and he was staring at the sunlight streaming down around him, encapsulating him in an otherworldly bluish light.

For the longest time, she stood and watched him, transfixed by the beauty of Grant Roberson. Tall and strong, broad-shouldered, he seemed the embodiment of all that was truly wondrous about Scotland: its independence, its beauty, stark and unapologetic. He sought answers for riddles that no one else even knew existed. And yet he was like a hawk, fierce and alone, protecting what was his while at the same time giving comfort to those who depended upon his strength.

He should have frightened her. The sheer magnetism and power of the man should have made her cautious. Oddly enough, she felt more comfortable with him than with any other man she'd ever known. Any person she'd ever known.

Why had she told him the truth about her past? Had it been a test of sorts, a measure of him as a man? Or had she simply wanted him to repudiate her once and for all, and end the suspense? Yet he'd not done what she'd expected. He'd acted as if it had not mattered at all. As if she were no more than a stranger, a woman of mystery who was telling her sordid tale to a passerby. How odd that she was both pleased and disappointed.

She should have known better than to dare anyone, because Fate always ended up shaking its finger at her, delivering a blow in equal measure to the one she'd attempted.

Very slowly, he turned his head, raised one arm, extending his hand to her. His gaze was unreadable; his expression somber and unsmiling.

She didn't say anything, merely descended the three steps and walked to where he stood. The light was so brightly colored that it seemed as if they were in an underwater cavern.

She looked up into his face, knowing she was being foolish for being here, but unable to stifle the surge of happiness she suddenly felt. If there were repercussions for this moment—and she'd discovered there always were repercussions for foolish deeds and heedless moments—she would pay them willingly. For now, she was content to stand here with him.

"You're going to kiss me, aren't you, Your Lordship?"

"Grant," he said. "Have we not progressed enough for that?"

"It's not proper, Your Lordship, and you of all people know that I should observe the proprieties."

"Propriety is an odd subject to bring up in the same breath as a kiss. Besides, what happened to friendship? Did you not offer a moment ago to be my friend?"

"I've had a few minutes to reconsider the offer," she said. "Earls do not make friends of fallen women."

"Is that what you are? It seems to me they would be the very best type of friends. They would not lecture you endlessly on your responsibilities and burdens. Instead, they might kiss you."

Gently, he placed his hands on her shoulders.

Run away, Gillian. Run away before he captures you as ably as you earlier wished to ensnare him.

"You promised."

He drew back. "I did, didn't I?" An instant later, he smiled. "Then you must begin."

"I must?"

"Unless you don't wish to kiss me."

What a very foolish comment.

She rose up on her tiptoes. "In the spirit of friendship," she said, and brushed her lips over his.

He pulled her to him with no subtlety whatsoever, and deepened the kiss. She gasped, and he inhaled the sound of her surprise, pressing his lips against hers.

He wrapped his arms around her and pulled her up

into his embrace, and she in turn entwined her arms around his neck and held on as he kissed her.

Finally she pulled back, and when he reached for her, she held up one hand and shook her head. Someone, of the two of them, must have a little sense.

"Your footmen are still here," she cautioned.

He nodded and kissed her again.

Moments later, she'd finally caught her breath. For safety's sake, or perhaps for prudence, she took a few more steps away from him. He smiled at her caution, but didn't reproach her.

"I've been taking advantage of your library," she said. There, a change of topic, something without passion or temptation.

"Have you?" His voice sounded disinterested, but he was smiling.

"I have. I wanted to find something about your experiments, but I could find nothing about electrics."

"Nothing published for the general public, I'm afraid. I have several papers from associates of mine in Italy. I would be more than happy to share them with you. Do you read Italian?"

It was her turn to smile. "Of course I don't, and well you know it. What would a girl from Edinburgh be doing reading Italian?"

"Then I shall have to read them to you. Shall we adjourn to the laboratory, Miss Cameron?" He held out his arm, and she walked toward him and placed her hand upon it. Together they mounted the steps and crossed the floor to the door leading to his laboratory.

Michael and the second footman were standing behind the long table on which they'd placed the glass bottles. At a nod from Grant, the two men bowed and left the room.

"There, now my footmen are nowhere to be seen."

"Your experiments, Your Lordship," she said, directing his attention to the bottles in front of him.

"Grant," he corrected.

"Gillian," she added.   ·

They smiled at each other in perfect accord.

She leaned against the table and watched as he began to arrange what he needed. First came the odd arrangement of metal discs in their cage. Then a second machine consisting of a crank and a large flywheel around which a wire was wrapped. A second pile of disks was placed beside the first, and Grant connected a wire to both.

"What is it?" she asked, reaching out with her hand to touch the very strange apparatus with the crank.

He pulled her hand back.

"I don't want you shocked," he explained.

"Shocked?"

"Have you ever walked across a carpet and then touched the metal latch of a door? A spark emits from the contact, and it's called a static charge."

She nodded.

"This will produce the same type of charge, only stronger."

"But why would you want to do such a thing?"

"For a variety of reasons," he said, smiling. "To create a better compass. To create a form of power. Because it exists."

"It's what you're going to use to ignite the gas, isn't it?"

"You're a very good student, Gillian. Would you like a demonstration?"

She nodded again. "I would."

"You might wish to step back," he said. "As a precautionary measure. I never know how strong the gas might be. It seems to vary in intensity."

"Are you not afraid that you might be injured?"

"I am as safe as I can be. Electrics are inherently safe, if one uses common sense."

She didn't feel the least bit reassured.

Instead she moved to where he indicated at the back of the room near the windows, and folding her hands behind her, leaned against the wall. She watched him intently as he began his preparations. First, he moved one of the bottles away from the others, and closer to the engines. Secondly, he began to crank the strange machine with the flywheel. It seemed to work in conjunction with the other two machines to produce a spark at the end of a wire. Grant held it in his left hand while he removed the cork from the greenish glass bottle with his right. Only then did he touch the wire to the lip of the bottle.

The explosion was so loud that she lost her hearing for a moment. The bottle shot off the table and nearly to the door before falling to the floor and shattering into a thousand shards.

"Did you see that?" he exclaimed with all the excitement of a boy.

She nodded, speech impossible at this moment.

"Would you like to try it?"

She shook her head, still unable to talk.

"Are you quite certain?"

Finally she was able to speak. "I can assure you,

Grant, I have never been more certain of anything in my entire life."

He glanced at her. "You're upset."

"The bottle could have exploded in the other direction," she said. "It could have hit you. Or shattered in your face."

"Of course it couldn't. The opening was toward me. The force of the blast would have carried it toward the door, which is why I asked you to move. I'm a scientist, Gillian. I have done this experiment many times."

She frowned at him, uncertain whether she was annoyed or still frightened.

"You were worried about me, weren't you?" He placed the still glowing wire on the edge of the table and then turned to her. "You truly were?"

"An exceptionally foolish emotion," she said. She was no longer frightened, but she was annoyed.

"You mustn't be," he said. "But thank you for the compliment."

She glanced at him curiously.

"It's always a compliment when a beautiful woman worries about a man."

"You are insufferably arrogant, Your Lordship. And possibly very lucky. You must take more care."

"Have I taken on an apprentice who's going to lecture me now?"

"Someone must, I suspect."

She folded her arms across her chest and regarded him impassively. "Are you never afraid that you're going to set the palace on fire?"

He didn't look up as he answered. "There was a time when I thought it should be razed to the ground," he said surprisingly. "All manner of evil was once done here."

"What type of evil?"

"It's better if you don't know," he said, glancing at her quickly and then away. "I myself would have preferred to never know. Now I'm beset with memories, and I'd much rather not have them."

"Then why make this building your laboratory?"

"The palace is only stone and brick. It doesn't retain thoughts, feelings, or memories. Only people do. Therefore, it is for me to dismiss those memories."

"Sometimes memories remain with us."

"Only if we allow them."

She sat in the overstuffed chair at the other side of the room and regarded him critically. She was not yet his lover, or quite a stranger. Every time she saw him, however, she discovered something new about him. What did he see in her as the days passed?

She sat forward, propping her elbows on her knees and planting her chin on her knuckles.

There was such a vast gulf between them: lineage, history, interests. But there was as much that linked them: grief, loneliness, need, and the grandest of all of these: a physical awareness that thrummed between them.

She watched him as he straightened up his workspace. "Are you not going to explode the other bottles?"

He smiled. "I'm thinking that it would be wiser to do so outside. The gas seems particularly strong this time of year. There's an area to the rear of the property that I've cleared for just such experiments."

"I commend your restraint, as well as your wisdom."

"So, the apprentice approves?"

She stood and walked to the other side of the table, bracing her hands on the edge. After a moment, she slid her hand across the table, and it sat there for a moment before he did the same thing, covering her hand with his.

"I don't want you harmed," she said. "Whether I remain at Rosemoor or not, I would not like to think of you causing damage to yourself."

His expression stilled. "Are you planning on leaving?"

"Not now, but one day."

He didn't answer, didn't comment, but he moved his hand, suddenly intent on his equipment.

"You can't think I would stay here for the rest of my life."

His fingers stilled on the apparatus, his hand resting against the metal coils. Slowly he removed them, placing them on the table. He didn't speak, neither to condemn nor to cajole, or even to question her further. But his gray eyes were suddenly smoldering, and she wondered if she'd angered him.

He walked around the table.

"Why are you smiling?" he asked. "I confess to not feeling much humor at the moment."

"You look so determined," she said. "As if I am some citadel that needs to be stormed."

"Do I? A marauding knight, is that what I am? I believe the first Earl of Straithern was similar in disposition."

"I wonder if most great families began with marauders."

"How else?"

He was only a few inches from her. His eyes hadn't warmed, and his expression was still somber. Her smile faded the longer he stood there, silent, intent, and almost intimidating.

"What do you want of me?" she finally asked. Unwise words, perhaps, especially as he answered her.

"I want you."

His thumbs brushed beneath her chin as the heels of his hands gently pushed her head back. "Shall I kiss you again, Gillian, simply to ensure that the experience was what we both remember?"

"Do you want to?"

He ignored her question.

"Then I'll take you to my bed."

"It's morning," she said, shocked.

"Do you think that people only make love at night, Gillian?"

"I've never given it any thought," she said. Assignations with Robert had been done in the darkness, furtive couplings when they could both escape their households.

Before she could say another word, he bent his head and kissed her. This kiss was not like the one in the chapel, or even the cupola. Sensations overwhelmed her to the point her words vanished immediately. His lips were warm, his tongue intrusive and hot, capable of inciting so many emotions that she couldn't keep track of all of them. Abruptly she was in a vortex, spinning in a world suddenly dark and swirling with a multitude of bright colors.

Her hands reached out to grip his shoulders. He was her anchor. He was creating these wonderful sensations, and yet he was the only oasis of safety in her altered world.

Her last cogent thought was that she should be fleeing from him, and not holding tighter.

Chapter 17

Grant bent and lifted Gillian into his arms, taking her to the back of the laboratory, to a series of rooms hidden by a raised panel in the wall. He'd never known about the hidden rooms until after his father's death. He'd made them his own, installing a comfortable bed in one for when he was too tired to make the trip back to Rosemoor. A second held a small room where he sat and transcribed his notes, and the third chamber was for his manservant, never far away.

He set her down near the bed, but didn't kiss her again. He would not attempt to convince her, would not cajole her, because he wanted her to be here of her own volition.

This would not be seduction but rather complicity.

She didn't speak, as if knowing somehow that words would scratch at this moment like a diamond on glass. Instead she looked down at herself and then pressed her fingers against her bodice as if measuring the swell of her breasts. Slowly, she began to unbutton each fastening.

When the bodice was open, she turned, bending

her head, one hand holding up the mass of hair at the nape of her neck.

"Would you unfasten my skirt ties, please?" she asked softly.

His fingers trembled on the knot, and for a moment he was tempted to return to his laboratory for an implement to slice his way through the blasted thing. At the last moment, before reason was buried beneath desperation, the knot finally loosened, and he had succeeded in his task.

He should have known that she would be different, that once she was set on a path, she would not veer from it but embrace it wholeheartedly. She slowly turned and faced him, her fingers plucking at the sleeves of her bodice and slowly drawing them down. She removed the bodice first, and then stepped out of the skirt, retrieving both parts of the garment and laying it over a chair. But still, she didn't turn from him, didn't ask for time or privacy. Nor did she ask him to avert his eyes from her disrobing.

Sunlight bathed her body, brushing against the ivory of her shoulders, the perfection of her arms. Shadows pooled at the base her neck and between her breasts.

Paradoxically, he wanted her to slow her movements so he could look his fill, and to hurry so that he could see her naked.

He knew, from previous experience, that layers of underclothes lay beneath her dress. A chemise, drawers, corset, and no more than two petticoats, if she'd been truthful.

But Gillian was as swift with these as she was in her decision, evidently. Each time she removed a garment, she folded it neatly and it joined her other clothing on the chair.

"How very neat you are," he said, gently teasing her.

She inclined her head but didn't speak. Perhaps she thought if she did so it might break the spell that stretched between them. Nothing could. The entire building could explode and he wouldn't care. His conscience could suddenly awake, and he'd ignore it. Only one thing could keep him from bedding her, and that would be Gillian herself.

Blessedly, however, she remained silent. Not one protestation of virtue slipped past those lovely lips. Not one look of regret entered those beautiful blue eyes.

She left her chemise on while she bent and removed her shoes, holding on to the bed with one hand for support while the other hand stretched toward him. He grabbed her wrist, placing a kiss along her fingers.

She smiled, but still did not speak.

Her stockings, plain and serviceable white, were next. She slipped the garter down her thigh first, then over her knee, past her calf to her ankle. She bent and retrieved it, but before she could place it on the chair, he took it from her and held it like a talisman in his hands. It was warm. Gillian's warmth.

He wanted a kiss, but she stepped back.

The stockings were quickly dispensed with, and then suddenly there was not much between her and nakedness. He removed his coat and threw it, not as neatly as she had, atop her dress. He would just as soon have torn the buttons from his shirt, but he forced himself to patience, and restrained himself in the face of her smile.

While he was turning to remove his shoes, she divested herself of the rest of her garments. It was only when he saw the chemise hit the chair that he realized she must be naked.

He turned slowly, each tiny clicking second marked in his mind as important and rare. Again, she did something totally unique and so Gillian-like that he almost expected it.

She stood in front of him, her gaze unwavering. Her hands were at her sides, her palms pressed against her thighs. Her shoulders were straight, her pose that of one of the statues outside the palace. But this female form was not draped in a diaphanous garment. No toga covered her. She was without artifice or covering of any sort, not even false modesty.

He raced to be as naked as she.

He reached out and placed his hands on her upper arms, noting the difference in the textures and shading of their skin. She was pale, a delicate ivory, and he was nearly brown. The contrast was startling and oddly arousing.

Now, right at this moment, at this exact second he should halt, draw back his hands, and give her a moment to arrange her thoughts. At this exact second, he should give her time to refuse him, or banish him from the room. Would he go? Reluctantly, most reluctantly, but he would go. All she had to do was say the word, and he would turn and gather his clothes and leave her.

He actually gave credence to the idea of saying such words to her. He almost said to her: *There is time, you know. There is time for you to refuse me. This must be your decision as well as my need.*

But he was feeling selfish, and not inclined to give her the opportunity to change her mind. Instead he closed the distance between them, until her breasts were brushing against his chest, and his cock felt the springiness of the hair at the apex of her thighs and began gloriously hardening even further. He had been semi-erect ever since he'd seen her before dawn in the light of the lantern. He'd been erect ever since he'd kissed her, and now he was an iron pole, harder than he could ever remember being.

Sex was as necessary as water or food; one of the elements to life that should never be ignored. He'd never stinted himself, never refused an invitation. But he was less lover than he was animal at this moment. Nevertheless, he forced himself to breathe deeply and loosen his grip on her arms. He savored the delicate touch of her nipples against his chest, and gently pushed his cock down until it was aiming at her like an arrow. Still, he did not move further, didn't force himself on her. Nor did he speak, simply experienced the sharp pleasure-pain of need.

Her breathing was as rapid as his, but her hands were at her sides. He wanted her to reach out and touch him in curiosity or wonder or even admiration. But she did nothing, surprising him yet again.

He wanted them to have been lovers for months and years. He wanted to avoid all the awkward phase of getting to know what she liked and what he liked. He wanted to simply know her as well as he did himself. He would pleasure her with his mouth and fingers and make her nearly beg for release.

She sighed. A gentle, almost innocent sound that almost made *him* beg at that moment.

Slowly, so slowly that the moments were measured not in a heartbeat but in days, she raised her hands and placed them on him, sliding them, fingers splayed, through the hair on his chest and up to his shoulders to link behind his neck. And then she swayed against him using her body like a brush, painting a picture of her nakedness against his skin, letting him feel the softness of her thighs and the dampness at the juncture of them.

She rubbed her breasts against him as he stood there, speechless, wordless, amazed, and delighted. Her eyes were fixed on his face, and not once did her gaze lower, not even when his cock slipped between her thighs and nestled there like an animal seeking its burrow, homeward bound.

He bent and kissed her, an almost savage caress. There was no gentleness, no tenderness, only a hunger he couldn't hide.

She met him measure for measure, her tongue dueling with his, her openmouthed gasps a signal that she was as nearly desperate as he. He bent over her as she fell back against the bed. He almost slid into her then, but he'd never been a selfish lover.

He bent to lick a nipple, and it stiffened in response. He did the same for the other, and it, too, was just as quick to harden. His hand slid down her body, exploring, the tips of his fingers gently smoothing over her belly to the top of one thigh, then the other. He combed through the curls that had so welcomed his cock, his fingers seeking proof that she was as aroused as he.

His finger softly flicked the flesh between her legs, and she made a sound in the back of her throat.

Her eyes, dazed, opened and fixed on his face. He spread the dampness over the swollen folds, and smiled. Tenderly, he kissed her, and when she would have deepened the kiss, he pulled back and suckled a hardened nipple.

Her breathing grew even shallower as her hips tilted, and she seemed to reach for his hand. Biting her lower lip, she lifted her hips off the bed. He increased the speed of his finger, and then slowed it. Faster and slower, over and over, once and again and again.

"Yes," she murmured as he kissed her lightly, and then bit her nipple softly. She gasped, and he licked the nipple.

He gently pushed two fingers into her, sliding in and out. Her hips arched in time to the movement.

"Yes," she whispered, her voice sounding low and husky. He took that as an invitation, entering her with a slow, deliberate movement.

Her eyes opened, her gaze still filled with pleasure. Her legs widened, and she whispered, "Yes."

Grant pulled back, and then thrust forward. She widened her legs, planted her feet on the bed on either side of his legs and lifted herself up, grinding her body against his. He moved one hand between them, sliding his fingers against her slickness. Her eyes flew open, and she stared at him, the look in her eyes helpless and yielding. Stroke after stroke, she matched his thrusts. Her breathing was as ragged as his, the beat of her heart as rapid, measured by his open lips against a trembling nipple.

She moaned in response, and he bit the flesh at

the juncture of her neck, and then licked where he'd bitten.

He pulled her tight against him, thrusting, driving his hips forward. He ground his cock into her, incapable of restraint, insensate and desperate for his waiting orgasm. His buttocks clenched as she widened her legs still further and took him deep. Her hips tilted, her body arching up to meet his, her internal muscles milking him with each downward stroke.

He could feel the heat of her body as she found her pleasure. He held his fingers against her as her hips slowly lowered to the bed.

A second, an instant, a heartbeat later his head tilted backward, an inarticulate cry emerged from his throat, and he was lost in mindless, piercing pleasure.

Perhaps she was a fallen woman because right now, with her cheek against Grant's chest, with his arms around her, Gillian was content. For however long she could retain this emotion, she'd be grateful for it.

She could feel the beating of his heart against her ear, and placed her hand flat against his chest. Slowly, she traced a path from one male nipple to another, claiming him with her fingers. Was it possible for emotion to be carried from her heart to her hands? Could affection, fondness, gratitude, and perhaps something even deeper, something she didn't want to name, be transmitted by touch?

He reached out and placed his hand on hers, pressing her palm against his skin.

"Gillian," he said.

She kept her eyes closed, but she smiled.

"Dearest Gillian."

At the endearment, she opened her eyes to meet his gaze.

"It's a fine morning, is it not?"

"A very lovely morning," she said, smiling at him. "Or afternoon. One of the loveliest I can remember."

Delight traveled through her as he bent to kiss her. She raised her arms and wrapped them around his neck, and then a moment later pulled back and pressed her palms against each side of his face.

"No wonder other women think you are so handsome. You truly are."

He looked a little discomfited by the comment, and she smiled even more.

He kissed her lightly on the nose and moved to sit up against the headboard.

When he'd first brought her here, she'd no other thought in her mind but him. Now she looked around the room, surprised it was as large as it was.

The four-poster bed in which she lay dominated the room. A small bureau sat against one wall. A fireplace took up most of the second wall, while a small washing stand was set against the third. The small window revealed a bright, sunlit day.

Blazing white squares of sunlight framed the bed. Gillian reached out her hand, feeling the warmth on her skin. The day was a beautiful one. Too precious for regrets.

Or thoughts of death.

"Why would anyone want to harm you, Grant? Or your brothers?"

"A question I've asked myself numerous times," he admitted. "The only answer I can come up with is the better to inherit the title. But even that doesn't make any sense. The closest relative is an elderly second cousin. Even so, I've asked my solicitor to do some checking on him, to ascertain that his financial condition isn't so dire that he's willing to do anything to ascend to the title."

She sat up beside him, needing to be close.

He bent and kissed her, a sweet kiss that led to something deeper and more emotion filled. As he laid her against the pillows, she looked up at his face, a face she'd known for such a short time but which was coming to mean a great deal to her. She placed one hand against his cheek, her thumb brushing the corner of his lips.

Was it so wrong to want to be loved? Society would say it was. If other people could read her mind they would declare her an outcast, a fallen woman with only thoughts of her own pleasure. They would be right, for she had no concerns for a society as narrow and condemnatory as it was.

Earls might occasionally—and surprisingly—marry doctor's daughters but they do not marry fallen women.

Very well, if she had nothing in her future, she would certainly enjoy the present.

She pulled him down to her, threading her fingers through his hair and gripping the back of his head to keep him in place. With all the skill of which she was able, with all the passion she felt flowing through her, she kissed him. Not because he was the earl, but because he was Grant, and she wanted him, needed him, desired him, or all three.

Impatiently, she pushed away the sheets that came between them, until she could feel his long and naked body over hers. He was hard already, and she reached out one hand to grab his shaft and guide him into her.

He reached out with one hand and cupped her buttocks, jerking her to him on each downward stroke. She bit back the sound she made, and then let it escape. He felt so good. They felt so good. She wrapped her feet around his calves, holding on to him as the sensations began to grow.

He shuddered, his arms braced on either side of her. He pinned her to the bed with the force of his thrusts. She planted her feet on the bed and pushed up, desperate for that last bit of feeling. Finally she was over, the crest reached; the precipice descended in a flurry of outspread legs and arms and halted breath.

"Tell me about your lover," Grant said. The request didn't surprise her; the fact that he asked now did.

"Robert? He was someone I knew in Edinburgh."

"Tell me about him."

She turned her head. "Do you truly want to know about Robert? Or do you simply want to know about my fall from grace? What led me to turn my back on my parents, society, and all the manners and lessons I'd learned in my lifetime?"

"I think they're one and the same question," he said softly.

"I fell in love," she said, turning her head to survey the ceiling.

After all was said, there was no other explanation. She had been rapturously, deliciously, foolishly in love. She had seen his smile as a demonstration of his devotion. She'd repeated every word he'd said to her in the quiet of her mind, seeing a meaning that never truly was there. She'd thought him constant, and worried about him, and considered his opinion each time she made a decision. She'd spent a great deal of time being involved in Robert, never noticing, until it was over, that he did not demonstrate the same devotion toward her.

She had been a young and impetuous fool, a comment she made softly now.

Gillian hadn't even suspected that he'd been using her for ill until the day she'd gone to his home. He hadn't met her in the garden as they'd arranged. She had news for him, the greatest and most monumental type of news. When she'd been worried enough, and desperate enough to travel to his home, a place she'd been socially since his father and hers had business together, she'd been met by his sister.

She could close her eyes and be transported back to that instant in time. She was standing on the broad stone steps of the McAdams town house. Mary had dismissed the maid who'd opened the door to greet Gillian herself. She'd not invited Gillian inside, and her expression had been rather cruel. Or perhaps Gillian only felt that way now, looking back. The scene had, no doubt, been played out many times before, and would be so again. A foolish girl, a man without honor, and the inevitable betrayal.

"He isn't here, Gillian. He's at the Andersons'. He and Helen are deciding the date of their wedding."

"Wedding?"

"Didn't you know?" Mary asked, her smile brittle. "Robert's engaged to be married."

Only later did she pull apart the words and give

them weight and meaning, but at that moment, Gillian was still youthfully naïve and innocent. No one should be that innocent.

She pulled out a small note from her reticule, something she'd jotted down in case she missed Robert.

She handed it to Mary. "Would you see that Robert gets this?" she asked.

"Why bother, Gillian? You aren't important to him."

She'd ignored Mary's words, to her great sorrow.

At the time, she'd not given any thought to the idea that Mary would go directly to her parents, and Robert's parents would go to Gillian's home, to confront her father and stepmother and Gillian herself.

Through it all, Robert never came. Why should he? He had scores of other people to rid himself of the complication of a discarded lover.

"Being in love, I've found, does not strip the intellect completely from your mind," Grant said now. "All lovers have lucid moments. Did you never think he was being false?"

She smiled. "I confess I didn't. I never thought it. How foolish is that?'

"Young and innocent, perhaps, but not truly foolish," he said.

"And have you been in love very many times?"

"I was desperately in love when I was younger," he said softly. "But circumstances change, and so do emotions."

She remained silent.

"Unfortunately, the lady in question was already married. Not happily but well. She was all for indulging in a liaison, but I wanted something more permanent."

"And respectable, no doubt, bearing in mind that you're an earl."

"Not because I'm an earl," he said, "but because I found myself very much wanting to set up a household with her. To meet her across the breakfast table. To ask whether she slept well, or to know that she did because she'd been in my chamber all night."

She felt herself warm, not from his words as much as from the image of Grant being a solicitous husband.

"Did you have no one to guide you? No one at all? Where was your father?" he asked.

She smiled ruefully.

"When you have children, Grant, you'll discover that you can control a great many things about life but you'll not be able to control who they love. I doubt I would have listened to him even if my father had counseled me."

She stared up at the ceiling, remembering the idyllic interlude. How different those days were from this moment, as a stream is from the ocean. She smiled at her own whimsy.

"What happened to your child?"

She froze.

He was lying on his side facing her, his head propped on his elbow. Slowly, he pulled down the sheet, and after a moment she gave up the battle, allowing him to bare her body. Gently, he placed his hand across her stomach, marking the faint lines there with his fingertips.

"You've given birth, Gillian."

She closed her eyes, waiting for his words, feeling shock wash over her. Of course he'd seen. Of course he would have known. Passion had stripped the sense from her.

Several moments passed, and still he didn't speak.

She moved, sitting on the opposite side of the bed. She'd never told anyone the story, never shared her grief with a single soul, and now it felt too heavy not to be revealed.

"What happened to your child?"

She lowered her head, wishing he wasn't so curious. Or that he was as arrogant as she'd first thought him. There was a gentleness to his tone, a kindness and a warmth to his voice that made the account all the more difficult to tell.

"When they discovered that I was with child, my parents sent me to live with a second cousin. After all, I'd brought scandal to the family. I didn't learn until much later that she had plans to give my child away. I suppose I was a fool, thinking that I could live as I had once done, with no punishment for my crime."

"Is that what happened to the baby?"

She shook her head. "I knew that I would die before I simply gave away my child. So I left. Another bit of foolishness. I had a little money, but I did not expect to be robbed, to have my valise stolen. In less than a day I had no money, no belongings, and no future."

He didn't question her further. She smiled. It wasn't a pretty story, but not quite as dire as Dr. Fenton had portrayed. "Dr. Fenton found me standing on a street corner in Edinburgh. He intervened before I was forced to sell myself, however. He took me home, and he and Arabella cared for me."

He didn't say anything, only sat up, moving close to her. She could feel the warmth of his body, and for a moment was tempted to simply turn to him. Passion, however, would only delay this tale; it wouldn't erase it.

"I was too ill, frankly, to care very much about anything. I seemed to survive for the baby. If I ate, it was for him, more than for me. When I slept, it was exhaustion more than a wish to rest. But when he was born, everything changed."

She took a deep breath. "He was the most beautiful baby I'd ever seen. He was perfectly formed, with a full head of hair. He had blue eyes, my blue eyes. The first time I held him, I knew that nothing would ever be the same again. I found love, the most pure and beautiful love in the world. It didn't matter that Robert had deserted me. He'd given me this amazing gift."

Grant didn't speak, but she felt the touch of his palm on her bare back. She stood, oblivious to her nakedness, and donned her chemise. Slowly she walked to the window, surveying the sunny afternoon at Rosemoor.

"I had one perfect day. One absolutely glorious day of happiness. Not many people can say that for a span of twenty-four hours their life was absolutely perfect, that there was nothing in that time but joy." She heard him rise, and wished he'd remained on the bed. Instead, he came and put his hands on her shoulders, pulling her back against him.

"He lived only a day. Dr. Fenton said such things happen. A baby's heart sometimes doesn't beat as strongly as it should." Her tone was level, as if she'd told the story before, when the truth was that she'd never spoken of her son to anyone.

"Dr. Fenton was very kind," she said. "He took me in when no one else would, and gave me a home. He gave me a position as Arabella's companion. He was very kind."

"And he's never let you forget it."

"He does not mean to be the way he is."

"*You* are too kind."

She smiled. She turned her head slowly and regarded him. "All I ask is that you do not tell me that you forgive me. You have no idea how tiring it is to be forgiven so often. Dr. Fenton does so endlessly."

"Would it make you feel better if I didn't forgive you?"

"Actually," she said, "it wouldn't matter. You've no right to judge me. No one has. I cannot help but wonder what people would do with themselves if they simply lived their own lives and didn't involve themselves with the actions of others. Whatever would they do with their time?"

"Perhaps they would spend it less in philosophy, and more in passion," he said, gently turning her so she faced him.

"I am sorry, Gillian. Stupid words, because they don't say enough."

He bent and kissed her, and then pressed her cheek against his bare chest. Only then did she realize she was weeping, soundless tears that wet her face.

Chapter 18

Grant looked around his laboratory and realized that there was something missing from his study of the newest theories, something he didn't quite understand. Or perhaps it had nothing whatsoever to do with his experiments, and everything to do with the fact that he was performing them alone.

Where was Gillian?

Ever since he'd left her a scant hour ago, he'd been wondering at the wisdom of his actions. Everything she'd said about her reputation was probably true. As long as she remained at Rosemoor, she was safe from rumor and conjecture. Or was she? Surely, if he simply commanded it, people would not speak of her in shocked whispers. The servants wouldn't gossip. No one would look askance at her. Part of him knew that such an autocratic view of the world was doomed to fail. People would do as they wished behind his back. To him, they would be polite to the point of being servile.

But to Gillian?

He had no right to damage her further. He would be no better than that idiot Robert. He was angry at both her and Robert, the lover about which she so fondly spoke. How dare she not guard herself with more care, treat herself with more reservation? Give herself to someone who would understand the enormity of the great gift she offered?

He must tell his valet to order new shirts. The material of this one felt almost coarse, but then it could be because he was remembering the touch of Gillian's skin.

Where was she? Michael had brought him hot water for bathing, and assured Grant that he'd done the same for Miss Cameron.

"She didn't speak, Your Lordship, other than to thank me." Michael smiled, and Grant couldn't help but wonder if Gillian had made another conquest.

Another conquest?

He'd be a fool not to admit that such was the case. Despite his grief, despite his anger, despite the fact he was certain someone was trying to kill him, he couldn't relinquish the thought that his life would be a great deal grayer without Gillian.

She interested him, and made him laugh. He was confused by what he felt for her, and the fact that he couldn't stop thinking of her. None of which was her fault, and all of which was because of her.

She enlivened a room simply by entering it. She made him forget what he was concentrating on, a singularly novel experience. She amused him and elicited his compassion, to such a degree that he felt himself, oddly enough, feeling pain where she was concerned. No other woman of his acquaintance had ever summoned his empathy before, and he wished there was someone to whom he could go and confess his utter state of confusion.

Why did he feel rage when she'd cried? He'd never felt that way for any other woman or for any other individual, for that matter. What did that make him? A man without caring or concern for his fellow man? Or had he simply been too occupied with his own concerns, too impatient to be involved in the lives of others?

He certainly wasn't too unavailable to be interested in Gillian, and it wasn't simple lust that kept her at the forefront of his mind. If he'd had only a physical awareness about her, he'd be able to dismiss her after today. Instead, he suspected she would become more and more important to him.

Vitally important to him.

What the hell had he done? Something he couldn't undo and wouldn't if he had the opportunity. Something he'd forever remember, even when he was an old man on his deathbed. Something he had to rectify even now.

Perhaps to the rest of the world Gillian would be a fallen woman, an unfortunate girl who generated whispers and warning lessons. To him she was simply Gillian, lovely, large-hearted, intelligent, and possessed of the ability to charm him utterly. For that reason, he should protect her, even from himself.

But he'd never lied to himself, and now was not the time to begin. Nothing but death could keep him away from Gillian Cameron.

Gillian hesitated at the door to his laboratory, watching him for a few moments before he caught sight of her. In the past few hours they'd loved each other, and she had revealed her grief. She had shared with him the depth of her pain, and the loss of her child. The Earl of Straithern knew more about her than any other single individual in the world, and that knowledge, more than their shared nakedness, made her suddenly shy with him.

"You're here," he said, looking up from the table and seeing her.

"Yes."

"What are you thinking?" he asked. "You look as if you want to run away."

"It would be easier."

"Would it? Don't you find that it's better to face a problem than run from it?"

"Is that what you are?" she asked. "A problem?"

"I think I am," he said, coming around the table. "At least from that look on your face. Are you wishing it hadn't happened?" he asked as he approached her. "Are you thinking that you shouldn't have come to Rosemoor? Are you wondering about whether or not people will think differently of you now?"

"Will they know?"

"Not from me," he said.

"I'm under no illusions as to what other people might think. I clearly broke the rules once. And did it again. Perhaps I should be punished for that."

"I didn't take you for a martyr," he said.

"I am not a martyr, Grant. But neither am I ignorant of society's reaction to what I've done. I have not acted in a way that is expected of young women. My parents disowned me for it. My friends shunned me. My relatives were disgraced, and the man I loved . . ."

"Was not worthy of the title," he said.

She smiled. "You might be correct. I thought he would act differently."

"Tristan and Isolde? You and he were going to live idyllically somewhere where society's rules and regulations do not apply?"

"It does sound ridiculous now that you verbalize it."

"Just naïve," he said. "There are countries other than Scotland where the rules are not so puritanical. Where a man and woman can live outside the boundaries of society."

"Like Italy?"

"Exactly like Italy," he said.

"Is that why you spent so much time there?"

"Actually," he said, "I spent time in Italy in order to be close to scientists I admired. And to be as far away from Rosemoor as I could," he added surprisingly. "We can create our own country here, if you like. A place where we decide the rules."

"Do you want to make me your mistress, Grant? Because of what I told you? Do you think my virtue is for rent?" she asked, careful to keep her voice emotionless.

"I have wanted to bed you, Gillian, from the moment I met you. From that first day you arrived at Rosemoor. When you drank tea and surveyed me with your cool gaze. I was enthralled from that moment. Should I be punished for the truth?"

She didn't quite know how to answer that.

"Are we going to be lovers?"

"I sense an inevitability to it." He smiled.

"And if I protest? If I run away to Inverness or Edinburgh?"

"I would find you," he said easily. "But I would certainly feel a measure of guilt that my actions drove you to such a foolish thing."

"And if I should enjoy being your lover too much?"

"I would be inordinately pleased. I would probably be insufferably proud of that fact. And flattered. I've never had a woman behave that way toward me. Perhaps I do not induce strong feeling."

They were both tiptoeing around each other, throwing down little pieces of their souls like rose petals, and then bending to pick them up when they went unnoticed. Perhaps it was time for less delicacy and more truth.

"I could love you," she said. "Women do, I think. Women fall in love while men fall in lust."

"You think that's what I feel?"

"I don't think you know what you feel, Grant. I think it surprises you as much as it does me. I do know that we have the ability to hurt each other. Badly."

"But love, Gillian?"

They studied each other for a long moment, and thankfully, he didn't press her for an answer.

Michael entered at that moment, bringing Grant his luncheon. He placed it on the sideboard, bowed once, and disappeared again.

"Is he always around?"

"Almost always," Grant said. "Does it bother you?"

"A little," she answered, and wondered if that confession marked her as hopelessly bourgeois. She wasn't used to servants obeying her every desire.

"Are you hungry?" he asked. "It's been hours since breakfast."

"I didn't eat breakfast," she said. "A certain impatient earl was waiting for me."

"Then you must eat," he said.

He joined her at the sideboard, and as she watched, a little bemused, he lifted the top from a small tureen to reveal a rose-colored, creamy bisque.

"Cook prepares a wonderful fish stew," he said, ladling some of the bisque into a small bowl. He took a silver spoon from where it rested on a snowy white linen napkin and filled it with the soup, holding it out for her as if she were a child.

"I can assure you, Your Lordship, that I can feed myself quite ably, thank you."

He didn't say a word in reply, but the corners of his mouth lifted into a small and almost tender smile. He stood there unmoving, and she had the decided impression that he wasn't going to cease in his efforts to feed her.

"Very well," she said somewhat crossly, and opened her mouth. The bisque was delicious. She closed her eyes to savor it.

Cook had used numerous spices to give the bisque a robust flavor, something that wasn't excessively fishy but had a hint of heat to it. Perhaps she'd added some carrots and potatoes as well. When she opened her eyes, Grant was smiling at her, and the spoon was full again.

This time she shook her head.

"A roll, perhaps," she said. Without waiting, she grabbed one from the silver tray, sliced it in two, and held one part out to him.

"It's only fair," she said when he initially refused. "You must eat as well."

"My appetite isn't for food," he said, and wiggled his eyebrows at her.

She smiled and bit into the roll. It was, like anything Cook made at Rosemoor, absolute perfection, light and flaky and crusty all at once.

He held out the spoon again, and she allowed him to feed her. She really should move away. At the very least, she should protest again. But she didn't. Emotions seemed to pulse in the air, a beat of rhythm that her heart strained to match. There was something almost pagan in the silence, something almost wicked and abandoned in the simple act of nourishing each another.

She pulled back, and he finally relinquished the spoon to her, pulling up a chair and assisting her to the small table as if he were a footman. For a moment she thought he was going to leave her, but he did so only momentarily, long enough to procure another chair from some other place in the palace.

He sat opposite her and poured some wine into a goblet.

"Wine and bisque and an earl for company. It will be hard to go back to my normal way of life."

"Must you?"

She felt light-headed, almost woozy. For a moment, she thought it might be simply being so close to him. What was the scent of the soap he used while shaving?

How very odd. What had he asked? Something dangerous. Something wrong.

She was finding it very difficult to concentrate. She stared at his mouth. She wanted to lift her hand and place her fingers against the fullness of his bottom lip, but, surprisingly, her arm wouldn't obey her instructions. She lifted her gaze to his and watched as he frowned. She wanted to reassure him that she was fine, but suddenly she wasn't at all certain she was.

She raised a hand with difficulty, pressed it against his chest. But then it appeared in front of her, fingers wiggling.

"Help me," she said, but the words came out garbled. She couldn't understand them herself, so she tried once again. Speech was suddenly beyond her as the world began spinning.

She was a child again, twirling with her arms spread wide around and around and around until she collapsed on the ground in a burst of giggles. Instead, she slipped soundlessly from the chair and sprawled at the Earl of Straithern's feet.

"Help me," she said once again, but the cry was deep inside her mind.

Chapter 19

For the second time in the same day Grant carried her to his bed, but the thought in his mind wasn't passion this time but panic.

He picked up the bell on the corner of the bedside table and rang it fiercely.

A discreet rap heralded Michael's arrival. When Grant called out, the young man opened the door and bowed from the waist. Grant didn't have time for demonstrations of obeisance. Not now. Not until he knew what was wrong with Gillian.

It was more than a faint; even he could discern that. Her color was ashen, her lips bluish, and he feared it was no coincidence that she'd succumbed to illness so quickly after eating the bisque.

His noon meal.

Had he inadvertently poisoned her?

Anger flooded through him, made his voice brusque and imperious. "Fetch Lorenzo," he told Michael. "Use one of the carriages, and if one isn't ready, then tell him to use a horse. And if a damn horse isn't sad-dled, then tell him to run."

Michael nodded his understanding, Grant's desperation evidently getting through to the young man. When the footman turned and left the room, it was without any gesture of servility at all.

Grant had never felt as useless in his entire life as he did in those next few minutes. He prepared a cold compress for Gillian's forehead, sitting on the edge of the bed and bathing her face gently. But she didn't awaken, and her breathing seemed worse then before.

He'd fed her the bisque himself.

Would he ever be able to live with himself if anything happened to her?

He pushed aside that thought, concentrating on smoothing the damp cloth over her pale face. What the hell should he do?

It seemed to him the longer he sat there, the softer her breath became. She couldn't be allowed to fall into a stupor like James. He angled his arms behind her, raised her until she was almost in a sitting position, albeit leaning against him. He stood, holding her upright and thinking that she should weigh more. She was a slip of a thing, a willow. She should be a more substantial physical presence.

He breathed into her hair and said a quick, unaccustomed prayer. The Almighty didn't take bargaining well. Grant had already offered up his earldom for James's survival and God had remained unimpressed. What could he surrender now that might render God kind? His own life, perhaps.

"She's done nothing wrong, God," he said in the silence of the room. "Nothing but be herself and seek out my company, for which I will forever be thankful. If we have sinned, then blame me."

Perhaps it wasn't wise to alienate the Almighty at this moment.

Where the hell was Lorenzo?

"You look exceptionally lovely today, Miss Fenton."

Arabella looked at Lorenzo out of the corner of her eye, but she didn't turn to address him fully. Almost as if she couldn't be bothered to be polite.

If he didn't know better, Lorenzo would have thought that she was a countess already. She certainly had the bearing for it, as well as the ramrod-straight back. If he didn't mistake it, she wore a whalebone corset that was so tightly laced she was not able to breathe correctly. If she were truly a student of medicine, she'd know that tightly laced corsets were detrimental to a woman's health. Thank God most women preferred them as loose as possible.

"I didn't expect to find you in the conservatory," he said, sitting down beside her without waiting for an invitation. If he waited her for her to notice him, or even be polite, he might well stand there for an eternity.

She had a book in her lap, but then she always had a book in her lap. She glanced at him, her expression easily interpreted. He'd annoyed her, he could tell, simply by interrupting her reading.

What would her life be like when one of her children demanded her attention? Or would she simply turn them over to nurses and nannies and governesses until such time as they were ready to go off to school? That was the English upper-class way, was it not? No wonder most of the English were cold and withdrawn people. They'd never experienced love, not even from their own parents.

Arabella, unfortunately, appeared as cold and as un-approachable as any woman he'd met in this gray and unforgiving climate. He couldn't imagine the Grant he'd known in Italy being married to such a woman.

Elise was warm and beautiful, dispensing her affection to anyone coming to their home. She was open and loving, and the most wonderful mother he could ever imagine. There were times when even he dismissed her passion and yearned for her nurturing. She was his friend, his wife, his confidante, and he missed her every hour. Had it not been for his deep friendship and sense of obligation to Grant, he would have returned home within a day of arriving at Rosemoor.

While it was true Scotland was ruggedly beautiful, he was not prepared for the cold. Even with the season rapidly turning to summer, the breeze still bore a hint of chill. He'd not been warm since coming to Grant's home.

"Have you read Linnaeus?" he asked Miss Fenton now, feeling an obligation to be civil to the woman who would soon be marrying his oldest friend.

"I've read both Linnaeus and Le Clerc, sir."

"Ah, *Systema Naturae*. An excellent text, as I recall. What is it that you're reading now?"

He glanced over her shoulder. "Elizabeth Smithwell. *Blessed Herbal*. I have not read this book."

"It details the medicinal properties of plants, sir. I would recommend it."

"Do you never read anything else, Miss Fenton? A shocking novel or a ladies' magazine? Do you never involve yourself in fashion? Or good works? I think you would find that if the interests grow larger, so does the intellect."

She frowned at him, apparently understanding the subtle nature of his comments. Good, at least she wasn't a stupid woman; for all that she was an unpleasant one. Why on earth had Grant decided to settle himself with her? Why not a woman he met in Italy? Or someone he could easily meet in London?

Why not Miss Cameron?

Why this particular woman who, although she was pretty in a superficial way, was possessed of a remarkably sour disposition? She had beautiful eyes, when she deigned to look at something other than a book or a suppurating sore.

She had potential, he had to admit that. She could easily be a beauty, if there were some expression on her face other than annoyance. Her hair looked as if it had been impatiently styled, as if her maid had not had an opportunity to finish it before Arabella waved her away.

"May I inquire, sir, exactly what you wish of me?"

"To spend a few moments in your company," he said easily. "Grant is an old friend of mine. Would it not be wise for us to become friends? You are to be his bride, are you not?"

"I cannot imagine why," she said.

He simply looked at her, uncertain how to reply.

She went on, "It's not as if you and I will grow to be great friends, sir. Nor is it even certain that we shall see each other very often. Do you not live in Italy? And if that is the case, why should I occupy myself with attempting to get to know you, to become your friend when it's all too evident that you will not remain at Rosemoor? If I do indulge any time whatsoever in attempting to know you, have I not done a disservice to my studies? So I ask you again, sir, what advantage is it to me to attempt to be pleasant to you?"

"I know of no advantage," he said, silenced by the sudden notion that nothing he could say would have any effect on her. She didn't want to know him, and so he would remain unknown.

"Then, if you do not mind, sir, I would like to go back to my book."

"A countess would be more welcoming, Miss Fenton. You are going to be a countess."

"I am to live at Rosemoor, sir. The dowager countess will remain as matriarch to the people living here. I can serve them better by learning how to treat what ails them more so than talking them to death."

Lorenzo forced a smile to his face, hoping that it appeared somewhat sincere.

Blessedly, he was prevented from attempting to find something to say in response to the very rude soon-to-be countess by the appearance of the true one.

"There you are, both of you," the Countess of Straithern said. She sailed into the room like a merchant packet, solid and determined, her black dress adorned with black bugle beads. Unlike Arabella, her hair was styled perfectly, in a crown of braids atop her head. A jet brooch no doubt containing a lock of hair from each of her dead sons was her only adornment.

The air was becoming thick, almost sodden, as if it had recently rained. It was too humid in here for a person to remain for long. He stood and bowed slightly to the countess, offering her his seat.

She declined the offer, instead turning to Miss Fenton. "Where is your companion?"

Arabella shook her head instead of speaking, a choice that quite obviously annoyed the countess.

"I did not see her at breakfast, or at luncheon. When I asked Agnes as to her whereabouts, she stammered something about an adventure. Therefore, I can only surmise that Miss Cameron is off doing something she should not be doing."

Arabella didn't look the least displeased to learn that Miss Cameron was missing. Perhaps she was relieved by Gillian's desertion. Or was it the fact that Grant, as well, had not made an appearance since dinner last night? Was Arabella Fenton so cold and unfeeling that she could not even summon the emotion to be jealous?

Lorenzo fervently hoped that his friend was being foolish, and with Miss Cameron, and that the two of them were attempting to find a little enjoyment before his wedding.

"Well?" The Countess of Straithern was not pleased with Arabella's silence. One of her black leather shoes tapped impatiently on the slate floor of the conservatory.

When Arabella remained silent, the countess turned to him. Before she could even frame the question, he held up his hands in surrender. "I believe that they went to the marsh this morning, Your Ladyship. Beyond that, I can only guess that Grant is in his laboratory. I would have no idea of Miss Cameron's location."

"Was there something Gillian was to do for you, Your Ladyship?" Arabella asked. She actually closed her book to do so, looking up at the countess with a small smile. The look of amiability, however, did not quite make it to her eyes, and he had the sudden and distinct impression that Arabella Fenton did not like the Countess of Straithern, and that the emotion was returned.

"No," the countess said, "I merely wished to ask her a few questions."

"Perhaps I could supply the answers for you."

"I doubt it," the countess said shortly.

"Gillian has not returned to her room, Your Ladyship," Arabella said. She smiled at the countess, so faintly that it might not have been a change of expression at all. "But I am never disturbed by Gillian's vagaries. She has a habit of wandering around at night, for example. She does not sleep well, you see."

For a long moment the two women stared at each other. What was going on between them? What knowledge did they share that Lorenzo was not privy to? He was simply grateful that he did not live in this place of swirling secrets. He had not confided such to Grant, but he did not like his estate, preferring the sunny climate of Italy over this dark and dour place. Rosemoor might well be a kingdom fit for an earl, but there was not enough love and warmth here, and too many questions.

"Perhaps she cannot sleep because of a troubled conscience," Arabella said.

"I would have thought you'd evince some loyalty toward your friend," the countess said. "After all, she is your companion, is she not? If you dislike her so heartily, why have you not dismissed her?"

"It is my father's decision, Your Ladyship, to have Gillian as my companion. Not mine. She and I do not suit in a number of ways. She does not appreciate my study of medicine, and I dislike her constant meddling in my life. When I become the Countess of Straithern, I shall dismiss her. It will be my first official duty."

The countess did not respond, choosing to focus her attention on Lorenzo. "Are you certain you don't know where Miss Cameron is?" She studied him intently, as if to measure his words against the truth itself. He debated, for a moment, telling her of his suspicions, that Miss Cameron and Grant had each found a compatible person in the other. But while the countess evidently prized loyalty, she evidently did not understand that Lorenzo did as well. Grant was his friend. Let Grant divulge his plans for Gillian to the countess. Or if that was not something his friend chose to do, then let him explain Gillian's absence.

"I regret that I cannot answer that question, Your Ladyship."

She only nodded, once, in response to his comments. As if Lorenzo was answering in exactly the way she'd expected.

"When you see my son, would you convey to him that I wish him to call upon me at his earliest convenience?"

He held back his smile, thinking that of the two of them, Grant was possibly the more stubborn.

But his answer didn't indicate either his amusement or his certainty that Grant would do no such thing. "Of course I shall, Your Ladyship," he said, bowing slightly.

"This is a miserable place for a conversation," the countess said, looking about her and frowning at the foliage as if in chastisement for its plentiful growth. "I shall adjourn to my parlor, and the two of you shall join me."

"If you will excuse me, Your Ladyship, I have letters to write home." Letters filled with thankfulness. Elise would read them with some surprise, he was certain. But he had never valued her more than he did at this moment.

"Nonsense," the countess answered. "I wish to speak to you of Italy." She turned, as if expecting perfect obedience, and left the conservatory.

Lorenzo bit back his sigh, turned, and extended his hand to Miss Fenton, who promptly ignored it. She brushed past him, almost pushing him out of the way. Lorenzo glanced at the bench, and realized she'd left her book behind. He leaned down and retrieved it. The corner of a page was bent back, and he straightened it.

Before he could follow her and return it, Arabella was there, grabbing the book from Lorenzo's hands.

"Thank you," she said in a tone that left no doubt he'd angered her again.

Without a word she turned and followed the countess, not unlike a small boat in the wake of a larger ship. At least Miss Fenton was wise enough to obey the Countess of Straithern without argument. Perhaps the young woman was blessed with some common sense, after all.

He entered the Green Parlor to find that the room was aptly named. All the furnishings were in shades of green, and surprisingly, the colors didn't clash. There were stripes and flowers mixed in with hues of emerald, pale greenish-yellow, and olive. It was, however, essentially a feminine room, one almost overpoweringly so.

Lorenzo nodded at Dr. Fenton, who sat at one end of a settee facing the fireplace. The good doctor looked as uncomfortable as Lorenzo suddenly felt. But at least the older man didn't have the added disadvantage of being placed in close proximity to the countess. She sat not three feet away in an overstuffed wing chair, both hands braced on the arms as if it were a throne. Miss Fenton chose to sit on the other side of her father.

The countess frowned at Lorenzo as he waited for Miss Fenton to take her place beside the doctor. Either she disapproved of his manners, his attire, or his very existence. At this moment it was difficult to tell.

He sent a commiserating look toward the doctor, but Dr. Fenton looked away, not unlike a trapped animal that refuses any kindness before its death.

Why, exactly, was he here again? Ah, for Grant. His own wife had added her urgings to his decision.

"You must aid him, Lorenzo. Had it not been for him, we would have no future at all."

"It is my intention to do so, my dear wife," he'd said. "But I dislike leaving you for so long." He glanced down at her stomach. Although there was no sign yet, she was pregnant with their eighth child.

"We'll be fine, my dearest. And so will you. A parting at this time would not be a disadvantage for either of us."

Lorenzo had only smiled at the time, remembering how very irritable she became in the first months of pregnancy.

He couldn't help but wonder what Elise would think of such a gathering. The four of them all seated together, he and Dr. Fenton nodding as if they had some professional affiliation, when the other man had no notion that Lorenzo was a physician as well. Arabella was sitting beside her father, her arms jealously around her book, guarding her knowledge with more ferocity than her affianced husband. The countess was supremely composed and as regal as a queen, regarding them all a little as if they were rodents unexpectedly discovered in the pantry. And him? He wanted to be home in Florence with a desperation that had its roots in loneliness.

He wanted the cacophony of his children, the serenity of his beautiful wife, and the manipulative machinations of his in-laws. If it hadn't been for Grant, he wouldn't have married Elise at all, thanks to those greedy vultures. Her dowry was decimated; his fortune was not substantial enough for them. Grant had stepped in and given them a wedding gift, an amount of money so large that it had nearly staggered Lorenzo into silence, at least for a few moments. But he hadn't turned down Grant's generosity. To do so would be to lose Elise, and he wouldn't allow that to happen. So he'd stifled any pride that might have reared up at that moment, and accepted the gesture with the munificence it was offered. From that moment on he was determined to do anything in his power to repay his friend.

That's why he was cold and lonely, and missing Elise, and seated here in this parlor that could well have done with a fire. Was the countess as parsimonious with her wood and coal as she was her smiles?

A fire might have added to his comfort, but Lorenzo wasn't at all certain that he could ever warm up to Grant's future wife. What a terrible mismatch.

The countess looked at Arabella and without even a smile just flicked her fingers at her.

"You will serve, Arabella," she commanded.

For a long moment the two women regarded each other. Was Arabella thinking of rebellion? It seemed not, for in the next moment she put her book down on the settee beside her and leaned forward. Her movements were brisk as she handed the countess the first cup of tea, doing so with an almost challenging look.

Lorenzo took his cup from her and smiled, murmuring his thanks.

She didn't respond.

He wrapped his hands around the cup, and wondered how long it would take before his fingers lost their numbness. Was no one else in the godforsaken country ever cold? Were they all lizards? No wonder Grant spent five years in Italy.

"Will you be staying long, Count Paterno?" The countess smiled at him, and if the expression was a little forced, he could well imagine the reason why. Arabella was glaring at her as if to dare the older woman to say something critical.

He smiled back at her. "Not much longer," he said. "My wife expects me home soon."

The door was abruptly pushed open, and a footman dressed in immaculate livery stood in the doorway staring at the countess. His face was ashen, and from his harsh breathing it was evident he'd been in some haste to reach the room.

"Your Ladyship, forgive me."

The countess would have spoken, but the footman looked directly at Lorenzo. "The earl needs you, sir. There is some urgency."

Lorenzo stood, nearly spilling the rest of his tea as he set it down on the table before him. Both the doctor and Arabella stood as well.

"What is it?" Arabella asked.

"Can you hurry, sir?" the footman asked, coming to his side. "He's asked specifically for you."

"Is he ill?" he asked, concerned.

"It's Miss Cameron," the footman said. "I think she's dying."

Chapter 20

Grant moved backward a few steps, wrapping his arms around Gillian, supporting the whole of her weight. Perhaps if he made her walk, he might cause her to awaken. For the next quarter hour, he half dragged her around the room, cursing the chamber's small proportions. If he'd been at Rosemoor, he'd have had twenty feet in either direction, but as it was, there was only a few feet between the bed and the wall.

"Gillian, you cannot leave me like this. You cannot bedevil me on the one hand, and simply disappear from my life on the other. How will I survive? What will happen to my days if I do not see you in the morning? What will I do in the evenings without the sight of you at dinner, without your sparkling eyes teasing me?"

What would he do without her?

He was finding it more and more difficult to fall back into the role of earl. How very odd that with her he felt as if he were in Italy again, unencumbered by rank, simply enjoying his life.

She did that to him. She brought him freedom, and he hadn't realized it until this moment.

He heard Dr. Fenton before he saw him. The man was shouting as he walked down the corridor, the openness of the building echoing the sound of his orders.

Dr. Fenton hesitated beside the rotunda, and only then did Grant realize that he'd brought Arabella with him.

"Is she ill? What has befallen her?" She ducked beneath Dr. Fenton's outstretched arm when he would have held her back, and came up to Grant. She pushed Gillian's hair away from her face, the better to study the paleness of her features, no doubt.

"You must lay her down," Arabella commanded.

When he made no movement toward the bedroom, she frowned at him. "We need to cover her with a blanket and get her to drink some warm wine," she said.

He remained where he was.

"We need to do as Arabella said," Dr. Fenton said gently. "We will care for her, Your Lordship."

Grant took a step back. "The better for the poison to travel through her system? Would it not be best for her to be encouraged to rid herself of what's in her stomach?"

"How do you know she's been poisoned?" Arabella asked. She pulled on Gillian's shoulder, and he took another step away, turning slightly so his back was to the woman.

"Your suggestion has merit. If she were awake," the doctor said. "As it is, she might choke and die." Dr. Fenton took a few steps closer to Grant. "You can leave her in our care, Your Lordship. She must be warmed, and a few spoonfuls of red wine must be coaxed into her system. Please note, Your Lordship, her lips are bluish even now."

What Grant knew of medicine could be placed in a thimble, but he was possessed of good common sense.

"I don't agree with your treatment," he said, realizing that he probably looked the fool to both of them.

The responsibility he felt for Gillian's condition nearly suffocated him, but that was not something he could articulate to these two people. Neither of them looked as worried as he felt. Arabella, especially, looked almost feverish to have a patient to treat.

"Where's Lorenzo?" he asked the doctor, but Arabella answered.

"Your friend went to his room when he heard Gillian was ill. My father and I should be allowed to treat her." She came closer, and he simply ended the discussion by striding from the room, still carrying Gillian in his arms.

"Do not follow me," he said, when it was obvious that was just what the two were doing. Michael appeared at the opportune moment, and he gestured to the footman with his chin. "See that they are escorted back to Rosemoor," he ordered.

He crossed the sunlit space and down the long, wide corridor stretching the length of the palace. He rarely came this way, preferring to ignore the presence of the two wings that jutted off to the right and left of the building. He remembered, all too well, what he'd found in these rooms.

Reluctance halted him at the door to the wing. The key was still in the lock, as he'd expected it to be. His steward inspected the grounds and all the buildings periodically, since he'd been tasked with the good working order of Rosemoor. The man would see to it that the roof was repaired and the door hinges were oiled, and the rooms themselves repainted when necessary. MacTavish was a wonder, but as Grant turned the key in the lock and pulled the door open with one hand, he wished the man was not quite so good at his job.

The doors to the rooms were open, allowing sunlight to spill into the hall. At the end of the corridor was a large plaster bas-relief stretching from floor to ceiling of the Greek god Bacchus. In front of it was a small tiled pool.

He reached the pool and stepped down into the water, knowing that it would come to a grown man's waist. Evidently his father had enjoyed games of a sort enjoyed by emperors of Rome.

Gillian was already cold, and as he lowered her gently into the water, she began to tremble. He pushed her down, submerging her until even her face was covered, and then pulled her back out. She coughed, gasped, and coughed again, and this time her eyes opened, rolled back in her head, and shut again.

For hours, it seemed, he dunked her repeatedly. He gave no thought to his own comfort although he did have an errant thought that his valet—a man who gave no heed to either Grant's title or his thundering frowns—would be certain to demand an explanation for the condition of Grant's clothing.

Dear God, let her live.

Gillian's garments clung to her body. He could see the outline of each stay, and realized that he should have loosened them earlier. His fingers fumbled on her wet buttons and he managed to undo two of them. The rest would have to wait until later.

She moaned again, which he thought was a good sign. Now he needed to make sure that she rid herself of what poison she did consume.

He carried her back to his laboratory, the pristine marble of the floor dotted with a water trail, and gently deposited Gillian in the large overstuffed chair against the wall. Turning to the cabinet behind his tables, he stood staring at the array of bottles he kept locked there. What the hell could he use?

"You do not do the expected," Lorenzo said from behind him.

Grant turned to find his friend bending over Gillian, forcing her eyelids back to examine each eye. She was still not conscious and her color was even more ashen than before.

"I've never been so glad to see anyone in my life," Grant said. "What the hell can I use for an emetic?"

Lorenzo smiled and reached into a leather case he held, producing a small brown bottle. "Our minds travel alike, even though our hearts go in divergent paths, my friend."

He reached Lorenzo's side, but his friend refused to surrender the bottle.

"Why are you so certain it's poison?" Lorenzo asked.

"Because of what happened to Andrew and James. Because I would have eaten the bisque myself if she hadn't been here. Because I'm certain that someone's trying to kill me, and they might succeed in killing Gillian."

"Then we must ensure that this person is not successful," Lorenzo said.

His tone might have been light, but the look on his face was not. He didn't argue, which was one of the reasons that Grant had summoned him from Italy. Friendship brought silence, sometimes, but more importantly, it conveyed trust. At the moment, Grant needed someone to help him, not someone who would question everything he was attempting to do.

Lorenzo scooped Gillian up from the chair, sat, and placed her on his lap. Before Grant could comment or protest, Lorenzo held the bottle to her lips.

"At least you did not ask me for the antidote to poison. A great many of your countrymen think that because I come from Italy, I know a great deal about ways to kill people."

"If I thought you knew anything," Grant said, "believe me, I would have sought your counsel."

"You simply needed me to remove those two from your vicinity, is that it?" With a jerk of his head, he indicated the other room. Only then did Grant realize that Arabella and Dr. Fenton were still in the building. He could hear Arabella's voice from here.

"Miss Cameron would not want you to witness what will happen next, my friend. Women do not, on the whole, like to be ill around their lovers. You can busy yourself bidding your guests goodbye."

Grant was torn.

"Your guests will not leave," Lorenzo said. "Your manservant is holding them back with great expertise, but I fear he is nothing to your bride-to-be's determination."

The two men exchanged a look.

"You must handle them, my friend. I will stay with the little Scottish kitten. I am a very good doctor. I will stay with her until she wakes."

"If she wakes," Grant said.

"Go and see to your stubborn fiancée. I will treat the kitten."

When Grant didn't move, Lorenzo smiled. "It is a smitten man who will gaze upon an ill woman with such favor."

"I hardly think I'm smitten, Lorenzo. She ate something meant for me. I'm simply trying to save her life."

"Then leave me to my duties while you attend to yours, my friend."

For several minutes after Grant left the room, Gillian didn't make a sound. Lorenzo had to bend closer to hear her breathing, it was so shallow.

Lorenzo waved the bottle in front of her nose until she took a startled gasp. Not only was it an emetic, but it had a foul odor and had succeeded, more than once, in summoning a patient back from unconsciousness.

Her eyes flickered open once, and then her head fell back.

"Miss Cameron! Can you hear me?"

Frustrated, he slapped at her face, at first gently, and then with more force.

A paroxysm of coughs escaped her, a fact that pleased him enormously.

The poison might be fast acting, in which case he could do nothing. But he was not about to fail now, especially since it was very clear his friend had feelings for this woman.

Quickly he unfastened the rest of her buttons, and pulled apart her wet dress. With great difficulty he loosened her stays and slipped his hands between them and her chemise.

She was as cold as the grave.

"Miss Cameron?"

He began to rub her torso with both his hands, attempting to warm her. He laid her back against the chair arm and briskly scrubbed at her skin.

She made a sound, a response, and he smiled, inordinately pleased. Perhaps it wasn't too late after all.

He held the bottle to her lips, and she made a protesting movement of her head, another sign of consciousness that he rejoiced in seeing.

Lorenzo persisted until she finally roused enough to take a sip. The liquid didn't stay in her mouth, however. Slowly, patiently, he managed to get a little of the emetic down her throat. A few moments later it had the expected results. He reached for the bucket holding the bottle of wine, and held her hair back as she was ill.

When he lowered her back in the chair, she was even paler than before. Her lips weren't quite so bluish, however, and her breathing seemed less shallow. He forced her to swallow more of the emetic, and when she was ill again, he repeated his actions.

He didn't care how sick she became, as long as she survived.

"No," Grant said, "you can't see her."

He stood framed in the doorway of his laboratory,

irritated that Dr. Fenton and Arabella were invading his privacy. This room was rarely seen by any inhabitant of Rosemoor, and he wanted it that way. He especially wanted no memory of Arabella in this chamber, and he pushed that thought away to examine more closely later.

For right now, he wanted them gone so that he could return to Gillian's side. However, the two of them seemed just as intent to ignore his every word and care for Gillian themselves.

"Your Lordship, if she has truly been poisoned, she may die without treatment," Dr. Fenton said. He took a step toward Grant, but Grant simply put both arms up on the frame of the door, effectively blocking the entrance to the room. The only other way to his bedchamber was through the hallway and Michael's room, and he doubted if either one of these determined personages could find their way through that maze.

"You'll have to get through me to get to Gillian," he said. "As angry as I am at the moment, that will prove to be an impossible task."

"I do not approve, Your Lordship," Dr. Fenton said, pulling himself up to his full height and looking as if he were ready for battle. "Gillian is under my protection, and should not be examined by a strange man."

"Nor by a foreigner," Arabella said.

Grant didn't bother to hide his disdain. "Dr. Fenton, you do not approve of anything Gillian does. I don't care what either of you think of Lorenzo. He's a very talented doctor himself."

"I doubt he knows our methods, Your Lordship,"

Arabella said. "He might not be versed on the newest treatments."

"I trust him implicitly," Grant said, deliberately allowing them to construe what they would.

"I must insist, Your Lordship," Dr. Fenton said, a comment that elicited a smile from Grant.

"So do I, sir," he said, taking a step back into his laboratory. He reached out and closed the door in their faces, and just for good measure, locked it.

Chapter 21

If death were a color, it would be grayish brown. If it had a smell, it would be sour, like the earth deprived of the sun, and if it had a flavor, it would mimic the taste in Gillian's mouth exactly at that moment.

Some tiny little person wearing giant hobnail boots was stomping through her stomach. In addition, she ached in places she'd never even felt before this morning, as if God were calling attention to the fact that she was alive, but not quite whole. Instead, she was composed of aching bits that were barely held together.

She would have moaned, but it seemed too much of an effort.

When had she becomes so ill? In the middle of the night? She tried to open her eyes, but her lids felt so heavy that it was an effort to do so. Better to let sleep cascade over her like a waterfall.

Water. Cold water. What a very unpleasant dream.

Grant had been there, solicitous and angry by turns. He'd demanded that she do something. Why couldn't she remember? Everything was a blur and yet some memories seemed sharper than normal. She slid her hands beneath the covers and felt for the pillow beneath her head. A moment later she buried her face in it, and waited for the nausea to pass.

Slowly, she rolled over toward the middle of the bed. Please, no, she couldn't be sick again. Her stomach was already so sore.

"Ah, you've finally awakened. Are you still feeling ill, Miss Cameron?"

She opened her eyes to find Lorenzo bending over her solicitously. She would have answered him, but words seemed impossible at the moment. He seemed, blessedly, to understand.

He reached out his hand, placed it on her forehead, and pushed back her damp hair.

"Your stomach, she is not settled, true?"

Gillian only closed her eyes in response, hoping he would take that for an assent. Again, it seemed as if he understood exactly what she was feeling.

"I've had to give you some powerful medicine, and the effects are very bad. But they should wear off soon, and then I'll give you some warmed wine perhaps."

He didn't linger on any description of food or beverage, for which Gillian was deeply grateful. Instead he slid something across the sheet to her. Her hand reached out and brushed against the cold sides of a porcelain bowl.

Evidently she was not through with being ill, and how perceptive of him to recognize it.

Lorenzo bathed her face a few moments later. The cool cloth felt wonderful against her skin. What a gentle touch he had. She could imagine all his patients in Italy missed him desperately. When he would have raised her to a sitting position, however, she protested weakly.

"Come," he coaxed. "Rinse your mouth at least."

She did so, and when he offered her some wine, she took a sip from the cup he pressed to her lips. She managed to swallow a little of the bitter liquid. Perhaps now he'd leave her alone.

"Is your stomach settling?"

"Not really," she said, when she lay back again. She reached out, grabbed her pillow, and pressed it to her midriff. He covered her first with a sheet and then the blanket before removing the bowl.

"How long?" she asked. Two words seemed to be the limit of her ability to speak.

"Until you feel better? With each person, it differs." He shrugged. "A day, perhaps. Maybe two. For now you should not worry how much time it takes, and simply rest. Your body has been through much and must recover."

"What happened?"

"I think I should let Grant tell you," he said.

She would have nodded, but suddenly the effort to do so seemed monumental. Had he put something in the wine? Before she could ask him, she drifted off to sleep.

It didn't matter that he was the 10th Earl of Straithern. If anyone found him here, Grant would be hard-pressed to explain his presence or the fact that he was packing a valise for a woman who was, as the world would see it, a stranger.

The very fact that he'd entered her room would be seen as shocking, let alone his actions of the past five minutes. He'd already carefully folded her four dresses and was now picking her chemises and stockings from the drawer in the bottom of the armoire. He really should have called in one of the maids to do this, but he didn't want to alert anyone at Rosemoor to what was happening at the palace.

The sad fact was, besides Lorenzo, he didn't know exactly whom he could trust. Therefore, it was better to trust no one at all.

He lifted the last of her belongings from the armoire. He'd never before invaded a woman's domain, never packed a woman's possessions while wondering at the history of them. Did she wear this when she met Robert? Had Robert ever seen this chemise? Had she owned this as the daughter of a prosperous Edinburgh merchant?

She'd gone from being, if not a cosseted daughter, then certainly a privileged one, to being a servant. That, alone, wasn't enough to anger him. Gillian wasn't the type of person to inspire pity. He felt admiration, perhaps, for her strength, and empathy for her grief. But her wardrobe made him pause, and think of what the last two years must have been like for her.

Her nightgowns were worn, the embroidery at the yoke faded from so many washings. The hem at the cuffs was frayed and had been carefully mended with small, telling little stitches.

His mother's clothing could barely be housed in one room, yet Gillian's belongings were easily packed into half a valise.

That errand done, he left her room quietly, so as not to alert Arabella in the adjoining room. He didn't know what he would say to her.

"What is this about your stealing one of Cook's helpers, Grant? And where do you think you're going with that valise?" His mother moved out into the hall, planted her fists on her ample hips, and glared at him. "Do not frown at me, son, I am your mother despite your age or your rank. I do expect an answer from you, Grant."

"Are you certain you're ready to hear it?"

She looked a little less irritated, but she stood her ground.

"Very well, Mother," he said, halting directly in front of her. "I am moving to the palace."

His mother paled, and he could well understand why. She'd avoided the structure ever since his father's death.

"It will not be for long," he said. "Just until I ascertain exactly who wants me dead, and who's responsible for James's and Andrew's death."

She took a step backward as if to refute everything he had just said. "What do you mean?"

"Someone tried to poison me, Mother, and they nearly succeeded with Miss Cameron. They did succeed with my brothers."

Her trembling hand hesitated at her throat. "You cannot mean—" Her words abruptly stopped, and her expression softened for a moment before her face firmed. "I cannot believe you, Grant. These are wild tales, and such things do not happen. James and Andrew died of a blood disease."

"Talk to Dr. Fenton. Better yet, speak to Lorenzo."

He brushed past her.

"Who would do this, Grant? If this is true, who want my sons dead?"

He didn't respond. There were no answers he could give her.

"Is she with you? Miss Cameron? Is she with you?"

He didn't halt, didn't turn.

"Have you no care for this family's reputation?"

He stopped at that.

"Have all my efforts in the past twenty years been for nothing, Grant? Will you join your father in trying to destroy this family?"

He turned slowly, walking back to her in measured steps.

"Do you care more for reputation than life, Mother? Are James and Andrew your beloved sons now simply because they're dead? They can't be loud or troublesome. You'll never get another letter from school about James, and Andrew will never concern you with his choice of bed partners. They'll never spend money lavishly, and they'll never bring their friends home, and they'll never embarrass you again."

"How can you say such a thing? I mourn them every day."

"Do you? Or are you simply thankful that they had the good manners to die in a discreet and genteel way? I would prefer to have them alive, Mother, boisterous, and rude, and scandalous."

"Do you hate me so much that you would say such things?"

"I think you choose martyrdom over life, Mother, and for that, I pity you. I think the living frighten you. Why else would you hole yourself up at Rosemoor as if it's a mausoleum?"

"Guilt."

Startled, he could only stare at his mother.

"Guilt, my dear son, and I have no intention of ex-

plaining that to you. Think what you will, Grant, and
do what you will. I cannot alter your course."

She turned and began to walk in the direction of
her chamber, leaving Grant to suddenly wonder what
she was hiding.

Chapter 22

When Gillian woke again, her first thought was that she was being punished not only for loving Grant, but for bedding him. Her second thought was that she was grateful Grant wasn't in the room, this observation being made after lifting her head and recognizing the room as Grant's bedchamber in the palace.

How long had she been here?

"Ah, now you are feeling better," Lorenzo said. He smiled, approaching her with a tray in his hands.

She sat up gingerly, surprised she didn't feel worse. But before she could wave away the food he brought her, she realized it wasn't breakfast on the tray, but a treasure trove of items any woman would adore: a silver-backed mirror and brush, a long comb with wide teeth, the better to disentangle one's hair. A toothbrush, basin, and a small ewer of water sat next to a jar of something called Lady Pomeroy's Mouth Treatment.

"I think you are the most wonderful soul on the face of the earth," she said, sitting up fully. "Whatever made you think of all these things?"

"I am married, little one. A man who loves a woman will tell you that a woman's mood matches how she looks. Or how she believes she looks. You see, I have seen many beautiful women who do not believe they're beautiful. I have seen women who are, how you might say, plain. But they think they are beautiful, and so they act as if they are the loveliest creatures in all the world."

She sat back against the pillows and regarded Lorenzo with more favor than she had before. "I suspect you're very wise in the ways of women. Does it come from a great deal of experience?"

"I confess that I have a great appreciation of women. I do not act upon it, however. I have a beautiful woman of my own at home."

She would have asked more questions of Lorenzo, specifically what had happened to her, and how long she'd been ill, but he bowed and disappeared, leaving her alone in the bedroom.

How very strange that she could remember nothing beyond yesterday afternoon. Or was it even yesterday? She had come to the palace, to watch the experiment with the marsh gas. Something she probably shouldn't have done at all. But she'd wanted to, and it seemed more and more difficult to disobey her inclinations where Grant was concerned.

They had loved; she couldn't forget that.

She arranged the pillows, taking longer at the task than it required, before subsiding against the heavily carved headboard. Slowly she began to comb her hair free of tangles. Why had she gone to bed without braiding her hair? Had she fallen ill? If so, why was she not being treated by Dr. Fenton or Arabella?

The questions would not cease, but she had no way to ascertain the answers.

She laid the comb down, feeling almost too weak to continue with her chore. She disliked being ill. On the whole, she'd been healthy most of her life. True, there were colds and an occasional fever, but she'd never felt as she did right at this moment, as if the strength had been leached from her.

She laid her head back against the pillows, closing her eyes and allowing herself to drift off into a light doze. She was roused some moments later by the sound of a door closing, and then a low voice she recognized only too well. She opened her eyes and gripped the comb almost like a weapon, wishing she had the strength to finish combing her hair. She must look like a disheveled horror. But the task seemed beyond her, and even a smile was a chore.

When Grant entered the room, she pushed aside the thought that her heartbeat escalated, and she somehow felt a little better.

"It is not entirely proper for you to be here," she said. Her voice was low, but there was determination in her glance. Still, he took another step toward her, only stopping when she held up her hand.

He smiled. "We haven't been very proper together, Gillian."

"Yet you are the very one who warned me of your nature," she said, plucking at the sheet. "Are you not given to an excess of propriety?"

"Did you find me excessively proper yesterday?"

He didn't back off, or turn and leave the room. Instead he came and sat on the edge of the bed as if he were a predatory animal and somehow knew how weak she was, almost injured by emotion. His smile, however, bore not one hint of triumph. Instead it seemed to be an almost confused expression, as if he were experiencing the same paradoxical thoughts as she. *Go away. Come closer.*

She wasn't to fall in love. She had not planned on it. In fact, she had given herself numerous strict lectures, especially upon arriving at Rosemoor. She didn't want to experience this feeling deep inside her stomach as if she were weightless, as if she had run quite a distance and could not quite catch her breath. Or as if there were a yearning inside for something she couldn't quite name.

She closed her eyes and shook her head, and she could feel him lean closer. When he spoke her name in that quiet voice, barely above a whisper, she shook her head again.

"Gillian," he said once more.

Suddenly she wanted to be honest with him, expose every single one of her thoughts, reveal every emotion, allowing herself to be vulnerable in front of him. But to do so would be to also expose the nature of her need, the depth of her potential despair. How very foolish she was to ignore the past. Yet for the first time she felt that she might be safe enough to be weak, to surrender for just a little while. She needn't be so careful of herself.

But caution held her mute and restraint came to her pride's defense. What would she do if he repudiated her? What if he was kind? What if he was understanding, but distant?

I love you, Grant. She could almost hear the words she might speak to him. What if he nodded and smiled perfunctorily? What if he patted her hand with an absent gesture, avuncular in his cruelty? What would she do? How could she bear the pain?

Perhaps it was best not to know his reaction. She would remain in blissful ignorance, an inhabitant of this strange and coddled world.

It was her own fault, after all. She had ignored all the warnings.

"How are you feeling?"

"Like someone beat me from the inside out," she said, and then wondered if she should have been more delicate in her response.

His smile faded. "I expect you will, for a few days at least," Grant said.

When he reached for her hand, she simply let him take it and cradle it between both of his.

"What happened?" She might have frowned at him if she had the energy, but as it was she simply pointed her comb in his direction.

"Do you remember eating my lunch?"

She shook her head, and then decided that was not wise since it made her unaccountably dizzy.

"No," she said. "The last thing I remember is the morning." She felt herself warm.

"The marsh?"

His smile was back.

She did frown at him now. "No," she admitted. "Later."

"When we made love."

She looked away, toward the fireplace. How intricate the carved mantel was, and how strange that she hadn't noticed it before now.

"I'm grateful you didn't lose that memory," he said softly.

How could she?

"I became ill after eating your lunch," she said, determined to get him back to the subject at hand. "Was it soured milk or tainted meat?"

"No," he said shaking his head. "I suspect it was deliberate, Gillian, just as I'm afraid that you were an unwitting victim."

She let her head fall back against the pillow. She knew she was still recuperating, but surely she should be able to reason with more clarity. "Are you saying I was poisoned?" she asked. "And that it was meant for you?"

"Yes."

She met his gaze. "I hope you're wrong," she said.

"I'm not. Even Lorenzo concurs."

"Dear God," she whispered.

"I'm keeping you here until you've recovered, or until I've determined who is behind this."

"You can't," she said. If she felt stronger, she would have countered his announcement with more vigor. As it was, she was grateful to have the strength to speak.

He stood and walked away, hesitating at the door.

"I'm the Earl of Straithern. I can do anything I damn well please at Rosemoor. And do not, I beg you, implore me to think of your reputation. What good is unsullied honor when you're dead?"

"So you're going to keep me here for my own good, and let the world go fiddle?"

He leaned up against the doorjamb and folded his arms. The perfect posture for an earl, an aristocrat.

Yet he didn't seem so much an earl at the moment, as much as he was simply Grant.

"Exactly."

"I'm your prisoner, then?" she asked incredulously.

"If you choose to think of it that way," he said, his voice low. "I choose to think of it as keeping you safe."

He took a step toward her, and then hesitated. "I'll send someone to be with you if that would make you more comfortable. Agnes? If not her, are there any of the other young girls at Rosemoor you'd choose? I'll have a footman stationed outside your door, if you like. And one in the corridor."

"Everyone knows I'm here, don't they?"

"Arabella and Dr. Fenton are both aware. I'm certain the entire staff at Rosemoor knows by now."

"And your mother?"

"Yes," he said.

"So, regardless of what is done from this point forward, the damage has already been done." The damage was done the moment she agreed to come back to his laboratory, but she didn't bother to make that comment.

"This is Rosemoor. I will not allow anyone to say a word about you, Gillian." As autocratic a statement as she had ever heard from him.

"You cannot rule the world, Grant," she said softly, the enormity of her dilemma occurring to her. "However much you wish to, you cannot change people's opinions, and even if they say nothing at all, they will think it. A dozen duennas would be a good thing, and perhaps a witness or two that we did nothing wrong, nothing scandalous."

She met his gaze. "But we can't do that, can we?"

"Do you regret it?"

Perhaps she would have been a better person if she could have said she did. No, there was something in her own nature that called out to her to push away the restrictions of the past two years, to become as emboldened as she felt deep inside. Perhaps she was too like the girl she'd been in Edinburgh, the one who'd fallen in love with Robert deeply enough to push aside all the tenets of her upbringing. Perhaps she hadn't learned anything after all.

If she were truly wise, she would seek the countess's influence in securing another position. Perhaps she would even go back to her parents' home, and beg admittance, or room and board in exchange for caring for the little ones. How very odd that none of those opportunities seemed preferable to this moment, staring at the Earl of Straithern and wondering at her wantonness.

How very strange and how very wrong of her.

For most of her life, she'd been sheltered from the privations she might have experienced had her father not been so wealthy or loving. But in the last two years, she'd known hardship and grief. She'd looked around her and seen what other people perhaps had always known, that life was not necessarily pristine or kind. Simply living could be brutal, and joy should be cherished when it was found.

And passion? Passion should be treasured as well because it didn't often exist. Passion was like a sunbeam on a cloudy day or a shooting star across the heavens. Passion was one of those emotions that should be held tight to the heart and cherished.

She'd known passion with the Earl of Straithern, a blinding, yearning need far in excess of anything she'd ever felt for Robert.

"Do you regret it?" he asked again.

She shook her head. "Regret is foolish, isn't it? We cannot undo what we did."

His expression changed, became sterner, as if he were angry but attempting to hide his feelings.

"Did you care for me? When I was ill?"

"Lorenzo was with you the entire night."

She looked down at the comb in her hand.

"Do you disapprove?"

She glanced up at him. There was no doubt of his annoyance now.

"Was there no one else in attendance?" she asked.

"No."

"Why didn't Dr. Fenton treat me?"

"Because I don't exactly trust Dr. Fenton," Grant said.

She stared at him. "You cannot be serious."

"My brothers were poisoned, Gillian. How do I know that Dr. Fenton did not orchestrate their deaths somehow?"

"Anyone could have tampered with your meal," she said.

"Exactly."

"But why? Why does someone want you dead?"

"If I knew that, I'd know the identity of the person doing this," he said. "Who do you want as chaperone, and I will summon her. But do not, I beg you, ask for Arabella."

"I would not," she admitted. "Even though being in attendance at a bedside makes her very happy." A moment later, she apologized. "Forgive me; I should not have said what I did. She excels at treating the ill, and gains great pleasure from it. She should be commended, not castigated."

"Whom do you think would suit me, Gillian?"

They regarded each other for a moment.

"You do not think Arabella will suit. Whom should I choose?"

Perhaps it was because she felt so weak, or because she still hurt so abominably, but the answer came without restraint. "Someone warm, someone who is given to demonstrations of affection. Someone to offset your occasional coldness. Someone who would make you laugh. Someone who would make you see the absurdity of things. Someone who would dare you to be more human."

She had angered him, she could tell. There was a tightness to his smile now, and his chin looked as if it had been formed of granite. His gaze did not veer from her, his eyes seeming to bore right through the sheet.

"You did ask," she said. "It is no good giving me that very aristocratic look of yours. I am not afraid of you, Grant."

He startled her by smiling. "Do I have an aristocratic look?" he asked. "If so, I was unaware. Most of the time, I am simply involved in my own thoughts. Not how my face might appear to others."

"Oh, you're very handsome, but very distant. Stern and stiff as if you were very, very conscious of who you are, or want to remind other people of it."

"Do I have any other flaws you'd like to correct, Miss Cameron?"

She'd offended him or angered him. Either way, it was better than him remaining at her bedside, solicitous.

She shook her head just once, and suddenly he was gone. He simply closed the door behind him with a smart click of the latch. She was alone, staring at the closed door and wishing she could call him back.

He was not cold, damn it. Nor was he so involved in being an earl that he forgot he was a man. He was perfectly capable of humor, of feeling emotions.

Why did she think he was distant? He'd never acted that way around her. But he should be, perhaps, if for no other reason than kindness. It was all too evident that someone wanted him dead. Why should he encourage her to feel anything for him when he might die before his time?

Did he want her to mourn him, and what an unprincipled, sorry excuse for a bastard was he to even ask that question? Hell no, he didn't want her to mourn him—he didn't want to die! A long and happy life was suddenly a prize held just beyond his grasp, and it angered him that he wasn't entirely certain he could reach it.

He walked into his laboratory to find Lorenzo there, sprawled in the chair.

"Have I done something to deserve that scowl, my friend? Did Miss Cameron complain of my treatment? Is that why you have such a fierce look on your face?"

"I am annoyed on general principles, Lorenzo."

"The lovely Miss Gillian, perhaps? Is she the cause of your annoyance?"

Lorenzo was his greatest friend, but there were some things Grant didn't share with even him, especially how he felt about Gillian. "Women are not worth the effort it takes to endure their presence," was the only thing he said.

"On the contrary, my friend. Women are the only thing worth the effort it takes. If you have not discovered that for yourself, then I'd truly pity you. Earl or not, you are a poor man indeed."

"Why the hell does everybody keep reminding me of my title?"

"Because you keep reminding everyone of it as well. The very way you carry yourself, your speech, and your very glances. I think you have become more the earl since you have returned to Scotland than you ever were in Italy."

"I have responsibilities, Lorenzo. Especially now."

"I understand your grief, my friend. It is not an easy thing to lose those you love. But you will not honor their lives or console yourself over their deaths if you make yourself miserable. They would not what you to simply cease feeling."

The very last thing he wanted to discuss was his emotions. They swirled around him as it was, threatening to drown out his intellect. "Are the kitchens salvageable?" he asked.

"Indeed, they are. Whoever built this Pleasure Palace of yours was not frugal. Your new cook's eyes lit up upon seeing the space where she would have to work. Myself, I think she would be just as happy never leaving this place."

"And the testers?"

"A very odd task you've given me, my friend. I cannot wait to tell Elise what duties I was given to perform: the catching of mice."

"Better a mouse should sacrifice his life than a human being," Grant said.

"There were a number of men in your employ who would have volunteered for the position of taster. For all your disposition, Grant, you inspire great loyalty."

"Is there something about me that brings out comments on my disposition? Is there something special about this particular day?"

"I take it, then, Miss Cameron has remarked upon it?" Lorenzo asked.

"She has."

"Such remarks are not to your liking?"

"Why do you look so decidedly amused, Lorenzo? As if she has done something deserving of commendation?"

"I think she is not so afraid of you. Even in Italy, there were a great many women who might have been attracted to you, my friend, had it not been for your frowns."

"I have not had much to smile about of late, Lorenzo."

"Perhaps you've forgotten how. Perhaps Miss Cameron will remind you. I was against this idea of yours, in the beginning," Lorenzo confessed. "But the more I give it time, the more I think it would be a very good thing for both of you."

Grant turned and regarded his friend.

"What idea is that?"

"Keeping her here, with you," Lorenzo said.

"It's for her own protection."

Lorenzo smiled and stood.

"This is not about Miss Cameron. Nor is it about us being here together. It's about something more important, Lorenzo. Our very lives."

"Life itself is unexpected, Grant," Lorenzo countered. "We never know if the next day will come. Ah, but if you can enjoy the night before, who cares?"

"I don't have your taste for hedonism, Lorenzo."

"Pity. If you did, I believe that your life would be a great deal more enjoyable, my friend. Perhaps you should be cautious, Grant, but enjoy the circumstances as well."

Lorenzo smiled as Michael entered the room, brushing past the young man on his way out the door. "I shall do what I can to keep the wolves from your door, Grant. In the meantime, I suggest you take advantage of this opportunity. Have a little enjoyment. Enjoy the circumstances."

Grant waited until he heard the sound of his footsteps on the marble floor. He knew the building so well, he could tell when Lorenzo had approached the rotunda and was nearly out the door.

Only then did he turn to Michael. "Have you obtained all the items on my list?"

Michael bowed slightly. "Yes, Your Lordship, I have. Everything is in the wagon outside."

"See that it's unloaded," Grant said. "And have one of the maids ready the room across from the rotunda. I'll be sleeping there."

Michael bowed once more and left the room without further need for instructions.

Enjoy the circumstances? Was Lorenzo daft? Gillian was dependent upon him, to guard not only her reputation, but her life.

There was nothing to enjoy about the circumstances. Nothing at all. She could have died. The world would have been a much less pleasant place, a thought he'd never gotten around to telling her. Nor had he ever told her how much he enjoyed their conversations. He'd become accustomed to her presence at Rosemoor, finding that she enlivened his home somehow. She'd been here only a month, and she'd changed his life.

He often strode through the grove where she liked to walk in the morning, and he'd stand beneath one venerable oak and put his palm on the trunk as he'd seen her do once or twice. As if she was communing with the tree or feeling the beat of life beneath her hand.

He found himself standing on the veranda outside the ballroom, surveying all of Rosemoor and wondering what she saw when she looked at the view he'd always taken for granted.

He discovered that he had perfect recall when it came to what she said, and could play snippets of conversation over and over again in his mind. Nor had he ever before been able to remember the tone of a woman's voice.

Enjoy the circumstances? He would be the worst idiot in the world to even give credence to that idea.

He was never going to forget how she looked sitting there pale and wan against the pillows. Her appearance seemed to bring out a protective nature he'd never known he possessed until today. He wanted to lay her gently down on the bed, cover her with the sheet and blanket and ensure himself she was warm. He wanted to take the comb from her hand so that she couldn't point it at him imperiously, and then play lady's maid. He'd finish combing her hair, smoothing it away from her face.

He could stare at her face for hours, measure the purity of it, the exact width between her eyes and the color of them, a dark blue so deep in color they appeared almost black sometimes. He wanted to trace a line from the lobe of her ear to the tip of her nose, and then draw in the outline of her smiling lips.

He wasn't besotted. He was simply insane. Or wild with lust.

He worked in his laboratory for a few hours, annoyed that, for the first time, he was conscious of the passing of time. He wanted to check on Gillian, yet he stopped himself, holding out that task as if it were a reward for his dedication. A few more notes, a few components of the experiment, and he would allow himself to visit her.

They shared a meal, although not in the same room. He'd taken the dinner trays from Cook and fed them to cages of mice, watching them carefully for any signs of illness. When a half hour passed and they didn't appear affected, he called Michael and had him deliver the tray to Gillian.

"Ask her if she requires anything," he instructed Michael.

"I shall, Your Lordship," Michael said.

"Be sure to tell her that if she needs anything at all, we can provide it."

Michael bowed.

Before Michael left the room, Grant called him back. "Tell her I'm sorry for the coldness of the meal, but that it was unavoidable."

"Yes, Your Lordship."

He ate his own dinner at the table in his laboratory. The pleasure of food had been stripped from him, to be replaced with caution.

A quarter hour later, Michael knocked on the laboratory door.

"Miss Cameron would like to convey her thanks to you, Your Lordship. She said the dinner was delicious, and that it didn't matter that it was cold."

"And you? Michael? Have you eaten?"

"Not yet, Your Lordship, but Cook is holding back something for me."

"Take the rest of the evening off, I shall not need you."

"Are you certain, Your Lordship?"

He could count on the fingers of his left hand those things he was certain about, but he didn't say that to Michael. Instead, he only nodded. Before the young man left the room, however, Grant called after him.

"Is she well?" He amended that question a moment later. "Is she feeling better than she did this morning?"

"She looked very well, Your Lordship."

It wasn't the answer he wanted. He wanted Michael to be able to say: *Yes, her cheeks are rosy, and she smiled at me, Your Lordship. Her eyes flashed intelligence and temper and impatience. She was quick with her questions and with her praise, and she laughed in delight over some silly remark.*

Michael would say none of those things, even if they'd been true. But he might say, with a young man's candor: *She is a beautiful woman, Your Lordship. She has a certain radiance about her, a certain fluidity to her movements, as if she dances when she walks.*

Michael wouldn't say that to him because Grant was the Earl of Straithern, and evidently, he was determined to impress that fact upon everyone he met. At least according to his friend and a woman he very much wanted to impress.

There, the truth of it, the whole unpalatable truth. He wanted to be more than a man in her eyes. He wanted to be greater than he was. More intelligent, more talented, more instructive, more learned, more of a man.

"Thank you, Michael," he said, releasing the footman. "That will be all."

After Michael left, he extinguished one of the lamps and walked to the window. Unlike a great many of the rooms in the palace, this room had a series of windows. He could see outside, and the world could see in. There was nothing shocking or horrifying to witness. There was nothing in this room that would offend the sensibilities, except for an earl who was on the verge of becoming a fool.

How odd that he'd never before realized how lonely a life he lived. Even in Italy he was alone, and he'd counted those years as the best of his life. What was it that Lorenzo said? Something about women being afraid of him.

He'd had a mistress while in Italy, an older woman who was mature enough to know that he could not give her anything permanent. Had he at least given her affection? He'd deeded a house to her and a carriage, and enough money to keep her in comfort for a good number of years. She had been appropriately grateful, but he didn't think she was grief-stricken when he left for Scotland.

Until this moment, he'd not given her one thought.

What sort of man has an intimate relationship with a woman and then banishes her from his thoughts with ease? A man with other things on his mind, perhaps. Or one who never quite lowered the barrier between himself and others.

He was not cold or distant. He was simply involved in his work, that's all. He had many friends, many acquaintances.

Yet he'd arranged to marry a woman he'd never met because he couldn't be bothered to search out a wife. Or because he'd known the search would require him to feign interest in someone other than himself. He'd be forced to demonstrate emotions he wasn't at all certain he possessed.

Dear God, he *was* cold and distant.

Until Gillian came to Rosemoor.

He'd felt desire before, knew passion in its many guises, but he'd never felt it as quickly as he had around Gillian. He wanted to know all the nuances she experienced. Did her blood heat as quickly as his; did her heart race as rapidly? Did she feel as if she were soaring high above the earth when pleasure came to her, and oddly sad later, when nature forced them to separate? Strange questions he'd never before thought, let alone wanted to share.

She was grace and beauty, and life. A woman of such disparate temperaments that he was fascinated despite reason or prudence or his own nature.

Nor did he ever want to share knowledge with anyone the way he did with her. He wanted to tell her of his work today, that he'd put aside the marsh gas and chosen another experiment, that of magnetizing a surface electrically.

There was no one else he could tell. No one who would care.

Did she fascinate him simply because he was lonely, and because he hadn't had a woman in his life for some time? Or was it because he dreaded and regretted the idea of marriage?

He didn't know what the answers were, but he did know he was tired of asking himself questions. He just wanted to forget for a while. He wanted to forget who he was and the past that would not let him go and the future that stretched before him like a long and dusty—and lonely—road. He wanted, strangely enough, to be someone entirely different from who he was.

Enjoy the circumstances? Not damn likely.

Michael brought her dinner, and although she thought at first that she wouldn't be able to eat, her appetite returned at the sight of the roast beef. There was crusty bread as well, and something that tasted like pear tart for dessert. The hot chocolate was absolutely delicious, and the bread was flavored with onions. She opened a small porcelain container to find it filled with mustard, a rich, spicy mustard that made the roast beef taste even better, if that was possible.

Food seemed to have more flavor than it ever had. Could it be because she'd despaired of living to see another day? In her hazy recollection of illness, she remembered being afraid, so desperately afraid that she'd felt cold from the inside out.

Her dinner done, she lay back against the pillows and stared up at the ceiling. There were touches of wealth even here, in a room Grant rarely used. A large decorative plaster rosette was carved in the middle of the ceiling, and in the center of it hung a chain supporting a massive crystal chandelier. A rope mounted on the other side of the room was connected to a pulley, and evidently lowered the chandelier so the candles could be lit and then the whole apparatus hauled back into place.

Before bringing her dinner, Michael had moved an armoire and a vanity into the room. On orders of the earl, he'd said, bowing to her. She hadn't been surprised at either item. Grant was evidently determined to keep her here, but her prison would be luxurious.

She put the tray aside and slipped from the bed. Someone had placed her dresses inside. The bottom drawers were filled with her chemises, stays, and stockings. Had Michael performed such an intimate chore? Her face warmed as she thought of the footman handling her garments.

In the vanity drawer were her silver-backed brush and comb, a gift from her parents on her eighteenth birthday and one of the few items she'd taken from her childhood home.

She found a wrapper and donned it, feeling slightly dizzy as she raised her arms. Gillian realized she didn't have any energy, but that was to be expected after being so close to death.

Who would want to hurt the Earl of Straithern? Or had someone tried to poison her? She brushed her hair, wishing that whoever was kind enough to fetch her clothing also had had the foresight to acquire hairpins. But she removed a ribbon from one of her chemises, and tied back her braid as well as she could.

She looked like a schoolgirl, someone innocent and

without knowledge. None of the experiences of the past two years seemed to show in her eyes, as if being poisoned had wiped grief, sorrow, and disillusion from her memory.

She needed to be brave and go in search of Grant. She needed to tell him that she had to go back to Rosemoor immediately. It would not do to have rumors accompany her to Edinburgh or Inverness. Being the Earl of Straithern's mistress was hardly suitable experience for employment as a milliner or a seamstress.

That would be the proper course of action, the right thing to do. She should leave Rosemoor at once, seek employment, and begin her life over again.

She must see Grant and tell him so. She'd demand that he allow her to return to Rosemoor. Once there, she'd simply tell Dr. Fenton and Arabella—and the countess as well, she supposed—that she had been too ill to return earlier. They would never need to know about that afternoon. But she would, and she'd keep that memory forever.

What was this excitement she was feeling? Her chest seemed to vibrate with the pounding of her heart, and her breath seemed tight with anticipation, all because she was going to see Grant.

She should run in the other direction, as quickly as her feet would allow her. She had to leave Rosemoor with all possible speed, and become the demure Miss Cameron once again. Gillian of the wild thoughts and abandon must disappear forever. Again.

Grant was not strictly to blame. Her own nature was at fault. She stared at herself in the mirror and wondered at the brightness of her eyes.

Gillian, you cannot have him. Even on a temporary

basis. Even if he compels you to remain here, you cannot love him. To do so would be the greatest foolishness of all.

She had begun to care. Worse, she had begun to care for a man who was too high above her, a man who was to be married soon.

But oh, there was something about the way his hands moved, something about the curve of his lips when he was amused. He was a marvelous lover, and there had been no awkwardness between them, only joy.

She stretched out her hands and remembered how she'd wrapped them around his manhood. She could still feel how hot and large it had been. Her cheeks warmed, and she was not surprised to see a blush appear in her reflection. She was no virgin, but in some ways she was still innocent, perhaps. But innocence had never protected her from the world; it had made her, instead, unprepared for life.

Once, when she'd consulted Robert about plans for their wedding, he'd quickly changed the subject. At the time, she'd thought it was just because men were not as interested in ceremony or social gatherings as women. The subject had evidently bored him, and she'd ended the conversation by smiling at him fondly. That was before she'd learned of Robert's perfidy from his sister.

What a coward he'd been, to let someone else tell her that he'd been a liar and a cheat.

She, at least, would summon her courage and face Grant.

Gillian stood and pushed back the bench and then replaced it. Let her find the strength to leave him. She

didn't even notice that she said the words aloud, or
that they sounded oddly like a prayer.

He extinguished the last of the lamps and left his
laboratory, closing the door harder than it required.
Sound traveled well in the palace, especially stripped
of furniture. She would know that he was done with
his experiments. Would she expect him? Or would she
insult him again? Or, even more troubling, would she
tell him a truth no one else dared?

He found himself walking too quickly, and his
knock on the door was peremptory and impatient.

At the sound of her voice, he grabbed the latch
and pushed it in. She was standing by the vanity he'd
brought from Rosemoor, facing the door. Her hair had
been combed and plaited loosely, the braid tied with
a pale blue ribbon. Tendrils had escaped to frame her
face, and by the glow of candlelight she looked exqui-
sitely lovely and too fragile to touch.

"I came to see you," he said foolishly.

"I was coming to your laboratory," she said, her
fingers plucking at the wrapper she wore.

He'd retrieved the garment from Rosemoor himself, and remembered sliding his hands over the needlework. The embroidery was in raspberry and lemon
and plum colors, something almost essentially Italian
and not at all Scottish. He wanted to tell her that, but
the words simply stuck to the roof of his mouth and
refused to be given voice.

He came into the room and closed the door softly
behind him.

"How did your experiments go?" she asked.

At this moment, he couldn't remember what he had

done all day. He stared at her blankly as if his wits had gone begging. "Some magnetizing work," he said, and hoped she would not ask any questions. He'd stammer, he knew it, or worse, sound like a blithering idiot.

When had he become so inept?

"You look well," he said. "Better than you did earlier."

"I'm still weak," she said, and shook her head as if to chastise herself for it.

"It's to be expected," he said. "You nearly died."

"Did you bathe me? The day it happened, did you bathe me?"

He'd never seen her blush before and suddenly wondered if her demeanor was different around him. Was she freer in her emotions, and in her speech? She was nowhere near as quiet with him as she was in other company. Nor had she ever been.

"In a way," he said. "But I'm surprised you remember. I dunked you in a shallow pool. The water was cold, and I was trying to keep you breathing."

She nodded as if he'd solved a riddle.

"I can't stay here, Grant."

So, she was determined, was she? He was as obstinate.

"I thought we had already discussed this point. I have no intention of allowing you to leave here, especially since I'm not certain you're safe."

"From someone who wants to poison me or from you?"

He began to smile, charmed by her irritation. "Are you asking if I'm yearning for you? Of course I am. But you're hardly well enough to be my mistress."

"I won't be."

"Then our discussion is ended."

She folded her arms and regarded him somberly. "You'll let me return to Rosemoor?"

"Absolutely not."

"So speaks the earl."

"Or the lover," he said. "I think, perhaps, it's more the lover than the earl. But however you wish to interpret it, it remains the same. You're not leaving the palace. Discussion will not work, charm will not, even arguments will have no effect on me. You're not leaving."

"You really are insufferable," she said.

"Do you know that you've insulted me more in the last month than anyone has in the last five years?"

"Have I?"

"Should you be looking so inordinately pleased at that fact?"

"I do believe you need to be teased a little from time to time, Grant. There are moments when you are too much the earl."

He studied her, wondering if she were speaking truthfully now, or still teasing.

"My title comes to me through birth, and not because of anything I've accomplished on my own. Unless, of course, you count simply surviving as an accomplishment. Which, given the state of my two brothers, should not be completely discounted. My title also exists to pin the whole of the responsibility for Rosemoor and the rest of the estate to me, to one person. I am the titular head of my family, and the person to whom all responsibility ultimately leads."

"I have angered you, haven't I? For that I apologize. I did not mean to do so."

"Do you truly think me a dilettante?"

She glanced up at him. "No. But what you said also explains something else."

"Should I ask?"

She smiled. "You work with electrics to leave your name to something, don't you? You want people to remember you as more than the 10th Earl of Straithern."

He stared at her, wondering how she'd come to know him so well.

He smiled. "When you're feeling better, you'll have to see the magnetizing work I've done. I'd be very interested to show it to you."

"You're trying to charm me."

"Of course I am," he said perfectly agreeably.

When she didn't respond, his smile broadened. "Come now, you can't tell me you have no interest at all. You're thinking to yourself: What can he positively want me to see? What can he have been doing all day?"

"I am not thinking any of those things," she said.

"Have I remarked upon your stubbornness? It's an admirable trait to have, especially as a scientist."

"I am not a scientist," she said.

"You have the curiosity of one. In addition, your intellect is deep and broad enough to encompass almost any subject you choose."

"How do you know that?"

She unfolded her arms and held them behind her. A more approachable stance, perhaps, but he knew better than to move closer.

"Because of your choice of reading material." He nodded toward the chair where he had placed all the books he had found in her room at Rosemoor.

She looked where he gestured, and then glanced back at him, her face turning a very delicate rose. "It was you," she said. "You went through my things."

"There are some chores I do not leave for my servants, Gillian. I didn't want to send Michael to pack your belongings."

"So you did it yourself."

He nodded. "I was very impressed by your readings of Camus."

"I also read novels," she said. "If you think that I'm given only to elevated pursuits. I adore novels. Lurid gothic tales."

"Heroines in distress?"

She nodded.

"What would one of those heroines do in this circumstance?"

"Scream."

"Do take pity on Michael," he said, amused. "He works very hard and retires early."

"I didn't say I was going to scream."

"You don't envision yourself as the heroine?"

"Occasionally," she said, elevating her chin just a trifle higher. "Especially when my own life seems either too boring or too painful to experience. I like to slip into some other person's life occasionally. Don't you?"

At his silence, she smiled. "Of course you don't. You're the Earl of Straithern. Who would ever want to exchange your life for a fictional character's? Who wouldn't want to be you, I wonder?"

"I don't know if you're correct about that," he said. "Especially during the last year."

Her blush faded and her face became unnaturally pale. Her gaze looked stricken.

"I am sorry. How foolish of me to have forgotten."

"You aren't a foolish woman, Gillian. In fact, you're the least foolish person I know."

"Stop being charming, Grant. Stop trying to snare me with words."

He took a few steps toward her. She stiffened but otherwise didn't move.

"Is that what I do? I snare you with words?"

"You do, and it isn't well done of you. Your voice becomes low and your eyes almost gleam and I forget everything but how handsome you are."

"All that?"

He took a few more steps toward her. She frowned at him.

"Stop."

"I shall," he said gently. "I will attempt to be as ogre-like as possible."

"No, I mean stop where you are. Don't come any closer."

"I should like to buy you all sorts of perfume," he said. She looked startled by his pronouncement. Good, it was about time she was disconcerted by him instead of the other way around. "Something woodsy and elemental, I think. From the Orient. Something that hints at spice."

"I will refuse your gift," she said. "That would be the wisest thing to do."

"You are more disciplined than I. I cannot imagine ever turning down a gift that you might give me."

"Oh, but you see, that is where you and I differ. You have the power to ignore what society might say about you. I don't."

"What if I gave you some of mine? I have enough power for both of us. I shall let it be known that no one will speak ill of you. That you are to be accorded all the rights and privileges of a . . ." His words stumbled to a halt.

"A mistress? A friend? A constant companion? A beloved intruder? Who shall I be to the world, Grant?"

"Is it important that you are anything to the world?"

"So says the earl."

"No, that was most definitely the lover."

He was close enough that he could extend his hand, his fingers threading through the hair at her temple. She didn't move away, didn't implore him to cease his actions. If anything, she leaned into his hand, and for a second she closed her eyes as if she were somehow savoring this moment, keeping it safe for her memory.

"Don't leave me," he said.

Her eyes flew open. Her gaze locked on his.

"Do not leave me, Gillian. I am not a man given to begging. I don't believe I've ever had to. But this is the closest I will ever come to it. I will offer you reason, and rational words, and money if necessary. I will give you excuses, or platitudes, or even outright lies. Whatever it takes to keep you here, I am more than willing to do."

"Please, Grant."

"Give me a day. Two days. A week."

"For you to find the killer?" she asked.

"That would be the wisest answer, wouldn't it? I should tell you that's exactly what I will be doing, and time is what I need. But it wouldn't be the truth, and I find myself wanting to give you the truth, if nothing else."

"Why?" she asked softly.

"So I can get the taste of you out of my mind. So I will not dream of you any longer."

Her flush was back, her cheeks pink.

"Am I being too charming again?"

"You know you are," she said.

She lifted her hand and brushed her fingers delicately across his cheek. "You really have no right to be so handsome. It doesn't seem quite fair that nature bestowed on you rank, wealth, and masculine beauty."

He felt his face warm at her words and felt like a young boy in the throes of his very first love, uncertain and desperately eager.

"While you have the power to unman me with a smile," he said gently. "Nature granted you beauty, character, wit, and intelligence, Gillian. Who is to say which of us the more gifted?"

"No one would ever expound to you about the virtues of my character, I'm very much afraid."

"Now it's your turn to stop," he said firmly. He grabbed her hand to place a kiss on her palm, and then folded her fingers over as if to keep the kiss sealed inside. He held her fist within the cradle of his hand. "I will not have you speak about yourself that way. I will not have you say those things. What happened to you was unfortunate. Perhaps it was a scandal, certainly it was a tragedy. But do not make it the cornerstone of your life, Gillian, nor measure your character because of it."

"Then what makes the measure of a person?"

"The way they treat others," he said easily. "The way they can think of others before themselves. The way they empathize with those who do not know the meaning of the word."

She covered his hand with her free one, and they stood there for a moment linked by their touch. She lowered her head until he couldn't see her expression.

"Stay with me," he said again.

"I should be the one to beg you," she said softly. "Beg you not to offer any more blandishments, or promises, or a future." She didn't say anything further for a moment. When she lifted her head, he was shocked to see her tears.

But before he could speak or enfold her in his arms, she stepped back, pulling her hands free.

"Please, Grant."

"Will you stay?"

She sighed, and didn't answer. But a moment later, she nodded, just once.

He would be content with that, for now.

The Countess of Straithern's chamber overlooked the entire east lawn of Rosemoor, a sweeping vista that led down to the groves and beyond that to the marsh Grant was so fond of exploring. The suite consisted of three rooms: a drawing room, a bathing chamber, and the bedroom. She would not like to relinquish it, but she had always known that the time would come when she would have to do so.

How wonderfully ironic that she must surrender her home to Arabella Fenton.

But first she wanted to ascertain if she was correct, after all. The first shock had passed, and there was nothing more to do but face the truth squarely. She'd never been a coward, for all that the world thought her possessed of a retiring nature.

One of the maids told her where she could find the girl. Not in the library, as she had supposed, or in her chamber, intent on one of her ubiquitous books. No, Arabella Fenton had surprised her and was sitting on the veranda overlooking the western view of Rosemoor, and the curving road that led to the palace and beyond, to Edinburgh.

Dorothea sighed and opened the French door, stepping up the few inches to the stone floor of the terrace. The design of the terrace was Italian, a loggia, she understood it was called. The intent was to capture the warmth of any fair day. Balusters carved from stone and only about three feet high lined the space shaped like a Maltese cross. A few boxes of flowers added color, and a statue or two, always women barely dressed, added what she supposed was considered a classical flavor.

The day was bright, the warmth from the afternoon sun welcome. Dorothea walked to the bench where Arabella sat. On her lap was a book, open to some grisly drawing or another, but her attention was fixed, instead, on the palace.

Right now, Dorothea could cheerfully strangle her son. Grant should be here to deal with this situation, but her son was unfortunately not present. Instead he was scandalously holed up with the woman he'd evidently made his mistress.

"Men will act in despicable ways, sometimes," she told Arabella. "But I've heard it said that the worst rakes make the best husbands."

Arabella didn't greet her, merely turned her head and regarded Dorothea with a look that was not far from contemptuous. So startled was she by the girl's expression that Dorothea abruptly decided against sitting beside her on the bench. Instead, the countess walked some distance away and leaned against the balustrade.

"Did you find that to be true, Your Ladyship?" Arabella asked. Her voice had an edge to it, an almost grating tone.

Dorothea turned her gaze from the palace and back to Arabella, and for a long moment the two women regarded each other.

"He says that someone tried to poison him, Miss Fenton," Dorothea said. "That's why he remains at the palace."

"I've heard that tale myself, Your Ladyship. I was not, however, allowed to examine Gillian."

"I have not questioned him as to his alliance, Miss Fenton. He would not allow that. But Miss Cameron has remained with my son of her own volition. Of this I'm certain. I have interviewed Michael, and he has assured me of this fact."

"I don't care what Grant is doing," Arabella said. Her voice had lost the grating tone. If anything, it was dispassionate, and genuinely without emotion. "I fear he is taking advantage of Gillian, however. She's too emotional, and believes in love."

"You do not, Miss Fenton?"

"Of course not." She closed her book and stood. "I have found, from an early age, Your Ladyship, that love is a word most people use to excuse all sorts of horrible behavior."

"My son has always tried to do the honorable thing, Miss Fenton. He knows how much his father shamed this family, and he's tried, all of his life, to make amends."

"By all means, no dishonor must be allowed to touch the Roberson family," Arabella said, smiling. "What a pity that isn't true."

Secrets pulsed between them, but Dorothea suddenly knew there was no possibility that she and the younger woman could ever confide in each other.

She must summon up her courage and ask Dr. Fenton for the truth.

Chapter 23

Gillian had marshaled all her defenses to keep Grant away, but it appeared it wasn't necessary since Grant was avoiding her as ably as she was prepared to avoid him. Her reasoning was to protect herself. What was his?

She'd expected Dr. Fenton to come and visit her. But no one came to the palace, and at first she thought it was because she'd been well and truly repudiated. Only after speaking to Michael had she learned that no one was allowed at the palace. Evidently Grant had created a fortress for them, a place where no one was allowed and she was not permitted to leave. Even Lorenzo scarcely made an appearance, and when he did so, he only bowed slightly to her and sent a frown in Grant's direction.

Any hope that she'd be able to escape the consequences of the last week disappeared the moment she received a terse note from Arabella. Consisting of only one sentence, the message managed to convey contempt, irritation, and superiority.

Do not be so foolish as to forget what happened before, Gillian.

The irony of her imprisonment was that she hadn't seen Grant for a week. For the first few days, she'd done nothing more than sleep. She'd been exhausted, but how much of that was from the poison and how much from the treatment for it, she didn't know.

During the latter part of the week, she began to feel better, so much so that she began looking for things to do. She was unaccustomed to inactivity, and it grated on her nerves not to have a chore to do or a duty to accomplish.

She spent hours walking the grounds of the palace. Behind the structure was a series of gardens that had been allowed to fall into disarray. She amused herself by attempting to reason out the original plan of the ornamental hedges. On some mornings, she spent time pulling away the dead leaves. When that occupation palled, she sat on the bench in the center of the maze and simply watched the world around her.

Today was the most glorious day. It was hours after dawn, but the air still felt cool, the grass still retaining a hint of dew. Everywhere she looked there were signs of nature feeling proud and jaunty. Birds did not simply sit on the branches, they walked sideways from one end to the other as if to converse with their neighbors. The squirrels that abounded at Rosemoor chattered noisily to one another. Did they share secrets of where the best nuts were stored? Or were they simply gossiping about their fellow squirrels? Butterflies flitted from flower to flower, and even the bees seemed to hover in the air in clumps, as if the gardens behind the palace were a companionable place.

There was no one to whom she was responsible; she had no duty to perform. Not one person would mark her absence, or demand her presence. For the first time in her life she was truly on her own.

All her life, she'd tried to be a credit to her father, to not shame her family. Yet she'd ended up straying so far from society that she was no longer bound by their approval. Unknowingly, she'd alienated Dr. Fenton and Arabella as well. Therefore she was all alone, subject to the whims of only one person, Grant Roberson, Earl of Straithern.

He and he alone was her link to civilization, the source of information, the repository of secrets, her only friend. Yet even he had been scarce of late.

How very odd that despite that, for the first time in a very long time, she felt happy, at peace. Was this what she'd needed all this time? A period of healing, a time to be nothing but herself, a space in which no one required anything of her except for her to simply be Gillian.

There was a time when she'd despaired of ever surfacing from her grief, but at this moment she was as far from sadness as a giggling child.

As the quiet hours unfolded in the garden, she realized that the world could be a beautiful place; she could experience joy.

The prayer was more a thought than an entreaty. *Thank you for all the beautiful memories. For all the joy, however short-lived, thank you. For the ability to experience beauty, thank you. For this sensation of sitting here and watching this small, perfect corner of the world, thank you. Most of all, for the ability to feel an emotion other than despair, dear God, thank you.*

Perhaps that's what this interlude at Rosemoor was

to teach her. Not to love as much as to begin living again.

What would life bring her? She wasn't certain; she didn't know. Choices, of a certainty. Opportunities, perhaps.

She must not be afraid. It was time she began living. Resolutely, she stood and walked back to the palace.

"You think you are so restrained, my friend," Lorenzo said, "but you are not. Perhaps the years in Italy have made an impression on your cold Scottish heart."

Grant frowned at him, but the expression only made Lorenzo smile.

"You must breathe deep now," Lorenzo commanded.

Grant did so, never swerving his eyes from his friend's face.

"You do not like to be given orders, I think." He moved aside the folds of Grant's shirt so that he could better listen to his chest. Grant remained silent.

"You have passion, Grant, and fire."

"Is that what you learned from listening to my heart?" Grant asked, fastening his shirt.

Lorenzo ignored his sarcasm. "I think the little companion has pulled it from you. You are like Vesuvius, calm on the outside, but just waiting to erupt."

"A volcano? Hardly."

"Cough."

Grant coughed, while Lorenzo pressed his hand hard against his chest.

Finally Lorenzo released his hand and stepped back, regarding Grant solemnly. "If you are dying,

Grant, then you are the healthiest dying man I've ever treated. All my patients should be as healthy as you."

"Not for the lack of someone trying," Grant said.

"What are you doing about that?"

"I don't know what else to do," Grant admitted. "I can create electricity. I can be God in my laboratory and replicate lightning. Why can't I protect those in my care?"

"I think, perhaps, my friend, that you are requiring too much of yourself."

"On the contrary, Lorenzo," Grant said. "I don't think I'm asking enough. If I were an honorable man, I would simply be done with it, and marry Arabella Fenton. After all, it was my suggestion, my instigation that she is even here. I would banish Gillian from the palace with all possible speed. Do you see me doing that?"

"I think, perhaps, you are done with being proper, Grant," Lorenzo said, smiling. "You have been exceedingly proper in all the time I've known you. It is time for you to have a little enjoyment of life."

"You make me sound like a prig."

"Not at all," Lorenzo said, picking up a dark brown bottle on the table. He frowned as he read the label, and then slowly put the bottle down, moving it away from him with the tip of one finger. "You are just in need of a little affection. I do not think, however, that it is fair to subject Miss Cameron to the gossip of Rosemoor."

"What are people saying?"

"It is not for me to repeat the words of others, Grant."

"I hate this," Grant said, threading the fingers of

one hand through his hair. "I hate this whole damnable mess."

"Then send her away."

"I can't." Grant turned to look at his friend. "I don't want her to go, and it's dangerous for her to stay. I tell myself that I'm protecting her, but who will protect her from me?"

"Is that why you've stayed away from me for a week?"

Grant turned his head and suddenly she was there, framed to the doorway. Her cheeks were pinked by the sun, her hair a little mussed by the wind. She held a wildflower in one hand, and a bonnet in the other. Her gaze was direct, allowing no artifice.

Lorenzo melted away with the practiced tread of the discreet.

"People will think that we're lovers, regardless of what you tell them. People will talk, and it never seems to matter if they're telling the truth or not."

He looked at her. "Do you want to go back to Rosemoor?"

She walked closer to him, but stopped on the other side of the table. "Shall I tell you the truth? Or should I be wise for once?"

"I should tell you to be wise, but I'm too curious."

"I should leave. Return to Rosemoor."

"But you won't."

"No, I won't."

"Has my caution finally made an impression?"

She shook her head. "I don't believe so. I think it was the garden."

"The garden?" He began to smile. "Why the garden?"

"It's a beautiful day, Grant. A day of promise, I think. But it may rain tomorrow."

"It may," he agreed.

"Why should we not simply accept the day as it is now, today, and live it fully?"

"I used to think my Italian neighbors did the very same thing."

"Shall we have our own Italy?"

He didn't know what to say. Several responses came to mind and were dismissed as quickly. But before he could frame an answer, she held out one hand to him.

"Have I shocked you?" she asked.

"Try delight, instead."

She smiled.

Gently, he gripped her hand and pulled her to him. She offered no resistance, simply linked her hands behind his neck, smiling into his face.

This moment should be stopped for all time. He wanted to remember this particular moment always. Gillian, with her teasing smile with a hint of wickedness to it, and something else, some other emotion he didn't want to name.

He reached out, gripping her waist with both hands. In a swift movement, he raised her so that she was sitting on the edge of the wooden table.

Grant bent and kissed her, lost in the sensation for several long moments. He heard her sigh, and smiled, pleased.

He wanted to bring her pleasure. He wanted to mark himself in her memory until she would never be able to forget him.

"Are you feeling brave?" he asked, pulling back.

His hand spread across her bodice, his thumb

brushing against a hardening nipple. Pleasure spread through him at the sound of her soft moan.

She opened her eyes, slowly smiling at him.

"Why?"

"I have always wanted to do an experiment," he said. "Will you be my assistant in this as well?"

She tilted her head a little and regarded him silently. "Now? I'd much rather you took me to your bed right now."

"Even if I promise you it will be pleasurable?"

"Very pleasurable?"

"I promise."

"Very well," she said.

He cleared off the table to the left of her, and moved the Volta engine closer.

She didn't say a word in question or protest, but her eyes grew slightly wider as he reached behind her and slowly began to unlace her dress.

"I will not hurt you. I've always wanted to know what the sensation would be like."

"What sensation is that?" she asked, and then licked her lips.

He finished unfastening her dress, congratulating himself on the expertise with which he did so, especially while not looking. He pulled the dress down off her shoulders, past her plain and serviceable undergarments. She unfastened the corset from the front and separated it, then folded down the large split opening of the chemise. Grant bent and suckled on her right breast, playing with the nipple with his tongue. He glanced upward to find her sitting with her head tilted back slightly, her eyes closed, an expression of rapt intensity on her face.

"Does that feel good?" he asked.

"Yes," she said, sighing.

He bit at the nipple gently, and then suckled it again, leaving it wet. With his left hand, he reached over for the wire that emerged from the Volta engine.

"Do you trust me?"

She opened her eyes and focused her attention on his face.

"Yes," she said simply.

"I want to touch the wire to your nipple. Will you tell me what it feels like?'

"Only a small shock?"

"I have not recharged the engine, and you might not feel anything."

"Am I to be your experiment? Will you send word to Italy of your results?"

"I might even write a paper," he said, smiling. "I observed the results of my experiment in the process of seducing a beautiful young woman. I placed her on my table in my laboratory, and undressed her to the waist, revealing a magnificent pair of well-matched breasts, full and high, with coral nipples pointing upward. They entice my fingers and my lips, and I find myself distracted by the chore of keeping the nipples wet." He bent and sucked at her breast as her palms held his face.

He pulled back, continuing with his imagined research paper. "With her complete agreement, I agreed to attach the wire to the Volta apparatus to see if there was any effect on the impudent nipple. Or to see if such a charge is an enticement to the sexual act."

Slowly, he drew the wire toward her, giving her time to rescind her agreement. She said nothing, only watched intently as it grew closer. When he touched it to the end of her nipple, she smiled.

"Did you feel anything?"

"I did," she said. "A very curious sensation. Almost as if you were rubbing my nipple with your tongue."

"The effects of the experiment," he continued aloud, "are uncertain at best. The subject has not complained, and instead seems to encourage further experimentation."

"Do I? Are you going to use it everywhere? And if you do can I use it as well? Shall I touch your cock with that wire, and see if it grows more animated?"

"I regret to state that you will have no difficulties in making that object twitch. Every time it's near you it becomes animated."

She smiled, and he dropped the wire for a more pleasurable pursuit, that of kissing Gillian.

"You are a very able apprentice," he said, his voice low and promising.

"Then the teacher should reward his student," she said. "Some sort of acknowledgment of my talents."

"When I was at school, our headmaster used to give us bookmarks when we excelled at our subjects."

She shook her head gently. "That will never do."

"You cannot simply negate something without offering an alternative."

"Perhaps an evening in your bed," she said, smiling.

She trailed her hand down his arm before linking her fingers with his. She brought their joined hands to her mouth, kissing his knuckles.

"No," he said, and pulled her to him. "If I am the headmaster," he said, "then I set the rules. No student is ever allowed in my private quarters unless she proves very, very adept."

"I thought I had," she said, her smile once more in place.

The fingers of one hand gently stroked the upper curve of her breast, while the other hand supported it, a thumb tenderly strumming across the nipple's surface. For a moment he concentrated his attention on her left breast before moving to the right. His concentration was intent, his expression rapt as her nipple responded to his ministrations.

"I will always be able to feel the texture of your skin," he said softly. "It seems something so intrinsically yours, Gillian. As if I could touch a thousand women and know them by the curve of their breasts, by the smoothness and suppleness of their skin."

"Must you choose this moment to talk about your future conquests, Grant?" she asked with a smile.

He didn't look up, almost as if she hadn't spoken. "Stay with me."

Now he looked up, to find that she was looking directly at him, that expression back in her eyes.

"You aren't asking for a week this time, are you?"

"Not a week, a day, or an hour," he said.

"Forever?" she asked, and he simply nodded.

Suddenly all she wanted to do was to lose herself in pleasure. She didn't want to think; she didn't even want to really feel. Not the emotions of the heart, anyway. She wanted to be a sensate being, a creature that reveled in pleasure for the sake of it.

"Make love to me," she said, leaning forward. She pressed both hands against his face and looked into his eyes. "Make love to me all night," she demanded. "And when the dawn comes, make love to me again. And perhaps I will say yes. If you're good at it. If you give me enough pleasure."

A mischievous smile appeared on his face. "Are you daring me, Gillian? I would be cautious if I were you. Never tempt a hungry man with a bite of food."

"Is that what I am now? Only a bite?"

He bent forward and took a nipple into his mouth, drawing heavily on it. His cheeks hollowed as his fingers curved around her other breast.

A line of fire streaked through her, prompting her body's response. She felt herself dampen for him as her blood beat heavily and pleasure mounted. He gently bit her nipple and then pulled back, his lips still wet from his kisses.

She kissed him hungrily, craving his mouth in a way she never had before. She was the one who deepened the kiss, and fisted her hands in his hair.

Maybe some of her need—her ferocity—communicated itself to him immediately. He moved between her legs, wrapping them around his waist, and then pulled her gently to the edge. She was dimly conscious of the fact that his hands were on her bottom beneath her dress and that he was making swift work of her undergarments. There was nothing circumspect about the way he removed her clothes. Nothing that would impede his possession was allowed to remain in place.

Suddenly, blessedly, he was inside her and she was gasping against his mouth.

More, please; more, please. More, please, until she was so filled she couldn't breathe or think or feel anything. More, until she could only experience pleasure and it became the beginning and the end of all that she was. She pulled him to her, whimpering in frustration.

She wanted so desperately to climax, and at the same time wanted to remain poised on the precipice where need and yearning and lust and pleasure mingled to become one unique sensation.

His fingers left her breasts and burrowed beneath her skirts, pushing them back.

He looked down to where they joined. "Look at us," he commanded.

She bent her head to see him entering her slowly. As she watched, he pulled out almost completely, engorged and thick and slick with her juices.

Her hands clenched into claws and she scraped at his clothing. "Now," she said softly, a yearning plea for him to return.

He did so, so slowly that she almost wept aloud. Her fingers flexed against his shoulder and then curved around his neck, bringing his head closer, that delicious smile closer to her mouth.

She wanted him to be faster and more intrusive, but he teased her by pulling back, and whispering in her ear.

"Is this enough pleasure, Gillian? Is it enough?"

There was no time for play, for pretense. There was too much urgency. She wanted passion and forgetfulness. She beat at his shoulders, but he only smiled, and then bent forward, kissing her very softly on the lips. It was a teasing kiss, an avuncular kiss, betraying none of the passion and the need she felt.

He let her skirts drop over them. To the rest of

the world they might have been a startling sight, the Earl of Straithern engaged in a carnal dalliance with a companion. Her breasts were exposed, her lips swollen from his kisses. But none would see that he was sliding slowly in and out of her, tormenting her with a teasing, controlled possession.

"Well?"

She laid her head against his shoulder, surrendering.

"Is it enough?" he asked. The calmness of his voice was at odds with the ruddiness of his face and the grip he maintained on the edge of the table.

Her tears came without warning, surprising her. Once, perhaps, she might've tried to hide them, but she just flung her head back and stared up at the ceiling, a sound like a half gasp, half laugh escaping her.

He was giving her exactly what she had wanted. Every inch of her body was rife with sensation, and she could feel nothing but him. Everything centered on Grant, on his teasing smile, on the touch of fingers on her skin, and most of all on the feelings that he was giving her, slowly entering her and then pulling back, in control and command not only of his body but also of hers.

"Is it enough?" he whispered.

"Yes," she said.

Remember this, her mind urged, even as her body peaked. *Remember this*, a last refrain as he finally crushed his mouth on hers, and swallowed her sob.

Her hands opened the stopper of the cobalt blue bottle with practiced ease. She lowered a long-handled spoon down the neck of the bottle, scooping out a portion of a grayish powdery substance. Powdered leaves of belladonna, a most favored plant, useful for nervous system disorders, diseases of the eye, and bladder dysfunction.

She'd once heard it said that poison was a woman's weapon. How foolish. Although this could be construed as a poison, it was also a valuable medicine. She used medicines to cure. Yet if the soul were not clean, what did it matter that the body was healed?

That's when the medicine became poison. A stronger dose became the means of ending a life. It was kind in its way, sparing the victim a lingering pain. While it was true the first few moments of ingesting the poison were difficult to endure, the agony was of short duration.

Too short a duration for evil to truly be eradicated.

There were some sins for which there was no reparation, just as there were some sinners who did not accept the need for atonement. In those cases, she simply did what she must, and ended their lives with less care for their eventual pain. If they screamed for release near the end, it was what they deserved.

She was well aware that there were some people who would look upon what she was doing as wrong. But these same individuals would deny the need for justice in all but the most egregious cases. Life was not necessarily kind, nor was it virtuous. It was for the brave to demand integrity and fairness.

The truth was that she was ridding the world of those who defiled innocence, who were evil. She would never be recognized as a savior, she was certain. Nor would she ever be completely forgiven for what she was doing.

There were those, however, who might wonder in the quiet of the night whether she was to be applauded for her zeal and whether she was more saint than sinner.

She didn't care either way.

Nor was she disappointed when she occasionally failed in her attempt to kill the wicked. She simply reevaluated what went wrong, what she needed to do next. If she failed, she tried again. She always succeeded eventually.

Look how long it had taken with James.

She turned and smiled at the skeleton arranged on the bed, the skull carefully placed on the pillow as if he slept. Dear Roderick—it was a pseudonym, of course, since no one would understand if she used his real name. But she'd engaged the services of an enterprising young man—who was satisfied with a paltry sum and some medicines to ease symptoms of a personal nature—to disinter him. No one else knew that the skeleton belonged to the very first of her victims, an old man who beat his wife and nearly starved his children. The world thought him buried in the churchyard where he lay alone and without visitors. But he was her constant companion, a reminder of not only what she must accomplish but what she'd already done.

Lorenzo would have a great deal to tell his wife when he returned home to Florence, not the least of which was this improbable gathering in Grant's library.

The evening was advanced, the day had been a long

one, and he would much rather have sought his own
bed than be in the library, enduring the company of
Dr. Fenton and his daughter.

What would Elise have to say about the two of
them? He could only imagine his wife's comments.

*She is very forward for a female, Lorenzo. Has she
no grace? For a beautiful girl, she seems almost to
have a dislike of her appearance.*

*And him? Why are his spectacles always dirty? You
are never so unkempt, my darling.*

He smiled and held up his glass, bowing slightly
from the waist. "It is excellent wine," he said to Dr.
Fenton. The older man simply nodded.

It was Arabella who corrected him. "It isn't my
father's wine cellar, sir."

Of course it wasn't, and his remark was merely
meant to be gracious in a fashion, not to be interpreted in the way she had.

Having witnessed her behavior at various occasions
at Rosemoor, Lorenzo decided that Miss Fenton was
not comfortable in social gatherings. She seemed to
hold herself apart, almost as if she were viewing other
people from afar. Yet perhaps he was judging her too
harshly. He and Elise had the same reaction to society. As long as their little ones were around and they
had each other, they were complete. They required no
other entertainments.

Yet he couldn't help but wonder if Arabella would
ever warm to Grant, especially after his interlude
with the companion. What woman would still marry
Grant, having been spurned publicly in such a way? A
greedy one, perhaps. A vengeful one?

"I'm very surprised, sir, that you never mentioned you were a physician. Was there some reason that you hid your occupation from me?"

Lorenzo bent forward and pulled the silver tray a few inches closer. He poured himself some more wine from the decanted bottle. When he offered to refill Dr. Fenton's glass, the older man shook his head.

"I was doing so at a request from my friend, sir," he said. More than that, he would not reveal. Grant's conclusion as to his own health was a private matter, and he would not reveal it to the doctor, or in Arabella's company.

He wished, fervently, that Miss Fenton would disappear, that she would go somewhere women congregated at Rosemoor. Where was that, exactly? To the library? Not a bad decision in Miss Fenton's regard, but since they were sitting in the middle of the library, that was hardly a solution. To one of the many parlors in this very large house? No doubt she would meet the countess, and from what he'd witnessed at dinner, he doubted the two women wanted anything to do with each other.

He took a sip of his wine, tasting the bitterness for the first time. He wouldn't make the remark to Dr. Fenton, but he would tease Grant about the fact that his cellar was turning to vinegar.

What would Elise say about Grant's improbable liaison with Gillian Cameron? For the first time, his friend was behaving with little thought to his customary rigid standards of behavior, and Lorenzo wanted to applaud the change, at the same time warning Grant that there would be repercussions for his actions.

Grant looked happy. In fact, he couldn't remember Grant ever looking quite so happy, even in all those years of living in Florence.

Gone was the man who would never escort a woman of dubious reputation to a public gathering for fear word would reach the community of English émigrés. Nor did Grant seem concerned as to the wagging tongues in the neighborhood—not like he'd been when people speculated as to his bachelorhood in Italy. He'd always been so inordinately careful not to sully the Roberson name. But he'd acquired a reputation all the same, one that would have horrified him had Lorenzo ever bothered to reveal it—Grant was known to the shopkeepers and Italian neighbors as *L'Inglese Rigido*: the Stiff Englishman.

He really should toast Miss Cameron. She'd accomplished what five years of Grant's living in Italy had not: made him a happy man.

"We could have conferred on a great many cases," the doctor said, evidently feeling a necessity to be affable.

Lorenzo had nothing against the doctor, and admired him for a great many attributes; however, his treatment of Miss Cameron was not one of them. He had been openly critical of her actions, and condemnatory to the point of prudishness, a reaction that Lorenzo did not quite understand.

Loneliness was a terrible malady, and when it struck, there seemed to be no true remedy. Medicine might work temporarily, but it could cause more problems if a dependency was begun. Alcohol was the same. The only true therapy for loneliness was the company of another person, the laughter of a convivial soul, the presence of a caring and compassionate individual, the solace of passion.

The world looked askance at such arrangements, temporary or otherwise, unless they were sanctioned by religion or societal approval. The world would forever condemn Grant and Gillian's liaison, which was a great pity. Loving each other might heal both of them.

"I would have enjoyed the discussion," Lorenzo said. "Unfortunately, I have plans to return to Italy soon."

"I would have thought you'd extend your visit somewhat longer," he said, "especially in view of what recently occurred."

"I believe that what recently occurred," Lorenzo said with a small smile, "only concurs with Grant's diagnosis. I doubt, Dr. Fenton, that he is dying of a blood disease. I do, however, suspected someone is trying to do him harm."

"I would have thought that a friend would remain at his side," Arabella said.

Lorenzo turned his head to regard her.

"You disapprove of my departure?"

"If Grant truly believes his life is in danger, it seems to me you would remain close to him."

"It is Grant who has insisted I leave, Miss Fenton. He holds great store for loyalty. And family."

She gently removed the glass from his hand and re-filled it, giving it back to him with a delightful smile, one of the most genuine expressions he'd ever seen from her during the extent of his stay at Rosemoor.

Arabella stood, bent to kiss her father on the cheek, and then left the room.

"Miss Fenton?"

She turned at the door.

Lorenzo retrieved the book from where she'd left it beside her chair. "Your book," he said. He glanced at the title. "A very heavy tome."

"My journal," she said, taking the book from him. Her smile had disappeared, but not so the brightness of her eyes. They sparkled at him, as if she were laughing and yet restrained her humor.

He watched her leave, and hoped that Grant had the good sense to get out of this marriage before it occurred.

Chapter 24

Grant lay beside Gillian in the darkness, thinking that what had begun in morning had ended at midnight. His body felt like a separate entity, a very satisfied and exhausted entity. His mind, however, was wide awake and racing with thought.

Gillian was unlike anyone he'd ever known—courageous and stubborn, opinionated, and fiercely herself. She was no more an angel than he was, but there was something about her that spoke of true innocence despite her experiences and her past. She did not have the nature to do evil or be unkind. Candor was part of her nature. While her words might sting a little, she directed them only to him, and he was more than able to withstand their occasional scorch.

To maids and footmen she was unfailingly polite. Even to Arabella, who occasionally strained the limits of his temper, Gillian was patient.

Was that why he felt so acutely protective of her? Did he perceive her as one of the innocent, and he had tried during the whole of his life to shelter the innocent?

Or was it something else entirely?

Whatever this interlude might bring was uncertain. One thing was abundantly clear, however. He could not marry Arabella Fenton.

"If you loosen your arm," she said softly, "I promise not to run away."

He realized his embrace was too tight, and moved his arm from around her waist, moving back a little on the bed. She brushed the hair out of her eyes as she looked over at him.

"What did you say to me?" she asked.

"When?" he asked, even though he knew quite well what she meant.

She shook her head from side to side, gently chiding him. "Was it Latin?"

"In a way. Italian."

She held his hand with one of hers and then reached over and kissed him full on the lips. A gentle, soft, and tender kiss as if she would waken him from a dream.

"What did you say?" she asked against his lips.

He smiled. He couldn't remember everything. Some of his words had been impassioned, surprising even him with their emotion.

"*Siete la mia speranza, il mio futuro.*"

"What does it mean?"

He rose up on one elbow, facing her. "The Italians are very inventive when it comes to love. *Siete bei quanto l'alba.* You are as beautiful as the dawn. *Rendete me il tatto potente.* You make me feel powerful."

"And the other? You won't say?"

It would be wiser if he didn't. *Rimanga con me.* Remain with me. *Non desidero vivere senza voi.* I don't want to live without you. And the most telling of his remarks: *siete la mia speranza ed il mi futuro*. You are my hope and my future.

"Should I ask how you became so expert at what the Italians know of love? Or should I simply pretend that you did not make that remark?"

"I confess to nothing," he said, bending to kiss her. "I'm sending you to Italy," he said abruptly.

"Italy?"

The idea had just come to him, and the more he thought about it, the more appealing it became. He would send her there, and after he'd made arrangements for Arabella, he'd send for her.

Life was suddenly a great deal brighter than it had been a month ago. Or even a moment ago.

Would she marry him?

It wasn't honor that kept him silent, but instead a curious reluctance. She couldn't refuse.

"I have a villa there," he said instead. "Where I lived before I returned to Scotland. It would be safe for you. Lorenzo will escort you, of course."

She placed her hand on his bare chest as if to restrain his thoughts.

"I don't want to leave," she said.

"And I want you to do so, in order to remain safe. Which of us will win, I wonder?"

"So says the lover?"

"No," he said, reaching for her. "So says the earl."

Rosemoor was too large. Despite the fact he'd been here for weeks, Lorenzo found himself lost twice before finally finding his assigned chamber. The first time he didn't mind being directed by a young, comely maid. The second time, a tall and rather supercilious footman haughtily announced the directions, managing to annoy Lorenzo greatly.

All in all, he preferred Italy, his comfortable home with the sound of children and not all these trappings of wealth.

His stomach burned, and Lorenzo grabbed at it, thinking himself constitutionally ill-equipped for Scottish food. But at least it had been spicier than the pap he'd been forced to eat in London. Perhaps because Grant employed a French cook.

He probably had eaten too much of the bouillabaisse, but it had been exceptionally good. Or perhaps he shouldn't have had the last glass of wine. Elise would have fussed at him about the lateness of the hour and his consumption of spirits.

Elise. How he missed his wife.

Once in his chamber, he sat down on the edge of the bed and pressed a hand to his stomach, letting out a small groan of discomfort.

He belched, but there was no attendant release of discomfort. His stomach felt like it was on fire, and so, too, did the base of his throat.

Uncomfortable still, he stood, poured himself a glass of water, and drank it down. Instead of helping with the pain, it seemed to make it worse.

He was never ill.

His scientist's mind began to piece together what was happening to him. An ulceration of the stomach? He would have experienced signs before tonight. He'd always been able to eat anything he chose without any kind of ramifications. No, tonight's pain was different, something altogether unique.

How very odd that he'd gotten sick after drinking bitter wine.

His stomach spasmed and he doubled over, falling to his knees at the end of the bed. He grabbed on to the curved footboard and pulled himself up, only to be felled by another paroxysm of pain. It felt as if a dozen spears had pierced his body, and he was bleeding. He even tasted blood as he wiped his mouth.

He doubled over again, and this time nearly lost consciousness. He would have shouted for help, but he found himself curiously unable to speak. He staggered backward, holding on to the bedpost.

Realization came to him then, and the horror of it nearly felled him. Lorenzo reached for his case, for the brown bottle he'd taken to the palace. His vision was blurry; so much so that the rug only inches from his eyes seemed so very far away.

He thought of Elise, but then the pain came again and he could only concentrate on the agony.

Dorothea, Countess of Straithern, stared in horror at Dr. Fenton.

It had been twenty years, but she felt just as she had the night she'd discovered the truth about her husband.

The evil was back. The evil that had once permeated Rosemoor and had been banished for the last two decades because of her fervent prayers and a benevolent God had returned.

"Tell me," she said. When the only answer she received from the doctor was a sympathetic glance, she spoke again. "Tell me the entire story, Ezra."

The man wouldn't look her in the face. But a few moments later, he began to speak.

She felt her eyes widen and a sound almost like a groan emerge from her before she cut it off with a handkerchief and her fist. It would not do to become hysterical at this moment. An excess of emotion never accomplished anything.

"Dear God," she said. "Why did you never say anything?"

"My wife and I decided that it would be wiser if no one knew. Until you asked, Your Ladyship, I thought the past well and truly buried."

It was a very good thing that she knew this parlor intimately. She took a series of steps backward, hoping that the chair was where it normally was kept, beside the marble table at the left of the fireplace. She felt the seat against the backs of her legs and subsided gracefully into the chair, placing both hands on the wooden arms and waiting for the light-headedness to subside.

She wanted, very much, for Dr. Fenton to leave, but good manners was the habit of a lifetime. An ability to retain one's aplomb is what separated the upper classes from the lower. She leaned back and focused on her breathing, wishing she hadn't instructed her maid to lace her quite so tightly this morning. She looked quite well in her black, but appearance didn't matter if she disgraced herself by fainting at Dr. Fenton's feet.

Perhaps she should adopt the fashion of an eccentric older woman and simply walk around her home attired in nothing more confining than a loose, sack-like dress. Perhaps she might ask Grant to build her a small house on the estate, someplace where she would be content to be odd and deranged.

"Did you not think that bringing her back to Rosemoor might awaken some memories for her?"

"She has lived not an hour away from Rosemoor all her life, Your Ladyship."

"How delighted you must have been when Grant proposed the match."

"Not delighted," he admitted. "Although a part of me thought that being the mistress of Rosemoor would be a fitting reward for what she'd had to endure."

"We have seen a great deal over the years, have we not, Ezra?"

"Your Ladyship," he said, bowing. "You know you only have to call upon me and I will be at your side."

How very odd that it seemed almost like a romantic declaration.

Perhaps it was the light-headedness that brought about the thought. Strange, she had never thought of Ezra in that way. She had never thought of any man in that way ever since her husband died. How very curious to feel the rapid beating of her heart. No doubt it was the effect of the shock she'd received.

"I, too, had thought the past well buried, Ezra," she said softly. "But I do not think it is."

His glance was troubled. "Nor do I, Your Ladyship."

She smiled, and bless the man, he understood it was a gesture of dismissal and bowed once more, nearly backing out of the room as if she were a royal personage. A queen, perhaps.

The queen of disaster.

* * *

Sometime later, Gillian rolled over to face him. He lit the lamp so he could see her more clearly.

"There are not that many people who would wish me harm," she said. She looked at him for a moment as if she were considering something. Then she turned and reached for the lamp on the table. She fumbled for something in the bottom drawer, and then handed it to him.

"My list," she said.

"I beg your pardon?"

"I had to consider that I might well have been poisoned on purpose, Grant."

"So you made a list?"

She nodded.

He held out his hand. For a moment, he didn't think she was going to surrender the paper to him. Would they argue about it? He hadn't had a quarrel with a girl since he was in short pants. Normally his title and his charm prevented the necessity of one, but he and one of the village girls had tossed clods of dirt at each other, until she'd been reprimanded by her mother, a woman who'd spoiled Grant's fun by appearing terrified that he would tell his father. He had agreed to remain silent, not telling the woman that he rarely even spoke to his father, let alone confided in him.

How odd that he would think about that now as he waited patiently for Gillian's cooperation.

Perhaps he thought of her as that long-ago girl, the only person in his childhood besides his brothers who had been unimpressed with his consequence.

She finally surrendered the paper, and he looked at the list.

"It's not very long," he said. "I believe you're right. I have more enemies than you."

"That's because you're older than I am," she said blithely. "Much, much older."

"Do not try to pass yourself off as having just escaped the schoolroom, Miss Cameron. I put your age as substantially past that."

She looked a little affronted. "I'm an ancient crone," she said finally, evidently deciding not to take offense. "I'm old as water." She squinted at him. "And you, Your Lordship? How old are you?"

"Old as knowledge, and as wise as experience," he teased.

"Perhaps you only look old because you've had a very full life. A great deal of wine, a great many women, a great many experiences, all in all." She sat back against the headboard and regarded him.

He wasn't about to respond to that goad. Instead he turned his attention back to her list. He knew only one name on the list, and it surprised him. The remaining two names were strangers.

He knew who Robert McAdams was—the man she'd loved, the father of her child. When he did speak, it was to ask a question about the next name on the list. "Mary McAdams?"

"Robert's sister. She believed that I was trying to trap Robert into marriage. I don't believe she liked me very much."

"Do you actually think they would do you harm?"

"No," she said. "I didn't begin my list that way. I didn't ask myself who would wish me dead. Instead, I thought of the people who would be relieved if I were dead."

"Arabella is on the list," he said, and turned to look at her.

"Yes." It was the only comment she made.

"Have you no names on your own list?" she asked in the silence. "No enemies or would-be enemies?"

"On the contrary," he said, glancing over at her, "my list would take pages, I'm afraid. Competitors, people I knew in Italy, perhaps even a relative or two."

"Any women on that list?'

"One or two. Perhaps we might as well add Arabella to my list."

She truly didn't want to hear about other women he'd loved and left behind in Italy. But she asked anyway, because she was curious, because he was looking at her expectantly, and because asking about the Italian women meant she didn't have to think about Arabella.

"Have there been very many? More than two?"

"Three," he answered. "I was in Italy for five years."

"One must evidently replace a lover periodically. Do they wear out?"

He laughed long and heartily, but she noticed that he didn't answer her question.

The knock on the door subdued them both. They looked at each other like naughty children caught in the act of stealing biscuits from the kitchen.

"Stay here," he whispered.

She gathered up the sheet, refraining from mentioning that she was effectively trapped in the bed since her clothing was either still in the laboratory or across the room in the armoire.

"Your Lordship?"

Grant stepped from the bed, uncaring that he was naked. What a glorious physique he had, and such a lovely bum. She forced herself to look away. Now was not the time to indulge in a bout of lust.

Michael called out again, his voice sounding breathless, and afraid. Was he ill? But it wasn't disease he brought to the palace.

The door opened, and his mother stood there. His mother never came to the palace.

Grant turned, hurriedly grabbed his dressing gown and held it in front of him.

She didn't say a word for a moment, simply stared beyond him to where Gillian lay in the bed.

Before he could demand a reason for her presence, or why she'd invaded his privacy, she turned to look at him. His questions faded beneath his surprise. His mother, the indefatigable, the strong, had tears in her eyes.

"It's your friend, Grant. Lorenzo."

"Lorenzo?" he asked. A sick feeling spread through him as one single tear rolled down her cheek. "What about him?"

"He's dead, my dearest. Oh my dear Grant, Dr. Fenton thinks it's poison."

Chapter 25

How was he going to explain this to Elise? Or to Lorenzo's seven children? How was he going to be able to sleep at night with this suffocating guilt?

Grant sat at the end of the bed in Lorenzo's room. On the floor, where Lorenzo had collapsed, was a scrawled word, carved into the wood with one of Lorenzo's ubiquitous jewels. *Bella.* Beautiful in Italian. How like Lorenzo to be thinking of Elise in his final hours.

Why the hell had he summoned Lorenzo to Rosemoor? The idea that there was a killer in his home enraged him. Who was creating havoc in his life? Who was so arrogant that they chose to act as God?

There was nothing he could do for his friend, but as far as the others at Rosemoor, he could care for them, protect them. How? He'd done a poor job so far.

Poison, Dr. Fenton had said. He would have to go along with the good doctor's diagnosis. But then, Dr. Fenton had been the one who diagnosed Andrew and James as having a blood disease. Then Gillian had been poisoned, and he'd had to alter his diagnosis.

Dr. Fenton's ineptness concerned him, almost as

much as the thought that Rosemoor was becoming a dangerous place to live.

He stared down at the floor, at the nearly illegible word. *Bella*. What had Lorenzo's thoughts been in those moments? Had he regretted being in Scotland? Had he longed for home?

Suddenly a female hand pressed against his cheek. He looked up to find Gillian standing there, sorrow in her eyes.

"You shouldn't be here," he said. "I wanted you to stay at the palace." But he reached out his hands and gripped her hips, pulling her to him before burying his face against her skirts. "You shouldn't be here," he repeated, but he didn't lessen his hold, and she didn't move away. She placed both hands on the back of his head, as if to hold him steady. Her wrist was against his face and he kissed it gently, infinitely grateful for the silence of her compassion.

He wanted to be anywhere but here. He wanted to be somewhere where there were warm breezes and deeply blue sky, and the riotous blooms of Italy in the springtime. He wanted to eat olives and thinly sliced ham and hard goat's cheese on a hard crusty roll and wash it down with a raw red wine. He wanted the sound of mandolins and laughter.

But he would never again experience those things separately or together, without Lorenzo coming to his mind.

"This shouldn't have happened," he said, pulling back.

She didn't argue him out of his reasoning. She merely pressed a kiss on the top of his hand. A nurturing gesture and one he hadn't expected.

She bent and knelt in front of him. "It's only normal, I think, to blame yourself. But unless you poisoned Lorenzo," she said, "you were no more responsible than I am.

"You are a good man, Grant Roberson."

"Am I? I am capable of so much hate," he said, a pronouncement that surprised her, he could tell. "I have hated one person in my entire life, but that hatred has lasted me the whole of it. It's fanned my ambition, no doubt. And my coldness. But I find I hate again, Gillian, and I'm frustrated because I don't know who to hate. What kind of man does that make me?"

"A normal one, perhaps. Even frightening, to some."

"Do I frighten you?"

He lifted his head and stared at her. There was warmth in her gaze and in the softness of her smile. Right at this moment he needed someone to care for him unconditionally, to touch him with affection, to love him.

"Gillian," he began, but she pressed two fingers against his lips and would not let him speak further. He didn't fight against her gentle touch, uncertain what he would have said, but suspecting it would have been inappropriate for this moment and this circumstance.

Instead he wrapped his arms around her, grateful for her presence, and her understanding.

"I want you to leave," he said. "Return to the palace and wait for me. I'll have Michael escort you."

"I'd rather stay with you," Gillian said.

"Please," he said, pulling back and taking her hands in his.

"Very well," she said, "if you insist. But is there nothing I can do?"

"No, there is nothing either of us can do at the moment."

She didn't speak, only leaned forward and embraced him.

Finally, he stood. "Go back to the palace and wait for me. There's something I must do."

She looked concerned. "Grant, come with me."

"I'll join you in an hour, no more."

She didn't look convinced as he hesitated at the door of Lorenzo's room and studied her for a moment. He didn't confide his sudden and startling suspicions to her. Not because he distrusted her, but because he didn't want to hurt her.

Grant turned and strode with measured steps down the corridor. His mind rebelled at his thoughts, even as he realized that his conclusions made perfect sense.

He didn't bother to knock, only pushed past the footman, pointing toward the door, banishing him without another glance. He marched into the Flower Room and slammed the door behind him. Only then was he calm enough to stare down at his mother.

"Did you hate him that much?"

She put aside her needlepoint and looked up at him. She had regained her composure in the past hour. Her tears for Lorenzo had faded, and her poise was evident again. But he noted that she didn't seem confused as to his question.

"Your father?" his mother asked. "Of course I

hated him," she said. "What decent person wouldn't? But I also loved him, and for that I will always ask for God's forgiveness."

"Did you hate him enough to countenance the murder of his children? To hide the identity of their murderer? To plot against me?"

"What are you talking about?"

"Dr. Fenton. He killed my brothers."

This time she looked shocked. Her hand went to her throat, as if to measure the pounding of her heartbeat. "He could not have."

"Why are you protecting him even now?'

"Protecting him? What are you talking about?"

"It would have been easy enough for him to poison Andrew and then James. He was their doctor."

She sat back and regarded him steadily.

Finally she spoke. "Why would he hurt me so very much? Especially when he went to such an effort to shield me?"

Now he was the one confused.

Before he could question her, she stood, putting some distance between them. She didn't face him, but stared at the painting on the wall, as if the bouquet of flowers held some answer for her.

"I don't understand," he said.

"I know you don't," she said, sighing.

She turned and faced him, a queenly presence in her black dress.

"I tried to keep you from knowing what kind of monster your father was, but I failed. But I succeeded rather well in keeping you from knowing what I'd become, didn't I?"

He walked to the window and stared outside. It was past midnight, and raining. He could almost feel the moisture seep past his skin and into his vitals. A perfect night for death. A perfect night to talk about that night so long ago.

"Your father had a penchant for little girls," she said, the revulsion evident in her voice.

"My father had a penchant for children," he corrected. "The gender didn't matter."

He'd gone to the palace the night of his father's death, never expecting to find room upon room of unspeakable horror: children arranged for the delectation of a man without morals or scruples or decency.

He'd been beyond repulsed by what he'd discovered.

"Fool that I was," the countess said, "I was still in love with your father. I'd attempted to entice him to my bed, not realizing that I was much too old to interest him."

Grant held up his hand to forestall any further comments, but either she didn't see or didn't care, because she went on with her story. "I went to the palace that night to seduce my own husband. I didn't know what kind of games he and his friends from Edinburgh played, but I was determined to interrupt them."

"Didn't he forbid you to enter the palace?"

"Of course. It was the first time I ever disobeyed him. The last time, too."

He turned to look at her. He was concerned about her color. She looked pale, and suddenly old. He went to her side, led her back to the chair, and sat on the ottoman opposite her. He reached for her hands, holding them between his.

"You needn't continue, Mother."

"Oh, I must. It's a story I had no intention of ever telling you, Grant, but perhaps it's about time I did so."

He nodded, focusing on her hands. She wasn't wearing her wedding ring, and he wondered how long it had been since she'd worn it, and why he'd not noticed until now.

"When I found what the palace was truly being used for, I was horrified. Horrified doesn't seem to be a strong enough word," she said, her voice harsh. "I don't think there is a word to describe what I felt. I entered the front door and was allowed to pass without comment from one room to another looking for your father. Not one person attempted to stop me. It's as if they wanted to shock me, wanted me to know. I eventually found your father and I will never forget that sight as long as I live."

She closed her eyes and took a deep breath. He thought her story done, but she grabbed his hands and held them tightly. "I returned to Rosemoor and found the dueling pistols that had belonged to your grandfather. He was always so proud of them, and their history, and since he had no sons, I was the one who learned to clean them and prime them periodically. I took both of them and returned to the palace. And I shot your father. In the head. Right between the eyes," she added very matter-of-factly, as if she were discussing the color of the parlor curtains.

"I've seen mice scurry just like the men your father brought from Edinburgh. When they were gone, I summoned Dr. Fenton." She looked at him. "He was new to the area, and young and scared, but he was as horrified as I to discover what the palace was being used for. The children were all orphans, did you know?"

"No," he said, "I didn't."

"We never talked about your father's death. The world thought him a suicide, but I think Ezra always knew. All I cared about was getting rid of the horror."

She pulled back, leaned her head against the back of the chair.

"I didn't care how much of the Roberson fortune I used to find homes for those poor children. To finance their education and provide some type of future for them. I prayed they could forget what had happened to them."

"Did Dr. Fenton help you find homes for them as well?"

"He did more than that," she said, her voice dull. She looked directly at him. "He adopted one of the children. A little girl. A little girl named Arabella."

His gaze flew to hers.

"Isn't it odd, but I didn't know until yesterday. I suspected. I wondered, but I didn't have the courage to confront Ezra until yesterday. He finally admitted Arabella's past."

"Why didn't you tell me?"

"Would it have made a difference? Would her past have changed what you feel for her?"

He stood. "I would have understood her," he said, events abruptly sharpening into focus. "I would have known."

The countess frowned. "Known what?"

He headed for the door.

"Where are you going?"

"To find Arabella."

And stop a killer.

Chapter 26

Even thought it was the middle of the night, Gillian busied herself with tasks in the laboratory, feeling every moment tick by on a sluggish clock. A quarter hour had passed, and Grant was still not with her. Her heart ached for him, and for Lorenzo, never to be reunited with his beloved Elise.

She was stacking the metal discs in the Volta apparatus when she heard the noise, easily recognizing the sound as the great carved doors of the palace being opened. In moments, Grant would be with her. She finished her task and washed her hands carefully, ridding them of any of the copper sulfate solution. After drying them, she straightened her skirts, adjusted her bodice, and felt to make sure her hair was still in place. Now was not the time to be vain, but still, she wished there was a mirror in the laboratory.

But it wasn't Grant who stood in the doorway. Arabella stood there, her face pale, her lips nearly bloodless, and her blond hair sodden. She dropped her rain-drenched shawl on the floor, looking wild and terrified.

Gillian forgot her own concerns and walked toward the younger girl. "Arabella? What is it?"

"I hate this place," Arabella said softly, her voice barely more than a whisper. "I told myself I would never come here again. But you made me come back. Not once but twice."

Arabella turned, staring out at the darkened corridors of the palace. A moment later she stepped into the shadows.

Gillian followed cautiously, uncertain of Arabella's mood.

"Have you no idea what this place used to be, Gillian?"

Before she could answer, Arabella spoke again. "It used to be hell." She turned and faced her. "When I was a little girl, I knew this was hell, just as I knew all the demons in residence. I even met Satan. I was his favorite."

"Arabella?'

"He liked my hair. Did you know that I kept cutting off my blond hair because that's why I was chosen? They said I looked like an angel, and what sort of man wouldn't want an angel? So they dressed me in white and brushed my long blond hair and sent me off to consort with the devil. No matter how I cried, and no matter how I promised I would be good, I was his darling over and over again."

Her voice was soft and barely audible, but the rotunda echoed sound, enlarging her whisper until it seemed to carry through the entire building.

Gillian lit one of the gas sconces on the wall, and only then did she see Arabella, standing on the top of the curved steps.

If anything, the girl was paler than before, and now she was trembling, her hands stretched out and pointing at empty spots along the wall.

"Grant's father used to have parties here," Arabella said. She descended the steps and stood in the middle, throwing out her arms and twirling slowly in the darkness. There was no moonlight, nothing but the faint patter of rain. She stopped and looked up at Gillian.

"He held his orgies here. Orgy, a word I learned much later. The Pleasure Palace, where all the little boys and the little girls he found lived."

Suddenly, she didn't want Arabella to say any more. Gillian wanted to silence the girl, send her far from here, banish the look on her face, and the residue of horror in her eyes. She didn't want to know.

Arabella tilted back her head and surveyed the roof of the cupola. "I promised my father that I would never tell anyone."

She looked at Gillian. "I had nightmares for years, Gillian, and when I woke from them, I was always told that it was nothing more than a bad dream, that I was safe. It took years for me to realize that I would never be safe until there was no longer a Roberson left alive."

Gillian had a sick feeling in the pit of her stomach. "Arabella, what have you done?"

"What a very stupid question, Gillian. How silly of you. You know exactly what I've done. I studied for years, Gillian. I studied and studied until I figured out exactly how."

"Where is Grant?"

"You really should not have eaten his lunch, Gillian. It was meant for him. How can I succeed in killing him if you're always about?"

Gillian took a step backward, but Arabella only smiled. Of course, *Bella* didn't stand for beautiful. Lorenzo had meant Arabella. He'd known.

"You killed him. You killed Lorenzo."

"Of course I did. He saw my book."

Horror vied with compassion. Gillian wanted to wrap her arms around the younger girl and hold her tight. "I'm so very sorry, Arabella," she said.

"Are you, Gillian?"

"I am."

Arabella shook her head. "You aren't, not really. If you were, you would never be here with Grant. I tried to warn you, but you stayed here with him. Once evil touches you, it scars you, Gillian."

She slowly began to mount the steps out of the sunken circle, heading toward Gillian. Her smile was otherworldly, the expression in her eyes calm acceptance.

"It isn't that I mind, Gillian, you must understand. If you loved him, that would be fine with me. If he loved you as well, I wouldn't care. If he were anyone other than who he is. But he has to die, because he is the Earl of Straithern."

"He isn't anything like his father, Arabella. He would never do such a horrible, horrible thing."

"He is a Roberson. He has evil blood. The world cannot afford any more devils."

"Is that why you've come here? To kill him? He isn't here, Arabella."

"No," the girl said amicably enough. "He isn't here, but you are."

Up until now, Gillian hadn't felt in danger, but looking into Arabella's eyes, she was suddenly, terribly afraid. If there was madness in her look, there was reason enough for it. That knowledge, however, didn't make Arabella less terrifying.

"You've had relations with Grant, have you not?"

"Is that what you think?"

Gillian took a cautionary step backward, and then slowly turned her head, measuring the distance between the rotunda and a door with a lock.

"Even now, you might be with child. You might be spreading the bloodline. Creating demons in a world where there should only be angels."

Arabella didn't halt, but came steadily closer. "Father wanted us to be like sisters. He wanted you to be someone I could tell about the palace. I never did, though, did I, Gillian?"

"No wonder you didn't want to come to Rosemoor," Gillian said, her fingers pleating the fabric of her skirt.

"I was nearly ill when I saw the building. And every day, you looked toward the palace with such yearning in your eyes. Poor Gillian, you never saw the evil."

"And you saw too much."

Gillian took two more steps backward. The action seemed to halt Arabella's advance. She smiled, and for a flash of an instant, Gillian could see the beauty of the child she'd been.

"Arabella, please. You can't do this."

"I have to," Arabella said reasonably. "Don't you see? I have to kill you, and then I will kill Grant. And then my task will be done. There was a reason I was brought here as a child. At first, I didn't understand," she said, shaking her head gently. "But then it came to me. I was the one who had to avenge all those poor children."

"James and Andrew? They never did anything to you, Arabella," said Gillian as she took another step backward. She needed to reach the bedroom on the other side of the laboratory. There was a lock there, and Arabella wasn't strong enough to go through a metal lock.

"They were Robersons. That was enough. Can't you see that, Gillian?" she asked impatiently.

Gillian turned and began to run, hearing Arabella's footsteps directly behind her. She raced through the laboratory, and was attempting to lock the door when Arabella threw herself against it.

She managed to clamp the door against the younger girl's arm, but Arabella pushed against the door with all her strength and threw it against the wall. Gillian didn't remain in the bedchamber but escaped into the laboratory again, tossing items at Arabella to halt her advance.

Nothing seemed to stop her.

She grabbed a bottle from the table, and threw it at the younger girl. The bottle shattered, liquid splashing on Arabella's arms. Only when the younger girl began to scream did Gillian realize that she'd thrown the sulfuric acid.

Arabella came at her with her hands outstretched, fingers formed into claws. The girl was screaming, incoherent curses Gillian couldn't understand. All she knew was that Arabella wouldn't be stopped and that she suddenly had a knife, the same knife Grant used to trim the wire for the Volta apparatus. Arabella must have grabbed it as she raced around the table.

Gillian started to run again. Arabella grabbed her skirt as she rounded the end of the table. Gillian fell to her knees, grabbing at the windowsill for support. Arabella kicked her hard on her thigh. Pain streaked through her as she landed on her back, lashing out with her uninjured leg. When her foot connected with Arabella's knee, the other woman grunted in pain and seized Gillian's ankle with one hand. She raised the knife and lunged forward.

Gillian felt the blade enter her thigh and screamed.

She wasn't going to die this way, not at the hands of a madwoman. Not when she'd just begun to live again.

One of the wires had come loose from the Volta apparatus and dangled from the edge of the table. Gillian scurried beneath the table, out of Arabella's reach, and pulled at it with all her strength. The machine was made of iron and filled with bronze and silver discs, and for a horrifying moment Gillian didn't think it would budge. No, it was moving; she could hear it slide across the wooden table.

Arabella bent and began to crawl toward Gillian, a calm and reasoned expression on her face. Her eyes, however, were lit with a fierce brightness, and there was a strange amused smile on her face. She raised the hand holding the bloody knife, and struck at Gillian again. She was so intent on murder that she wasn't paying any attention to Gillian's actions, and didn't see the Volta apparatus until it fell on top of her, pinning her legs.

Her howls of pain filled the room.

Arabella rolled over, pushing at the apparatus. The wire at the end of the fully charged machine sparked, and then curled as if it were alive. Arabella flinched when the wire met her skin, trying to draw away.

The floorboards began to smoke, a plume growing not far from the other woman. Arabella's chemical-soaked skirts burst into flames. Gillian realized, in horror, what was happening. She'd thrown the bottle of acid at the other woman, and now Arabella was acting as a conductor. Arabella screamed, pushing at the machine again, but it was too heavy to dislodge.

Gillian scrambled on her hands and knees to the head of the table, reaching for the buckets of sand stored there. But before she could reach her, Arabella was completely engulfed in a pillar of orange and yellow fire.

She threw the sand on top of Arabella, deliberately trying not to hear the horrible sounds emerging from the young woman. She was crying, but not in a recognizable voice. Arabella sounded like a little girl, a frightened and terrorized child.

The flames would not go out. Gillian grabbed the second bucket and a third and then raced into the other room to see if there was anything she could do. She pulled the curtains from around the bed and returned to Arabella's side. There was no sound. Only the crackle of the flames spreading along the floor where the acid and copper sulfate had spilled.

"Gillian!"

She heard her name being called and wondered

if Arabella had somehow learned to speak in a male voice. She turned to see Grant standing there. Suddenly he was pulling at her, dragging her from the room.

He was there, really there, solid and sane, touched not by wickedness or evil but intelligence, kindness, and concern. A generous man, a man she loved with her whole heart.

"She's going to die," she said. She tried to turn back to Arabella, but he lifted her into his arms and carried her through the door. "We must help her." Her last sight was a strange, isolated fire, yellow and gold flames, and Arabella's shape somehow melting inside it.

"It's too late, Gillian," he said in the kindest of voices.

"Your laboratory is going to burn."

"It's going to explode," he corrected.

They were out of the palace by only feet when the first of the explosions occurred. In her mind, she could still hear Arabella's words, and the eerie cry she'd made as she lay dying. *The demons are coming.*

She closed her eyes and held on to Grant, an anchor in an uncertain and suddenly terrifying world.

"As the Earl of Straithern," Grant said stiffly, "I am also empowered to act as magistrate. I feel that I should detain you for something."

"Under what charge, Grant?"

Lorenzo, Count Paterno, frowned at Grant, who stared back, the look on his face carrying not one whit of friendliness or gratitude that his friend was alive.

Grant turned back to the doctor. "I'm speaking of Arabella, sir. Surely you knew."

They were sitting in Lorenzo's new room, a spacious chamber overlooking the west lawn. Lorenzo was sitting up in bed, looking wan but alive. Gillian was seated in an invalid chair beside his bed, her leg bandaged and elevated. The cuts Arabella had inflicted had been deep, but she would heal. As far as Lorenzo, he would heal as well.

Arabella was not so fortunate.

The palace was still burning, but there was no chance she might still be alive. The chamber that had been Grant's laboratory had been an inferno since the blaze began six hours earlier.

Dawn was bright on the horizon, the morning promising to be a new and brilliant day. Everything was just as it had been the day before, except that it wasn't. The secrets of Rosemoor had been revealed, and they were too raw and horrible to discuss. Gillian had not spoken of her confrontation with Arabella to anyone. Nor had she mentioned what kept her frozen inwardly. Not Arabella's revelations, but another thought, one even more horrible to contemplate.

Had she always trapped her emotions behind silence? Had she always been adept at hiding what she felt, even from herself? Emotions seemed fiercer, and stronger than they ever had before, as if they were pulling at her to pay attention. Between Dr. Fenton and the countess she had not been left alone all night. It wasn't difficult to determine that they were concerned for her. As for Grant, he was never far from her side, but they had not spoken as lovers, nor even as friends, but remained distant as they once had been, the earl and the companion.

Or had they ever truly been distant? From the very beginning he'd had the ability to open her heart.

She turned and looked at him sitting beside her, and he glanced at her. Slowly, he reached out and touched her sleeve, his eyes warm, his smile reassuring.

"I didn't know," the doctor said, removing his spectacles and cleaning them with the edge of his waistcoat. He replaced them, staring down at the floor. A moment later, he retrieved a book hidden between his body and the side of the chair.

"Arabella's journal," he said, handing it to Grant. "I'd no idea she was such a prolific writer. She wrote it all down." He sighed. "All of it." He looked up at Grant. "But you're right, I should have seen it," he said. "I should have known. I should have remembered that she treated Andrew for an inflammation of the lungs."

"And James?" Grant asked.

Dr. Fenton shook his head. "I don't remember. Perhaps he came to my surgery on a day I was not there. She could easily have prescribed him a medication filled with belladonna."

"Belladonna?" Gillian turned to Lorenzo. "*Bella*. Not beautiful, after all. Or Arabella's name. Did you know? Is that why you wrote it?"

Lorenzo looked confused for a moment and then began to smile. "She might as well have told me." He looked at the book on the table beside him. "She was always carrying it with her. As if she wanted someone to know that she was poisoning people. Almost as if she taunted them to discover her secret." He sighed. "She had the page marked, and I remembered it when I became ill."

"Is that how you survived?" Grant asked. "Because you knew what the poison was?"

"I survived, my friend, because I had already treated Miss Cameron. I took the emetic as soon as I realized. If I had not treated her, it would not have been with me." He shrugged. "Fate, perhaps."

"Why did you let us think you were dead?" Gillian looked from Grant to Lorenzo. The two men still looked as if they were angry at each other.

"I was too weak to protect myself from her," Lorenzo said. "I doubted, my friend, that anyone would believe me. She was a beautiful woman. A beautiful woman should not be a killer."

None of them responded to that comment.

"It was the good doctor who understood," Lorenzo said, looking at the older man. Dr. Fenton still sat slumped in the chair, his gaze on the floor. At Lorenzo's words, he raised his head.

"I knew, God help me, the minute the footman summoned me to the count's chamber."

"So you told the countess that he'd died," Gillian said. She wrapped her arms around her waist, but she could still not rid herself of coldness. Even her bones felt chilled.

Dr. Fenton nodded. "I didn't wish to lie, but I agreed with the count that it would be safer. Until we found Arabella. But it was too late." He looked away, as if his tears were shameful things.

"Did she kill more people than Andrew and James?" Gillian asked, directing her question to Grant.

Grant turned to her. "I wouldn't be surprised," he said, thumbing through Arabella's journal. "She evidently considered herself a crusader. A righter of wrongs. Those who were deemed innocent were spared. Those who were evil were not."

He looked at Dr. Fenton. "God knows she had enough grievances against my father, but why kill my brothers?"

"Because of their blood," Gillian said, the words hard to speak. "Because of your father." She folded her hands together tightly, and focused her gaze on them. "A bloodline. The innocent were not spared because they were offspring of evil. Wickedness."

She raised her gaze to Dr. Fenton. A question had been torturing her for hours. A question that kept her from sleep. Now it sat on her tongue, just ready to be voiced if she could find the courage. "Did she kill my son? Because I had sinned, did he have to die?"

Dr. Fenton looked at her, shock contorting his features. For the longest moment they simply stared at each other, neither one speaking.

"I cannot say, Gillian," he said, his voice breaking with emotion. "God help me, I don't know. The symptoms would be similar for belladonna poisoning and a heart malady."

Grant placed his arm across her shoulders. He had not been far from her during the last few hours, as if to assure himself that she was fine. She wasn't fine. She would always wonder about the fate of her child and whether Arabella thought he should be punished for the sins of his mother. Nor could she forget Arabella's story, a glimpse into a horror too terrible to remember.

Before she could summon up the words to reassure Grant that she was composed and calm, that she needed no comfort, he leaned close and whispered, "I'm here."

Just that quickly, she knew. Any doubt, any reservation, any fear was simply swept away, and in its place the knowledge that she was captive in this emotion, bound to this man for all of her life. If he banished her from his side tomorrow, she would survive it as she had so many other circumstances, but she would not cease to love him.

Love was not a convenient emotion. There was nothing kind or gentle or sweet about it. Love violently jerked you from your moorings and washed you out to sea. Love was a vast and fierce wind, a spear to the heart, a thunderclap, a bolt of lightning.

She might not have wanted to fall in love, but she had. She might not have wanted to love an earl, but she did. The emotion was simply there, like the color of her eyes and her height—a fact of her being.

Dr. Fenton was saying something but she ignored him, choosing instead to stretch her hand out toward Grant. It wasn't the proper time to acknowledge what she felt for him, but perhaps it showed in her eyes, in the soft smile she sent him.

His hand left her arm to link with hers, their fingers warm.

No one could take away her pain. No one could truly understand it. But Grant's simple gesture made her wonder if it was possible to share the experience of living. Could you love someone enough that you could ease his hurt? Would the simple comfort of a touch be enough?

His grief clung to him like a cloak, just as she suspected hers did. But in that moment, Gillian suddenly experienced a soothing calm, a feeling that she wasn't alone.

Perhaps love was a blessing after all.

Chapter 27

Grant heard someone come into the library, but he didn't turn from the window. If it was Dr. Fenton, he didn't want to talk about Arabella at the moment. The man was grieving, taking on too much guilt for his adopted daughter's actions. Lorenzo? He could barely face Lorenzo, feeling his own guilt about the agony both his friend and Gillian endured.

But it was not, blessedly, either man.

"You have not summoned the fire brigade," the Countess of Straithern said, speaking of the footmen who were regularly trained in putting out fires at Rosemoor. "In fact, I was told that you specifically ordered them not to extinguish the blaze. It's been a day, Grant, and the building is still burning. Do you want the whole of the estate to go up in flames, then?"

She moved closer to him.

"Not the whole of the estate, Mother," he said. "Just the palace." As if to accentuate his remarks, another explosion occurred, this time smaller than the others. The fire had already reached the chemicals stored in one of the unused rooms. "I don't think I could walk into that building again."

"I know that I could not have," she said softly. "But I've found, son, that my memories come with me."

She drew closer, and he wished she would simply leave. He had not yet come to grips with the knowledge that she'd killed his father. One part of him understood completely, and knew that he probably would have done the same. Another was still a young boy made earl too soon.

His father was responsible for the deaths of his sons and for ruining dozens of lives. Arabella was only the means of performing that murder. His father's actions had begun the series of events that had led to all the tragedy at Rosemoor.

"What are you going to do, Grant?"

He smiled. He'd been giving his future a great deal of thought in the last twenty-four hours. "Perhaps I should leave Rosemoor," he said. "Go back to Italy, where life is much less complex."

"There are going to be enough Robersons in Italy," she said surprisingly.

He turned to look at her.

"Dr. Fenton and I have decided that we should escort Lorenzo home. It is, after all, the least we can do. Besides, another country sounds like a blessed idea. I have not stirred from Rosemoor for too long." She glanced over at him. "We have wounds, both of us, Grant. Yours have time to heal. And you have a dynasty to begin. Sons and daughters, all proud of what their father has accomplished. Most of all, Grant, you have your happiness to find."

She looked through the window to where the palace still burned. "Perhaps one day, you will build another structure there. A building to house your experiments.

And you will make sure that only good memories are held within its walls."

She patted his arm, and then turned to leave the room.

It was time for her to go.
It was time for her to leave.
It was time.

Perhaps she should be afraid. Perhaps she should be concerned about the future more than she was, but she couldn't feel anything beyond the pain. It lingered there behind her eyes in the form of unshed tears, and was present in the heaviness of her heart.

How was she to do this?

How was she supposed to marshal her strength to leave him? Somehow. That was the only answer. Somehow, she was supposed to endure this, and somehow, one hour would pass and then another until a whole day had elapsed. One by one, the days would merge into weeks.

Grief was so familiar to her, such a friend. Perhaps it was the only emotion she would have in the future, stronger than love or hate.

She'd known all along that it would be this way. She'd considered it, dispassionately, reasoning that if she were fortunate enough to find love, then she would pay any price for it.

What makes a woman so foolish that she will brave anything for love? The look in a man's eyes? The promise of his smile? The memory of passion or the longing for it? Was it simply loneliness? Or had she gone against every caution in her heart because she'd loved Grant from the first, in a way she couldn't understand, with a strength that humbled her?

Somehow, she would have to go on, and somehow, she would endure, and somehow, perhaps, someday, she would remember this time as an odyssey. *Remember when you lived at Rosemoor? Remember when you loved a man by the name of Grant Roberson? Remember love?*

If she were lucky, perhaps she'd lose her memory. Would nature ever provide that release?

Dear God, help her.

Help her be strong, resolute.

"Where do you think you're going?"

She turned to find the countess standing there, glaring at her imperiously. Gillian smiled; she was no longer afraid of the woman, had not been since the night they shared chocolate.

"I am leaving."

"I can see that," the countess said. "Where are you going?"

Gillian didn't respond.

The countess stared at her for several long and uncomfortable moments.

If the woman wanted embarrassment, she would get none from her. True, what she had done was wrong as the world saw it. If her own daughter had engaged in such behavior, Gillian would have been appalled and shocked. But there had been too much sorrow and too much tragedy at Rosemoor to worry about a few bent and broken rules. If she and Grant had stolen some happiness, then they should be congratulated, not castigated.

The countess stared down at the valise in her hand.

"You cannot leave," she finally announced, almost as if it were a command.

"Yes, Your Ladyship," Gillian said tiredly. "I can." She turned and continued walking down the corridor. She'd already said her farewells to Lorenzo, and Dr. Fenton was to meet her at the carriage.

She would stay at the doctor's home only until her leg was healed, and then she had other plans. She missed her father. He was a good man, if a bit strict. But his love for her had always been strong. Perhaps he would welcome her return. If he did not, she would find employment somewhere. She had her wages, enough money for lodgings for a time, and determination. She'd take small steps, and one by one, she'd carve a life for herself.

How odd that she was no longer afraid.

"Are you going to say goodbye to Grant? Or are you simply going to disappear? I would have thought him deserving of a little more decency from you."

Gillian stopped but didn't turn.

She couldn't say goodbye to Grant. She could not look into his beautiful gray eyes once more. She simply couldn't. But before she could articulate her reluctance to the countess, the older woman marched up to her, grabbed her arm, and propelled her down the hall.

"Your Ladyship!"

"No," the Countess of Straithern said firmly. "You have acted in a daring manner for the whole of your stay at Rosemoor. I will not have you retreat into a shell of decorum now."

"I beg your pardon?'

"Oh pish," the countess surprisingly said. "Simply put, don't be an idiot, Gillian." With that rather surprising announcement, the older woman opened a door and nearly tossed Gillian into the room.

Grant was standing at the window. At her entrance, he turned.

"I am to tell you, according to the countess," Gillian said, frowning at him, "that I am leaving."

He didn't respond to that news, simply turned and faced the window again. "Have you ever wondered why you cannot see the stars during the day? Yet they are there."

"No," she said, "I confess I have not. I was always more interested in what was around me than in something so very far away."

"The stars offer us a respite from what is very close. A way of looking at things differently, a different perspective."

She didn't know what to say. She'd never before heard him sound so philosophical.

"Change goes on around us constantly. We're unaware of it because we're locked into our own little worlds. We're the center of it, and it's only until some event knocks us off that axis that we look beyond ourselves to find that all this time, things have been changing and we never knew. We think life is solid and formed, but it's actually a molten mass, forever moving. Forever changing.

"You're my change," he said, turning to face her. "You've managed to alter my entire world. I could never begin another experiment without wondering where you are, or go to my bed without wishing you were beside me. Even sitting down to dinner is different, because I expect you to be there. And all this time, I never knew. I never realized."

"I did," she said softly.

"I was going to offer you Italy, but it seems as if my mother and Dr. Fenton have plans to escape there."

"I know," she said, having been apprised of his plans by the doctor. "I think it's beyond time."

He looked at her.

"They were forever stealing glances at each other. Didn't you see?"

He shook his head.

"You shouldn't be walking on that leg."

She didn't answer him.

"You should be sitting."

She ignored the admonition, but when he pulled a chair to her side, she sank down gratefully into it.

"Sometimes, we don't see what's in front of us," he said, his tone one of annoyance.

"Or we do, and we're willfully blind to it," she countered.

For a few moments, they were silent. But then, they'd always shared silences with great companionship, as if the absence of speech merely facilitated the transmission of their thoughts.

"This could be a happy place," he finally said. "Rosemoor could be known as a heaven on earth with the right people living here."

She didn't respond.

"A woman with optimism in her heart, despite the pain and the grief she's known." He looked straight at her. "A woman who believes in joy. A woman who isn't afraid to live."

"At one point I was," she confessed. "But all we

have is today, Grant. We might as well live it with great enjoyment."

He smiled. "You would have liked Italy," he said. "As it is, you'll have to content yourself with Rosemoor."

She raised her gaze to his. "No," she said.

He reached for her, but she waved him back.

"I've become very quaint, you see. I crave normalcy in my life. A certain respectability. While being your mistress is exciting, it isn't what I want."

Grant smiled. "The whole of my life has been dictated by what other people might think. Strangers who had no inkling of the life I lead. My father's sins are not mine, but for years I've been circumspect in all my dealings, as if being perfect might hide the horrible secret of the Straithern line."

She didn't say anything in response.

"I've decided that I don't give a damn about propriety, just at the moment you do."

She still remained silent.

"We shall play at being lovers secretly," he said, "while on the surface we're very proper. We shall be the very souls of propriety, I think. Or perhaps I will let it be known that I adore you, just so there is no confusion as to my feelings."

"You will?"

He nodded. "I might even speak Italian to you in public. People will think I'm besotted, but only you will understand the true meaning of my words. Little secret phrases, I think. Outwardly, however, we shall be the epitome of all that is starched and decorous."

She shook her head.

"Do you really think you can leave me?"

She nodded. "It is very difficult."

"I think it would be damn near impossible," he said, obviously annoyed.

"Perhaps," she admitted.

"But we'll never know, because it will never happen."

"It won't?"

He walked to her, holding out his hands. She placed hers within them and allowed him to pull her up into his embrace.

"Stay with me at Rosemoor. Make this a happy place, my dearest Gillian. Let it be known throughout Scotland that there isn't a hint of grief or sorrow or loss here."

He slowly put his arms around her.

"Do you not feel anything for me?"

"I love you," she said, and watched as his face changed. He grew somber, his eyes warming as she spoke. "I love you enough to tell you my fears, and my hurts. I love you enough to be weak around you, and not protect myself so much."

He pulled her closer.

"When you come into a room my heart beats faster," she began. "I want to smile when thinking of you. I want to cry when I know you are in pain. I want to be your help mate, even though there are times when I want to bedevil you. I want a world with you in it. I want a place at your table. I want to roll over in the middle of the night and know that you are by my side. I want to feel delight in your arms, and laughter and tears."

"Yet you don't want me," he said, frowning at her. His eyes, however, were a soft, warm gray. "If the position of countess isn't enough of an inducement to stay, there is Rosemoor. You'll be mistress of Rosemoor, but I doubt if a few bricks will change your mind."

She pulled back. "Countess?" She began to blink rapidly, but the tears still fell, blurring her vision. "I don't care about being a countess," she said.

"We've got some jewels, I think. A few sapphires and rubies. Do you like jewels?"

"I don't know," she said, "I've never had many."

"You could be my assistant. You're a very good assistant. I'm rebuilding my laboratory."

When she didn't speak, he frowned at her. "Well?"

"All in all, I'd prefer the title of wife, instead."

He smiled as he bent his head. "I think we can arrange that," he whispered, and kissed her.

Next month, don't miss these exciting new love stories only from Avon Books

In My Wildest Fantasies by Julianne MacLean

An Avon Romantic Treasure

Rebecca Newland is desperate to escape a loveless engagement. Devon Sinclair is his family's only hope for averting crisis, but a forced marriage can't be the answer. When Devon rescues Rebecca on a stormy evening, their happiness may depend on their ability to save each other.

Not the Marrying Kind by Hailey North

An Avon Contemporary Romance

Harriet Smith and Jake Porter went to their graduation dance together, but Harriet was devastated to find out Jake had only asked her on a dare. Sixteen years later, Jake's back in town. Harriet thought all she wanted was to make him pay, but happily ever after may be the sweetest revenge of all.

Blackthorne's Bride by Shana Galen

An Avon Romance

When a drunken priest marries the wrong couple, Lady Madeleine's escape from her money-hungry suitors is hardly a consolation. Her new husband, the Marquess of Blackthorne, is fleeing an infuriated duke. But will the struggle to save their marriage, as well as their lives, prove to be too much?

Taken by the Night by Kathryn Smith

An Avon Romance

Six hundred years have taught Saint one thing—it is better to stay away from humans, and save himself the pain of loss. Ivy is no stranger to vampires or the passions of men, but Saint is the first to tempt her. As they search for a killer and fight to protect those they care about, Ivy and Saint will risk everything for a chance at a love that will last forever.

Visit www.AuthorTracker.com for exclusive information on your favorite HarperCollins authors.

REL 1007

Available wherever books are sold or please call 1-800-331-3761 to order.